A CAPITOL
DEATH

A CAPITOL DEATH

Lindsey Davis

MINOTAUR BOOKS
NEW YORK

First published in the United States by Minotaur Books, an imprint of St. Martin's Publishing Group

A CAPITOL DEATH. Copyright © 2019 by Lindsey Davis. All rights reserved. Printed in the United States of America. For information, address St. Martin's Publishing Group, 120 Broadway, New York, NY 10271.

www.minotaurbooks.com

Designed by Steven Seighman

Map by Rodney Paull

The Library of Congress Cataloging-in-Publication Data is available upon request.

ISBN 978-1-250-15270-1 (hardcover)
ISBN 978-1-250-15271-8 (ebook)

Our books may be purchased in bulk for promotional, educational, or business use. Please contact your local bookseller or the Macmillan Corporate and Premium Sales Department at 1-800-221-7945, extension 5442, or by email at MacmillanSpecialMarkets@macmillan.com.

Originally published in Great Britain by Hodder & Stoughton, an Hachette UK Company

First U.S. Edition: July 2019

10 9 8 7 6 5 4 3 2 1

A CAPITOL
DEATH

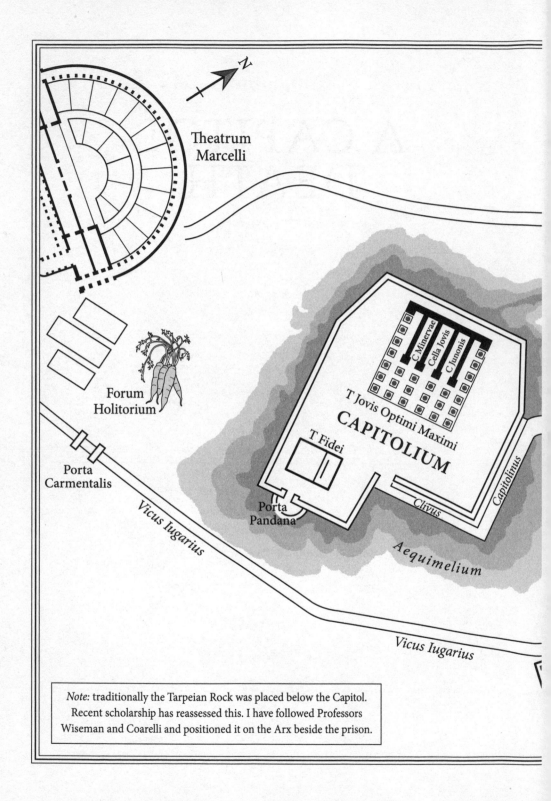

Theatrum
Marcelli

Forum
Holitorium

Porta
Carmentalis

Vicus Iugarius

CAPITOLIUM

T Jovis Optimi Maximi

C.Minervae

Cella Jovis

C.Junonis

T Fidei

Porta
Pandana

Clivus

Capitolinus

Aequimelium

Vicus Iugarius

Note: traditionally the Tarpeian Rock was placed below the Capitol.
Recent scholarship has reassessed this. I have followed Professors
Wiseman and Coarelli and positioned it on the Arx beside the prison.

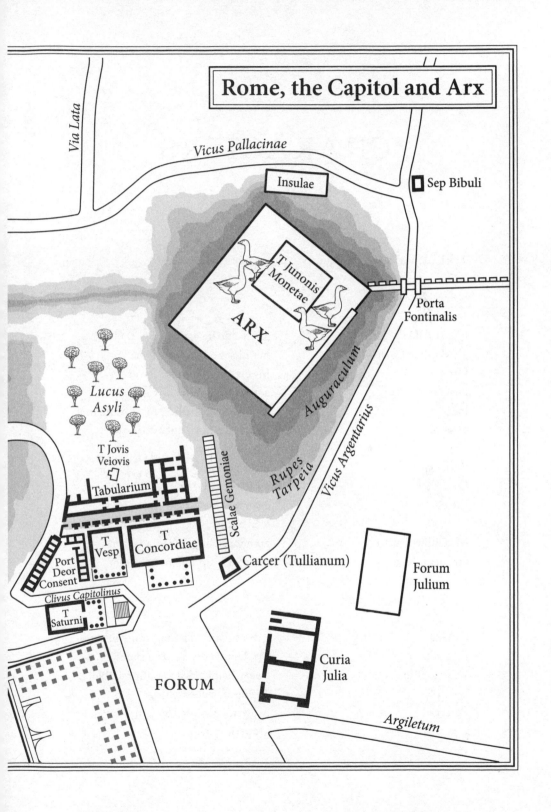

Rome, the Capitol and Arx

Via Lata

Vicus Pallacinae

Insulae

Sep Bibuli

T Junonis
Monetae

ARX

Porta
Fontinalis

Auguraculum

Lucus
Asyli

T Jovis
Veiovis

Tabularium

Vicus Argentarius

Scalae Gemoniae

Rupes
Tarpeia

T
Vesp

T
Concordiae

Port
Deor
Consent

Carcer (Tullianum)

Forum
Julium

Clivus Capitolinus

T
Saturni

Curia
Julia

FORUM

Argiletum

CHARACTERS

T. Fl. Domitianus Germanicus	a conquering general

On the Aventine

Flavia Albia	a sensible investigator
T. Manlius Faustus	her husband, a dark horse
Dromo	his classic, not-very-clever slave
Fornix	a prize chef, can cook a goose
Paris	a runabout, heading for dipsomania
Gratus	a slick steward, got everyone's measure
Barley	a shy new dog
Drax	a jealous old dog
Prisca	a shrewd businesswoman, tells it like it is
M. Didius Falco	an honest auctioneer, a father
Helena Justina	a mother, a problem-solver

On the Capitol and Arx

Gabinus	a dead man, not a big contributor
Egnatius	his deputy, dead man's shoes
Valeria Dillia	a very helpful witness (unreliable)
Larth	an augur, skywatching
Percennia	his wife, with her feet on the ground

Lemni	an augury assistant, knows the odds
Alichsantre	another augur, nervous (seen the signs?)
Callipus	a hutless caretaker, living with his mum
Callipina	his houseproud mum
Geminus	her younger lover
Nestor	a Praetorian with an agenda
Feliculus	an elderly goose-boy with anxiety problems
Geese	sacred to Juno, troublemakers
Florentina	a very unlucky bird
Old Romulus	a talkative bar-owner
Genialis	a jailer, strangulation on day rates

On the Campus Martius

Quartilla	a mistress of stitchery
Naevia	a wronged woman
Children	good actors, very cute
Successus and Spurius	colourful painters
Lalus	a chariot-gilder, an agitator

On the Palatine

Aepolus	a worried bureaucrat
Hylus	wardrobe master to Our Master

On the coast

Ostorius	an ambitious manufacturer
Cincia	his wife, pushing him
Susuza	their buxom niece, with a stylish career plan
Castor and Pollux	recalcitrant donkeys

On their beat

Scorpus	a vigiles inquiry chief, who has his methods
Julius Karus	doing unspecified work for unspeakable reasons
Taurus and Zenon	two trusty vigiles, up for it

Plus full supporting cast: a triumphal procession of soldiers, sweepers, workmen, priests, tour guides, tourists, the imperial transport corps, scenery builders, Dacian and Chattian "prisoners," actors, dancers, musicians, flower-strewers, drinkers, slaves, drivers and bearers, and, of course, idiotic members of the public.

Almost nothing is known of the procession's infrastructure and management. No ancient source addresses the logistics . . .

—WIKIPEDIA

One woman with a list could do it easily.

—FLAVIA ALBIA

ROME:
THE CAPITOLINE HILL,
November AD 89

———————

I

Domitian was back.

I state this in completely neutral language. Your slave must read it out to you with no hint of judgement. Even if he or she is a highly educated, clever specimen, who cost you thousands (or decades of being nice to the horrible aunt who first owned them), restraint must be shown. We don't want a nasty execution, do we?

Domitian was back, so everybody had to look out. For me to imply that the Senate and People of Rome felt a happy respite had ended when their emperor reappeared would be risky, as risky as trying to evaluate what Our Master actually achieved during his absence abroad. *That* is on record—I mean, he told us. His summer-long campaign on the Empire's borders was so politically glorious and valorously punitive that he was to be awarded a Double Triumph. He had asked the Senate for it, so the Senate would bleat their agreement because even an implicit death threat works.

A Roman triumph is a huge public event to celebrate a military commander who has successfully completed a foreign war. He rides through the main streets in a big fancy chariot. In a ceremonial procession, the general and his troops are welcomed home with wild enthusiasm; their glittering booty is admired and their exotic captives are derided or, if the poor souls look miserable enough, even pitied. It takes a very long time, costs squillions and leaves behind vast quantities of litter, which the public slaves are too tired to deal with. People behave badly. All the temples are open but there are never enough toilets. Often more divorce follows than after a Saturnalia.

To spend a full day watching a march-past is supposedly wonderful.

This is Rome. Romans love street festivity. To me, they are a simple people, who never learn from their mistakes. They call it tradition. The barmier a ritual is, the more they love it.

So, our emperor was back. A triumph always has to be *over* someone: it must celebrate Rome conquering barbarians, our hairy, obstreperous enemies. Rome knows how to make foreigners feel sorry they exist. This double event was meant to show the world that the warlike Domitian had brilliantly walked all over the Chatti and the Dacians. They saw it differently, but they were a long way away and wouldn't be coming to argue.

We citizens, lucky us, were to be reminded of what a dazzling emperor we had. At least until the day it happened, Domitian was camping with his troops outside Rome, as he was supposed to do. My father, ever the satirist, kept reminding us that some poor mutt in the past had had to wait five years for his triumph, but my mother, a realist, said Domitian would not be thwarted. He studied rulebooks, as paranoid tyrants do (omitting the rule that rulers should show kindness to their people). Being so meticulous, he would probably remain outside the city boundary until the triumph—though that put him rather too close to the Campus Martius, which contained the Saepta Julia where my family had its auction house. On the other hand, being Domitian, he might well decide to come in secretly, to listen to what people were saying about him in case it was treasonous so he could take revenge.

He would not camp out any longer than he had to. He was famously impatient. He would be nagging the planners to move faster. He would also want to keep close personal track of all the arrangements. Our podgy overlord liked to control every detail. He hand-picked army officers and was prone to dismissing freedmen suddenly from the palace secretariats, simply because in his view they had been around too long to be trusted. He took everything to heart. Any fault in the ceremonial would be seen as a deliberate insult to him; any omission or failure would be fatal. My husband, who was a magistrate that year, had been involved for weeks in preparations; like so many in Rome, he was now depressed and anxious. He regularly came home moaning it was all a nightmare. Pressure on the official organisers probably caused what happened one evening on the Capitol.

It began with a man falling to his death off the Tarpeian Rock. It looked like suicide. Unfortunately for those who tried to hush things up, an old woman saw him drop. With no idea of tact, she kept insisting loudly that someone had been up there with him.

She made this claim to everyone she met in the street, her neighbours, their visiting relatives, barmen, stallholders, the teacher at the infant school at the corner of her road, and some feral cats she fed. A busybody took her to the vigiles to report what she had seen. That might not have mattered since the vigiles know all about discretion, which avoids having to write reports for their prefect, but she found other outlets: because of the Triumph, Praetorian guards were crawling everywhere "for security," so when the daft crone spotted one making himself unpleasant in a bar where she sometimes had a tipple, she rushed up and parked herself there to regale him with her tale.

The guards don't bother with discretion. Any word longer than two syllables sounds intellectual to them, and intellectuals are bad people. The big idiot would have listened to her anyway, wondering if this was a plot. Praetorian cohorts are taught that it is their noble role to deal with anything that could be embarrassing to their emperor. The one whose tunic sleeve had been grabbed by the witness's skinny fingers went back to camp, muttering. Some loon on the commissariat thought, Ho! Dealing with stuff is what we lads do, so let us bravely deal with this . . . But a crazy old lady, who actually admitted her eyesight wasn't brilliant, was too hard to interrogate. They soon passed on the story to a civilian committee.

In a superstitious city, such an unnatural death could be seen as an omen. A bad one. In any case, if some heartbroken soul found his life too much to bear and jumped to oblivion, Domitian would be furious that a sad man with mental troubles had spoiled his day. He might even feel that having mental troubles was his own prerogative. Either way, he was unable to punish the victim, who had so selfishly put himself out of reach by dying, but he would lash out. Somebody would cop it.

The first committee shunted the problem onto another. Every group connected with the Triumph looked for a way out, which they hoped someone else would process. Time passed, as usual in bureaucracy, but this difficult agenda item would not go away.

The scene of crime, if it ever was a crime, was their big problem. The Tarpeian Rock is an execution place, starting in mythical history with a get-rich-quick wench called Tarpeia, who tried to betray Rome to a besieging army for a reward. Instead, she was crushed under a heap of shields and thrown off the Arx, the citadel. At the heart of Rome, this outcrop of rock is somewhat prominent. Not only is it an important part of the Capitol but the Capitol is where a triumph traditionally ends. Sacrifices to Jupiter and other rites occur up there, as the honoured general formally completes his task, hands back the symbols of his military power and sighs with relief that he can now go home for supper.

Nobody wanted Capitol Hill to be defiled. At the time, it was awash with workmen and temple assistants, preparing for what would be a very religious day. Jumping off the rock was the wrong kind of sacrifice.

Then things got worse. The dead man was identified.

Oh dear. He was named as a project manager involved in the Triumph. This could still have been downplayed with the right wording, except that he was in charge of transport. So not only had he been assembling a multitude of carts to amaze the crowds by carrying loot and other wonders— but his remit included the chariot. *That* chariot. The big beast at the climax of the procession. The specially designed chariot in which our emperor, valiant suppressor of the Chatti and Dacians, was to ride.

If someone who was meant to be buffing this fancy quadriga had killed himself before the Triumph, it was sad enough. Any suggestion that he had been murdered was a ghastly taint on the occasion. All the gods would be attending Domitian's party: you don't want gods to notice that your transport manager has topped himself, or been topped.

Well, all right. Maybe the gods can be paid off with a few wheaten cakes but, Hades, you don't want Domitian to find out. He would be standing in that chariot all day, continually brooding about why the man who prepared it for him had not cared enough about his Triumph to stay around and watch.

Men on committees despaired; some succumbed to heart attacks, or said they had, before they rushed to hide in country villas. After the usual period of faffing, just long enough to lose any useful evidence, of course, someone finally applied a fix. It was solemnly decreed that they had better find out what had really happened. One of the committees dumped the problem on the aediles.

There are four of these magistrates. By definition they are among the most practical officials in Rome, though they have a big staff of experienced slaves to help them. Each man looks after a quarter of the city. The aedile who managed the Capitol swiftly claimed he already had too much to do, what with keeping top temples tidy for Domitian's big day. He inveigled a colleague into helping out. He knew one of the others was a soft touch. This was Tiberius Manlius Faustus. My husband.

Of course, I knew what he was intending from the moment he came home and sheepishly admitted he had let himself be commandeered. I am Flavia Albia, a private informer. I specialise in domestic situations that require investigative skills. I know what husbands are like. But I had married this man on the understanding that ours would be a sharing partnership. So, Tiberius, the sly rat, passed his task to me.

II

It didn't work out quite like that. He made a big show of worrying about his problem until, as he had intended, I said, "You will have to give the job to me."

"That wouldn't be right."

"Don't be ridiculous." I had been married two months now. I had all the wifely phrases. I promised him family rates on my fee.

"This is just right for you," Tiberius assured me. "You'll love it!"

He was right, because somebody needed to get down to asking straight-forward questions and I am that kind of girl. Nevertheless, I said a few words back. They were frank and forceful.

He knew perfectly well I could have done without this. Still establishing our household, I was breaking in staff: a new runabout, who needed to learn our habits, and a new chef, who had to be told Tiberius loved fish but hated bones, plus we had recently acquired a stray dog. Since a terrible accident on our wedding day, my husband had been unwell—though not sufficiently indisposed to prevent him making the dog a kennel, which apparently needed to be painted up, by him, like a Greek temple. It even had its own little terracotta antefix on the roof.

You might think that, while helping to organise an imperial triumph, Tiberius was very busy. Even so, it seemed a man must have priorities. For mine, what came first was finding a way to attach a broken antefix that he had picked up in a salvage yard for next to nothing because it had lost its fixing-hole.

At least there are worse hobbies. As an informer, I had had many weeping female clients so I knew the alternatives. With possibilities that include nose-picking, gambling, buggery, sloth, drink and listening to his mother too much, count yourself lucky if your man's worst trait is playing with his Greek-style acroterion.

See that as a euphemism, if you like. Old Katutis, who writes up my notes for me, may strike it out in any case.

Enough of that.

The Triumph had already caused us personal anxiety. Traditionally they begin before dawn and continue, winding at a snail's pace, for many, many hours. In the past, the grand processions for especially show-off generals have taken several days, although Domitian would not claim that. This was his third time. He knew the perils. He had to stand up all day in his chariot, a bruising journey that would require patience and strength, not to mention tempering his victorious expression with modesty, which is a hard trick to pull off. By the time he finished the ritual and was led off to a banquet, all the food would be fly-blown and naughty slaves would have spat in the drink.

What worried me was that in the line ahead of Domitian the senators and magistrates would be on foot. They had to hike through the city, across the Plain of Mars, past many theatres and markets, down through the entire length of the Circus Maximus, then back along the Forum on the Sacred Way and finally up Capitol Hill by a very steep flight of steps. The day would be a killer for any who were elderly or impaired.

I had a particular fear. My husband had been struck by lightning. He survived, but he was damaged, both physically and mentally. He now took life cautiously, never knowing from day to day whether there would be pain or confusion, whether new effects would trouble him or previous misery would reoccur. This made him frustrated and angry, so I had to be careful too. We got by, but if Tiberius Manlius tried to walk the route, wearing the heavy weight of a toga and with very few rest stops, he might not manage it. Even if he could, completing the circuit was bound to do him harm.

I had been watching him closely, yet probably had not seen all he suffered. He sometimes hid his trials. Oh, he was fine, we told everyone. He could still do everything. He was a good husband, helping me put together our new house, and he even ran a construction business. But he was not the man he had been. Tactfully I suggested the procession would be too much. Then, after dodging a flare-up, I made him accept this.

I wrote my boy a sick-note. His mother was dead; he was an orphan. I had to do it.

I did ask him first. I have more sense than some wives, which was why he married me. I felt like Calpurnia begging Julius Caesar not to go to the Senate that day, though without the excuse of a bad dream. The feeling did not stop me: I had already had one husband killed in a street accident and I wasn't going to see Tiberius brought home to me dead on a pallet too.

Since my family knew the Prefect of the City, who was in charge of Rome until Domitian came back, I addressed a pathetic plea to him. In the chaos of trying to organise the Triumph, the noble Rutilius Gallicus was heading for a nervous breakdown. The old duffer had no energy to argue with a woman who knew how to write a good letter; besides, I was suggesting I might ask the Vestal Virgins to intercede. I never would, as they are ghastly women, but Rutilius could not be sure. The poor sap stood no chance.

Rutilius Gallicus suggested that my husband might join the leading men when they went to salute the Emperor before dawn. Then, as the procession began, Faustus could slip away in a closed litter through the backstreets and spend the day quietly at our house. Later, he was supposed to make his way to the Capitol for the ceremonies at the Temple of Jupiter.

I viewed this as a forgettable promise. Stuff Jupiter. It was Jupiter who threw thunderbolts about. Jupiter had caused the lightning that struck down Tiberius. Even though the god had graciously deigned to spare his life, I would never forgive that. All-seeing Jupiter didn't notice my wedding procession? Never spotted my bridegroom in the way? Even divine beings should be taught by their mothers to take care when playing with their toys. In fact *my* mother always ensured any dangerous toys silently went missing.

I might have managed to keep Tiberius Manlius off the Capitol, but he had not escaped other burdens of his office. Aediles are famously in charge of checking market weights and so forth, but they also run big public events like the Games. Domitian's Triumph came into the same category. Tiberius had to help.

Four men in their thirties with logistical talents and public ambitions should be enough to knock together a carnival, I thought. Mine claimed it was more complicated. As Tiberius said in private to me, Rome may be a great power, capable of magnificent civic and military feats, but if a situation can be a pig's arse (some committee term, apparently) it will be.

"And this is a pig with dysentery. We have a Praetorian prefect who thinks he is organising, because of the army connection, a committee of palace freedmen who *know* they are in charge, and a clerk with a bunch of ragged public slaves who is doing all the work. Heaven knows where my colleagues and I are supposed to fit in. We get stuck with the rubbish jobs as usual. If something involves buckets and mops, the other beggars all think they can pass it to us."

"Buckets, darling?"

"For horse dung."

"Lots of that?"

"Shitloads."

"I expect you have done calculations . . ." Tiberius was that kind of man. He would have counted the horses, obtained an ostler's estimate of how much solid waste per horse should be expected over a twelve-hour period, measured by both weight and volume, and he would prepare an adequate rota of slaves to collect it. Luckily I saw him as a treasure—otherwise he would drive me nuts. "Any chance you can siphon off some for compost on roses?"

My treasure glared. I subsided, knowing when not to irritate such a top-notch co-ordinator.

Still, common sense was needed. "It's just a straight line," I muttered. "Surely a man with a noteboard can run this? You only have to muster the various groups:

- *one*, captives
- *two*, plunder
- *three*, floats with tableaux
- *four*, senators and magistrates
- *five*, general's guard of lictors
- *six*, the four-horse chariot
- *seven*, unarmed troops in clean uniforms, all shouting, '*Io triumphe!*' and singing ribald songs.

"Give each group a start time, then make sure they keep moving along. One woman with a list could do it easily."

As a woman, I was used to making sensible suggestions. Nobody listens.

"Musicians, dancers, masses of incense and strewing flowers," added Tiberius, gloomily. "Each of those is full of potential for chaos. Two white oxen to be sacrificed. *Spare* white oxen for when the originals get tired. Medics to stretcher off people who collapse. Law-and-order located at suitable points for unavoidable arrests . . ."

"The slave who has to hold the general's crown and remind him he is only a man."

"Never mind that—the important slave is the one who has the jar for when the general feels desperate for a pee," said Tiberius.

"That slave never gets a mention from historians! But I suppose Domitian can't jump down and go dashing into a public latrine if he is caught short." I laughed, then paused. "I reckon the pee-jar is some novelty introduced by the sanitation-conscious aedile, Tiberius Manlius Faustus."

My husband did not dispute it. Normally he would have enjoyed himself pretending it was an antique tradition that he had uncovered, written up in a hallowed scroll he had found deposited in the Temple of Ceres. This evening he had no heart for that. He was worn out. He hunched on a couch, where he had subsided, groaning, when he came home for supper. His slave, the useless Dromo, had followed his master out at dawn and back again at dusk, falling over his feet. Dromo had dropped straight onto a sleeping-mat in the courtyard. I myself removed my loved one's shoes before I sat and talked to him.

I gazed at him with open concern. Aware he was being assessed, he straightened slightly. He had a strong physique, which fitted his new occupation as owner of a building firm. He could carry the crazy folds of a Roman toga lightly enough, while still looking as if he would be a match for any old republican, ready to stomp back to his plough. He was tough, grey-eyed and sure of himself. My kind of man: at leisure, he liked reading but when he wanted an activity, he could paint a kennel.

"What is the conquering hero supposed to do?" I continued, hoping to distract Tiberius from his weariness. "Stand with his feet apart, looking innocent, while he discharges a hot torrent through the base of the chariot? I know he traditionally has a big breakfast beforehand. What if—"

"Military training." Tiberius let himself be drawn into a conversation that was not entirely fantasy on my part. I have attended enough family picnics to know what needs to be planned for a day out. "The manual must include a drill for crossing your legs. When you're going into battle, you can't have lads putting their hands up and whining, please, sir, can they be excused? Generals have to lead by example," he said. "Iron bladders."

This was guesswork. Tiberius had never been in the army. I refrained from pointing out that Domitian had never gone through basic training either. Becoming a prince at eighteen had spared him an early stint in the legions, so as commander-in-chief, he was winging it. He had won the soldiers' respect by awarding them a massive pay raise. He was not unintelligent. "I think you should give one of your dung-buckets a very good wash and put a gold ribbon on the handle."

"Good idea!" Tiberius roused himself. "I have married an invaluable wife. Planning cannot be skimped. I shall need to sort out a particularly handsome boy to carry the imperial bucket. A signal must be agreed in advance for when he's wanted, and we have to train him to hand up the equipment into the chariot discreetly, not to mention supply a hand-washing bowl and a nice towel. So while I am absorbed in this critical stuff, dear girl, maybe you can help me with the other thing."

"What thing?"

"The Tarpeian Rock."

I spoke more frank words, but half-heartedly.

"Good lass! There is a big budget for the Triumph: I can get you a fee. Watch out for Nestor, when you run into him."

"Who is Nestor?"

"You will find out."

Tiberius ran a hand thoughtfully over his jaw. He needed a shave. If he shouted for Dromo to razor off his manly stubble, I knew what that meant. Our ancient forefathers, that stocky breed who wore their togas so lightly and could plough so well, had established the fine tradition that a Roman wife should support her husband—after which she was entitled to her matrimonial reward.

III

The first person I contacted was the witness. Best get it over with. She might be annoying. From what I had heard about her failing to keep quiet, she would be.

Tiberius had brought home a few garbled notes, in various wonky hands. Someone had scribbled a kind of address, which I tracked down next morning. At her home there was no answer, so I braced myself to poke about nearby, searching for the old woman—my work demands persistence.

False leads from nosy neighbours became unnecessary when the dame in question turned up of her own accord, just as I was writing a note to leave on her door. Someone must have told her a fancy messenger was there. Eager to be the centre of attention, she rushed home.

I explained I was working for an aedile. The eminent Manlius Faustus, I said, thought she might prefer to talk to a woman.

I made the claim without bitterness, even though I had been an independent operator for years. I tolerate Roman prejudice. Any businesswoman has to roll with it, whether she is selling fish or running twenty commercial premises. I had been in the same position all my working life, and I started when I was only seventeen. First I was Falco's daughter; now I had to grit my teeth and be the magistrate's wife. To begin with it had driven me wild, but I had learned that once I established my presence on a case, clients would accept me as the lead professional. "It's your quiet air of competence!" said members of my family—before they guffawed.

"My name is Albia, Flavia Albia," I announced to the witness.

"Am I supposed to have heard of you?"

"No. I like to be discreet."

My contact was a typical old woman. They are everywhere in Rome. Small, skinny, intensely suspicious, worn to a shred by Life, holding off Death with vicious tenacity. She fought Death as if he was a neighbour she had been feuding with for years, determined to outlive the upstart and pinch his Gallic hens before his family arrived for the funeral.

Thin wisps of grey hair wandered about as she moved, while cat fur and particles of old breakfast clung to her black dress. She could have been any age between forty and eighty. Most likely eighty. She was slightly deaf, wobbly on her feet and a little smelly.

"Ooh, I'd love to meet an aedile!" she croaked. I could have put her lunacy down to extreme age, but I guessed she had always been that way. I pretended the great man Faustus wished he was able to give her his time, but unfortunately the Emperor had him tied up from dawn to dusk, planning the Triumph. (I had left him at home, de-fleaing the dog.) "I suppose I shall have to manage with you, then," she conceded.

"Anything you tell me, I shall report direct to him," I promised. "Manlius Faustus is deeply disappointed that he cannot meet you personally. But, trust me, I am fully in his confidence."

She inspected me with great suspicion, even so. I was twenty-nine, so just about mature enough to satisfy her. The air of competence my relations deride probably means I come across as pushy. My dark hair was pinned up, my gown and embroidered stole were of good material, I had jewellery. My necklace and earrings were more tasteful than people wore around there: the old woman lived in one tiny room in a dark apartment block where the fashion was for rings that turn your finger green and, of course, snake bracelets. Still, she had picked up the hint. If she wanted the glory of sounding off to the authorities, there I was to take her story.

It was hardly the first time I had been viewed as unreliable. In fact, I was reliable enough to have formed the same opinion of her. I won't say she was doo-lally, but this was going to be a long morning.

I produced my usual waxed tablets and stylus, which I carried in a satchel, though I did not bother taking notes of our entire rambly conversation. It was punctuated by crashes, arguments and screaming babies in the tenement outside. We were in one of those multi-storey buildings carved into the Capitol on the river side, full of tiny lets and narrow corridors, not much better than slave accommodation, despite the apparently refined location. She had allowed me into her room, where she swept mouse-droppings off a stool for me. I sat tidily, keeping one eye out for the mouse, which I guessed would not be shy. I didn't want it running up my skirt.

I listened patiently. This old bird had caused the problem by constantly harping on what she claimed she saw. The whole point of an inquiry was to prove her wrong or right. I was easy about which way it went. All I wanted was to make a true report on what had happened.

"Your name is Valeria Dillia, I believe?"

It was. Someone along the way had got that right. Dillia had lived in the same room all her life, even when she was married to a day labourer. He died fifteen years ago. She would never want to move: she knew everyone and everything that went on in the neighbourhood. Yes, I bet she did.

The information I extracted over the next two hours contained nothing new. Nothing useful anyway, though I endured endless details. It was first thing in the morning. She had been shopping at a vegetable stall. She had bought artichokes, out of season but she had managed to bag them because she had got there so early, plus a turnip and a bunch of mixed herbs, rather bruised so money-off. This set it in context. Some investigators might have imagined the turnip lent authenticity. I am not so fanciful.

"You don't favour the Forum Holitorium?" That is the big vegetable market near the river, next to the Theatre of Marcellus.

"I'm not going to trudge all the way around there for my bits and bobs. Besides, they cheat you."

Tottering back the short distance from the stalls she did like, old Dillia had carried on around the hill for some reason. She saw something like a shadow fall suddenly from high on the Arx. She was quite sure that a moment beforehand a second figure had been on the Tarpeian Rock too.

"It was barely light?"

"Enough to see by."

"What made you look up?"

"I have no idea."

"Did you hear anything? A cry?"

"No. Well, I may have. That man at the vigiles told me I must have done. Hearing the shout drew my attention, he told me."

"Just say what you remember. Ignore the man at the vigiles."

I knew how they worked, inventing evidence and blaming easy suspects. If your house is on fire they will put out the flames and rescue your baby in his cradle, provided you can get them to turn up. If you are burgled, stabbed or run over by a cart with a blind driver, either solve it yourself or hire an informer. My rates are reasonable. Please do not ask me whether Falco is still working and, if so, can you go over my head to him? Not unless you want your eye poked out. If I am too busy, Nervius at the Porticus Aemilius will do a decent job. There is an idiot who talks big by the Diribitorium; whatever you do, avoid him.

"Do you really think you heard a noise, Dillia?"

"No. A movement caught my eye. It was like a dream. Almost a premonition. I glimpsed two people, but my gaze followed the poor man who flew down."

"That's natural," I assured her sympathetically.

Dillia was far from squeamish: "So then it was, hello, what's that? Splat, ooh, nasty! Next time I looked, there was no one on the top."

"You could tell the victim was a man?"

"I think I could. Well, people said so afterwards."

"Let's not mind what other people said, though of course now we do know he was male. What about the other person?" The one who mattered if they had pushed him. The one I had to find, if this truly was murder.

"I don't know."

Thank you. What a surprise.

"But you did feel you glimpsed a tussle going on?"

"It was my impression. But it was all over in a moment."

"Gone in a flash? Yet you had a clear idea the second person gave the first a shove?"

"I thought so. I saw it, but I wouldn't like to swear an oath. I don't want to get anyone into trouble. I don't want to get into trouble myself."

"You are not." I smiled my reassuring informer's smile, which fools nobody. "Valeria Dillia, would you mind if I asked you to come with me to the place it happened? I would very much like to know just where you were standing so I can visualise the scene."

"Has the aedile asked for me to do that?"

"Yes, he has!" I exclaimed warmly.

The aedile might have done. But we had established before we were even married that I work unsupervised. One thing I like about the eminent Faustus is that after he delegates some lousy job to me he backs off. Ever since I met him I had let him know he should have faith in my skills and judgement.

"I'll come along there, then," agreed Dillia, complaisantly. "If it's for him!"

IV

Time for culture and heritage.

Whichever list you follow for the Seven Hills of Rome, the Capitoline will always be on it. Other peaks may come and go. The Janiculan and Pincian are usually excluded, though both have their advocates as high-class places to live. That pimple called the Oppian once vied for listed status. I live on the Aventine, which is the outsiders' hill, yet long ago shouldered its way in there among the main seven. Always the Capitoline reigns supreme, smallest but most prestigious. Standing close to the river and at one end of the Forum, it has two peaks called the Capitol and Arx. There, dominating the city, stand the great Temples of Jupiter and Juno. Jupiter Optimus Maximus, Best and Greatest, is on the Capitol; Juno Moneta, the One Who Warns, stands on the Arx. He the betraying husband, she the nagging wife. He has the kudos but she has the money. So like real life.

Both tops provide fabulous views, but the Arx probably wins the contest. Both Capitol and Arx have steep sides running straight up, cliffs with limited footpaths and in part too rocky ever to have been built on. The Arx is specifically known as the citadel, because it can be defended. That even happened in modern memory, during the civil war after Nero: in the battle to be emperor, Vespasian's supporters held out on the Capitol against his rival Vitellius; the Vitellians set fire to the whole hill, captured and murdered Vespasian's brother, nearly caught his son Domitian (if only!), until only the arrival of the Flavian Army saved the day.

The temples then stood in ruins. Restored by Vespasian, who famously shouldered away the first bucket of rubble himself, the still-new buildings were later lost again in a terrible fire that destroyed half of the city during the reign of his elder son Titus. Titus began a magnificent new restoration; when he died it was quickly finished by Domitian. His huge Temple of Jupiter stood on the foundations of the original Etruscan building but had the most lavish superstructure ever. It was entirely built in white Pentellic marble, with its bronze roof tiles gilded so it shone visibly from all parts of Rome.

Although the great temple contains three internal shrines and shows Jupiter with Juno and Minerva on its pedestal, Juno has her own temple as well. For four hundred years all Rome's silver currency was coined there. Domitian moved the mint. He would.

The crags had once been crowned with trees, though now they were given over to temple enclosures. Thick groves used to run down into the middle dip. While Romulus was founding Rome, he established the saddle of ground between them as a place of asylum for fugitive slaves and criminals, who were invited to live in his new city. This bunch of pioneers stole and raped the Sabine women (what else does anyone expect of riff-raff?). When the Sabines tried to fetch their wives and daughters back, the citadel commander had a daughter of his own, Tarpeia, who approached the besiegers in their camp and offered them entry into Rome in exchange for "what they bore on their left arms"—she meant their gold bracelets. The Sabines threw heavy shields on her instead, and the greedy girl's corpse was hurled from the Arx.

Despite their principled refusal of Tarpeia's offer, the Sabines (so it is said) were still unable to break into the Forum because its gates were miraculously protected by jets of boiling water created by Janus, the two-faced gate-guardian. That's myth for you. No justice.

Rome survived. Its inhabitants forgot they were descended from criminals, becoming the snobs we know today. Tarpeia is cited as a moral lesson by parents of girls who plead for jewellery. Young girls duly curse her.

Tarpeia's Rock stands on the Forum side, above the state prison called the Tullianum or the Lautumiae, where traitors are incarcerated; alongside are the Gemonian Stairs where those traitors' bodies will be left to rot. This nice configuration of punishment places is perhaps what Juno is

Warning us about. If, at the conclusion of his Triumph, Domitian's chief captives were sacrificed, they would be strangled in the Tullianum by the jailer, though the word was that Our Master had not managed to bring home anybody who was that important or interesting. Certainly, as I stood in the street with Dillia, the prison appeared to be locked up and deserted.

To my amazement, Dillia now informed me she was the official cleaner. That, she said, was why she came around the hill to here after buying her vegetables.

"I am glad to have the point cleared up—but good grief! Is it a nasty job?"

"No, it's no trouble. One of the cells is a bit deep to get down into, especially at my age, but I manage. I keep them nice. The prisoners seem to respect that. They are always instructed to behave well, but they tend to suffer from nerves—you can imagine. Otherwise, they never stay long enough to make much mess. They just have a day or two until they are done in. After they are turfed out dead, I soon whisk around with a mop again. The jailer only comes in for stranglings. Lovely man, very clean habits. So on special occasions I do up the premises. He gives me a tip out of what he earns. We rub along well—we have done for years."

"Fascinating!"

I had heard that if ever a prisoner was a young girl, for instance the teenage daughter of the disgraced Praetorian Sejanus, the jailer had to rape her to avoid the crime of killing a virgin. I decided not to ask Dillia, who might hate to think of her clean-habits man having to carry out anything so sordid.

Then I did ask the question after all. Of course I was as curious as you are.

"He would. It's just a job," she answered, not batting an eyelid. Learning about people's different attitudes is an aspect of my work. As she saw me raise a cool eyebrow, Dillia insisted, "Sejanus tried to take over the Empire, didn't he? What kind of behaviour is that? It was right that his children were killed too—I bet that taught him. The jailer at the time must have done it in the line of duty, not because he enjoyed it. Besides, it's not going to affect the little girl for long, is it, not if she is strangled straight away?"

This is a popular excuse among serial killers too: "The women never suffered."

I felt depressed now, but Dillia perked up. We stood at the bottom of the Gemonian Stairs, which climb up to the corner of the Tabularium, that huge construction at the top of the Forum where archives are kept. The Tabularium was above us on the left-hand side; the Tarpeian Rock soared on the right. I put myself into searching professional mode as I made Valeria Dillia give her statement of what she saw and where.

V

We stared up at the Rock. Valeria Dillia gestured to where she had thought she glimpsed two figures, then where she saw the body fall. Given how tragic it must have been, and how much she wanted to dwell on it, her gestures verged on vague. Still, I have had worse witnesses. It is quite common that they insist they possess priceless evidence yet, when challenged, it evaporates.

I tested her eyesight. To Dillia, I blamed the aedile for suggesting this examination, though the idea was mine. I made her look down the street, across to the Temple of Saturn on the far side of the Forum, then tell me about people coming and going. She got about half of them right. She picked out the man in the long tunic who was turning up the Clivus Capitolinus; she counted the panniers on a donkey, though she could not tell whether the woman touting for business near the Curia was as young as she wanted men to think. Mind you, this is a regular problem for prostitutes' punters, even when they are right up close.

"The body is no longer here of course," I mused, fairly sure Dillia would know what was done with it.

"No, they took it away."

"You stayed to watch what happened?"

"That's natural, isn't it?"

"Who came?"

"Men."

"Vigiles? Public slaves?"

"I don't know. There was a commotion. Some temple officials, it looked like, popped up on the top and had a look down, gabbling and pointing.

Then people came scrambling down the steps. A bunch of the ones who are working up there for the Triumph, I suppose. Some of them managed to climb over to the bottom of the rock and they pulled the body out, hauling him by his heels onto the steps. The public had been shooed off by then."

"Not you?"

"Nobody bothers about an old duck like me. The workmen stood around looking at the dead man for so long I nearly went home tired, but then someone must have said something. They picked him up and threw him on a barrow that had been wheeled down here, so away he went."

I opened my mouth, about to ask where he was being taken.

"Don't ask me," said Dillia, sharper than she looked. I had interviewed people like her before. Now she would be over-confident, breaking in to answer the wrong question.

"Did they seem to know who he was?"

"They seemed like idiots."

"That sounds like a fair assessment," I said. "I wonder if he ever had a funeral."

"I heard he did. I would have gone," Dillia told me, "paid my respects, seen if they had a few bits to eat and any speeches. Only it was never advertised."

Thanking Dillia for her public-spiritedness in coming forward, I sent her on her way.

Well, I tried. She clung on. "Will I have to help the aedile again?"

"At this stage, I am not sure."

"Well, you know where to find me if he wants any more evidence. If I'm not at home, I shall be in the prison with my mop."

"Thanks."

"Are you going up on top now? Shall I come with you?"

Over-hopeful, ever-helpful—for a bad moment I thought she was glued to me permanently. Luckily, I managed to shake her off.

She had told me nothing new. I was now able to picture the man's fall, but I could have come here alone and figured that out.

———

I climbed to the top of the Gemonian Stairs. As I laboured up the crumbly steps that curve around first the prison, then the side of the big Temple of Concord, I reflected that if the Citadel was ever attacked, this would indeed be a hard way to take it. There are other routes up, though all equally steep. A crag is a crag.

At least it is until a Domitian comes along. He had new plans to dig out the ground that links the Arx to the Quirinal, boldly reconfiguring the hillside. To our emperor, Rome was a big sandpit where a boy as important as him was allowed to play all he liked. Juno's Citadel had stood and looked the same for eight hundred years, but the emperor's massive building programme never stopped. It showed no deference to sacred topography.

Domitian had built more grandiose public buildings than anyone, with many new works still at the planning stage. He had the funds. His father had filled the Treasury. The Flavians possessed tax-collectors in their ancestry; they knew how to gather in masses of cash, then make it work for them.

No one, I noticed, had bothered to repair the Gemonian Stairs. They are nicknamed the Stairs of Mourning. This may be because you can twist your ankle so easily and bust a sandal strap.

I had been up these cranky steps many times, when taken by my father to see the Sacred Geese of Juno. Falco had a fondness for those birds. If he fancied an omelette for supper, his innocent-looking daughter would be assigned the task of carrying home the eggs in her stole.

With my past-learned caution, I negotiated the cracked steps. At the top I paused, regaining my breath. Then I took a quick, wary look over the edge of the cliff, making sure not to fall down. There is no health-and-safety balustrade. A would-be suicide need not even take a run at it. All he had to do was be brave and jump.

Murder would be possible. Stand near the edge. Distract or overpower your victim, then a sudden big shove . . . Just ensure they don't grab your tunic and pull you over with them. Step away quickly. Dodge off before any witness can be certain they saw you.

The Arx was useless for evidence. Below on the cliff there was nothing to see, no snagged clothing, not even a trail of battered bushes to mark the victim's fall. Above, the ground was rough and rocky. Such a place could not retain footprints or other clues. All I found was goose-droppings and litter. Everything looked quite old.

What now? There seemed to be unusual activity everywhere, both here on the Arx and over on the Capitol. Extra staff were tidying the open spaces, while small groups of soldiers, in boots and red tunics but minus their armour, ambled about with no obvious purpose. Where could I start?

Between the Temple of Juno Moneta and the cliff edge is a flattish open space, the Auguraculum. The college of augurs operates there, regarding the Arx in general as their roofless temple, a major site for the pursuit of Etruscan divination. They don't practise as haruspices, who know about animal livers and how chickens feed; they are seers, who scan the heavens to interpret stars and the flights of birds. Favourable signs give validity to main events such as the appointment of consuls; claiming the signs are *not* favourable can be a useful device for politicians to delay proceedings . . .

"Oh, never in our city!" I hear you cry.

From the Arx, augurs who have avoided cataracts can see as far as the Alban Hills, more than twenty miles away. After Domitian built his fortress retreat at Alba Longa, they had a sightline straight there—but they would be aware of the terrible truth: if you can see Our Master, he can see you. And he will be looking. If he is in residence, he is always looking. Nobody needs to poke about inside a dead sheep to prophesy that.

Almost certainly a ceremony would occur up there, immediately before the Triumph. Only a brave haruspex would tell Domitian he could not proceed because a spot on some steaming entrails had forbidden it, but sky-watching augury is a more fluid art. These augurs would fix it. Birds would fly in the right configuration, no doubt of that. No crow would cross Domitian.

I saw that the standard preparations were being made so they could promise good luck for him. A small tent with an open top had been erected, squared to the compass points, within which an observer would position himself to stare at the sky. I could hear male voices coming from inside.

Relatives of mine had served in the legions. They had taught me various handy tricks. When approaching a tent, it is always a good idea to cough: this gives the occupants a chance to stop anything naughty they may be doing.

VI

A *hem!* Coming in!" I cried cheerily, before opening the tent flap. "Is there room for a little one?"

Two men were inside. One was an augur: his long special robe was folded up on the ground with his crooked stick on top of the pile. The other had to be his cheeky assistant. They were eating bread rolls. I suspected they had been discussing the races. It took me two beats to decide this was a right pair of confederates.

"I hope I am not disrupting anything religious—oh, no, it's your lunch-break."

Being an augur is a sought-after post for senators. This incumbent had to be a patrician, despite looking as if he came from the rough end of the scale.

Tall but gaunt, in a long black tunic and wearing sandals I wouldn't give a dog to chew, he carried himself with world-weary hunched shoulders, even when sitting on his cross-legged augury stool. He had a certain look about him. I wouldn't have left him in a room with my sister. Mind you, my brother would sort him: Postumus tends to fix people as if he is wondering which tool from his toy farm he will use to disembowel them. Don't worry: we have explained that he must ask us first. He is an obedient boy. So long as we like people, they are safe.

The assistant also gave off untrustworthy signals. If he were a mansio stable-lad, your horse would bite him—then you'd quickly learn he knew how to demand compensation. Done it before. Better cough up: he's had more practice than you.

He was using a stool, which he must have pinched from another augur. I presumed he helped to erect the observation hide, because he had a mallet under his seat, along with secretarial items that suggested he took notes of observations. He was around the same age as the first man, maybe fifty. Even so, this laddish chancer had persuaded his barber to shave his head up from his neck to above his sticking-out ears, leaving matted hair on top. It goes without saying that the remaining follicles were as oily as fish on a barbecue. If one of his lovers ran fingers through that thatch, the run-off would do to stop squeaks in cupboard hinges.

"Your tent is a bit draughty," I commented, as I came inside its leather walls to join them. Above us, the sky over Rome was blue—and completely empty of birdlife. Not that anyone was scanning for portents. The races were more important. They had been using a third augury stool as a camp-table for their food, so I moved the empty basket and sat down with them.

"Greetings, prescient ones. My name is Flavia Albia. I have been engaged by the aediles to solve the mystery of what happened with that man who jumped off the Tarpeian Rock. Perhaps you have enough ancient wisdom to foresee where my task will lead me." Clearly not. I sighed aloud. "No, that would have been too helpful."

They had been stuck in poses of surprise ever since I arrived. I must have been the first woman to be chippy with an augur since Romulus came home to his shepherd mother after cheating his brother Remus over who should found Rome. As they continued to stare, I added brightly to the man with vision, "Validation: I am the wife of Manlius Faustus, the poor plebeian aedile who was struck by lightning on his wedding day. I imagine that incident caused hot interest in augury circles. Also, sir, I am related to your colleagues in the Senate, the noble Camillus Aelianus and Camillus Justinus, if you know them."

He did not. My uncles, who were only marginally noble, would not want acquaintance with him, either: both Camillus brothers regard state divination as mumbo-jumbo. Justinus comes right out and says he would campaign against offal-peering and sky-watching, but superstition is so popular he could count on no support. Aelianus can be pompous, but even he would rather see a sacred chicken bubbling in broth with tarragon leaves and wild garlic.

The augur unbent: he introduced himself as Larth and his assistant as Lemni. I took these for Etruscan working names. The voice of Larth was slow and sonorous, the result of a life spent intoning. This man would make "Pass the salt" sound like a thousand-year-old prayer for abundant crops and fertile women.

Lemni, piping up like a market porter, took it upon himself to relay answers for his superior, who seemed simply too tired to continue. Overnight augury must be as shattering as any shift-work. I asked if they were there on the evening of the supposed suicide. Lemni confirmed it, though they had been absorbed in putting up the tent for that night's watch. It must be done correctly. Lemni boasted of his skills. I admired the tent's taut walls.

When the man jumped off the Rock, they heard a commotion so they went across to look as soon as they could. If you stop a ritual action you have to go right back to the beginning. By the time they had finished installing their tent according to the ancient rules, anyone else who had been present when the victim fell was gone. Lemni pretended the augur and he had behaved calmly at the top of the cliff, though Dillia had told me the reaction she saw was highly excitable. I believed her.

"Did you know the dead man previously?"

"We never heard his name," said Lemni.

Larth, the augur, abruptly roused himself, though he had to fight off a yawn. "I nodded greetings to the man on occasions. He had something to do with transport, I believe."

"Yes," I said. "Officials have identified him."

"He had been working out of the hut alongside Jupiter Custos."

Larth meant the temple caretaker's accommodation. That one-time hovel has been turned all magnificent. Its striking upgrade commemorates how the young Domitian's life was saved when he was hidden overnight on the blazing Capitol. Afterwards, Domitian converted the grim kiosk where he had cowered for hours into a whole new temple. Presumably the caretaker did not live in the shrine, but some adjacent cubicle. If he was lucky, it too had been gratefully upgraded.

"I know it." I explained: "I am familiar with the precincts here. Thanks to the deified Vespasian, doughty old chap, my father was for several years Procurator of the Sacred Geese of Juno."

"Quite an honour," returned the augur, perhaps satirically. The old emperor had certainly seen it as a laugh. Nevertheless, Pa was diligent: the geese had never had their welfare so tenderly nurtured, and he claims the honky avians loved him for it.

"Vespasian had a gift for finding the right man for a job." I simpered.

"Indubitably." I thought Vespasian might have chosen Larth, the augur, though probably not Lemni. "Do we remember your father?" Larth hinted.

"Marcus Didius Falco."

Oh, yes, they knew him! Falco would have transited the Arx like a rackety comet. A glance passed between them. However, the polite sky-watchers made no comment.

"So how come the dead carts-organiser was using the new élite hut? What did the caretaker feel about that?" I wondered. "Did he want a sub-tenant? Are they bunking up in the same rustic bed and sharing humble meals? Surely he cannot be happy."

"He was incandescent," confirmed Lemni, enjoying the suggestion that the transport man behaved badly to the caretaker. It was my first proper hint of a possible motive. "He was very harshly ejected."

"You did know the sweeper? You heard his complaints?"

"Too right! He now has to trudge up the hill every day to carry out his duties, which is very inconvenient, especially after he used to be right on the spot. This has upset his whole routine. He grumbles at anyone who will listen. Seated in the tent, we were at his mercy."

I tutted sympathetically. "Not still the same man who hid Domitian?" I asked.

"No, his grandson."

"Jobs for the boys? I beg your pardon, I mean of course 'a hereditary position.'" We all smirked. "Still, Domitian loves to remember how his skin was saved all those years ago . . . So where has the displaced care-taker put himself?"

"He went home to his mother."

"Ah! Is his mother happy with that?"

"No, she thought her great fledgling had safely flown the nest. She gave his room to a lodger who acts as her lover, so his nose has been put out of joint. She has been coming up here herself, sounding off about it like a pre-menstrual harpy."

Lemni finished eating. He handed me half a roll he did not want. I chewed it thoughtfully. The bread was good, but the strong cheese tasted as if it had been sliced with a knife that had recently cut onions. "So tell me," I mumbled, when my mouth was empty enough, "whose bright idea was it to park a transport man on the Capitol? Surely it's a road to nowhere."

"His own." The augur came to life again. He spoke with doleful disapproval, even though his role in life was to be a neutral conduit for divine will.

"How come?" I wheedled.

"He was like that." Even augurs can be drawn. When they are not pronouncing on the prospects for war or peace, they like gossip as much as anybody. "Upstart. Full of his own importance. It was to do with the Triumph. The carts and draught animals are kept down in the Campus Martius, but *he* thought he rated fine views and a high-end site-hut."

"Made his nasty presence felt," added Lemni. "He loved kicking out the keeper. Of course we are above tittle-tattle, but he was objectionable to anyone he bumped into. Everybody hated him."

"You too?"

"He kept away from us."

"Bullies like that can spot someone handy, Lemni!" Flattering him, I licked my fingers clean as I finished the roll. "I was asked to investigate a suggestion that this charmer may have been murdered. What you describe sounds like motive."

Both men tipped their heads and nodded. I asked whether they had witnessed any portents that foul play was due on the Capitol.

"None," said the augur. "But no one asked us to look."

That sounded like a get-out clause. They must be used to surprises. They have to pronounce on natural phenomena, exciting events like tornadoes, trees falling down on windless days, fish dropping from the sky. "What, no ravens cawing loudly, *He's a complete bastard. Someone's got it in for him?* You are no help!" I teased. "Still, in my line, what's new?"

"That stuff is a bit old hat," Lemni joshed back. "These days, if a lion whelps in the street we just call in the aediles to capture the mother and cub for public safety . . . I bet you love a victim who was unpopular with everyone," he said, grinning. "Such a large cache of suspects!"

"I like a challenge," I replied, as I got to my feet. "I see I am in for days of disgruntlement from this man's enemies. I wonder how many will tell me they loathed his guts yet swear *they* never gave him the heave-ho off Tarpeia's Rock. All of them will gloat at me that I can't prove anything against them, at the same time as they assure me they are ecstatic that he is dead . . ."

Lemni winked. Then he offered to arrange a private observation to ask the gods about my chances. Those two must be busy entrepreneurs: they had denarius signs in their eyes. I guessed their freelance work funded a huge investment portfolio—if I accepted their offer, I foresaw my budget withering.

I declined gently. I was already starting to believe my inquiry would be hopeless. I noticed they never suggested their bird- or star-watching could actually find evidence. "I have my own methods. Let me give it a try solo. Thank you, amiable ones. I have enjoyed our chat, but since you have no clues for me, I must tiptoe across to sniff around the janitor's hut where the dead man had been living."

They both reared to their feet in polite farewell. The augur bowed. Since lightning was so much a part of their work, Larth even asked whether I would like him to consult the gods about my husband's recovery. Lemni, who had spotted my scepticism earlier, was quick to say we could have mates' rates.

"You act for private citizens a lot?" I asked, as one freelance to another pair.

"Top-sector obs, with attractive money-off discounts. A certificate of prophecy on special papyrus for a small extra fee. Full reviews from satisfied clients. Answer a few simple questions and you are guaranteed to be accepted. Bird of choice."

"From a specific selection?"

"Crow or eagle. Or on our most basic fee-scale, which we do not recommend to you, Albia, Larth will do you any flock that passes over."

If they thought they could swing it on me, this off-colour pair had been living in the Citadel's rarefied atmosphere too long. But I said I would ask Tiberius, even though I guessed he would decide we preferred the future to come as a surprise. "My husband is very traditional."

"Oh, tight with his cash!" quipped Lemni.

"No, the aedile has always been generous with me."

"Understandable!" cried the augur, sounding just the wrong side of flirtatious while he eyed me up as if I were a particularly rare alignment of planets.

I had been squeezed in a tent with two dubious men for long enough. I lowered my eyes modestly and escaped.

VII

Ostentation does not impress me. While I walked down through the Grove of Asylum and up the other side, I shot baleful looks at the Temple of Jupiter Best and Greatest. It is too huge. Four times as large as the Temple of Juno behind me, garish with its golden roof and plated doors, flashing its massive topknot of a four-horse chariot, then there is more: as well as that careering quadriga, the three gods sit enthroned on the pediment, above a totally excessive glittering spread eagle, while on either side of them thrash other two-horse vehicles, carrying sun and moon divinities. In Olympus there is no escape from your relations. Gods from that fractured family also cluster on the roof, thinking about how lovely they look and where to go next for a love affair . . .

At ground level the sanctuary needed a good clear-out. As well as the bright white hexastyle double colonnade in front, with its single side colonnades, our emperor had dumped up here four ancient columns created from the rostra of captured ships. People collect this clutter then need to find a home for it. The entire walled precinct, covering most of the hill, was clogged with shrines, statues, altars, and as many trophies from forgotten wars as could be squashed in.

By comparison, the replacement hut, renamed the Temple of Jupiter Custos, Jupiter the Guardian, was neat and tasteful. It had an altar illustrating Domitian's night of adventure on beautifully cut marble panels. Jupiter extended a protective arm above the grateful Flavian youth as he courageously eluded capture. My mother corresponds with a doctor in Alexandria who suggested that extreme terror when Domitian was eighteen might have triggered his paranoia. Helena Justina had had to destroy the letter since anybody paranoid would call it treason.

The caretaker who hid him was not pictured. Still, he won his perks. The pretty little shrine of Jupiter Custos was sited in the lee of the big temple. Attached to the shrine was a modest staff lodging. Perhaps any caretaker was now obliged to keep a pile of rugs, under which any fleeing princelings could be concealed.

Some people say Domitian was hidden by a kennel-keeper. Rubbish! They have consulted the wrong encyclopaedia, some trove of lightweight scholarship that claims the caretaker looks after the dogs that historically guarded the Capitol. Idiots. Those would be the dogs that failed to bark when invasion threatened—which is why Juno's geese, who did raise the alarm, are treated regally and carried in processions on purple cushions. Centuries later the geese are still there, still doing a great job as thuggish security guards. Trust me, the dogs were banished. Consider this, easily fooled encyclopedia-readers: no frugal Flavian emperor will pay twice for the same service.

Enough. I could calm down. Other people were getting themselves worked up.

Two men were having an argument. Listening in, I waited for them to finish. When they seemed disinclined to pause, I took out a waxed tablet and pretended to make notes.

Being watched by a quiet woman with a scathing expression will eventually stop most men having a spat. For one thing, they end up wanting to sound off at her instead. Also, no one in Rome likes a stranger who turns up and carefully writes things down, in case something they have done or said gets reported to Domitian.

They stopped. They stared at me.

They were, I had gathered from their furious quarrel, the caretaker, who wanted to reclaim his hut, and the stand-in transport manager, who had grabbed the place from his dead colleague. Like his predecessor, the new bully meant to stay put. So long as he lingered, the caretaker would come here every day and give him hell for it. As the augur indicated, there would be no compromise.

Once they paused, I told them who I was and what I had been hired to do. I suggested the cart-organiser should go inside the hut where he could play with his logistical lists, while I had a few words with the caretaker. Later, I would come and talk transport. Neither liked it, but they were so curious, both grumpily agreed.

My first witness, the caretaker, was a pug-nosed, curly-haired precinct watchman of the standard swarthy type. Squat of build and short of polish, he was either an ex-slave himself or had slavery in his pedigree. He looked as if they had carved him out of bedrock; he behaved like the king of the heights. His name was Callipus. He was the kind of worker who moans that he has a one-man job that is very lonely—whereas in fact he spends all day leaning on a broom talking to people. He wore a neutral-coloured tunic with one sleeve missing, a man pretending to do manual work, though I guessed his duties were light.

I took no notes. I let him rant. I am famously intolerant, but I do sometimes quietly watch witnesses unburden themselves. It fills in time while I am wondering what the heck to ask them next.

I learned that he was employed to guard the mighty Temple of Jupiter, together with its environs on the Capitol, though he did not have to patrol the Arx: Juno Moneta had her own staff. His patch included the Temple of Faith, the Temple of Vejovis, many altars and statues, including the monumental altar dedicated by the Senate when the Empress Livia was seriously ill. There was also a famous contentious trophy that showed a Numidian prince called Jugurtha being handed over to Rome, an episode of murder, bribery and betrayal: Marius and Sulla in bitter rivalry over who deserved the triumph, thereby sparking civil war. My trophy is better than your trophy. My war is justified.

The caretaker kept the area clean and tidy. He prevented theft. His duties were to shoo away vagrants, shout at drunks, kick pickpockets, and try at least to deter the usual idlers who hang about hoping to pick up someone for sex. Shrines are sordid places.

I had assumed Rome's great temples were mainly at risk because of their huge deposits of treasure, gifted by the grateful over many centuries. Gold, said my witness, could be locked down in the vaults. Stealing from the cella upstairs—statuary, precious vessels used in sacrifice or a goddess's earrings—was such a serious crime that it was rare. The real worry for state authorities was a secret one: temples contain weaponry. Returning generals offer up arms they have seized. Since Rome, a self-professed warlike nation, was founded seven hundred years ago, there is a monstrous amount of this military paraphernalia. None can ever be removed. It is a gift to the gods.

You bet it is. Generals' wives don't want that terrible clutter in their fashionable homes.

What the weaponry meant, Callipus told me, was that Rome's fear of armed mobs could easily come true: all any rebel or gangster needed to do was break into a few temples and grab the mouldering trophies of their ancestors. One aspect does deter them, though: most Romans would not be seen dead carrying curly foreign swords and sickles or wearing exotic barbarian armour.

The Roman "trophy" was familiar to me: a tall frame made of crossed bundles of javelins, an empty breastplate stuck up like a very fancy scarecrow, with a helmet balanced on top, shields and flags added according to taste. A couple of these monuments were rusting away in the open air on the Capitol, pieces so old that, although in theory thieves could snaffle them, any leather was ready to disintegrate and even the ironwork would shatter under stress. No robber was likely to bother.

That explained, I thought drily, why if you wanted to murder an obnoxious transport manager, you wouldn't bother stabbing him with some ancient blade that might snap. You would push him off a rock instead.

"This is my busy time. It's always hard when we have a triumph," grumbled Callipus. "Every temple is thrown open so the gods can join the party, and there is endless talk of weapons. It gives the wrong people all the wrong ideas." I nodded sympathetically. He careered on: "Well, you see what I'm saying, Flavia Albia. I need to be here on the spot. I need to be really vigilant. And that swine landed me in it with my mother as well. She has already had enough of me and I can't bear the idiot she lives with. So the transport man had no business heaving me out of my proper hut like he did."

Callipus had wound up and come back to the point of his own accord.

"Let's get to him!" I said, breaking in anyway to remind him I meant business. "Tell me all about this interloper."

His name was Gabinus and he was a right stinker.

"Thank you, Callipus. You are the first person who has provided me with anything factual about the dead man."

There was more. Much more.

Gabinus was a pushing-and-shoving, throwing-his-weight-about, chancing-his-arm general menace. He was short and hated anyone to mention it. He was skinny, pigeon-toed, rumpled, ill-shaven, near-sighted and deaf to reason. He had mean beady eyes and a country accent. He wore a red tunic with black braid. He believed all women would fall at his feet; surprisingly, some did. He also had dodgy-looking business contacts who came up to see him here at all hours.

"Who were they?" I managed to ask.

"No idea."

"Isn't it your job to monitor oddball visitors?"

"No, not at the moment. With Domitian due to come up to the sanctuary, a Praetorian has turned up to do identity checks."

I would need to speak to him. Internally I groaned. I hate Praetorian guards.

"This is just what I don't need!" Callipus wailed. "People of all sorts wandering about here when we are trying to get the place nice for the Emperor's do."

He gave me a look. I was a person of dubious sort, wandering about. Luckily in my work suspicion of me is normal. I gave him a look back. I have interviewed a great many suspects. I ignore what they think. Even the ones who *can* think tend not to be trained in philosophy.

Crunch time: "Thank you for such a detailed portrait. I can certainly see why he annoyed you. So, Callipus, let me ask: if somebody shoved the ghastly Gabinus off Tarpeia's Rock—was it you?"

Apparently not. He said he had been at his mother's house. She and her abominable lover would both vouch for that.

Leaving wails of outrage rising like steam from a volcanic geyser, I abandoned the janitor to his indignation while I went in to question the dead man's deputy.

VIII

The caretaker's hut was a single room, fully furnished—what my father calls a bed-and-bucket bunk-up. The bed was a narrow cot; there was no bucket. Instead, since every state employee was entitled to one luxury to show how lucky he was, working for such a compassionate emperor, the caretaker of the greatest temple outside Greece had been allowed a very small table with a short leg.

Egnatius, the new transport man, leaned on the janitor's wonky table as he waited his turn irritably. Another wide-bodied, hairy-legged, self-righteous layabout, he managed to be both truculent and smug. His earth-tone tunic had two sleeves, to show he was a level up from menial.

Gabinus had taken squatter's rights; Egnatius now owned them as a self-claimed inheritance. He was sleeping in the janitor's bed, using his bowl and beaker, petting his cat (or more likely kicking it), while defiantly refusing to be ousted. However, that was no reason for him to keep the place decent. His crumbs were on the table and his mud was on the floor. His piss would have been in the chamber pot, but there wasn't one.

As soon as I came in, he told me he would not be kicked out by any two-quadrans female who tripped up the Clivus Capitolinus with the purpose of dislodging him. His voice was hoarse from snarling at people.

I stayed calm. I told him again what my real purpose was. "You want to be careful how you fill Gabinus' boots," I said. "It looks as if he was shoved off the Rock. What guarantee you won't be sent flying down after him?"

I would not normally threaten a witness straight away. I like to get to know them first. It helps me choose which picturesque death to suggest. Be apt. It does twice the damage.

Egnatius seemed to have taken over his forebear's objectionable manner too. "Get lost, bitch."

"All charm! Of course, you may end up pitchforked off the Rock simply by public demand."

"Why's that?" They never can resist.

"It could be you who shoved Gabinus."

For a moment the transport man boiled with the same umbrage that had so loudly overcome the caretaker. He was sufficiently intelligent to read my steady manner. I watched him think, then pause. I won't say he changed, but rather than storm in, he waited.

If he *had* killed Gabinus, I reckoned this Egnatius would have planned his actions with care. If he did do it, I felt I stood little chance of breaking him.

"You took over his job," I said. While he thought about that too, I organised a seat for myself. There was only one stool; Egnatius was firmly plonked on it. With one hand I swept the remains of a horrible breakfast off the tiny table, then from my satchel I removed a clean napkin which I spread on a corner so I could perch myself on that. An ample woman could not have done it.

I made sure my pose was not provocative. I adopted the style of an unpleasant spinster aunt. "Don't bother offering me the stool. I wouldn't want to sit where you may have farted."

I always found it best to establish that a hostile witness was not about to encounter what he expected from an aedile's wife. Egnatius would gradually work out that it must be a rather unusual aedile who had sent me to poke around. He might even spot that Manlius Faustus had taken an unusual wife.

I spoke quietly. "You installed yourself in Gabinus' job, so if somebody killed him, you are the prime suspect. If this case had gone to the vigiles, you would be in a cell right now, shredded by their whip-man—even if you are innocent, as you maintain. If the Praetorians had bothered with their lovely no-questions-asked procedure, you would be queuing outside a lion's cage, waiting for a big ferocious beast to eat you. So think on. If you want to keep your liberty and life, this is up to you, Claudius."

"My name's Egnatius."

"Claudius Egnatius, help me, if you want to help yourself." Calling people by the wrong name is an old ploy, often productive.

"You are a very annoying woman."

"So my family tell me. They love me for it. Even you will love me, I imagine, if I clear you of this very serious charge."

"What charge? There is no charge—"

"Skip it. You will be charged with murder, unless you give me cause to see someone else as a more likely suspect. Start now. Who had your colleague annoyed so much, they might have killed him?"

"Gabinus committed suicide." I glared sternly, eyebrows raised. "Didn't he?" Egnatius quavered.

"A witness says no."

"What witness?"

"Somebody public-spirited who came forward. Very believable. Until the killer is apprehended, their identity will be protected." It struck me I had better warn Valeria Dillia to start keeping quiet.

Egnatius was weakening. I saw a froth of nervous spittle at the corner of his mouth.

"Now listen, Claudius—"

"I said—"

"So you did. Give me your three names."

"Titus Flavius Egnatius."

A palace freedman of Vespasian's era, going by his position and age. I made a point of writing the name on my note-tablet. I could always squash it out later. I added a scribble that he could not read, though he tried hard: *all-round idiot*.

"So, Titus Flavius Egnatius, let's get to it. Why would Gabinus kill himself? You worked with him, did he seem depressed? Don't say he did. Come off it, I've only been investigating this for a day, yet I am sure he had no reason: he enjoyed throwing himself about in a job he thought important, and with a double triumph coming up he was at the peak of his career. Not to mention the money," I scoffed. "I guess there is a big bag of gold for whoever titivates the chariot?"

Egnatius, not as intelligent as he thought, made the mistake of boasting about the stupendous reward for pimping the Emperor's ride. Very gently, I pointed out that he, now he had snatched the job, had put himself in line for this bonanza. Cursing, he saw he had marked himself as the man with a motive.

I won't say I had Egnatius eating out of my hand. But from that point he began to answer, even though he did it cagily.

First, I asked about the sought-after job he held. I said this would help me put together a picture of the victim. I knew it would provide an insight into Egnatius too.

The transport brief for the Triumph was two-fold: beasts and the vehicles they had to pull. Horses and oxen were collected temporarily in fields on the outskirts of Rome, but immediately before the big day they had to be brought into the city and stabled. Stabling was a nightmare because of all the visitors flocking to Rome. "No matter how often we tell an innkeeper his place is requisitioned, they just take no notice. Then we turn up with our horseflesh but, bloody heck, there is no room." I nodded. It would be no good earmarking a billet, only to find the stalls filled with five Sicilians' mangy mules and a bad-tempered ox from Veii.

"Fodder's a problem?" I asked.

"Not a problem," he replied tetchily. "Just needs to be organised."

"And you can requisition merrily?"

Annoyed by my questions, the man just growled. Still, I was a daughter and a wife. I knew that scenario.

Gabinus, and now Egnatius, had to ensure he collected enough animals for the procession. Because it took so long, relays were needed, stationed in side-streets along the route. Nosebags would not suffice; the teams would need a proper respite. Crack squads of grooms had to be ready for discreet and speedy changes.

Security was vital too, so whenever a cart stopped for some reason, citizens could be stopped from jumping on it to steal its cargo of weapons, jewels, drinking vessels, statues or mechanical curiosities. I knew that at our family auction house they were preparing to sell many lots that had "fallen off" triumphal carts. My father was chipper with expectation, honing his spiel that anything foreign-looking was "a superb copy, almost as good as the real thing, heavily inspired by our recent triumph."

"Loading up on procession day must take a long time," I suggested. Being related to auctioneers teaches you a lot about this.

"Our lads have loading the fancy freight down to a fine art."

"Mainly good positioning and tying on tight?"

Egnatius ignored me. "It's the floats we loathe." Among the carnival sights that would sway through the streets were representations of towns, forests, rivers, battle-sites—or, at least, battles Rome had won. Along the Danube frontier there had been terrible defeats in recent years. The floats would not be carrying reproductions of the governor of Pannonia being beheaded during an incursion, or Praetorian guards suffering ambush and massacre at Tapae, near the Dacian stronghold. "The idiots make the flats and models top-heavy. Half the time they are impossible even to lift onto the carts."

"How did Gabinus get along with those people?" I already knew what the answer would be.

"He couldn't stand them. And they bloody hated him."

I wondered how many of these carpenters, swag-sewers, scenery-painters, glue-pasters and overall set-designers there would be, but I could not face asking. Reading my mind, Egnatius grinned.

I braced myself. Do your job, Albia. "Any particular bugbear?"

Egnatius gave me a name. Successus. A painter who specialised in towns. "He's a failure!" And Spurius, who did rivers. "He's a leftover."

Then there was Quartilla, a costume-maker, who would be dressing the various captives in typical Chattian or Dacian daywear. Egnatius gave no details on her.

He did mention Lalus, a gilder, who had to polish the pictorial elements of the special chariot. According to him, a trouble-maker.

"Is responsibility for this chariot yours overall?"

"Of course it's bloody ours," Egnatius sneered. "It's a vehicle, isn't it?"

"Sorry. I just thought a special chariot might be assigned a special chariot-manager."

"It is. That used to be Gabinus and now it's me. Normally we're at the palace looking after imperial litters and carriages."

"Wonderful."

He lost interest in being tetchy with me, as he went off into a rant of his own. "Bloody Domitian wanted elephants. An elephant quadriga—I ask you! Typical."

I raised my eyebrows as if sharing his disgust at the crazy idea. "Well, Egnatius, I have seen them on old coins, so it has been done. But getting them to stand abreast to pull must be demanding. Don't elephants really like to walk one by one in a line?"

Egnatius looked at me in astonishment. The concept of an educated woman, who absorbed curious knowledge, was completely new to him. He thought I was taking the fish-pickle.

"Well, we just told the poncy messenger to go back wherever he came from and remind all the crackpots he found there that when Pompey the Great tried to have an elephant quadriga it got stuck in the Triumphal Arch. Pompey Magnus had to climb off his chariot and wait for horses."

"Ouch! Nobody wants a repeat performance . . . So you are doing white horses?"

"Nice couple of teams from the racing stables," Egnatius confirmed glumly. "Just hope none of them gets colic. I'm up to my eyes with worry. I don't suppose you know this, Flavia, but Julius Caesar nearly came to grief once. He was driving past the Velabrum when the axle on his chariot actually broke. What a nightmare. I have to have wheels and a spare axle standing by. Just in case."

I did know.

No point telling him.

Nor did I mention that I loathe being called Flavia.

"You are giving me a good picture of this highly important job you do," I said, lashing on the flattery. "So was Gabinus good at it?"

"He knew his stuff."

"Really, or bluffing?"

Grudging at first, Egnatius felt obliged to correct my scepticism: "He was all right. He seemed as if he couldn't organise a wine festival in a vine-yard, yet somehow it would all happen. I have to hand that to him."

"And how did he treat you? I imagine that, as his deputy, he relied on you heavily."

"He was poisonous with me."

"I am sorry to hear it."

"No, he was like that with everyone."

"You didn't enjoy working with him?"

"I loathed him," Egnatius told me with feeling. "I'll tell you straight, I'm laughing my boots off that the filthy swine is dead. But I never killed him."

IX

Before I left Egnatius, I tried to screw more names from him. I said I had heard Gabinus was one for the women, also that he was regularly visited by peculiar types who came on business. His successor looked vague about the women, while implying the business contacts formed no part of his inheritance. I wondered.

Remembering my mental note to warn Dillia to be discreet, I made my way down from the Capitol precinct via the Clivus Capitolinus. At the top of the Forum, I walked past the Porticus of the Consenting Gods, then the Temple of Saturn and the Temple of Peace, to pass back around the prison and the base of the Tarpeian Rock for one further look. Carrying on, I bought a drink at a stall, sipping it slowly while I thought about progress. I handed back the beaker, then retraced my steps to the crowded apartment where the old woman lived.

The stallholder did not wash the cup, he just shook out any drips and dried it on his tunic hem.

Mother was right. Never buy drinks in the street.

My witness now had company.

"Well, well! Valeria Dillia, you sly thing. You didn't mention you have a follower."

"This her?" the follower mumbled to Dillia through his teeth, as he scraped the big outer leaves of a globe artichoke. It was not easy, since he had several front teeth missing.

He wore civilian dress but had a large sword openly slung around him. He was big, dumb and uncouth, so that and the sword told me: a Praetorian guard.

"This is me!" I whipped back. I doubted he was Dillia's son. He had his feet well under her table, though. I decided to set him straight right now. "I am Flavia Albia, wife to the aedile Faustus. My husband has commissioned me to investigate the death of Gabinus. And you are?"

"This is Nestor," said Dillia, almost proudly. She was standing beside him as he tucked into the treat she must have specially fetched and boiled up for him. She had provided a small flagon from a wine shop too, though I thought he received the pampering in a rather glum fashion. Praetorians are never much fun, but this one seemed even more morose than normal.

The artichoke looked fine, though small at the start of the season. At the moment it was all fennel, spinach, figs and grapes. Had this come up from Campania where there are three crops a year? The lucky eater had little bowls of oil and salt. "Nestor is very kindly looking after me since my terrible shock, with what I saw the other day."

We all knew she had not been shocked at all. Staring at me defiantly, the Praetorian pulled off the next leaf. The professional bully had enormous ears. When he was in full kit, they would be useful to stop his helmet falling down over his nose.

"Nestor!" I cried. "Oh, Nestor—I was warned about you!"

A faint sign of nerves crossed his scarred face, though immediately dissolved. Perhaps those were battle-wounds, but I thought bar-fights.

"Fame!" He leered, once more self-assured. Then he demanded more anxiously, "Who is saying things about me?"

I gave him a small mysterious smile as I seated myself daintily on Dillia's bed. This room was another meagre bunk-up with only one stool. Needless to say, the doting old dame had let the Praetorian have it.

I saw what was going on here. This must be the guard whom Dillia had met in a bar and inveigled into listening to her story. Instead of shaking her off, he had stuck fast. Now she thought it was wonderful to have a big strong lad to look after. He knew how to seem needy. With forty years of taking advantage of people, Nestor was turning up for food and drink on a daily basis. If Dillia possessed savings, he would keep turning up until he had siphoned off her nest-egg. Then he would flit.

Perhaps I had been an informer too long. Perhaps they were both lonely and had simply clicked. No, get a grip, Albia. He was a classic predator.

He had already finished the large outer leaves, gathered up the fine inner ones in clumps, pulled out the feathers and gobbled the choke greedily. He ran a fat finger around the oil saucer, licking up the residue. "Now then, Flavia!"

I applied an interested expression, openly fake.

He made himself sound, as he thought, helpful and kindly. "You don't need to worry your little head over what poor Dillia saw on the Rock."

"Why is that?"

"Because we, the guards, have got this one. Job covered."

I sighed. "Wrong, soldier. You, the guards, passed it on to the palace, who had to bring in the aediles, who have turned to me."

"Leave it, Flavia. This is my mission."

"No, Nestor."

"I am going to find out who did that to Gabinus."

"No, I shall pursue all the necessary enquiries, which were too difficult for you, the guards. You can stick to what you are good at."

I did not say what that was. *Intimidation and picking the dirt from between your hairy toes.*

He saw what I was thinking.

I flashed my annoying smile again. "Now then, Nestor!" I was mimicking his patronising attitude. "It is a relief all round that Valeria Dillia has a noble fellow like you keeping an eye on her. I shall make a note in my report that, without even waiting for an instruction, you have taken it upon yourself to protect this vulnerable citizen. Tell me your cohort?"

"Third," he admitted automatically, before he saw that my mention of him in despatches might not be a good idea.

"The Third!" I scribbled on my trusty note-tablet again. "I wonder if my husband knows your centurion." Tiberius knew no Praetorians, I thought—though he had somehow been able to warn me in advance that this man was to be avoided.

Nestor said he was currently based on the Capitol. He was the guard the caretaker had mentioned; his duties were to carry out security checks on anyone who turned up there in the days before the Triumph. "Were you stopping visitors when Gabinus took his tumble off the Rock?"

"Night off."

"He died in the morning."

Nestor looked oddly unhappy. "I was still at the camp."

"On your night off, does your officer send out a substitute?"

Nestor gave me a nasty look. "No, there is a barful of men who will tell you I was getting bladdered with them!"

"Do you mind telling me where?"

"I do mind."

"Be nice and tell me anyway."

Slightly to my surprise he named the bar. It was called Nino's, near the Esquiline Gate. "Ask Nino. He'll tell you." I would ask him, though I did not say so to Nestor.

"Thank you. You must be very busy, Nestor, with Praetorian resources so stretched. Somebody ought to be up on the Hill. I suggest you go back to your duties."

"I've got no secrets," Dillia intervened.

"Very well. I need a quiet talk with you. Worrying things were said when I was up on the Capitol. I have to impress on you the need to be discreet for your own safety."

"I can cover that," said Nestor.

I despaired. "What time does your watch end?"

Nestor stood up. He was not yet leaving, simply making himself look large and more imposing. I snapped that he had better present himself on the Hill. I had been on the Capitol and Arx all morning; I had seen no security checks. Suddenly efficient, he demanded I show him a permit to prove I had a right to go there.

This was becoming ridiculous. I pointed out that any free Roman citizen could visit the sanctuaries for religious reasons. But I thanked him for his diligence, gravely promising I would bring my docket for him the next time I was up there.

I would have to ask Tiberius to invent something.

To my surprise Nestor slung a cloak around him so it hid his sword, though he threw on the garment—a woolly brown civilian thing—with a Praetorian swagger; they always let people see they are bearing arms. Giving Dillia a smacking kiss, he departed. He must have been worried that, if his superiors heard of it, his absence from the tops might be frowned on. Myself, I thought those in charge might have given him that job simply to keep him out of their way.

Once he left, I decided not to upset his hostess by asking how he had latched on to her. Instead, I warned her not to talk any more to anyone about what she had seen. "Not until I find the culprit. Promise me."

Looking vague, Dillia promised.

In the end, I could not leave until I had gently suggested she exercise caution with her new friend. When I said best not to mention any valuables, at least until she knew Nestor a lot better, her eyes went to the bed. The money was under her mattress.

It must be uncomfortable. Every time she turned over, her old bones would be rolling on her savings. The mattress there was even thinner than the one I had seen in the caretaker's hut. Most of Rome was spending disturbed nights, trying to sleep on little more than a folded horse blanket.

X

I went home.

The Aventine is much larger than the Capitoline. Its double peaks are more spread out, without such an obvious dip in between. Our hill has an old antipathy to the Capitol where I was working: plebeian versus patrician. I would not normally have thought of it, but visiting the Auguraculum must have put me in mind of how Romulus and Remus each chose a divination spot when founding Rome. Remus, who wanted our hill, observed six favourable birds, but Romulus claimed he saw twelve above the Capitol. It ended badly. Lying beyond the ancient city boundary, the *pomerium* that Romulus ploughed, the Aventine had always been the hill of outsiders. We had even more temples than the Capitol, including the Temple of Liberty where slaves were traditionally freed. Diana of the Aventine, Ceres and many more stare balefully across the valley of the Circus Maximus to Jupiter, Juno and Minerva, the official top gods.

Around our temples there had always been a rude, rough, noisy, reeking district, packed with lowlife—and I don't just mean amateur poets in that tragic group, the would-be authors' guild. Only now, precisely because this hill stood apart and private, were the packed tenements being pulled down so the neighbourhood could be gentrified. If Tiberius and I managed to dodge the diseases that decimate the urban poor, we would have fancy fellow residents: big spreads were being developed into the lush homes of wealthy men, even men who would in our lifetime turn themselves into emperors.

One of the smaller properties under reconstruction was our house. Tiberius had bought it from an ex-client of mine. She died; we took advantage of insider knowledge, which is the norm in Rome. The back-scratching was two-way. Her stepson now rented a shop attached to a warehouse that belonged to Tiberius, who gave him favourable terms in return for a regular supply of the cheese he produced.

Stripped out and opened up, the house was airier and larger than we had first thought. It had the potential to be pleasant, even grand, if we wanted to spend enough money. The building yard alongside was a business Tiberius wanted to run. No fanciful hobbyist, he was developing a sound commercial practice. The disadvantage was that when you own a construction firm, your own house only gets attention in the gaps between paid projects. Some rooms had been hurried along and finished as a marriage gift to me. The rest remained bare, their function and decoration as yet undecided.

I had my own key. It was needed, because we had no door porter.

I walked through the porch, one feature that had been finished, into the small atrium, which was also decorated. I did feel I was coming home. It was the start of November. We had lived here for two months. Next January, Tiberius would stop being a magistrate and devote himself full time to the building firm, while I, too, would work from our new home.

The property was well-positioned. On a corner of Lesser Laurel Street, we were near good roads, close to temples, above major meat and vegetable markets. If we had built a tall tower we would have had fine views across Rome. But our house turned inwards in the Roman way. Its heart was an internal courtyard. There, or in the rooms adjacent if it rained, we sat privately or welcomed visitors. The best bedrooms were on the upper storey, overlooking this area. One day we would have an adjacent dining room with big folding doors. A carpenter was making them, or would be when he had thought out how to tackle them. Meanwhile, I was planting roses, like those my parents kept on their roof terrace; when I had asked Tiberius to sneak me horse-dung from the Triumph, it was with a real purpose.

This, then, was our delightful, contained domestic haven. As often happened, in my absence it had turned into lively chaos.

———

I stood at the edge of the courtyard.

Fornix, the new cook, was angrily banging at old pans in the corner by the passage that led to the kitchen. Each cauldron had layers of burned-on cinder that he would need to batter off. A row of brightened griddles showed where he had already been active, but it was noisy, hard work: Fornix was sweating. I decided not to tell him I had seen an out-of-season artichoke today or he would dive off to look for some. We had snaffled our fine cook from a celebrity restaurant; he liked a challenge.

Paris, our new runabout, was running about, trying to catch our new dog. In a stand-off I had missed, the watchdog had come in through the adjoining door from the yard; jealous, he had bitten our dog.

"What's her name?" gasped Paris, normally unflappable.

"I call her Not-My-Dog." The creature had adopted me. I gave her no encouragement.

"Barley!" That was the name Tiberius had given her, based on her light fawn colour. It was Dromo, his slave, who snorted this. "And it's not my job to look after her."

"No, we can all see that!" said Paris, dourly, as Dromo slouched and did nothing to help. Paris cornered Barley, who bit him as he grabbed her, though it was only a nip. She wriggled free then dashed into her kennel, crying and bleeding all over her blanket.

"Where is your master?" I asked Dromo.

"Gone out."

"Why aren't you with him?" It was Dromo's job to tail Tiberius, so he could take messages, fight muggers, and pretend to be an impressive escort. As far as I could see, this had never worked. Dromo was untrainable.

Tiberius liked to wander the Aventine, often in a rough disguise, seeking public misdemeanours for which he could extract fines. Staff at the aediles' office had told me, with nervous admiration, he was the most productive magistrate anyone remembered. I think they were afraid it would lead to complaints of over-zealousness. However, if any culprit raised a voice against his stern behaviour, Tiberius just threatened to slap them with another fine for insulting the office of aedile. He was always courteous, as if saddened that it fell to him to impose order. Other aediles could be ranting bullies. His manner was such a surprise that people thought it a privilege to be fined by him.

I asked if he had gone out on the prowl.

"No, he said he wanted a quiet walk around by himself."

I could see why that might be.

A man I had never seen before came out from the kitchen corridor, carrying a pile of disreputable pannikins for Fornix. Later, I would learn this was our chef's elder brother, who had come over to inspect his sibling's new place of work. They were both round-bellied and affable. Seeing me, the newcomer handed over the skillets, nodded to Fornix, then left rapidly.

As mistress of the house, I was aiming to be like my mother. Helena Justina was viewed as a sweet woman, a senator's daughter with the breeding that that implied, who stood no nonsense yet was welcoming to all. Apparently I lacked this art. When the cook's brother skedaddled, I was shocked at how fearsome my reputation must be.

Still, that can have its uses.

Two painters, who were supposed to be at work on a reception room, came out in the midst of a blazing argument. When they saw me, instead of cooling it, they increased the volume. Larcius, our foreman, put his head around the door from the building yard and remonstrated with them. Then, as they calmed down, he rounded on me accusingly. "Your dog had a fight with Drax!"

"She is not my dog, Larcius."

"You need to take her in hand. I can't have our Drax upset."

Drax, a skinny hound who whined a lot, put his snout around the doorframe, looking self-righteous. Drax had lived here even before we did. He had been guarding materials in the yard for years, often chained up and rarely fed much. He could hardly be blamed for feeling indignation that this pampered new pet had turned up of her own accord, only to be spoiled with her special Greek temple, not to mention her comfortable blanket, her elegant bowl (a wedding present, costly but hideous) and her personal fine-toothed grooming comb.

"I heard Drax picked the fight—and he bit Barley."

On his knees in front of the kennel, Paris succeeded in pulling Barley out, which confirmed that she had suffered wounds.

"She must have goaded him!" Larcius swore, full of bitterness as he retreated back to the yard. Drax barked, thinking he had made a point, then trotted after Larcius. Paris began cleaning up Barley.

I sat on the stone bench and let turmoil seethe around me. Dromo took it upon himself to join me. He said Tiberius had de-fleaed Drax as well as Barley, which the watchdog had taken badly; Dromo, who viewed it as an insult that we made him go to the baths—and actually strigil himself down—was taking Drax's part.

"How did your master manage to deal with their infestations?"

"Put them in half a barrel of water so the fleas floated off. Ugh! Then he made me catch them. The fleas. I wasn't going to catch the dogs. Drax hated being wet."

"What about Barley?"

"She just stood and shivered horribly, all dripping." Although she had had the nous to follow me home and get herself adopted, Barley was a nervous soul.

As soon as Paris had washed the blood off her, she came across to me. She put her nose on my thigh, then one paw crept onto the bench. Dromo stood up and stalked off; I had a suspicion he was scared of dogs. By the time I had smiled over that, Barley had managed to sneak up a second paw. She was medium-sized, with a skinny whippet's body and pointy nose, pale brown, with her ribs showing.

"You are not mine, Barley." I might be a magistrate's wife now, but I, too, had started life as a street child, unwanted and abused. She licked my hand. There was no way this dog could know how I had grown up in far-away Londinium, or that if she nudged the right dice in my direction, she would win our game, a walkover. Even so, three legs had made it to the seat already and as I turned to shove her down, the fourth came up so she was lying in my lap.

I did nothing about it. Instead I asked Paris to take himself up to the north of the city, when he had finished washing the blood off the dog blanket, in case he could find a bar called Nino's. "It's where Praetorians drink, so be prepared, it will be rough. If you can get the owner in a corner on his own, see if he remembers a guard called Nestor, supposed to have been drinking there the night that man jumped off Tarpeia's Rock."

Paris, who was beginning to enjoy helping me with casework, spread the wet blanket on the kennel roof to dry, then went off happily. He would stay at home to break up a dogfight, but he liked to be out and about.

Next I called across to Fornix to abandon the worst pots and pans: we would buy new ones, using my earnings. I hadn't been paid yet for the Gabinus case, but in Rome you live on credit.

I told Dromo to take Fornix to Fountain Court where I used to live. There was a kitchen supplier opposite the apartment block. Dromo loudly claimed this was not his job.

"It's not a job, Dromo, it's you being helpful. You will eat what Fornix cooks, won't you? Take your handcart so you can bring back purchases."

Fornix flashed me a scheming look, discreetly. I told him to obtain whatever he needed; he should tell the shop-keeper it was for me and payment would be sent later.

"Dromo, you could take the dog out with you for a walk."

"No, I can't. I've got my handcart to look after when we are out."

Barley snuggled deeper into my lap, letting me know she wanted to stay there. She might not be my dog, but I belonged to her.

As they left, Dromo yelled, "There's a man at the door! He wants you."

"Ask his name and let him in nicely, then."

No luck. Dromo had gone. The man let himself in. He looked back over his shoulder as if making a note of poor service. I could have been offended at this, but I recognised him and felt relief. My household badly needed someone who would, on his own initiative, make action lists.

The newcomer was taller than average, lean and refined. He wore a crisp white tunic with scarlet braid running over the shoulders; he looked like someone who might even have sewn on the neat braid himself. His manner was wry and intelligent; I knew he was competent. His name was Gratus.

I had first met Gratus when he worked as a very slick home steward for a slightly unpleasant man. He was at the point where that loyalty was wearing thin, so I kept in touch. When I first married Tiberius, Gratus had found me a housekeeper, though it had not worked out. Once a slave, I had heard that he had bought his freedom since then.

After the usual greetings, I explained, "We thought Graecina was too fond of vase mats and room rugs for our style. She, I am afraid, just thought we were nuts." Gratus, I knew, was a man with whom I could be satirical.

"Could this be the moment for you to poach someone else?" he asked frankly.

"Only if they can fit in here, Gratus." I was delighted by his offer. "As you see, we are somewhat informal. It is Saturnalia every day in our house."

"I dare say I can put a stop to that!" he answered. "Is that your dog?"

"No, but she thinks she is." I went so far as to stroke her head.

After congratulating him on his new status in life and the freedom it gave him to choose where he worked, I ran rapidly through employment terms, mentioned a couple of house-rules, outlined the staff we had, and those we badly needed.

By the time Tiberius came home, we had a new efficient steward. As Tiberius came in from the porch, he called, "There was a man outside. Since nobody was answering the door, I let him in."

XI

As the next visitor stepped out into our courtyard, his face fell. He had entered by the finely painted porch, then through our handsome atrium. We had no pool; our entrance was roofed. Instead we had placed in the hallway a solid marble table (only one leg mended, with the work done skilfully) upon which we displayed a huge Athenian vase where a characterful octopus crazily writhed. Our statement piece. Any of the oldest, wealthiest, snootiest families in Rome would yearn to own this. But a very good friend had given it to us.

Sadly, once people passed the octopus pot, any statements were much less impressive: this was the home of a new man, with a newer wife. We were living in a building site; we were too used to it to notice. With our ramshackle style, the visitor would not be offered silver snack trays with tots of ancient liquor. He would be lucky to find a seat.

He paused, looking wary. Big mistake. Our slave crashed into him from behind, then careered on in a mighty rattle of metalware and pottery. As the man stepped to avoid this buffeting, he moved into a sideswipe from the rolling bulk of our chef. Always have a big chef who enjoys what he cooks.

Fornix advised him to look where he was going.

"Good buying spree?" I called, as the chef hurried to his kitchen, eager to start playing.

"Tops!"

"Run after Dromo before he breaks things."

I could hear Dromo now indoors, muttering as he flung items off his handcart. He would hurl aside purchases, then spend an hour minutely inspecting his beloved cart in case it had been scratched during the unfair role of carrying things. Fornix rushed to rescue the new equipment.

Our new steward Gratus would have soothed things, but he had gone to collect his belongings.

The visitor had ink stains on his fingers. He was an obvious pen-pusher, stoop-shouldered and short-sighted from his work, dressed in white, the palace colour, and so supercilious he was probably a freed slave. I watched him assess the place austerely. He looked down, as if afraid he might plonk his sandals in something nasty. Having come in so far, he could hardly retreat. I could see his horror that the mistress of the house spoke with a good accent, yet had no maids attending her, only a shy dog peering around her skirts. The staff were lunatics. Whoever had let him in was unplace-able . . .

Tiberius, wearing his scruffy outfit, had waved a hand to me and slipped away to change.

I was flopping on my dolphin bench, completely relaxed, not going anywhere.

I can behave. The rules have been explained to me. Many times. There was nothing wrong with how my mother brought up her daughters, only the stroppy material she had to work with.

I made a gracious gesture, inviting the newcomer in. I produced a smile that Mother would have approved. "Greetings, stranger. I am Flavia Albia. Are you here to see me?"

He placed his posterior nervously on a portable chair, looking around what might one day be a peristyle garden. So far it had tamped soil plus a few containers. The roses were new-planted, the young climbers so spin-dly we had not yet given them pergolas. Rough-cut stakes leaned against a wall, for landscaping in some vague future. The best feature was the dog-kennel. Barley slunk from safety behind me, then high-stepped over to-wards it. She slithered in and snaked around, to lie with her long nose on her front legs, watching.

"I wish to speak with the plebeian aedile, Manlius Faustus. He lives here?" The man's hopeful tone said he did not realise it was the aedile, clad like a navvy, who had admitted him.

"My husband. Lovely person, I am so lucky. We have no secrets. What can I do for you?" The world of government service was a world of men. This one managed not to shudder at our ghastly liberal principles. I pressed on as if I had not noticed: "And who are you? I place you as holding a secretarial post."

He squeezed out his name, Aepolus, then admitted he worked on the Palatine. He was sitting with his knees tight together, arms folded, a tense, defensive posture. The pressure of unsought conversation with a nonchalant woman deflated him. He was trapped with me. He was in anguish.

Aepolus grudgingly revealed he was working on the Triumph. He thought this would put me off. I kept my terribly interested smile. "I can imagine! Doing all the work, receiving no thanks for it."

His eyes jumpily tracked a sudden noise. I was so used to a racket, I had not even noticed. Someone had dropped a girder in the yard, apparently. Loud banter followed. Drax had a barking fit. Such staff as we had in the house, plus the painters who had come out onto the upper balcony for another of their wrangles, were making their presence felt too, upping their volume to contend with the workmen's banter.

To the scribe's relief, Tiberius then came downstairs. He had tucked a stylus behind one ear as if he had come from writing letters. Nice touch!

A quick-change operator, he was now in a white tunic with a soft nap, clearly the home-owner. Tiberius smartens up well, even without Dromo's help. Aepolus did not recognise him as our door-keeper. Palace freedmen would have low expectations anyway: to them, aediles are ambitious rich boys who win elections, inflict themselves on the city for a year while they do as little as possible, then swan off to new pastures, leaving career officials to sort out their many mistakes.

First, Tiberius opened the yard door and yelled for less noise. This was so unusual, it worked.

Since we had not seen one another all morning, when my loved one took the bench beside me, he put an arm around my shoulders, leaning in for a hearty cheek-kiss as if he had just returned from a long sea voyage. Aepolus blushed. Tiberius made a don't-mind-me, you-two-carry-on gesture, causing the scribe to writhe in further misery.

"This is Aepolus, darling," I exclaimed, still cheerily in command. Aepolus must now assume I was the partner with the money. My husband could deny me nothing. "He is running the Triumph, he says. I think he must be the poor soul you spoke of, who is in charge of everything." Tiberius tickled my neck, still not speaking. He would communicate eventually. Assessing a situation in silence was normal behaviour for him, though Aepolus could not know it.

"I have a few points to discuss, sir. Delicate matter." Aepolus bravely tried addressing the master. In any other home, the domina would have rushed away to count finger bowls. I made no move.

"Good man. Carry on!" breezed Tiberius. Once again, he waved a hand to say his wife would do the talking.

"Aepolus, I am glad you came." I can sound helpful. Only people who knew me would see through it. "I assume this is about the event on Tarpeia's Rock. Perhaps you don't know, but as I have some expertise . . ." I saw no reason to specify what kind of expertise: let the silly man sweat ". . . I have been asked to assist our hard-pressed officials by conducting interviews. I have spoken already to a possible witness to the dead man's fall."

"Any use?" Tiberius asked, in a low voice.

"I felt she may be credible. To be certain needs more work." Turning back to Aepolus, I asked, "There is a Praetorian oaf who claims he has orders to monitor pedestrian traffic. Nestor. As far as I can see, he spends his time absconding. You don't happen to know who assigned this man a security role?"

Aepolus shrugged. "The duty commander, I presume."

"No one in your bureau asked for him?"

"Neither for him nor for a watch to be kept generally."

"No specific intelligence calls for extra caution?" asked Tiberius.

"No reason to fear for the Emperor," Aepolus confirmed. A glance flickered between Tiberius and me. Domitian was always afraid of being attacked, probably with good reason. "None more than normal," added the scribe, as if he saw what we were thinking. His tone was neutral. Neither of us commented.

"So what do you need to discuss with the aedile?" I was still pleasant, which struck our visitor as more ominous than reassuring.

Aepolus pleaded with Tiberius, "This is extremely confidential, sir . . ."

"We appreciate that." No help.

"I expect, my darling," I giggled, to break the stalemate, "you are being asked to dismiss me from my commission!" I saw the scribe look grateful—then more nervous.

"Not a chance!" Tiberius Manlius now came out in full positive mode. "Aepolus, the aediles were formally asked to decide what happened to the victim—"

"Gabinus," I inserted. "He was much loathed. If he was pushed to his death, there will be many potential suspects."

"My wife has been busy, you see! So," Tiberius concluded crisply, "this problem requires looking into, but we in the aedilate have neither the time nor, frankly, the skills. All official law-and-order bodies are up to their earwax in arrangements for the Triumph. But, Aepolus, if a man who had a key role has suffered an unnatural death, it is imperative to ascertain whether that impinges on the success of the day or even on imperial safety. Flavia Albia will, as a favour to me, attempt to discover the facts. She has a great talent. The city should be grateful she is available. Any more questions?"

"Will this inquiry be under your direction then, sir?"

Tiberius shuddered. "No fear! My wife is strictly independent. I don't want a divorce."

Aepolus gloomily agreed he had no further questions.

"I have some," I said.

Aepolus, who was yearning to escape, shifted uncomfortably again. Tiberius applied an interested face, similar to the one I had used earlier.

I opened my satchel, which I had previously hung on a dolphin bench-end. I took out my note-tablet. "Aepolus," I began, in a quiet voice, "tell me what work you are conducting for the Triumph."

He considered refusing. Then he thought better of it. "Forward planning and logistics."

I gazed at him, considering this tosh. Tiberius gazed at me, like a man watching a good farce. "Fill me in, Aepolus. Details, please."

"I fail to see what this has to do—"

"Let me decide what is relevant."

"As you wish . . . My unit is charged with co-ordination, keeping the various sections properly in contact with one another, ensuring a tight timescale, ascertaining problems and solutions, monitoring consistency."

"Important!" Clearly I doubted that.

"Essential," he claimed. His glance flicked to Tiberius, but once again he found no help there.

"This leaves me puzzled." I remained polite. "You need things to run smoothly. So tell me why you want to halt my inquiry." Aepolus played dumb. "Confidential palace business?" I smiled. He was not fooled. He was not meant to be. "Or, Aepolus, here is an idea: you have a personal beef. I am gathering a collage of notes about people who had reasons to resent the dead man. Gabinus was one of your colleagues. Pending the Triumph, he must have featured in your 'forward planning and logistics.' So did you, in the course of that, have a run-in with this man?"

"I do not feel—"

"It is a good question." Tiberius leaned in; he was now dangerously quiet. "Answer it, please."

"I—"

"Answer."

"Relations between you?" I insisted.

He might be a good clerk, slick as they come—which on the Palatine is extra virgin oleaginous—but Aepolus was unused to interrogation. Most of the people I talk to are liars, but once he had to, he came right out with his confession: "Gabinus was thoroughly obnoxious to me. Rude, coarse, foul-mouthed, quarrelsome and obstructive."

Tiberius smiled, while I openly chuckled as I said, "Goodness! Next thing, you will be telling me you did not like him!"

"He was completely impossible."

I stopped laughing. "So here is the crunch." Setting aside my notetablet, I asked: "Did you hate him, Aepolus? Did *you* push him off the Tarpeian Rock?"

Here it came again: "No," the scribe replied, with a defiant note. "I admit I wanted the earth to gape and swallow him, but I never did a thing about it."

XII

ell, they all say that. The ones who had not said it yet would join
in when I came to ask them.

We let the scribe go. He beetled out as if we had set the Furies on him.
Tiberius shook his head at me.

"I was kind! I was polite to him."

"Not bad for you," agreed my husband.

We took a moment to sit, hand in hand, beside each other on our
favourite bench, turning our faces to the autumn sun. In a few words Tiberius described his morning of tedious meetings. Then, at greater length,
I relayed my discoveries so far. Fornix brought out luncheon snacks.

Fornix and Dromo ate with us because in our household slaves and
employees counted as our wider family. Only the day-rate painters trotted
through the courtyard and went out through the side door to take their
break with Larcius and the workmen. They wanted to tell crude stories,
cruder than was permitted in my presence.

Paris came back from his errand. Competent and intelligent, he had
identified the bar called Nino's. This was good: the last thing you need is
a runabout who can never find the places to which you send him. I was
teaching him ploys to use on informing errands. I already trusted him with
a small petty-cash fund. Since working with me would often involve locations where drink was served, I hoped he would not become wine-sozzled.
Many informers have tipsy helpers—let's face it, many are hopeless drunks
themselves. But I wanted better.

Once he had identified Nino's, Paris first sat down with a cup of wine,
absorbing the atmosphere. This had results, because after a while an obvious

guard hurried up, in the traditional hooded cloak and with the traditional arrogance; he pulled the owner inside the bar for a deep private confab. From the description Paris gave me, it could have been Nestor. He had a drink, clearly paying with a huge tip, then threw filthy looks around and left.

When Paris in turn settled up, he made no reference to this and neither did the bar owner. The runabout announced he was on official business; he asked my question. Was a Praetorian called Nestor at the bar the evening Gabinus died? The barkeeper said he remembered Nestor. Of course he did. Nestor, a regular, was there with his cronies, all very familiar at Nino's. They stayed all night.

Paris had already become attuned to my work: he knew he had witnessed a stitch-up. "So was it useless, me going there?" he asked, sounding despondent.

"No, Paris. Never mind what the proprietor said. The little scene you saw speaks for itself. If the guard you spotted was Nestor, then I bet he was *not* drinking at Nino's, or not all the time. He went to persuade the barman to lie for him. What was more, you saw him pay for the alibi. He's pretty dumb because Gabinus died in the morning. It was early but an alibi for the night before is shaky."

"Will you find out what he wants to hide?"

"I shall try."

"On the face of it," Tiberius joined in, "there is no reason why a Praetorian should attack the transport manager. What contact could they have had before?" We could not know. But Nestor had stupidly steered me into wondering. "Even the unlikeable Gabinus would shy off pushing a guard around. Bullies attack the weak."

"Guards are used to people mouthing off at them, sir," Paris argued. "Everybody hates those pushy beggars."

I smiled. "Being up on the Capitol seems to make people officious. First Gabinus, now Nestor."

"Try to avoid him," Tiberius warned. "Even if we reckon Praetorians have a soft life in Rome, Nestor does look as if he came up through campaigning legions. He will be a dangerous figure to upset."

———

That was the point we had reached when we heard someone else knocking. After a stern glance from his master, Dromo for once went to the door. He sidled back with the usual message: there was a man to see us. For once, he had taken a name. Incredibly, it was Nestor.

Tiberius grinned. Knowing I hated contact with such types, he volunteered to take on the visitor this time. I grabbed a stole and my satchel, then nipped out through the side door, making a run for it.

XIII

Egnatius, the stand-in transport manager, had told me the processional floats were being built in the Diribitorium. This gave me a chance to visit my father. I loved to remind him of what a soft-hearted pushover he was to adopt a British orphan.

Falco operated as an auctioneer out of the Saepta Julia, down on the Campus Martius. The Saepta once formed a voting hall, but nowadays elections were an irrelevance, since benevolent emperors chose officials for us. How fortunate we were! The current one was especially keen on making decisions he thought too taxing for us.

Denuded of its democratic function, the Saepta had become a huge two-storeyed bazaar, frequented by strollers and posers. It housed jewellery shops and antiques boutiques, a trove of sparkly gifts for men with expensive mistresses or those who needed to appease their wives. Pa had fun deciding whether the wife or mistress was getting the biggest bribe, though according to him, most people who wandered through were maddening time-wasters. They picked up items, left grubby finger-marks, then moved down the arcades without buying. They were leisured men, who had never been told money is for throwing away, especially on artefacts that auctioneers claim are bargains.

Never say, "I'm just looking." One day some seller will run mad at this hackneyed phrase, and retaliate with a bout of mass killing.

Father was sitting in his office, like a glum toad. Occasionally he darted out to keep an eye on someone he deemed to be light-fingered. The increased activity caused by the Triumph would top up his coffers, but he was at the stage of moaning bitterly about the extra work. "And bloody soldiers everywhere."

"Our noble restorers of peace?"

"Thieving tossers."

After greeting him like a good daughter, I left him to it. My sisters and I go to the Saepta for a reason, but I could see he was in no mood to winkle out treats for me from the incoming goods. The main point of being connected to an auction house is to take first pick.

I took myself to the Diribitorium, as always wondering what clown labelled it with such a ridiculous tongue-twister name. The building was once a vast enclosed area, also used in voting procedures, so like the Saepta, it was now redundant for the fine purpose of elective government. It had had a legendary roof made from heavy larchwood timbers that were supposedly a hundred feet long. When these were destroyed by a city fire, a decision was taken that the Diribitorium could not be rebuilt as before so it stayed open-topped. Yet today it was so crammed I could barely see the sky.

The floats used in a triumph are tremendously high, people say three or four storeys, though that is nonsense as they have to pass under the usual street tangle of washing lines, or at least move through ceremonial arches. But they were lofty. Those towering constructions stood about in various stages of completion. Many were already hung with tapestries and painted scenery. Their wooden frames and panels, draped with stepladders and scaffolds, impeded my view. The noise was alarming: hammering of wood and metal, cursing that could be furious or simply routine, rehearsals with musical instruments, the cacophony of many conversations, all of which caused participants to shout ever louder. I made out several languages. Smells of paint and its colourings caught at the back of my throat.

Once my eyes grew accustomed to the hectic scene, I gradually identified groups creating specific projects. They were of all ages, perhaps family units because some had children there; even the children were working. There must be logic, even though it looked like a disturbed ants' nest. An official pushed through, with attentive clerks. Orders were rapped, questions asked, notes taken. Mainly the craft workers got on with whatever they were doing. I sensed resistance to supervision: when the officials moved on, gestures were made behind their backs.

Had that happened with Gabinus?

The Diribitorium had been built to hold all the male voters of Rome. This would have been a fraction of the populace, because elective government cannot be lavished on women, slaves, the young, the poor, outsiders or troublemakers who did not know your grandfather, but it would have been a big crowd. The place was massive. Now once again it contained hundreds of people; I had to seek out four. At first my task seemed hopeless. No one knew anything about any other workers, or so they insisted. Some swore at me for interrupting.

I refined my method. Refreshment-providers moved around, skilfully lifting their enormous trays over every impediment. I latched on to one. "Do you deliver to Successus and Spurius? The failure and the remnant, they are known as, apparently . . . No? How about Lalus the chariot-gilder?"

"What chariot?" Piemen did not follow politics. For them a triumph was just a big sales opportunity, never mind why. All they cared about was would the rabbits run out? If so they'd need a rat-catcher.

"Ever take drinks to Quartulla in the costume department?" He shook his head. "Oh, maybe it was Quartilla—"

"Well, you should have said!"

At last. He led me around a pile of thrones, wove through a collection of statues, barged aside a man who was cataloguing them, pushed among hanging swathes of newly dyed material, then pointed her out.

Queen of the wardrobe, Quartilla was hefty and bosomy. Of vague age and comfortable bearing, she looked like the aunt in every family who provides salves, socks, ghost stories and wise sayings. She controlled her section calmly, as if she had been kitting out "foreign prisoners" for decades. We all knew that when the mad Emperor Caligula held a triumph over Germany, he had so few real captives that a bunch of tall Gauls were rounded up for a short-contract impersonation; they had to dye their hair red, take German names and even learn to speak a Germanic language.

Domitian had already held his own triumph over the unconquerable

Germans, so he was now formally named Titus Flavius Domitianus Germanicus. Maybe soon he would be Chatticus Dacicusque. Maybe not. It might sound silly. He was notoriously sensitive.

Quartilla had noticed me. Little got past her. I said who I was, then owned up about what I had come for.

Quartilla assessed me, not hiding her scrutiny. She even came and plucked up the neck of my tunic, checking how the facing-braid was sewn on. She could tell I had done it myself. She seemed quite taken with another woman who worked, one who acted as if she knew what she was doing too. "Well, Flavia Albia, I hope they told you everything depends on me and my lot! They had to allow us a week or two over, so my men playing Dacians can grow their curly beards. Nothing can start without us."

"You won't have enough real Dacians?" I asked, knowing the answer.

"Real?" The round-hipped dame exploded into gusty laughter. She was loud enough for people nearby to glance over at us, though clearly they knew Quartilla's laugh; they lost interest. "None, darling. Our Master just bought off that bastard Decebalus, big king of the Dacian warforce. You don't collect useful prisoners through bribery. We needed a good massacre."

She was right about what had happened. After struggling to control trouble further along the Danube, Domitian had shied off more fighting. He agreed to pay the Dacians huge financial subsidies, which were going to continue for years. Roman engineers and other experts would be sent to help fortify Dacia against threats from tribes elsewhere. Dacia would give reciprocal assistance to Rome, some sort of free pass across their territory for our armed forces if they marched to whack different barbarians.

Their wily king took care to avoid capture: Decebalus had sent his brother Diegis to sign the treaty with Domitian. It had happened on the remote frontier, not in Rome. The Dacians were wary and Domitian was bright enough to realise his truce would be unpopular. It was said Diegis had received a golden diadem from the Emperor, symbolising that Dacia was now Rome's client kingdom. I bet in their mountainous stronghold they sniggered at that.

Prisoners were actually given back to us: Diegis handed over a demoralised bunch of Roman soldiers who, unknown to anyone in Rome, had been kept as hostages for the past five years since the massacre at Tapae. They were traumatised by their experience—Tiberius had heard about it. The poor shaken souls would not be on parade.

Shortage of captives meant finding substitutes. Quartilla launched into what might have been complaints about fakes, though she seemed confident she could pass them off convincingly: "I can't tell you the trouble I've had trying to teach my needlewomen how to sew baggy trousers. My actors are creating all Hades about having to wear them. They make them itch in awkward places."

I said I was sorry to hear that.

"Oh, you do what you can. I keep a pot of special cream handy—mind you, the boys have to rub it on themselves!" She reddened at her own joke. "Anyway, they know me, they do what I tell them. Now what was it you wanted, sweetheart?"

I duly asked about Gabinus, at which she frankly said he was a world-beating, big-talking, small-minded, bullying lump of animal tripe. No surprises. Then I said I had heard he was one for the women as well. She guffawed. Not her! He liked them too feeble to argue. I asked which feeble women he had dallied with, then. Narrowing her eyes, Quartilla claimed she had no idea. For the first time, I did not believe her. Later in the case, I might come back to ask again, but for the moment I left it.

I wanted to know what business she had had with Gabinus, and how it had gone wrong. Quartilla said he was supposed to supply carts for some of her "prisoners" to ride on, so they could act as too wounded and demoralised to walk. She had told him how many carts would be needed, he had trashed her figures, she had threatened to go over his head—

"Who to, Quartilla?"

"I'd have found someone. Now he's dead, I won't have to bother."

"Is Egnatius, the substitute, more amenable?"

"Egnatius couldn't substitute a jellyfish. Not if it lay on its back and begged him to. But I can handle him—with my hands tied and a blindfold on."

I felt bad, but had to ask, "Was your contempt for Gabinus strong enough for you to do something about it?"

This time Quartilla did not laugh. "Did I heave him off the cliff? Don't be delicate, Flavia Albia—go on, ask."

"You heard he was pushed?" I was watching her closely.

"Didn't need to hear it." She was easy with her answer. "He was too mean to jump by himself. Someone must have helped him take the leap. *He* would never have spared the world his nasty presence."

I told her wryly how witnesses admitted they loathed the man, but all swore they had not killed him. Quartilla laughed along, though gently, as if she knew how true this was, and how unfortunate.

"So where did your altercation with Gabinus take place, Quartilla?"

"There was more than one. He kept coming back for more. That was him all over. Nasty beggar never knew when he had been seen through and was no longer wanted. Never gave up . . . It all happened here. Where else?"

"You never went up to him on the Capitol?"

She fanned herself with one hand. "I have no time to go globe-trotting! And I wouldn't tiptoe into any stinking den of his. No, when he wanted a ruckus he had to come down to parlay. Every time I saw him on the approach, I had to stop myself grabbing a stitch-ripper to gouge out his tickly bits."

"Some people did go up on the Hill on the sly," I said. "I have heard of mysterious business meetings. Any idea what that could be about?"

Quartilla was a reasonable woman. "No, but you know what those horse-traders are all like, dear. Dodgy deals are in their sweat. He was always having to negotiate with diddlers—in fairness he couldn't help it. He needed a constant supply of fresh beasts, and they have them." Then she reconsidered. "I am being too nice! He dabbled his filthy fingers wherever he could. If he saw a chance to make a bit on the side, in he wriggled. Never mind whether it had anything to do with carts and animals. Gabinus would try anything."

As I prepared to leave, she pleaded, "You look like a fashion-conscious girl who knows about foreign stuff." I experienced that old twinge of unease, the fearful catch whenever somebody seemed to see through my pose of being Roman. Since I left Britain I had been well-trained, yet to me my position here would never feel secure. I knew where I really came from.

"You don't happen to know the difference between Chattian and Dacian cloaks, do you, Albia?"

"Just stick them all in torques," I advised. "That's good shorthand for 'barbarian.'"

Quartilla shook her head sadly. "I can't get torques for love nor money. Those grasping torque-importers saw us coming. Fixed a right little torque cartel. Prices have shot up high and mighty."

I suggested she ask the army's nail-makers to twist some wire rings, then dip them in gold or silver paint. Quartilla perked up. Even though military fabricators were bound to start out unhelpful, I could see her persuading them to help her out. They all have aunties. At heart, they would be frightened to say no.

Two very young children ran up to us, a boy and a girl being brought to show off their costumes to Quartilla. The excited tots wore richly coloured little tunics, with jewelled embroidery at the necks that had been exquisitely sewn by the young woman who had brought them along. "Give us a twizzle!" As she inspected them, Quartilla explained to me that they would represent captured royal children; they would ride on a float where a barbarian mother would sit half naked and weeping, while her husband stood in heavy manacles, gazing back through the procession towards the imperial chariot as if torn between admiration for his conqueror and apprehension of coming death. "Heart-rending!" The children were good-looking and sweet. Liking attention, they eagerly mimed for me how they would pretend to cry.

"This was why I went head to head with Gabinus," Quartilla murmured. "He was such a numbskull, he couldn't see the point. That crook wasn't going to give a cart for my loveliest tableau. Look at their pathos! And what outfits! An infant Caesar in his golden crib could wear those tunics. See all the work that's gone into them, Albia. They took days to do and, never mind the transport section, I'm having them on proper show."

A muscle-bound porter shouldering a dead-weight container dropped his burden at Quartilla's feet with a resounding clank. "Where do you want your chains?"

We jumped back, partly from the reek of garlic. "Oh, toss them anywhere! You just chuck them around, and if they land on someone's feet they'll have to grin and bear it. Don't you mind if you break anything here, everyone knows there's a big budget . . ."

While Quartilla engaged in a wrangle with the porter about his casual treatment of the ironwork, I asked the young woman if the cute children were hers.

"No, we are minding them—"

"Again!" shot in a seamstress nearby. It was pointed, though not vindictive.

"While their mother had to go to see a man about a loan."

"Again!"

Someone else said they ought to feel sorry for her this time: she had been truly landed . . . Conversations like this took place all over Rome on a daily basis.

"Little ears!" Quartilla dragged her attention off the porter, while fingers went to lips to warn against gossip in the children's hearing. I could see Quartilla was more easy-going with the troubled mother than her staff, though even they seemed fairly tolerant.

I had the impression these costume-makers were a well-established crew who had been together for a long time, content with their work, proud of their skill. Though she was a force to be reckoned with, Quartilla ran them with a light hand. She showed appreciation. They knew she would take on anyone in defence of them and their work.

I reckoned she would have bested Gabinus. She was proud of it. Despite him, her beautiful costumes would make it to the procession, where they would thrill the crowds. Romans would love to gloat over the distressed barbarian mother on the tableau cart, her proud warrior husband in his enormous chains, and their winsome, weeping offspring. Then they would let themselves pity the colourfully dressed "Dacian" family.

So, this woman had had no reason to shove Gabinus off the rock.

XIV

The same food-seller came winding through, with a new load of hot pies and spiced meat. He had a big water gourd slung on his back and a small cup for it, which he kept on the edge of the tray with two fingers. Quartilla helped herself to a drink, wiping the cup carefully first on the end of a stole that was wound around her ample waist. She instructed him to take me to the scenery painters; he accepted her command, setting off fast. He managed to sell snacks as he went, though in his wake I was struggling against the press.

Successus and Spurius had managed to commandeer a big area. They had set up a boundary tape, which people even honoured. I ducked under it. Inside, huge panels were hanging half done. I made sure not to knock against the still-wet paint, keeping in my skirts to avoid kettles of colours.

Two bulbous men in streaked tunics plied their brushes, with a couple of dark-skinned mixing boys in attendance.

"Piss off, woman." That must have been automatic. The painters barely looked my way. The mixing boys went on mixing.

"Aediles' inquiry."

"Got a docket?"

"Don't push it."

"Only asking."

"I don't need one."

"Fair enough."

Underneath their banter they were friendly. They looked like the fresco artists at my house, who worked hard, stopping for regular meals and chats about the arena, came early, stayed late, then went out for a couple of long, slow drinks until bedtime.

"Which of you is which?"

They told me, but over their shoulders as they continued working.

Successus was portraying a barbarian town full of long-haired disorganised rascals in beards and woollen hats; they were being overcome by handsome, barbered Roman legionaries who, sure as Hades, knew what they were doing. He said it was no particular town because he had never been told anything about them. He had never even been across the Tiber. He pictured all his foreign towns with pointed roofs, square windows and no columns.

"Columns are sophisticated. They say 'Roman.'"

"Or Greek?" I suggested.

"*Greek?*" he responded dismissively. Just another bunch of exotic foreigners. Paint them naked, being trampled underfoot, while their wives snivelled.

If ever Successus got bored he depicted a tree of no known botany, poking up above one of his roof gables. This had a nice softening effect, though he had to remember his brief was to show glorious military imperialism, not gardening.

On the other side of their cleared space, Spurius took on the grand geographical features of conquered territory. He was currently creating a river, his speciality, which he signified by a huge bare-chested, big-biceps river god, rising from elaborate water ripples. This was a standard god, because everyone knows river gods all have unemotional features and weed in their hair. He said you could never go wrong with weed, though even better were ripples; Spurius was strikingly good at ripples. Those I saw him do were the mighty Danubium's many curly waves, with currents rushing about in different directions. The river had to be clearly labelled with a name banner because of water gods all looking similar. A sign painter did the banner.

After establishing how much I admired their work, they stopped painting, gathered around and I set out to question them both.

"I have talked to a few people so I assume you hated Gabinus. What in particular had he done to you two?"

Set their backs up. Came around like King Rat of the dungheap, spouting as much heartache as he could, causing aggro, knocking their paints over, driving them nuts.

Was that all?

No. Not the half of it, they told me bitterly. He had maintained that their floats were too big for his carts. When they said the floats were the same size they had always used for triumphs, he claimed the rules had been changed. They demanded to see the new specification, with official stamps. He refused. It became heated, he behaved like a prick, and although he always did that because it was exactly what he was, on this occasion the outraged painters lost it. He was just too much.

Successus tried to knock Gabinus off his feet with a trestle plank, while Spurius told him colourfully what a prick he was. Successus missed, but when his partner used colourful language he employed the full paint chart, both earth tints and precious metals. So that was a colourful chat. Indeed, it was so lively, Gabinus reacted: he lashed out and punched Spurius. He was drunk, but landed a good blow. I was shown traces of the black eye. Or ebonised, as the painters called it.

"Was he often drunk?"

"Most times."

"Who did he drink with?"

"No one who saw him coming."

"You two ever share a bar with him?"

"No fear."

"So not a convivial colleague?"

"Lone boozer—thank the gods!"

"What was his watering hole?"

The noise around us seemed to be increasing. They leaned closer, now eager to co-operate.

"Any bar he was passing when he felt a thirst—"

"—or he went to that dump the Centaur."

"Right. I don't know it."

"You're lucky, then!"

"Really . . . Did being in a tipsy state stop him doing his job?"

"No, he was used to it."

Yes, they both hated him. No, they had not pushed him off Tarpeia's Rock. Honest, they were never violent men. But they would like to meet the man who did Gabinus in. They would each buy him a big drink to say thank you.

"If you know who it was, I suppose you're not going to tell me."

"Clever woman! But, honest, we don't know."

"Then give me a steer on his dodgy business contacts."

Too many to name. They just chortled.

XV

The food-seller was nowhere to be seen. Gone to lunch, said the painters. He wouldn't grab one of his own sausages: he knew what went into them.

I needed to move on. When I asked if they knew where the gilder hung out while he was working on the special chariot, they made a big fuss of pretending its whereabouts were confidential.

"State secret."

"Whyever is that?"

"Security. Some saboteur might damage it."

"Get away!"

"Give me a chance, *I'*d throw a pot of colour at it!" muttered Spurius, darkly.

"He gets colour everywhere, the messy dope," commented Successus, playing down the seditious threat. In fact both men kept meticulous work areas, protected with surprisingly clean dust sheets. "No, there's no hope for him. He's a republican. He's away with the dryads. I could paint him into a woodland scene, only he's too ugly."

"Whereas you think the Emperor is wonderful?"

"I'm not saying. You never know who may be listening."

"True! Informers are everywhere nowadays . . . So, Spurius, if you wanted to hurl paint over that chariot as a wild political gesture, where would you go to find the thing? Give a girl a break."

"Oh, all right, then."

The painters were all heart. A cynic might say it could mean they were guilty men bamboozling me, though I refused to believe that.

I found the gilder in a temple precinct. Since this is a state secret, never mind which temple. However, it was near the big new sanctuary of Isis, the one on the Campus, from where the Triumph would take its start. As he waited for a hot fire to melt a small crucible of gold, Lalus was leaning on a sphinx. Work it out.

He was a stick-thin, deeply anxious, extremely slow-working man in a tunic he had belted so tightly he was obviously squashing his liver. He looked ancient; he must have done that work for years. If he had ever had staff or colleagues to help with the gold, his perpetual worrying had driven them away.

The chariot was so important it was housed in its own temporary carriage house. That stopped pigeons shitting on it. Once he had accepted me as genuine, I followed the gilder to it. Within the gloom the monster stood, with blocks under its wheels. Lalus made me climb mounting steps and step inside. I had a brother and many male cousins who would grind their teeth that this privilege had been given to me, a female, who by definition could never appreciate the finer points of racy transport. Even Tiberius would probably have liked a go. All I wanted was to jump safely down again.

I was struck by how high up I was. The front rail would be above the level of the horses' backs. A driver would have a fine view right over the team's heads to the cheering crowds. The standing board was firmer than I expected. Inside was sumptuous, finely upholstered with a light padding. The top rail felt comfortable. I found myself pretending to shake reins.

Suddenly Lalus kicked the blocks away and hauled the beast into the open. He needed it out in the light so he could work on it. As the chariot rocked under me, I clung on nervously. It was very heavy, yet Lalus had more strength than he showed, and even with my weight, it moved smoothly like a boat on water. No friction jarred the massive wheels, so I was afraid it would sheer off of its own accord and run away with me.

Even to an amateur, this was a crack vehicle. Lalus discussed it intently. Apparently it had a superb turning circle and was a smoking good runner. A luxury ride, very few miles on it, just a few dings to the axle hubs, while the interior trim still smelt like new.

As soon as Lalus shoved back the blocks to hold it, I sat on the edge and scrambled down. "I suppose you'll tell me it's had one careful owner who never took it outside Rome. If I could arrange finance, I'd snap it up!"

"Two owners. Titus rode in it first. We don't tell Our Master. He won't want his brother's castoff." Lalus sniffed. I reckoned he would only reluctantly put this beauty in the hands of Domitian, or anyone.

The great curved front was decorated all round with embossed and painted garlands. Everything gleamed. I saw curious hooks on which could be hung a bell and a scourge, mythical symbols to avert the evil eye— which Lalus said he always tried to leave off on the day because the damned things scratched his gilding. Near the bottom, an oddly crow-like bird, impersonating an eagle, was having his bedraggled feathers touched up.

"Beaky is a character!"

"The bird-carver's joke. I can't do much with him—he always comes out looking as if he's been pulled backwards through a hedge." Lalus had begun brushing on molten gold. The recalcitrant Beaky would still splay his flight feathers at all angles, unlike the well-groomed silver eagles used as legionary standards. "Can't stop. I have to do this while it's right. We are not allowed any waste. I need to keep back some gold for the white oxens' horns. They won't allow me any extra. The Senate is so tight with funds, the plunder team have had to raid imperial stores for unused furniture to pass off as captured booty."

"I heard. My father runs an auction house. He shifted some ghastly big vases onto the commissariat. And, luckily for them, he can always lay his hands on mock-Parian statues with the wrong heads. If you really run out of gold, he may have some old-fashioned necklets that could be melted down . . ."

We had exchanged enough chat. I said we had better tackle what I had really come for. "Gabinus."

"Gabinus!" exclaimed Lalus. "You want to talk about him? Now that's a surprise! I hear the miserable bugger died."

"That's the issue. Tell me all you know about him. The word is, you and he were not friends."

"He had no friends. Even if he had, I would never have been one of them."

Lalus finished tending his graffito-like eagle. Still holding his crucible, he broke into a furious mime of a short-legged man with a stuck-out chest and a vicious sneer, marching about aggressively.

"You're good, Lalus! I feel I have now met the man and instantly taken against him."

For a time, Lalus kept in motion, acting his caricature of a bumptious offender, despite being himself so thin and precise. I persuaded him to calm down and say what had passed between them. It was a sorry story. Gabinus had upset the entire chariot team: Lalus, the coach-maker, the wheelwright, the tack-manager in charge of bits and reins, and the two grooms who would walk alongside to hold the outer horses' heads, even though Domitian was supposedly driving.

"I tend to be our spokesman." On the face of it, he was a good choice. When not agitated at the thought of Gabinus, Lalus became measured and articulate.

"So you and the others are guardians of the quadriga. You are the experts. Then what did Gabinus do to upset you all and why would he be so foolish?"

"The teams!" Lalus spat, almost unable to speak at all.

"The four white horses? Egnatius, the deputy, told me you have more than one set. You have to use reserves."

"What matters is that we use the right ones," Lalus raged. "Right temperament. First, that self-opinionated squit decided this time it would be elephants. Elephants! Pompey Magnus had elephants, but he had conquered Africa. Elephants don't go prancing along the Danube, yet Gabinus even put the mad idea to Our Master. Of course it went down a treat there! Thank the gods, sense prevailed. Bloody Gabinus was threatening to wreck everything—even after horses had been agreed, he kept interfering."

Lalus subsided into bitter silence.

"How?" I prompted. "Where would he source your white horses?"

"From the factions."

"The racing stables? Circus runners? Is that ideal?"

"No, it bloody well isn't!" Lalus exploded. "But this is the way, so there it is. We have done it before, we can manage. The whole thing about chariot racers is they gallop. They are trained to go fast, that's the point of them—they even love doing it."

I saw the problem. "But in a triumph, the poor beasts must go very slowly."

"You said it, Albia."

"Chariot horses keep trying to canter."

"If they speed up—and they will attempt to do so—someone who knows how has to slow them again. Not easy. They will fight him. They are keyed up anyway. All the time noise and movement is going off all around. The trumpets are worst, but the crowds will spook them. We have to get it right. Bloody Gabinus picked out the wrong team. Insisted we get them from the Greens. We told him he had to find a calmer four or the day would be a disaster."

"You cannot have the quadriga running away."

"We don't want any kind of crash."

"No, that would be an ill omen."

"It would smash the chariot!" Lalus protested, full of possessiveness. He showed no anxiety about harm befalling the Emperor. "All our work for nothing. Call himself a transport manager? Gabinus had no idea! Now you're going to ask me why he was so determined on his set." I had no need to ask: the answer was erupting. "Listen—the Greens want to boast that *their* team pulled the chariot. They made sure Gabinus went their way."

"They bribed him?" I had lived in Rome long enough. I was not shocked to hear it. The Blues and the Greens were the leading factions, the richest and loudest.

"The Whites own the team we want," Lalus confirmed. "Controllable and steady. Not winners, but lovely to look at and responsive to handling. They have had them in training, up to twenty miles a day, for weeks, so they are at peak condition. Fed them. Groomed them until they look exquisite. The Reds also have a very nice four that we identified as good reserves. We've been talking to the Whites and Reds about this for a long while. We had it sorted, but Gabinus decided otherwise."

I jumped in, turning tough: "So does that mean one of your colleagues killed Gabinus to stop him?"

"Not us."

"No?"

"No. Now he's copped it, we are laughing—but we didn't push him. We can prove we weren't there," Lalus told me. Yes, he was a man who thought ahead: he had an alibi ready. "The morning when Gabinus took his tumble off the Rock, all of us were somewhere else, brothers-in-arms together. We were holding a dawn meeting about how to overturn his stupidity. We were at the Whites' stables, so there were plenty of them present, and we also invited a group of the Reds."

"What were you planning to do? Offer him a bigger bribe than the Greens paid?"

"We thought about that. There was a lot of strife about how much we would be prepared to give him, and how we might find the money. Both the Whites and the Reds would have struggled, though it never came to that. In the end, we decided we hated him too much. Nobody could stomach giving him a fortune. He was too obnoxious. He would have gloated unbearably—anyway, we guessed he would say no. Worse than that, we could not trust him. He might have taken our money, then turned up on the day with the Greens' team anyway."

"What was the alternative?"

"Appeal to the City Prefect."

"Rutilius Gallicus is sensible. I'll vouch for it; he is straight."

"We sent in a petition. I said we should, even after Gabinus died. We worded it quietly, drawing on our experience. A mistake was nearly made, we said, but it can still be righted. We pleaded with Rutilius to suggest that Egnatius ought to act with us, not against."

Working men in Rome are always presumed to have little power. Even so, they do collaborate, often with surprising muscle. The trade guilds are deeply embedded and long-standing. The chariot guardians Lalus spoke about were a mixed group of professionals, but I could see them using their influence. The Prefect would probably listen, in the interest of providing a successful triumph; in fact, I thought Rutilius might have listened to them even before Gabinus died.

"I should think Gabinus was afraid of you."

"That had made him even more set against us." Lalus was a realist.

There seemed no more to ask. I was about to leave when Lalus threw in one last comment. He was using the informer's trick: catch them with some tease, just as they head off. I fell for it. People always do.

"Never mind suspecting us, Flavia Albia. You should be going after his wife."

XVI

This was a facer. I had been on my way, heading off through the temple's sphinxes and obelisks, but I stomped back to the gilder. "No one has mentioned a wife."

He shrugged. As so often, someone had thrown me a valuable nugget, but he immediately backed off, as if it was nothing after all. Witnesses can be so misleading. "Well, I might be wrong," Lalus hedged, "but we always believed he had one somewhere."

"I never even met him, but I can guess she led a terrible life!" I scoffed. "A name or address would be helpful."

"Can't tell you. He never talked about her—people just thought a wife existed. I never saw her. If you ask me," Lalus cheerfully condemned the man, "neither did Gabinus most of the time."

Absences would give the woman a motive to hound him, or worse. On the other hand, if his behaviour in the home had been as unpleasant as it was with his work contacts, she might have been glad he stayed out. Did she know he was dead? Was she pleased?

"I gather he had other women too. Do you know anything about that, Lalus?"

"Nobody special. Only girls he went with sometimes, working girls he grabbed for a night. They soon learned better. Never lasted. None of them had any real reason for doing him in."

"Not relevant to his death, then?"

"I can't see it. He flirted. Either they flirted back or they took a hike. Most women kept out of his way. Brave ones, the ones he couldn't bully, told him where to go. He didn't need to bother them twice—Rome is full of easy women."

"Any of them available to a man like him. He had a good job. He had money," I said.

"He had money," Lalus agreed, his tone more dour than usual.

"More than he should have?"

"Not for me to say."

"I take that as an affirmative."

"Take it as you like."

I was satisfied Lalus had now told me all he knew. I had an idea for following up his information. On my way homewards, I went via the Diribitorium, where I sought out Quartilla again.

The costume-maker was critically examining a rack of new red tunics, which she said were sent in by out-workers. These scarlet duds were for the troops who would march in Domitian's procession. They would shout obscenities along the route, while scoffing food that the public laid out for them on portable tables as their official welcome home. They were supposed to be unarmed—a good idea if they had too much to drink. As they would. Domitian would give them a huge amount of thank-you money; they would spend it eagerly.

If a general ever let them break the rule, the weapons they carried would be ornamented with laurel, that well-known meaningless symbol of peace. Another farce was that by tradition they were kitted out with special uniforms, supposedly silk. The material in the new garments seemed lighter than normal woollen tunics, though even to me it felt inferior. In view of triumph economies, I did not pursue whether the "silk" was real or faux.

Quartilla was venting dismay at the colour. The shade looked much like a madder dye, the cheapest available, rather than the better hue that had been ordered. I did not care whether the army were to parade in rusty sorrel, ox-blood, vivid scarlet or even washed-out pink, but Quartilla had become obsessive. "Now I've seen this tacky tint, I'll have to take a good look at the purple. If someone has skimped on these uniforms, what have they done about the Emperor's doings? Is his *toga picta* reduced to a mockery as well?"

Managing to sidetrack her, I asked if her own team were doing the gold embroidery on the all-over purple robes for Domitian. She mentioned specialists in metallic thread, sounding mildly dismissive. Then I slipped in my real query innocently: as someone who kept her eyes and ears open, had she ever heard that Gabinus was a married man?

Quartilla continued assessing the new uniforms. She tried one against a passing barrow-boy she commandeered, while she shook her head abstractedly as if a Gabinus spouse was news. Absorbed in her critique of the unsatisfactory red tunics, that matter-of-fact gesture was all the answer I would get. Around her, various members of her team, who might have heard what I was saying, continued their stitching while they showed no interest in our conversation.

"Did you ever hear where in Rome Gabinus lived?" I asked.

Quartilla finally looked up. Her gaze was straight. "When he hadn't grabbed someone else's hut, you mean? He organised imperial transport. Wasn't he required to doss down on the Palatine?"

Her reply seemed final enough and it made sense, so I went home.

XVII

There could be reasons why a married person would avoid their own household. Mine was topsy-turvy enough, I thought, as I approached my door. If his domestic world was similar, Gabinus might have been reluctant to face the chaos.

Maybe his wife was equally obstreperous. Like attracts like. A harridan. Perhaps she drove him out.

The new dog had already learned to distinguish whose key was being turned in the lock. Before I had the door properly open, Barley came up with her shy, wandering gait, testing my response; if I rebuffed her, she could pretend she had been passing through the hall by chance. I bent to give her a receptive pat, while I listened to hear what was going on.

It seemed quiet, so I ventured to the courtyard. The new steward was talking to Tiberius, making his acquaintance under the baleful glare of our slave. Immediately he saw me, Dromo exclaimed loudly, "I hope nobody thinks I will be taking orders from *him*!" He knew I must be the cause of the outrage, importing another tyrant who would have authority over staff; when the previous housekeeper left, Dromo had seen it as his personal triumph. In fact she had simply thought us lunatics and taken herself off somewhere more normal.

Gratus pursed his lips, assessing how the boy's statement was received. It was his first day. He was playing it gently. I trusted him to take a stand when needed. He was efficient and urbane.

I went across to the big bench. "Tiberius Manlius once made the mistake, Gratus, of taking Dromo to a play, which had a clever slave who ran rings around everybody else."

"Dromo secretly controls the household?" suggested the steward, drily.

"We all love a comedian. Don't we, darling?" I asked. Tiberius opted out of comment, as usual ignoring the fact that Dromo was a problem, *his* problem. However, he shoved the boy off the bench to make room for me. I had to brush away cake crumbs from the seat.

The new dog had sensed conflict. She stood on the edge of our circle, trembling. I pointed to her. "That dog has been cruelly treated in her former life. She hates raised voices. Let us all try not to threaten her, shall we? Dromo, you must continue to take instructions from your master. If ever you are unsure of anything, you may come to me for help—or now you can ask Gratus."

I held out my hand to Barley. After hesitation, she walked over to me, sitting down close.

"Good dog," said Tiberius, receiving a tail twitch for it. "All safe."

"See how kind your master is!" I urged Dromo, who scowled.

Change of subject. Stiffening theatrically, Tiberius assumed the attitude of an offended husband. "Flavia Albia, welcome home, you gallivanter! I hope I am not to be subjected to a string of appalling visitors, all asking me to rein in my wife!"

"Oh, you liked the Praetorian?"

"Not much. You dumped me in it there."

"That is what I have you for. But you offered. What did he want, darling?"

"Who knows?"

Gratus made a discreet gesture that he would leave us to our conversation. Although he gave Dromo no hint to do likewise, Dromo decided of his own accord that he would slink off too. Tiberius winked at me. As an afterthought, Gratus called back, "A lady visited, who said she is your mother. She told me this is a madhouse; she offered me a very good post with her instead."

"Theirs is worse," I replied gaily. "She was lying in order to steal you."

"She seemed a pleasant woman."

"That's a trick she uses."

Gratus went off, smiling. Even on a brief first acquaintance, he had worked out what kind of mother I had. I felt glad Helena Justina had met with favour. The last thing any household wants is a steward who skirmishes with your relatives. We did enough of that ourselves.

Left alone, Tiberius and I relaxed. He had a scroll case with him, a fancy silver one his uncle had given him, though he had not raised its lid. I leaned over to rearrange a cushion behind him in case he was in pain. He accepted the attention.

He told me Nestor had been a mixed bundle of attitudes. Self-righteous but evasive. His lofty Praetorian excuse for visiting was that he needed to check whether I, a woman parading herself on the Capitol, had had a genuine reason for being there. Could it really be true that my husband had sent me? What kind of husband would do so? Why? And did Manlius Faustus *know* that I was out on my own, unaccompanied?

Tiberius sounded dry. "I replied that if Nestor was suggesting that a woman who roamed about near temples might be looking for sexual dalliance, it was none of his business—and only *my* business if you start bringing home more money for it than I earn myself."

I mimed a horrified gulp. "They never joke. He'll have you—he will accuse you of pimping your nearly new bride."

"Oh, I think he was too intent on whatever brought him here."

Tiberius was annoyed about it. Nestor wanted me called off, just as the palace clerk, Aepolus, had done previously. Tiberius had assured the guard I was acting with full authority. Nestor must give any assistance I requested.

"I managed to shoot in a few questions for you, about Gabinus on the Capitol. Nestor knew him. He knew he was living in the hut, though he tried to belittle how much contact they had. I pointed out that Nestor ought to have stopped and searched those odd business contacts that have been reported. He looked as if I had caught him out for not doing it."

"He could be in on the deal," I suggested. "Gabinus and his business contacts could have bribed the guard to look the other way."

"That would not surprise me."

Nestor had fidgeted about for an hour at our house while Tiberius politely engaged with him. He could be very patient. Nestor kept blathering that it was his job to look for evidence. He insisted this task should be his, not mine, but as soon as Gratus arrived home, the guard left. He seemed leery of having his conversation witnessed.

Tiberius sent him off with a strong warning that Nestor had to allow me on the Capitol or the Arx if I needed to go there. "I said I would send an official note about it to the Praetorian prefects."

"That should alert them to Nestor's antics."

"So I thought! He knew what I was up to with the suggestion. Maybe he will rein back. I like your steward," Tiberius then told me. "He and I have arranged a signal now, for when I need awkward people to be pushed on their way."

"What signal?"

"I'm not telling you, woman! I can't have you spotting it when I want Gratus to get you off my back!"

He was joking.

He'd better have been.

"All right. Thank you for taking on the guard." Tiberius shrugged.

"One thing, though," I broached. "When you gave me this case, you cryptically said, 'Watch out for Nestor.' How did you know about him in advance?"

Tiberius pretended guilt. "Sorry! When the aediles were debating the Tarpeian death, Nestor presented himself at the Temple of Ceres. Even at that point, he was trying to take the investigation off our hands."

"Why didn't you accept his offer?"

"We are a civic body." For once my husband sounded pompous. "We chose not to deploy the military . . . Well, we thought he had a cheek," grumbled Tiberius. "We weren't going to let some damned soldier with his own agenda muscle in."

Typical. SPQR in lovely action.

It was my turn, so I described my afternoon at the Diribitorium and how I had been allowed a go in the triumphal chariot. That caused a mild huff, as I had expected. Trying out the quadriga could not be a privilege for girls!

"Were you scared, Albiola?"

"Certainly not."

"You can tell me. It's a very grown-up toy."

"I loved it." I can bluff. "I wanted to take a turn around the Campus Martius, but the gilder had to work on the decoration."

Thinking about the suggestion from Lalus that Gabinus had a wife, I decided I would go up to the Palatine. Quartilla was right that Gabinus probably had to live officially within call, in case the Emperor or one of the imperial court needed a chair or carriage. Even while Domitian was away, he had left a forceful empress behind in Rome; Domitian's imperial niece Julia had recently died, but perhaps other entitled ladies would need to take tisanes with the Vestal Virgins or secretly visit their lovers.

I had a mad moment wondering if Gabinus, who would know where his bearers took the women, might have tried to blackmail someone. Had he been silenced to avert a scandal? It seemed unlikely. Everyone said Domitia Longina, the Empress, was more likely to boast than feel guilty if she had affairs outside her marriage—tricky though marriage to Domitian must be. He did once kill an actor in the street because he believed the man had slept with Domitia. He then divorced her, but recalled her because he missed her. The Empress never publicly commented on any of it. That proud woman would have no truck with a meddler.

In fact, discretion must be a requirement of Gabinus' job. Since he had been in post for some time, I reckoned he must have been good at it. He could keep his mouth shut. I had to hope he had not hidden his wife with the same amount of discretion.

Tiberius offered to come out with me. We had a light supper first, during which I asked him what turned out to be a dangerous question. "Lalus was telling me about borrowing racehorses for the chariot. I cannot believe I don't know this, but which Circus faction do you support, my darling?"

Any bride should ascertain this crucial fact before her wedding. How many of us ever ask in advance? Never mind, How much is your dowry?; Where are you going to live?; or Do you want children? Never mind, even, Can his mother share your house? Your husband's team will dominate your daily life, not only in debates at breakfast, though that will be bad enough:

if he supports the wrong faction, there will be hideous rows with your male relations. Saturnalia may have to be cancelled.

My father and all the men he values have always sided with the Blues. With the Greens, the Blues have most supporters. The Reds and Whites, though older, are much less prominent. Domitian, a keen racegoer, had added the Purples and Golds, least followed of all.

Tiberius confessed he had a mixed family heritage. Uncle Tullius was for the Whites, his father and grandfather had been Reds men. He had decided to strike out on his own to resolve this conflict.

"What does that mean?" I was already apprehensive.

"I suppose, when the shouting starts, I stand up for the Golds."

"The Golds?" I stared, to see whether he was teasing me. He was serious. I view the races as a mindless occupation, yet I was shocked.

"They were new." Tiberius was unrepentant. "Somebody had to."

"*Voluntarily?*" This might be grounds for divorce. "It's not even an unfortunate family tradition you inherited. You *chose* to follow them? Never," I said, "just never let my father know his daughter loves a man who follows the Golds."

XVIII

W e took the dog. I talked to her. Always have an alternative for light conversation when you go for a walk after supper. Cover any frostiness with your human companion.

To reach the Palatine we had to drop down from the Aventine, then take a long loop around the Circus Maximus. The racetrack's proximity didn't help.

The Golds. Even I knew how, despite the Emperor's support, his two new factions had never taken off—all right-thinking people shunned them.

I could hardly believe what he had said. On the other hand, that was him all over. I had married an eccentric, unorthodox crank. Worse: it was the second time I had done so. I started to think I was attracted to freaks.

"Barley, Tiberius Manlius is an utter nut."

"What for?"

"You know!"

Those grey eyes were mischievous. He was enjoying this.

The palace was the place to go. I'd got that right.

Among the more famous marbled spaces in Domitian's new development were darker, older ranges of rooms and corridors. These had a sinister history, not so far surpassed by any excesses of our current ruler, though he was working up to it. For a hundred years the Palatine had been the scene of murder, envy, ambition, treachery and blood. Mad men and miserable women lived here. Many died too. They were starved, beaten, poisoned, stabbed by soldiers, worn down by disloyalty, kicked during pregnancy, assassinated.

This was also the haunt of the imperial freedmen who ruled Rome and the Empire, mainly unseen, generally with success. Alongside them, clustered like bats in an oddly elaborate cave, hundreds of slaves existed. There were hairdressers, pearl-threaders, poison-dispensers, wine-tasters, bed-makers, lamp-fillers, wardrobe-keepers, lyre-twanglers, sauce cooks. These anonymous beings mopped the marble, swept the courtyards, carried trays, waved fans, endured buggery, listened out for plots. Among them, in an only slightly mud-encrusted mews down under the crumbly salons of the long-gone Emperor Tiberius, lurked a set of mule-drivers, litter-bearers and grooms, who formed that gnarly team, the imperial transport corps.

In the mews there was a sense of expectation. Our Master was back. Those who had slumbered all summer with little to do were warily wakening. When Tiberius and I turned up, the drivers and bearers thought we were trouble, so they were happy to speak to us once they learned we were not. They ruffled our dog between the ears and told us anything we asked.

They had known Gabinus well; they knew his deputy, Egnatius. Egnatius had not yet been along to see them, not since his elevation to transport manager. He was now too busy running the Triumph from the special command post on the Capitol. Although the drivers and carriers spoke of him with more warmth than they showed towards Gabinus, they were not eager for the new boy's inspection. Once Egnatius turned up, it would signal that the Emperor was back in residence. Enough said.

Yes, Gabinus and now Egnatius were supposed to be on call for the Emperor at all times, night and day.

Yes, a billet had been assigned to Gabinus here. But, of course, in quiet periods he sloped off and stayed out. No, nobody ever knew where he went. All palace staff did it. Somebody would cover for him. Yes, even for Gabinus. You have to have a life.

Here in the mews it was known that Gabinus was connected to a woman, who had convinced herself, then tried telling him, that their on-off relationship was a marriage. He used to laugh about it. Sometimes she nagged him for money; he even gave her some, though not often. Not often enough, she used to claim. Naevia her name was, but no one knew where she hung out. Down in the town. Could be anywhere.

She had come up here once. Ponticus, a boy, the yard-sweeper, had seen her.

She was carrying a baby, but Gabinus had joked she must have borrowed it for the occasion. He was like that, all heart. He got rid of her, bawled at her, even threatened to hit her, ordered her not to come bothering him at his work. He must have done the trick with his bellowing because they never saw her again.

"I saw her," Ponticus piped up. "She was at his funeral. By herself. Weeping all through it, probably not for Gabinus but herself."

"So he did have a funeral?" I asked, wondering if anyone could tell me who had paid for it. Nobody knew. Tiberius tried to extract details of the funeral director, but they could not tell him that either. Gabinus' corpse was very quickly burned, with no feasting afterwards.

"Who received the ashes?"

Nobody here. His colleagues had certainly not wanted them.

Afterwards, a groom with no common sense had tried to persuade the lads to chip in for a memorial plaque, which they normally did for someone from their circle; everyone had stuck their hands into their belts and walked away quickly when they saw the collector coming.

"Did you have any reason to suspect that Gabinus was depressed?"

"No."

"No idea he might have killed himself?"

"Oh, he never did that! He wasn't the type."

"Anyone here have a reason to shove him off the Rock?"

"Nobody liked him, but no one would have risked trying. If it didn't work, Gabinus would have had them for it."

"If there was a tussle, could he have resisted? Was he strong physically?"

"Not very. He was too idle. He liked telling other people what to do. And he enjoyed his drink too much."

"Did he have debts?"

"Not specially."

"Where did he hide his nest-egg?"

"What nest-egg? He spent everything on whores or he drank it. Mainly the drink. A flagon never answered back. He liked that."

"Did he ever have other visitors? People he was doing business with, on the side maybe?"

"Not here. If he was fiddling, he'd meet them somewhere more secret. He wouldn't have wanted us to see anything going on."

"Would someone have landed him in it, if they knew?"

They smiled. You bet someone would.

I asked if we could see the room Gabinus slept in. Since Tiberius was a magistrate and I had asked so nicely, yes, we could.

Gabinus might have been the man in charge but he had the usual cramped, windowless quarters, little bigger than a dry-goods cupboard. A narrow bed, a crooked stool, a couple of leather bags with straps, containing a spare tunic and toilet items. A set of dice, in a little purse with counters. Often-mended boots. Three flagons: two empty, one nearly so.

"That's not many empties for somebody who drank a lot. If he went out to bars did he meet anyone special to drink with?"

His fellow workers did not know. Since nobody talked to him, he would never have said.

There was a slight sour smell, though that could be because nobody had opened the room since Gabinus died, which was now a couple of weeks ago.

We found a stylus and note-tablet, though the pages were empty. No diary, no plaques with family portraits, no lists, no calendar, no bills. Gabinus had left no written records.

"Very unhelpful!"

"Very normal."

Many businesses in Rome are run on memory alone. This is especially the case with disreputable ones. If Gabinus was involved in something he was not supposed to do, why would he keep evidence?

The property we inspected could have belonged to anyone. It was cheap and impersonal. That might have meant Gabinus kept other things else-where, but I thought it more likely this was all he had. All he bothered with. He was a man who cared for no one else: that was clear from everyone I had spoken to; he probably cared little for his own comfort and pleasure. Truculence and bloody-mindedness were his only character traits. Anyone would say his sudden death was no loss.

XIX

It had been a long day. I was exhausted. As I discreetly monitored
Tiberius, I knew he was tired too. We came up from the bowels of the
palace and slowly made our way home.

Rome already had a sparky atmosphere: lively commerce was under way
both for keyed-up locals and wide-eyed visitors. More proprietors than
usual were standing in their business doorways, looking out at whatever
was going on. Waiters, furniture-makers, sponge-sellers invited possible
buyers in. Quantities of trinkets and statuettes were being shifted at ludi-
crous prices. Children stayed up late. Notices advertised rooms for hire.
Women were offering hires of another kind. Loud voices of groups in bars
gusted into every street, while the narrow alleys were alive with deals,
fights, music, and the scent of food grilling. People in the evening crowds
shoved, leered and swore more than normal; I was glad to be with Tiberius.

Up on the Aventine, in familiar streets, it felt safer, though I knew that
was an illusion. When we finally reached Lesser Laurel Street, I was ready
to be indoors.

Slippers were waiting for us near the front door. A tray with wine tots
and olives stood on a goat-legged serving table beside our courtyard bench.

"Welcome home," said our smooth new steward. "I shall lock up now
you are back, shall I, sir and madam?"

"Thank you, Gratus," we replied meekly.

I had lived alone in a derelict tenement for many years; I was trying
not to giggle. Mind you, this new concept of "home" was no more ridiculous than having acquired a husband who shamelessly cheered for the
Golds.

XX

Next day I started out stuck for ideas. So far, I had worked with a view to discovering all I could about the late Gabinus, his character and his habits, hoping to unearth the right clue to what happened to him. An informer must go forward on the premise that such a clue exists. If the day ever comes that you cannot pretend this to yourself, it is time to give up.

We had the usual story: everyone hates the project manager. However, this time the object of loathing was not simply an inadequate official who ought to be retired or moved on, yet was basically a man doing his best in trying circumstances—too few resources, not enough time allowed, nit-picking superiors. This time, the swine deserved it.

That left me with far too many suspects who might have wanted to end the misery of working with him, plus too many more who mainly encountered him on special occasions, such as the Triumph, yet who still loathed his overbearing attitude and choices he made that affected them. It sounded as though he was equally horrible to everyone. I thought if he had picked on a special victim, it was probably the yearning wife. I wondered why she was so keen to have him, but I wonder that about a lot of wives.

I would find her. She would appear eventually.

I was hopeful I could track down the dubious business contacts too. For one thing, whatever scam those people were involved in, with Gabinus dead they would need to switch it elsewhere. His successor looked obvious as the next collaborator. They might have to come up to the Capitol again to try out Egnatius.

So, when I set out on foot next day, my plan was one I sometimes used:

having dug out all I could in my first round of interviews, I would go over that work again. I was going back to the Capitol. I would look for extra witnesses and perhaps re-interview yesterday's too.

It was a bright morning, though in November not hot enough for the sun to evaporate the puddles left behind by last night's drunks. As the reek rose from the back-streets, I cursed their bladders, adding insults about puny male equipment. Tiberius, famous for fairness, would say not all drunken revellers are male. I concede that sometimes desperate women need to make the acquaintance of dark alleys. I know people who have. My advice is, only go out partying with a really nice man who will stand guard.

Amused by these thoughts, I carried on with a disapproving air, like a particularly snooty Vestal Virgin.

All right, that could describe any of them. Like a Vestal whose haemorrhoids were hurting badly today.

I made the ascent on the Clivus Capitolinus, the route the Triumph would take. I felt subdued. However sure of myself I normally was, the knowledge that people wanted to withdraw my commission had dented my confidence. However, I did have in my satchel a small tablet Tiberius had prepared to validate me, bearing a huge seal and written in extravagant language. He had enjoyed creating it.

I brought Barley, though the Capitol was not a hill for anyone to choose when they wanted to walk a dog, especially while it was crawling with soldiers and extra workmen. Nor was it ever a place to trot about with a smile on your face, greeting other pedestrians with murmurs of "Lovely day!"

November. Most Romans thought it was already time for winter tunics. Only a crazy Briton would be bare-armed and happy with the weather.

People did not come up here for recreation. The Temple of Jupiter Best and Greatest, symbol of Rome's endurance, spread its wide arms as a monument to be viewed from afar. Ordinary folk who felt pious would offer prayer and sacrifice at smaller, friendlier local shrines. Today there were no big official assemblies in the precincts, so apart from men preparing for the ceremony everywhere lay quiet. The Capitoline triad, Jupiter, Juno and Minerva, could look out at Rome, Rome could see their temple, but the Hill seemed almost deserted.

Egnatius was not in the caretaker's hut. I could not find the caretaker either—he must still be at his mother's, sneering at her lover or having one of the quarrels with his mother that Larth and Lemni had mentioned. Incandescent about her fancy man, Lemni had said.

I strolled around to the Temple of Faith, sniggering to myself because the goddess of good faith was supposedly the patron of diplomatic relations. How did her responsibilities cover Domitian holding a triumph for buying off the Dacians?

From there I looked down at the Theatre of Marcellus and the vegetable market, then walked back. Hmm. Barley sniffed a few smells with eager interest but I was less happy.

A scatter of tourists was admiring the big temple's architecture at close quarters; one group was even being led around by a local guide. He was thorough; they were fading. When he finished discussing the Temple of Jupiter, he turned the group around to gaze out over the Forum, while he told them they were now looking down where lambs for sacrifice used to be sold in an open space called the Aequimelium, according to a learned reference by Cicero, although the hillside was prone to rockfalls and collapse . . .

Newcomers to Rome would have nothing to tell me. I left them being informed that the Porta Pandana, a gate in the fortified part of the hilltop, was always closed at night. They were receiving their plethora of facts sadly. If this guide had said he knew a good snack bar nearby, he would have been given a much bigger tip. They never learn.

I carried on behind the Tabularium. Another guide was intoning Ovid to his group. "The Temple of Vejovis was consecrated above the Place of Asylum. When Romulus surrounded the grove with a high stone wall, 'Hither flee, whoever you are,' the hospitable city-founder promised, 'you shall be safe.' From such low origins the Roman people rose! But let me tell you who this god Vejovis is—young Jupiter. Regard his youthful looks. Witness his hand, which holds no thunderbolt. Originally almighty Jove was unarmed. With him stands also a goat: nymphs of Crete are reported to have furnished milk to the infant god . . ."

Holy custard cakes! I had endured sight-seeing with a maudlin guide who spoke peculiar Latin; we had had it in Greece, when I was travelling with my parents. I sympathised.

Vejovis was the ancient temple of "not-yet-Jupiter." Outside was indeed a cult statue—"Originally cypress wood, which assumes a high polish, but which was destroyed by fire a decade ago, lately restored in marble by the generosity of Domitian . . ." The guide was wrong: the god brandished a bundle of arrows—he was obviously *not* unarmed. A rebel among the tourists pointed this out. It went down badly.

Barley approached the goat statue, sniffed it and backed away a few steps, as if she wanted to play. I called her, leaving behind the guide's sing-song recitation of how the little temple—note its new brick columns, its elegant travertine decoration—was unusual in its width, due to its transverse cella caused by space limitations, as it was encircled by the Record Office . . . The helpless group was being hammered.

I could not bear a grisly lowdown on the Record Office, which is often used by informers when in search of official documents.

As I walked on, I found myself wondering whether the mysterious "business colleagues" Gabinus was said to have met at his borrowed hut might be nothing more than transfixed tourists. Did he moonlight as a hired escort, hauling people around Rome's famous sites? Was he killed by some maddened traveller, desperate to escape his spiel?

I had crossed the Asylum. Running to greet me came some old familiars of my father. I was wary, even though I knew they were simply curious. Believing it an attack on me, Barley plunged in among them. There was no point trying to call her back: she had not even learned her name, let alone obedience. Anyway, I was too late. My untrained dog was pelting around the Arx, barking hysterically, in hot pursuit of Juno's Sacred Geese.

XXI

One of many fowl facts my father had taught me was that, to protect their family, ganders will tackle anything, yet in the end they are no match for foxes or dogs. Or, he added, for confident young women, so stop whimpering . . . The creatures on the Arx acted as if Falco had forgotten to tell them that.

Selective breeding had produced a choice white strain, heavy in the rump and upright. Those lumps of couch-stuffing were symbolic of faithfulness and bravery, famously nosy and intelligent—though in my opinion not bright enough. Barley was making snowy down fly. They did their best to retaliate, pecking off fur, but with her thin body she could switchback more bendily than a mountain road to get out of their way.

They made a raucous noise. The birds led a pampered life, hanging around until some crisis required them to flap in and save the day. Then they let the world know about it. They despised dogs. For them dogs, like sentries, shamelessly sleep on duty. When silent besiegers climb your citadel in the hours of darkness, only loyal gooseys honk the alarm. Geese are top birds. Geese absolutely know it. These birds were shouting the fact all over the peaks.

Falco reckons their reason for alerting the Citadel was not a longing to be carried in processions upon purple cushions. They feared that if marauding Gauls arrived, any geese the greedy Gauls ran into would be grabbed by their sturdy necks, force-fed dried figs through a metal tube and their livers turned into a rich pâté. Juno, Queen of the Heavens, their mistress, could not save them from being spread on bread rolls.

Helena Justina, on the other hand, contends that fattening goose livers was devised by Egyptian deviants. Gauls, she says, have a kinder cuisine: they would rather make yolky omelettes or, better still, roast the birds whole with star anise and ginger.

"Whatever you say," says my father.

"You never mean that," she retorts.

Regardless of my parents' controversy, historically Juno's geese had heard the Gauls creeping up the rocks. Their frenzy alerted a certain Marcus Manlius—who bore, I now realised, the names of my father and my husband: heroic men in any crisis. Every schoolchild knows what he then did: face to face with the first Gaul over the battlement, Manlius threw him off. So for the death of Gabinus there was an interesting precedent. Not that it helped my inquiry.

More pressing matters claimed me. I had no time to ponder myths. Barley and I were in big trouble with the holy honkers.

The dog was haring around like mad, but those geese weighed in lustily. There were a lot of them, big-bodied, necks extended, beaks open. Wings wide, they ran at the dog on flub-dubbing pink feet. When I see a dog in difficulty, I race in to help. Using the downhill slope for lift-off, one of the spoiled birds took flight. When it came at me, Barley went bonkers. As I ducked, shielding my head, the dog leaped up at the attacking bird. It veered away while she continued to spring up and down, almost shoulder high.

The goose landed, but bounced itself airborne again for another attack, which it luckily aborted. All the Arx resounded to barks and honking. Wildly excited, Barley was still making precious white feathers scatter. The geese could not deter her. I could not catch her. I failed to steer the geese away too. Like feasting Celts (if you believe historians), they had no idea why they were fighting but were keen to keep going. A good peck-up was their idea of entertainment.

Barley bounded at a goose, gripping its angrily wagging tail. As it swung around in outrage, its hard golden beak landed a vicious peck. The dog squealed. She let go. Her victim scampered off in ungainly haste.

Worse followed. Unable to distinguish between play and purpose, the dog then accidentally jumped me from behind. It was so unexpected, I fell over. The ground around the temple was splattered with green slime;

after a short skid, I landed full length—right on a goose. I am compact but a grown woman thumping down on top of it was too much. I had a soft landing, but the goose went limp.

Nobody would believe it was an accident. Our fracas outside Juno's temple had now become sacrilege. Barley and I faced religious penalties. Since I was married to an aedile, I knew what that normally meant: the death sentence.

The bird lay on the grass. I stroked its neck. Kindness and pleading failed to revive the stupid thing. Another great goose loyally joined in, first taking a look, then hanging around beside the body. They are famous for never abandoning a wounded flock-mate.

I had no such scruples. Clambering to my feet, I pointed to the ground beside me, which somehow convinced the dog to come. I picked her up; she was bigger than our old family pet, Nux, but still medium-sized and manageable. As I moved off, clutching her hot, panting body in my arms, she buried her slobbering muzzle in my neck as if we were having a wonderful adventure.

So far, no one had seen it. Possibly the gods had noticed, but gods prefer to watch fornication or war. Now I heard people coming. As I gripped Barley, I muttered, "Get the story straight. We did nothing. Those naughty birds attacked us. It is not our fault!" Barley licked me.

Temple attendants reached the scene; we froze in a heart-rending pose. We were shocked. We were frightened. We were still encircled by aggressive geese and, once someone came to rescue us, we were seriously thinking of sending for our compensation lawyers.

In Roman law, can you sue geese? Discuss avidly; cite precedents.

The goose-boy, as he was always called although he looked about ninety, turned up with his piece of herding stick. All still-active geese hurried over to greet him. Not bothering with the live ones, he fixed on the unresponsive carcass. "What happened?"

"Poor thing fell over."

"I'll have to make a report."

"Don't expect any help from me. My dog has been bitten. I want to submit a complaint."

"Save it. He's going to get a fine."

"She's a bitch."

"Makes no difference."

"She's innocent. She never bothered geese before."

"How long have you had her?"

"About two weeks. Just pop the bird in a sack, and I'll take it away," I volunteered, thinking this was a way to impress my new cook, Fornix. "Come spring, you will be awash with goslings—you'll soon make up the numbers."

The goose-boy scoffed. He didn't even need to say it was more than his job was worth.

He might have forgotten that when Didius Falco became Procurator of the Sacred Poultry, sometimes he collected omelette eggs but it was not unknown for a "sick" bird to be culled during his check-up visits. Then while he went off on more interesting business, he might send me home with something solid in a grain sack.

Various temple attendants were making attempts to round up the agitated flock. Juno's revered priests waddled in circles, holding their arms wide, while the geese simply nipped underneath and made off. The goose-boy rolled deploring eyes. Instead of helping, he let them all get on with it.

I remembered his name was Feliculus. He was a stringy public slave in a clay-coloured tunic, with hairy arms and a downbeat attitude.

"You are Falco's daughter."

"Afraid so. His eldest."

"I could tell by what you said about the sack. We miss your pa up here."

"He is a memorable character."

"I was sorry when they did away with his post," Feliculus mourned. "He was wonderful with the geese. Always considerate to me as well. Such a good listener. I suffer from black thoughts. Discussing it with him has helped me understand a lot of my problems. I made progress while he was procurator. Falco explained how talking to poultry all day for forty years was bound to erode anybody's social skills."

My adoptive father does have his soft side, which all his children deploy when suggesting gifts for birthdays. I said, "Falco will be very glad to know he was of benefit."

"Please give him my regards." Digging into a pouch at his belt Feliculus produced a ragged length of string, which he must keep for rampant dogs. Tiberius, the fond master of our house, had lavished a leather collar on Barley; I put her down and tied on the string, so she could devote herself to trying to chew it off. With her attention claimed, I was free to ask the goose-boy if he knew anything about Gabinus. A good informer wastes no chances.

We paused while Juno's priests and their assistants, sweating and much out of breath, brought back Juno's sacred flock to their official minder. Both birds and priests now looked rumpled. I had the impression it was not the first time the élite temple squad had carried out his job for him. "Just helping out with the inquiry into the Tarpeian fatality," he excused himself airily. They were snooty as Hades but he had them in control. He must have used his way with livestock to herd them around.

He gesticulated with his stick, mainly to steer away the temple retinue. The temporary drovers obediently dispersed. Left with us, the geese insisted on mobbing their carer, who had probably hand-reared some of them. After pleading for him to stroke their heads and pet them, they cooed at him lovingly before they returned to their normal occupation of destroying anything that looked like grass. Any gardener in that precinct had a soul-destroying job.

Feliculus and I shared a useful chat, though only after formal preliminaries. Informers sometimes pay in coin for evidence, but more often we extract it by listening. This is harder to recover through your invoice system, though clients who bother to pay up approve because it is a cheap item. So, first, I had to suffer tedious views on poultry-keeping.

"White geese are held in great esteem, as you probably know, Flavia Albia. They are delightful characters, very tame once they know you, not at all as fierce as people think."

"Not unless your dog annoys them."

"They will take offence at any strangers. It's their nature. If you were to keep a pair at your house, they would soon snuggle up with your dog in her kennel."

I hoped no geese ever heard that our kennel was a decorative Greek temple. Barley would be mobbed again, this time by would-be lodgers.

"But they are generally docile," Feliculus maundered on. "They can live for twenty years, you know. Looking after them is no trouble. All I have to do is move them to better grass or put grain for them in the bottom of a bucket of water. Every night I steer them into their lovely houses that Falco improved so much. Now they have learned the daily routine, they expect it. If I happen to be thinking too deeply about my troubles, they will even come knocking, to remind me it's their bedtime."

"Good heavens!"

"Everyone moans about their droppings, but the splods don't smell— well, it's nothing but grass, is it? Everything dissolves when it rains, or it can easily be washed off with water and a broom."

"So," I insinuated gently, hoping to drag this barnyard chat towards more useful subject matter, "while you were out poo-sweeping, did you have any contact with that man who died, Gabinus the transport manager?"

Feliculus sneered. "Oh, yes. His honour brought himself over here."

"Really?"

"My geese didn't take to him, not at all!"

I had never envisaged that loathing for the victim might be shared by this feathered flock. If they could speak, would they too tell me they found the man unbearable, yet swear they took no part in killing him?

Or had the Sacred Geese of Juno ganged up and run him off the rock?

XXII

I have had my bad times." Feliculus was thinking about himself again. As with most depressives, whatever originally caused his unhappiness, self-obsession had taken over as his problem. "I often have thoughts of ending it all. Your father used to talk me out of it. He would say, 'You are up here on the roof of the world, Feliculus, with the finest views in Rome. You have an important role in society, a good life out of doors, free food, and pets who love you. The geese need you, Feliculus. You have to be strong for them.' A lovely man."

That did not sound like my father, who was more for telling people to snap out of it. *Try a little light woodwork, or sex in the afternoons . . .* Still, it gave me an idea. I asked, "Was Gabinus prone to dark thoughts too? It's said he may have committed suicide. Was fellow-feeling how you came to know him?"

Feliculus turned stroppy. "Him? You are joking!"

"I am sorry. For a moment I had a picture of you two helping each other by talking your misery through . . ." I saw them gloomily dissecting methods of self-elimination and the risks involved: falling on a sword, the Roman way, though you had to be rich enough to own weapons; poisoning, where some interfering person might have an antidote handy; drowning yourself, if do-gooders along the Tiber Embankment were looking the other way. Or there was jumping from the Tarpeian Rock— even if you changed your mind halfway down, it would be too late . . . "Gabinus was living in the custodian's hut on the Capitol, I expect you know that. He sounded very happy to have grabbed it. Why did he come over here to the Arx, Feliculus?"

"The first time, people he was meeting one evening didn't know the way, so they came up the wrong peak. He hiked over here to fetch them—seemed anxious to haul them off before they started talking with me." That sounded as if Gabinus was up to no good. He had not wanted Feliculus, or anyone else on the Arx, knowing who those people were or what they had come for. "After that he used to strut around here because he knew it stirred up the geese. He enjoyed causing trouble. He would make out I wasn't up to the job."

"I'm sorry to hear it. Don't let it upset you. I gather he was like that with everyone . . . Did you manage to get anything out of his visitors before he stole them away? Who were they?"

"No idea. The geese were in a fit, so my whole attention was on calming the situation. The strangers never said who they were, not to me."

"Did you only see them the once?"

"Once was enough. There was quite a big group—they even had children. It was the nippers my geese got all worked up about. They always run after little ones, as soon as they spot them coming. High little squeals of 'Nice birdies!' are a natural signal to attack."

I knew how they felt. Roman parents think their children sweet. Not me. I had never tried aggressive honks to scare them, but when next faced with some spoiled infant in its dear little tunic and gold bulla, this was a thought . . . "Sounds as if it could have been his own friendly family visiting Gabinus."

"I don't think so," said Feliculus, sneering again.

"Why not?"

"What friendly family could a man like that have? Anyway, when he came over here looking for them, there were introductions and very polite handshakes. They looked uncomfortable, as if they didn't like his attitude. For some reason they needed a meeting, but they were wary of him and unhappy with the situation."

"So, not his familiar aunts and uncles? Were they foreign, then? Visitors to Rome?"

"Tarentum. They came from Tarentum," Feliculus told me, as if hailing from the heel of Italy made people dangerous foreigners. As a slave, he himself could have come from anywhere, but he chose to claim Rome as his; he was snobbish towards all other places.

"How did you know that? Presumably they had not cried, 'Don't chase us! We are special, we come from Tarentum!' while your geese were having a go?"

"You're a one! When you talk, I can hear your father."

"I learned it all from him . . . 'How could you tell that?' would be Falco's first question."

Good grief, enough! I was twenty-nine: I did not need a patriarch taking over.

"I told you it was evening. They got in, but must have wasted time coming to the wrong place. They went off to his hut with Gabinus but they can't have known that the gate to the Area Capitolina would be locked after dark." *The Porta Pandana is always closed at night.* I had heard so that very morning. Who expects to learn something useful from a local guide?

"So these bods strolled over to the Capitol, held their meeting, but stayed too long with Gabinus until they found themselves the wrong side of the Pandana, locked into the temple precincts? I see it! They had to rouse the gatekeeper, who would have been suspicious. It was him who asked their identity. So, Feliculus, you later went for a gossip at the Pandana?"

Feliculus looked annoyed to be rushed. "I knew him, so I went to find out. I wanted to know who upset my geese. I have to give in reports, you know."

"Yes, you told me. It was the gatekeeper who said they came from Tarentum?"

"I don't know. He must have done. Somebody told me. Maybe Lemni."

"You know Lemni? Lemni at the Auguraculum?"

"Everyone knows Lemni."

"All right. The gatekeeper told you Gabinus forced him to let the Tarentines go out."

"Yes. That miser never gave the keeper a tip for unlocking the gate, so he was furious afterwards."

"One more person who hated Gabinus," I grumbled. "Probably not enough to kill him, though. Or it might depend how far into his supper he was, when loudly roused after hours."

"He lost his job," Feliculus told me, one public slave on behalf of another, indignant at this cruel trick. "The day after the incident, Gabinus made a complaint about him being over-officious—he could talk! So the gatekeeper was moved to a new post. Nothing was his fault, but management don't care. They whistled him out of Rome to a farm somewhere. A new boy came to the Pandana, who couldn't fasten a bootstrap, let alone lock up a gate. Don't ask me where the old one is. He was dragged off and vanished without telling me. And since you're bound to want to know, he went first. Gabinus fell off the rock later, so the gatekeeper couldn't have pushed him—though he must have wished he did."

I sighed. "Thank you."

"So that," concluded the goose-boy, dramatically, "is all I have to tell you, Flavia Albia. All except one curious thing the gatekeeper also mentioned. He didn't need to tell me. I copped a whiff for myself when they got lost on the Arx."

I waited.

"Those people stood out very noticeably. Believe me, I didn't get too close."

He was milking it. I couldn't wait: "Because?"

"Because they stank disgustingly of fish."

XXIII

Fishermen? Neptune's winkles! *Fishermen?* Barbs and bobbing floats: that was all I needed.

Feliculus had not actually seen this crowd hung about with nets or lobster pots, though such an occupation sounded plausible. Plenty of fish is eaten in Rome every day. Much of it is genuinely fresh and bright-eyed. If it's five days old you can never prove it; often it hardly looks flabby at all, though you find out when the stomach-ache kicks in.

Most seafood is unloaded on the coast, though. Why would a transport manager in the heart of Rome be meeting trident-wielders, bottom-trawlers, clam-diggers or prawn-netters? What monumental octopus glut would require an imperial mule train to deliver it? Did a gilt-head bream caught in their nets contain a wondrous jewel? Had they hauled up a turbot of such huge proportions they wanted to give it to the Emperor—a gift, they would say, while silently begging a reward, or at least a mention in a satirical poet's raw invective? Had Gabinus offered to negotiate for them at court? Why had wily sons of the sea failed to see such an offer was not needed?

Did the self-motivated crook reel them in, squeezing out a bribe to "smooth the way at the palace," but they spotted the dupe and took revenge? Cast him off the rock? Far-fetched, I thought. If he had been found with a filleting knife stuck between his ribs, I would like the clue more.

Better idea: look at it the other way. It might not be the briny people who were petitioners. Gabinus could have run some scam with them. He sought them out, dragging them to his meeting so he could fix up a deal to use imperial beasts of burden for private business; in this deal, the fisher-men "borrowed" transport that he supplied and he creamed off the profits. Everything I had learned about him said he enjoyed a fiddle. This man would cheat the Treasury, even if his lover was the Minister of Finance. So donkeys and mules would go moonlighting. The Emperor would be none the wiser that his baggage trains were trotting around in private commerce . . .

No. If the mules came home to their stable after hauling creels of squid, they would, in the most literal sense, smell fishy. Someone officious would notice. Someone who had not been included in any underhand pay-outs was bound to ask an "innocent" question of the last honest bureaucrat in some lacklustre secretariat, who would primly take it upon himself to alert an auditor who was looking for promotion and would trash Gabinus.

Of all the undercover trades he could have dabbled in, shifting seafood around was the least appealing.

Maybe the fishermen were going through hard times. Had they come here simply to beg Gabinus to employ a lad or two of theirs? Driving might look easier than rowing out to sea in search of uncertain tunny shoals. Driving for the Emperor might appear more lucrative than working on their local dock. Maybe my first assumption had been wrong: they *were* aunties and uncles of Gabinus, his own relations pulling family strings.

But flying jellyfish! Why were these people from Tarentum? Tarentum is in Calabria; that is a long way down the boot of Italy. It lies in the soft part of the instep, in the spot where a foot is maddeningly ticklish.

Of all the seafarers who might visit Rome, those from Tarentum were the most unlikely. It was just too far away. Anyone could come to watch a triumph but, given the slow speed at which news travels, I bet no one in Calabria had yet heard Domitian was having one. In any case, Calabria had no particular love of Rome, emperors in general, or the Flavians in particular. Putting together a long-distance journey to Rome would take time, advance planning, money and a distinct motive. Surely not worth it, just to see a plump man in a chariot? Even that scrumptious chariot I stepped into yesterday.

"Feliculus, were they Greek-speaking?" Tarentum is down in Magna Graecia, ultra-civilised in its inhabitants' own eyes because of its ancient heritage as a series of Greek colonies, yet barely absorbed into the Roman world. My father had had to travel there once. He reminisced of it as badlands. More of an outback even than the Pontine Marshes, another remote spot Falco disparaged.

"No, Latin. Strangers, though, with thick country accents. I could hardly understand a word."

To a native-born Roman, that could describe anyone from as little as five miles outside our city. Dialects went down badly. To fit in here, a standard intonation was vital: coming from Britain, that was the first thing I learned.

Of course Romans have an accent. They just don't know it. Try asking for a loaf in any other argot: you'll go hungry.

"Thanks, Feliculus. Were they buried in luggage?"

"No, they had nothing."

"So they were staying somewhere."

"Must have been. All you have to do is find an innkeeper who is complaining loudly about how they stank!" He had a nice line in sarcasm: "If that dog of yours had any training you could show her a sardine and she'd find their trail." His style was nice for a while. I could easily tire of it. "Or even, Flavia Albia, you can sniff the wind and follow your own nose—"

"Enough, Feliculus! I do know my task is hopeless."

"Your father would find them," the goose-boy badgered, "no sweat. Falco could do it. He would devise some cunning ruse to ferret them out. In a wink, he'd have them."

Time to go, before I socked this man. "I'll be off now. Any chance of that dead birdie coming home with me?"

Sadly there wasn't. That was because at the same moment I offered to nobble the carcass for a succulent supper, the "dead" goose suddenly stood up, ruffled its feathers with a petulant shake, then stalked away.

Some people never have any luck.

I was sounding like my father again.

XXIV

I looked out for Lemni, but the augury tent appeared deserted. I crossed back to the Capitol. I found Egnatius. I asked whether he knew of any contacts from Tarentum who had been engaged off-the-record with Gabinus; naturally he denied it. If his predecessor had had a scam, Egnatius would want to keep quiet and carry it on himself.

Much as I loathed Nestor, I would have asked him. But he was nowhere to be seen. Egnatius told me he had been ordered back to the Praetorian Castra; it was to receive a wigging, the messenger had said. That could be because Tiberius Manlius had tipped off his superiors. All the more reason to avoid the guard: he must know who had dumped him in it.

After Egnatius, I gave up on the Capitol. I came down on the river side, with Barley quietly following. We walked over to the Porticus of Octavia. It was new, rebuilt by Domitian after the last great fire, like everything in this area. Its elegant cloisters housed a library I liked. Fortunately so few Romans are scholars I could always find a space. In the Porticus of Octavia you can tie up your dog to statuary by Alexander the Great's great sculptor, Lysippus of Sicyon. You can gaze at prime paintings while you wait for your scrolls. You can sit down for as long as you like, among the world's best stolen art. The scrolls available are many, all beautifully cared for, filed neatly and scented with cedar oil to keep away bugs. And it's free.

All the scrolls were new copies, all recently catalogued. Only the librarian was old; when the fire swept the city, he must have been out of town. Sometimes he was helpful. Not today, though. He was grumpy over something. Perhaps Domitian's return had made him fearful his tenure might be reviewed. Perhaps the mighty cost of the Triumph would impact on his book budget.

He threw a bunch of scrolls and a map at me; I wasted a couple of hours looking up Tarentum on my own. After dragging through yards of tiresome history, I picked up that it was supposed to have been founded by Spartans born to unmarried women—"Bastards!"—after which had followed centuries of wars between the Tarentine Greeks and Greeks of other flavours, then Italian wars with Bruttium, Samnium and Lucania, before further wars with Rome. Typical. I could never be a historian. All this showed a fighting Spartan heritage, though not necessarily bastardy. It was too light on scandal to keep me from drowsing. The worst aspect of my job is that sometimes it is very boring.

Facts that looked helpful were not. During the Carthaginian Wars, amid anti-Roman feeling, Tarentine hostages who were being held in Rome were caught trying to escape; they were thrown from the Tarpeian Rock—even this was irrelevant to whether more recently Gabinus might have jumped or been pushed. So far, the only person I knew he might have needed to escape from was his wife, yet my information said *she* ought to have escaped from *him* but had been pleading for more contact.

After Hannibal was kicked out of town, thirty thousand prisoners were brought here to Rome, along with Tarentum's art treasures, including a statue of Nike, or Winged Victory. Some transport manager at the time had had his work cut out with bringing Nike home, making sure her gorgeous wings never broke off to leave her half clad in her gloriously flowing garments, like any young girl who had gone out in wild weather without a good cloak . . . But again, that expert's anxiety had no bearing on Gabinus, centuries later.

I knew Augustus had placed the Tarentine Nike in the Curia, among his spoils from Egypt; it was a none-too-subtle hint that he had received the Empire as his special favour from Victory. Senators now had to pour libations of wine and burn incense to Victory every time they entered the Senate House. It was supposed to make them carry out their duties more conscientiously, though I never saw how. My uncles said it only made them mutter against the cost.

A Victory, probably a statuette, rather than someone acting, would be stuck in the chariot with Domitian to show *he* was now top general. Again, surely not a problem for Gabinus? It was traditional. There must be space to squash her in, along with Domitian's massive sceptre, his laurel branch, and the slave who would hold a wreath above him. There had been no suggestion Domitian wanted the large Nike from the Curia to process with him. Mind you, knowing him, that was only because he hadn't thought of it.

I was exhausted. Tarentum lacked impact. Scroll-strolling faster, I found nothing about geography, industry or culture. Here in the Golden City, who cared what went on in a Greek-speaking, Spartan-derived, Hannibal-supporting coastal town in far-flung Magna Graecia? Why would anybody catalogue it? Pliny did, no doubt. I couldn't face him.

What was I doing anyway? How many informers would bother to visit a library in a hunt for background material? It is especially hard for a woman. The librarian tries to chase away your dog and is reluctant to help your research because even in a campus named after a woman, male readers take precedence. Let's face it, men are all they want.

An informer should persist.

Of course, the chance is you find nothing. I was sick of Tarentum. I went home for lunch.

Good move.

My fact-devoted husband swore he had no time to help me out. I knew he would. Scratching around in general knowledge was irresistible to him. So Tiberius delayed trundling out to an official meeting, put off his clerk-of-works' questions about positioning doorways and, while pretending to take no interest in Calabria, dived into his works of reference. He owned a lot. He grew up with a wealthy relative who encouraged literary interests—where "encourage" meant paid for, and book collecting was reckoned to "keep him from vice" or to stop him nosing through business accounts. Uncle Tullius was a wily bird.

Soon Tiberius assembled plenty of facts for me on the town founded by bastards. He liked that concept. Named for Taras, a son of Poseidon, who rides astride a dolphin, wielding a trident and signified by a scallop shell, he said Tarentum was populous and prosperous. Nero had granted it colony status, which meant he filled the area with military veterans. The Via Appia, Rome's main high road to the south, went that way, though being positioned inside the arc of the Gulf of Tarentum, some sea routes across the Mediterranean bypassed the port. It lay in an area that was famous for producing champion athletes. From its hinterland, Tarentum exported wool and finished textiles, plus fairly ordinary foodstuffs.

"Fish?"

"No mention. Too far to bring fish here, surely?"

I was still musing, when we were interrupted. My whole family descended on us, a ruse to try out our professional cook. Six starvelings, who appeared to have no idea that others had to work, swarmed in as if they owned our house: Mother, Father, gadfly sisters, solemn brother, brother's worrying pet ferret.

While Gratus set out seats, cushions and serving tables, Fornix rose to the occasion. Soon everyone had flatbreads, titbits, tots of something. The ferret, whose name was Ferret, was exploring the dog kennel.

Clutching slices of egg pie, my brother and Dromo were staring at one another silently, as they did. Postumus was often thought weird—"unusual," my mother called him gently. Meanwhile my teenage sisters fell upon the new dog, who ran behind me; unfazed, the girls rushed over to the fancy kennel with squeals of delight, then galloped out to buy garlands to hang all over it. Offended, Barley refused to go back inside (just as well for Ferret). Instead Barley ran away upstairs where, later, Tiberius found her hiding in our room. Thanks to Julia and Favonia, she knew where the bed was. Our rule of no dogs sleeping on it had come to an end.

On one side of the courtyard, I held a low-voiced conversation with Father about Feliculus and his depressed condition. We began with a mischievous analysis of the best way to commit suicide—definitely not by the noble Roman method of falling on your sword. Apparently this is very hard to do, which is why so many famous personages needed help from tearful slaves. Once we had trawled through enough off-colour jokes, my parent agreed to visit the goose-boy for one of their helpful talking therapies.

On the other side of the courtyard, Tiberius was entertaining Mother with my inquiry's twirl into Calabrian fishmongery.

Never go into the same profession as your parents. Not unless you wish to be beset with people praising their talents and charm. Give up. You are no match for such much-loved characters.

Helena Justina made what she would call helpful suggestions. I called it pinching my case. "The strong pong may not come from fishing itself but industry."

Helena and Tiberius were playing a game, tossing ideas at one another like beanbags. I ought to have given them a board and sets of counters.

"Garam?" he guessed. "Fish-pickle sauce?"

"True, that is notoriously smelly . . . But what about shellfish?"

"Mussels and oysters? The taste and tang of the Ionian Sea. What else is pungent?"

"Tyrian purple."

"No!"

"We are having a triumph. Don't you think, Tiberius dear, this could be relevant?"

"I do! Of course. Albia, your wonderful mother has cracked it!"

I grimaced. *Well, thank you, Mother!*

"Don't sulk. Use your contacts while you've got us," muttered Father. He liked to think he was good at anticipating daughters' filthy moods. It is true that I felt as if we were back in the days when I continually hid in my room to weep and write terrible poetry.

I signalled to Gratus.

I watched my excellent new house steward making mental notes: the family are loud and lovable—but keep an eye on the ferret and do not let them stay too long. Pretend not to notice the master is being a tease with his in-laws. When the mistress assumes a frozen expression, bypass her father with the flagon and even blank her mother as she demurely tries to grab it. Flavia Albia herself needs the wine.

XXV

I sent Paris to the Diribitorium. Our runabout was to find Quartilla, who had already grumbled to me on this subject, and ask if she knew the Tarentum purple-dyers. Whether she did or not, thinking ahead, I also wanted Paris to ask her the name of the Emperor's wardrobe keeper. While I awaited his return, I had to sit through intense discussion of what Mother's clue would mean, plus analysis of where everyone else thought I had been going wrong. They all had a lot of ideas on that.

Tyrian purple is the famous regal tint made from seashells. Invented on the coast of Syria, it uses thousands upon thousands of sea creatures, so it is costly and rare. Nero tried to ban ordinary folk from wearing it. Tyrian purple is a gift for kings. The queen who has everything will still welcome more, a sign of her fame and status. In the back of my mind I was aware that once, when my parents were travelling, my mother had bought up a huge bolt of deep-dyed cloth that she had brought home and sold to the palace for imperial uniforms.

Helena Justina did not care that as a senator's daughter she was barred from trade. She was no slouch at spotting a market and the only reason she had never developed this opening, to import luxury fabric from its faraway homeland was that she had learned of an alternative source in Italy. The beautiful turquoise waters of the Gulf of Tarentum bred molluscs that were equal to those at Tyre. "Calabrians have learned how to create the dye, so they might well visit Rome at a time like this."

Thank you, Mother.

———

Paris came back fast. He knew when it was best not to dawdle with a pack of nuts, watching boats on the Tiber. He brought me a name. I was glad to get out of the house. I needed to escape from people telling me, *Try to be more gracious, Albia.*

Of course I was glad to have a clever, well-read, intuitive, sharing parent—indeed, a complete set of them. Three times the value for a pair, as the auctioneers' manual has it. But you can be smothered under too much help.

I am not surly. I simply wished to run my own investigation. In my own style, at my own pace. Hands off, you irritating blighters. If I am doing this job, just leave it to me, will you?

The sun was shining as I tore over to the Palatine, barely muttering at all. The hills of Rome were glazed with autumn light, like the sheen on the pastries our chef had served for dessert. Afternoon rest had descended on the city. Its human inhabitants were sluggish, while domestic animals stretched out fast asleep. Even the bees in the gardens were parked up on petals, feeling the weight of collected pollen as they thought of the hard journey home, while ants circled aimlessly on warm stone as if they had forgotten what they came for.

In the corridors of Domitian's palace, tired tourists with bunions were stumbling on their way out. Their eyes hurt from staring at flawless gilt and marble in endless visionary architecture; they were desperate for a grubby bar beside a choked fountain where pigeons liked to roost. Clerks, cleaners, hopeful poets, plotters seeking hide-outs had all bunked off. The Praetorian guards had been thin on the ground all summer, because the Emperor had taken their crack units with him to the frontier.

It was quiet. It was virtually deserted. It was the kind of place, and moment, in which a self-possessed career woman could make her own luck. I could achieve what I came for simply through knowing the right name and the right way to ask for him. Then if I got myself taken there, I would know how to persuade him to share what he knew, with no thought of a bribe. My relatives would be amazed: Olympus! I did this without one of them holding my hand.

———

His name was Hylus. He had a pale moon face with a pointed nose. His tunic today was gamboge, with ivory braiding; it must be his personal choice while the Emperor was absent so Hylus was not obliged to endure the official white uniform but could branch out.

In fact, I was in white, though with a crocus hem and an amber stole. It had taken thought to put this ensemble together. I was visiting the imperial wardrobe master. You don't want a man who hoards a hundred cloaks with special brooches, plus a whole shelf of wooden hairpiece stands, to sneer at your dress sense. I needed him to feel favourable towards me while I picked his brains.

I owned up to sartorial diffidence in his presence. In Our Master's dressing room anything less than bombast was novel. Surprised, Hylus decided to like me. He suggested a larger pendant necklace would add impact. Maybe a darker stole. Ginger, perhaps, or even persimmon.

Once I had thanked him for his tips, I probed into what he did. "Hylus, I am surprised to find you here, not with the Emperor. Even on campaign, doesn't a long train of personal attendants accompany him?"

"Oh, yes. Everyone and the food-taster. Sir likes to have people he is used to looking after him. I came home early, with permission, to get together his triumphal glamour. He had an orderly for the soldiering stuff, so I risked leaving that fellow. I never do the breastplates. Metalwork is for a specialist. I loathe it." Hylus shuddered. "*Straps!*" he spat, as if denouncing poor drain hygiene.

We were on such good terms he gave me a private view of the special costume. He led me to a locked room where garments for the Triumph were hung up in semi-darkness. There was no armour. Triumphs symbolise returning Peace. Hylus was happy.

The wardrobe keeper threw open shutters. As we talked, I had a close-up of the gorgeous robes. The cloth itself was beautiful, yarns finely woven with precious silk for lightness and sheen, then deep, deep dyes in the very best colour. Triumphal regalia was by tradition a long tunic covered with naturalistic designs, on top of which went the luxurious purple toga, embroidered so it looked painted. Iridescent material had then been stitched all over in thread-of-gold, the tunic with victory palms and the toga with wide brocaded borders and many intricate designs.

These costume pieces were being supported on poles of such a thick diameter it emphasised the weight that would soon be on the imperial shoulders, simply through getting dressed.

"The fabulous outfit is to make him look divine," I mused. "But Jupiter has the advantage of a diet stuffed with ambrosia to build muscle. Domitian is said to be physically weak . . . Will our man be painted red?"

Why do rulers believe that turning their skin a peculiar colour makes them look godlike? Hylus sniffed. He said he would not remind Domitian of the special red paint. Hylus had enough problems day to day, coping with the premature hair-loss situation. "Our Master is *so* sensitive!" Domitian was an idiot. I said so. Hylus, who himself boasted rampant curls that were probably real, told me that when generals did colour their faces red, it was a nightmare afterwards removing stray dye that percolated onto the *tunica palmata* and *toga picta*. "Myth-makers should think about us, washing out their mess afterwards."

"Heroes never have to do their own laundry," I sympathised. "When does anyone in winged boots stop off to wash his smalls?" Locked in this intimate consultancy, we exchanged tips on sweat-stains, which I feel no need to write down.

Though fabulous, the garments carried a definite odour. Their long-lasting dye had an equally permanent smell of the shells from which the purple had come. Hylus said nothing would remove this unpleasant aspect. So the courts of the great stink even more than democrats suppose.

Nevertheless, the breathtaking shimmer compensates. Hylus now handled the folds, to show me how, with the slightest movement, light gleamed exquisitely. As he lifted and tossed material from hand to hand, admiring it himself, his movements were both casual and respectful. He knew it would not break. He loved it, yet was never afraid to touch, shake, smooth or rearrange the precious stuff in his care.

This was not pure adoration: there was a practical side to his appreciation. He knew what it cost. He knew where it had come from, who had dyed the material, who the negotiator was. Only one middleman brought the purple to Rome. This agent worked for the palace exclusively; he dealt with producers in Tarentum, oversaw quality of cloth, depth of colour, cost, transportation and delivery to the imperial workshops where garments were made up and finished. Hylus was in charge. He would issue an initial order, go to the workshop to check the finished product on arrival, sanction payment. He and the negotiator covered it all on a one-to-one basis. No one else was involved.

He had not heard of Gabinus. Well, yes, he had. The palace was full of gossip: the man was said to be unspeakable; Hylus avoided him. Gabinus would have had no reason to confer with the agent, nor would he ever have influenced any aspect of the imperial clothing collection. The only link Gabinus had with Hylus was straightforward: on the night before a triumph, a closed litter would be ordered from Transport on a special chit to take the robes to the temple where the Emperor stayed. Hylus in person would accompany this cargo. He would sleep alongside the purple outfit, then dress the Emperor before his salutation at dawn. He had done it before. There was a system.

Hylus would not ride in the triumphal chariot, though at all times he would be nearby. Whenever necessary, he would tweak pleats.

He had never even spoken to Gabinus, so here was one person in my case who genuinely had had no reason to kill him.

I was still trying to equate the agent who arranged Tyrian purple for Hylus with the group seen on the Capitol. Hylus thought his agent was not even in Rome currently. Material for the triumphal robes had been ordered many weeks before, because there had to be time for embroidery. With the Emperor coming home after a military campaign, there was also a need to obtain new outfits for his daily routine, so the agent had gone back down south to fix this up. Hylus received regular reports, so could tell me for certain the agent had not been here when Gabinus fell off the Tarpeian Rock. Neither could the Tarentum dyers have been in Rome, because they were hard at work fulfilling the next imperial order.

Before I left, I went up close and sniffed the robes more closely. The new Tyrian purple had been thoroughly washed and aired. Even so, the tunic and toga carried a definite whiff of the sea. Our Master and God would strut around smelling like a dead clamshell thrown up on a beach last Thursday.

XXVI

This required thought.

Hylus was adamant that his agent worked solo. That need not prevent him from having a large family, perhaps never mentioned to Hylus. In the run-up to the Triumph, the hypothetical family might have gone for a day out on the Capitol. But even with that pleasant theory of holiday merriment among the negotiating classes, two puzzles stood out: why did they smell of fish? (I ascertained that the agent himself whiffed of garlic, so he was a normal man of business.) And whyever would such a group arrange to meet Gabinus?

I came to the conclusion I could not be sure that the group seen on the Capitol actually were Tarentine. Someone had got that wrong. Feliculus could not even remember who. I now felt he had passed on only what he had been told and his informant would never have known Feliculus would be talking to me. Perhaps someone had lied, but more probably this was just an error.

Suppose not. (Test everything.) Feliculus had suggested he obtained this "fact" from Lemni. If so, could I trust Lemni? Why would the augur's assistant invent it? He seemed a bright spark—more helpful than most. I would not expect him to fib outright. Or was that because I saw him under the eye of Larth, the augur, his watchful superior? Would Lemni have been more mischievous, or more casual, with Feliculus?

Could Feliculus have been fed false information on purpose? In my work I had to ask such questions, yet I could not see Lemni or anybody else giving the goose-boy the run-around. Up here on the Arx, everyone who bothered to notice Feliculus liked him. Otherwise he was ignored—a public slave doing his work; simply invisible. The sacred status of his flock gave him notional protection; anyway, those geese pecked hard. Only someone as crass as Gabinus would interfere with either geese or guardian.

Even to myself I seemed to be nitpicking. It was down to past experience. People do tell lies to informers. Sometimes there is no reason for them to do so. They mislead on principle. Nobody wants Truth coming out. Any onset of Truth-telling makes people feel uncomfortable, even when this dangerous commodity will have no bearing on their income, their status in the community, or whether their girlfriend will still like them.

Long-held secrets do escape. So many Saturnalias have been ruined by people with too much wine inside them letting fly: "This has gone on long enough. It's time for the Truth, Drusilla!" *Don't say it, you idiot!*

Next thing, Drusilla tries to silence him by whacking him with a big bread paddle. She—having even more wine in her so that she can put up with his horrible habits—whirls around, wobbles off balance, falls over. She lies helpless, whimpering. Even if she tries to get away, she can't. He grabs the paddle; he cracks open her skull with it.

With luck, he then conceals the body, trying to explain away her disappearance, until her mother, who never liked him anyway, hires an informer to investigate. Excellent. Some good comes out of it for my profession. Eventually, if the mother's informer is any good at all, the idiot has to face Truth, Whole Truth, Unpalatable Facts, Hideous Revelations, and Complete Ignominy for the rest of his life.

Which may be short. Murder is a capital crime. That ought to teach him to keep quiet, though in my experience it fails.

While these ideas were fandoodling through my brain, my feet somehow took me down from the palace on the Forum side. I often let my mind wander. Conscious thought can be an inhibitor. This especially applies in the middle of a case, when all you have to go on is a mish-mash of half-truths from witnesses who weren't looking properly, or else those curious stories people invent because they believe it is always vital to mislead the authorities.

No private investigator can compel members of the public to give evidence. To be honest, for me this is part of the fun. Any law-and-order bully can crash in demanding answers, which inevitably makes witnesses clam up. I have to be subtle: I must persuade them I am good to talk to. They *want* to talk to me. They trust me with what they know. It is a relief to share it, then to be reassured I will use it for the most good.

Until they unburden, I keep my mind open. Some might say it is like writing a poem—you drift into creativity, letting your soul guide you—but that's mystic tosh. I know that when my father has reached this stage in a case—when he gets himself stuck or tries to be too clever, my mother says—he often goes for a drink. He does hold a few set theories about how to do the job; this, he says, is his best. He relies on sitting at an uncomfortable table, thinking, *What crappy wine this* caupona *has taken to serving. Dear gods, what horrendous pit in Hades did they dig it up from?* while waiting not even for a flash of intuition of his own, but for the next event. Things always happen. "Hang around," Falco says. "Let Fate do the work." He taught me the job; he taught me such patience.

Today the waiting method was to work. Something had happened and I came upon it. Without my vacant musing, I would never have wandered where I did. I had no purpose in taking myself down to the top end of the Sacred Way. Once I woke up and saw where I was, I groaned and thought to make the best of it.

The Forum is a place of men. Solidly rich, obscenely rich, unbelievably even richer than that, or occasionally hard-up but begging a dinner from the others. They congregate, meet, greet, masticate, obfuscate, plan their next chance to fornicate, and generally mill around in a highly charged aura of business and sex. They could discuss religion or public administration, but why spoil their fun?

I go there when I have to. I am not afraid of men. A woman alone will not be mistaken for one of the tired Forum prostitutes if she carries a businesslike satchel, walks steadily and never meets anybody's eye. I cannot decide whether it is better to tackle catcalls by ignoring them or by snarling back a witty riposte. Depends. Too vague in ignoring, and you can end up with a pesterer glued to your elbow; too witty, and annoyers can turn nasty. If stuck, wave wildly at a stranger then speed up, as if you have spotted a friend. Fix on a big one. At the last minute dodge around this innocent person and keep going fast. The vigiles tend to congregate outside the Curia, so head for them, though don't actually ask for help or you will end up having to shake *them* off.

Which is worse, believe me. The Forum beat is assigned to the First Cohort, whose members (say my relatives with attachments to the Fourth) are little better than the vagrants they are moving out of temple porches. Almost as bad as the lawyers who are gambling on the basilica steps. Brothers to pickpockets and sons of loose women. Not as nice as the stray cats who occasionally manage to kill pigeons by the Black Stone. Not even as nice as the lost dogs.

Surprisingly, it was the First who bothered to deal with today's problem. That was: a body, which had been lying all morning below the Tarpeian Rock.

XXVII

Hello, hello, this was familiar! Hail and farewell, mysterious rock-battered corpse.

I was hours too late to see it happen, but for once Fortune had guided my steps to an incident. I could so easily have turned left at the Vicus Jugarius, strolled around the top end of the Palatine to the Porta Carmentalis, before I wandered home after a quick visit to the vegetable market, just in case I could find any of those artichokes I had seen Valeria Dillia serve up to Nestor. I was still hankering. With food, once you get an idea you have to keep trying until you fulfil your hunger. At that point you find the real thing fails to match your dreams. Still, if you have ever taken a lover, you are prepared for that.

Had I been chasing after vegetables, I would have missed the big event. Instead, I had found myself so near the site of Gabinus' death, I felt called to take another look. Something relevant might strike me. So back I went to where the old woman had seen the transport manager fall.

By the time I hit the Tullianum jail, there were five vigiles. The red tunics stood about in a typical bored formation. As they hovered on the fringe of the death-scene they were eyeing up women and sharing a packet of flatbreads, while they tried not to notice any crimes occurring, lest they had to abandon their scoff to intervene. I found them waiting for their senior investigator. He would need to trek down here from the station-house, after they sent a message for him. When the day shift had gone on patrol that morning he probably yelled after them: "Make sure you don't call me out to anything!" So now he would be slow to unglue his backside from his comfortable stool.

The station-house was along the Via Flaminia, currently clogged with traffic ahead of the coming Triumph. There were legionaries everywhere. En route, he was bound to run into military friends he hadn't seen for years, which would hold him up. For a body, why hurry?

Why? He ought to know why: because this was next to the Forum. He risked having the entire Senate piling out of the Curia in their broad purple stripes and tottering around the corner to take a look. He would not care if the noble ones gawped at the corpse, but he could do without three hundred of those pernickety fellows watching how he handled things.

"Is your man any good?" I could make a guess.

"Scorpus can manage a crime scene."

"Scorpus? I know him!"

I introduced myself to his crew, explaining my connection. The First are responsible for not only the Forum but the Quirinal, where I had worked a previous case, with which Scorpus was familiar. Their station-house stands very near the Saepta Julia, so Scorpus also knew my father. For added impact, I mentioned that my uncle had been an inquiry chief in the Fourth Cohort.

Laying out my wares like this immediately made me an acceptable person to gossip with. The vigiles, tough ex-slaves, would have liked conversing more if I was male but they were, after all, engaged in their traditional role of eyeing up women. Now here was a woman who actually strolled up and talked to them. That was highly unusual.

"So do we have a repeat performance?" I asked, playing it gently. I used my connections when I could but knew better than to push it. "Copycat?"

"No. That's why we called in the chief. He's going to love this!"

"I can imagine. Just when he's ready to go home for a kip, eh?"

I told them I was already enquiring into the Gabinus case for the authorities. They looked surprised but accepted it. I hoped my professional manner would convince them to discuss this new event, though I am realistic. It was more likely they just wanted to continue the rare treat of a respectable-looking woman chatting to them.

"You called it a crime scene. Is it?" Might as well make the chat purposeful, even if I was stretching what they had said.

They looked shifty, unwilling to commit. With Scorpus on his way, they knew better than to give a verdict, to me or anybody else. Scorpus would want to pronounce.

"That's all right. Save it. Let's wait for your man." I treated them like human beings. Most people can never manage that, even when the vigiles are heroically carrying them out of their burning homes. "So what are you allowed to tell me? What looks different this time, lads?" That was precisely what they should *not* tell me or anyone, but they readily spilled.

First, nobody had witnessed this one. Whereas Gabinus had died in the early morning, this must have happened in the dark, last night. Come daylight, all anyone around here noticed to begin with was what looked like a bundle of old clothes lying at the foot of the rock. For several hours, nobody took any interest.

Eventually a lone vagrant managed to clamber over there, hoping to pick up a wearable cloak. Once he came close, he realised that the enticing material was wrapped around someone. He reeled back, too moral to steal anything that had an owner wearing it, in case they jumped up and bopped him. A public slave, sweeping the Gemonian Stairs, spotted the vagrant from his elevated position when he stopped to wipe his nose on his arm. Since the authorities liked to keep people away from the Rock, this slave whistled to Zenon, a vigilis who was passing. Zenon shouted. The vagrant bolted. His colleague Taurus, who was just catching up Zenon after stopping at the flatbread stall, laid the suspect low with a flying tackle.

"Yes, I thought your snack-packet looked a bit battered!"

"Someone fell on it. Luckily it was Taurus, not the vagrant. The vagrant was lighter, but he stank even worse."

They ate the food anyway. They would have offered some to me but, as they sadly admitted, there was none left. That saved me having to give them either an enormous tip, or some worse thank-you present. Taurus was not the only smelly one among them.

"Where's the vagrant?"

"Done a bunk."

"You let him?"

"He had nothing else to tell us."

I nodded. "Well, it saves on paperwork."

"Stops him pissing in our holding cell!"

Scorpus turned up. He was broad in the beam and none too tall, as they all were, although, unlike the rankers, their investigator was a free man with a military background. No hair, no trust in women, no joy at a corpse turning up on his patch. Some manners. Some tact. Beard stubble: the manly man-about-the-alleys look. A bad limp; I had never dared ask how he'd got it. Astute: he spotted at once that there had been food, but it was finished.

He pretended not to remember who I was or that he had even met me. I carried on as if I had not noticed I was being blanked. The rule is that an informer who deals with the vigiles must prove they are worthy of respect; they have to do this every single time they come into contact. Like most rules, it is rubbish. Still, I knew it always happens.

Scorpus took over. He had the public moved back to where they would see and hear less, though he was vague about whether his order included me. I took that for professional courtesy, the most I would be granted. I stood my ground, though I kept quiet to avoid annoying him.

Before I arrived, the vigiles had been into the jail to fetch long poles with hooks. The apparatus was stored ready for incidents like this. The ground was too rough simply to climb over so, using their fire-fighting skills, the men stuck the implements into whatever lay by the cliff and hauled. For them, it was like pulling down a wall to gain access to the seat of a blaze. Scorpus, who probably never went to fires, stood watching with his thumbs in his belt. He was not the type to offer helpful tips.

When it came to removing bodies, these lads were handy. In Rome, they had regular practice. They dragged their burden in fits and starts across the rough ground below the Rock. As it came, it was definitely heavier and more solid than rags, several times causing them to adjust their hooks.

Once they had hauled it right to our feet, we saw what had alarmed the vagrant. A dead body was indeed contained within the wrappings: a human sausage in a stiff leather skin, which was tied on with rope. Feet in sandals had come out at one end. A head, face down, became visible when one of the men pushed back the leather.

Scorpus crouched to inspect the remains. I managed to peer over his shoulder without being sworn at. The top of the skull had been stove in, with blackened blood matting dark curly hair. "Fall damage?" one of the men asked, almost hopefully.

Scorpus shook his head. "Too deep. Much more than he'd get from knocking against the rockface. Something wide, flat-headed. A lump of rock? A club hammer? Done first. Then this wrapping-up job. Then fly-tipped."

"This one never jumped?"

"No, lad. Chucked off. This one had been killed first."

Gingerly, he pulled down more of the wrapping material. It was un-yielding leather, difficult to bend or pull aside. He gave up. At a nod, one of the men helped Scorpus turn the body over, still complete with this stiff shroud. It was a man's corpse, his visible skin a little blotched, either with bruising from the fall or simply the decay of death. No other wounds were visible.

A vigilis worked at one of the rope knots, which was amateurish. It would have been easier to cut through it with a dagger, but the night watch are unarmed. He soon freed it anyway. They opened up the leather.

The dead man was not young. His hair was part-shaved around the sides of his head, leaving his ears prominent. Any human character had left him. No cheeky-chappy light remained. He was dressed in a plain un-bleached, unbelted tunic, with no identifying jewellery; no pouch, purse or stylus bag was with him.

Scorpus and his men looked despondent. To them, a tragic incident now acquired added pain. It would be hard to find out who this person was, which made it near impossible to work out what had happened and who had killed him. This was a very public death, so high-level interest would be a menace. The scribes at the *Daily Gazette* would mention it. The scene was central; sightseers would come wandering around for days.

"Over to us!" Scorpus finally acknowledged me as he groaned at his task. "Nothing to go on, but half Rome wondering whether we're making progress. The big nobs wanting answers. Our prefect constantly on at us. All we can do is tidy up."

I gazed at him quietly. I sympathised, yet I hate the way the vigiles always resist outside help. "You could let me ask questions."

"Why?" he growled. "Have you got a special dispensation to grab anything that happens on the Tarpeian Rock?"

"Something like that."

"Get lost, Flavia! Leave it for the big boys, who know what they are doing."

"Up to you, Scorpus." I pretended not to care that I was being excluded. "You want this the hard way? You are the expert." He was already looking suspicious at how easily I seemed to give up. He knew me better than that. "I thought you had your hands full of gangster killings, Scorpus, not to mention that imperial spy they dumped in your office. But why should you let me help?" I asked dramatically. "Ooh, look—an answer! I can help you, Scorpus, because this death occurred so close to my own case—an official commission, remember. These events may be linked."

"No dice, Flavia."

His choice. He wanted to be intransigent. He thought it made him look tough.

I would not beg. So I did not reveal to this mighty inquiry chief that I had recognised the unyielding stuff the corpse was wrapped in. The vigiles were picking at it in puzzlement, but I knew what it was. Besides, when they allowed me enough space to look at him, I could identify the dead man. He was a witness I had interviewed.

I let a beat pass. Scorpus could stay down there wondering aimlessly, while I would nip ahead of him. Because I knew this: the body was wrapped in a leather sidewall from an observation tent. The dead man was an augury assistant. His working name was Lemni.

XXVIII

Scorpus was not entirely dim. He might sometimes wake up and put his left boot on his right foot, but he would notice it halfway through the morning.

Suddenly he spun around and fixed me with an accusing finger. "You're having me on, Flavia! You bloody well know something."

"Albia," I said routinely. "I told you before, Scorpus. Show some respect, please." Like many in the Empire I had been stuck with an imperial name, but had no obligation to like it or use it.

He ignored that. "What are you hiding? Who is this cove?"

I kept him waiting long enough, then replied haughtily, "Lemni. Some kind of assistant at the Auguraculum. A knows-it-all and runs-it-all fellow, according to him. I interviewed him alongside an augur called Larth—I think those are both working pseudonyms. They cannot have been given antique Etruscan-sounding names at birth. Who would know what poncy religious career a couple of innocent little babies would end up in?"

"Get on with it."

"I assume Lemni used to work with all the augurs, but I would start with Larth. He and Lemni seemed quite close when I saw them. They were setting up a tent for the observations that must be carried out ahead of Domitian's Triumph."

"That's buggered up the Triumph, then!" scoffed Scorpus, happily.

"If only!" I grinned. Camaraderie helps. I can fake it. "Find the mallet—the one for bashing in tent pegs for their guy ropes. I bet it will have Lemni's blood on it. What's bothering me is that Larth is supposed to be sitting inside this tent, doing the mystic business—but at least part of the hallowed structure looks to be wrapped around Lemni. So, is the rest still up there on top of the Arx? Where is Larth? And is he dead too?"

I had a vision of an equally lifeless augur, propped on a stool inside half of a broken tent. Scorpus was bound to regard that as moonshine, proof to him that all informers are a nightmare, while female ones are worst of all and fanciful with it. So I let it rest. I had asked the valid questions.

Scorpus changed.

"*Get lost, Albia!*" His voice suddenly dropped. The first time he ordered me to vanish had been routine banter: this was urgent. Scorpus had seen somebody heading towards us. I recognised him too: he had "militiaman" written all over him and it did not make me feel warm and protected. He was an imperial agent called Julius Karus whom we both saw as vile.

"Ha! Yonder comes an emissary from the Underworld. Your filthy friend."

"Dash up the steps, girl. Up that hill before he gets here!" Scorpus had become fully complicit with me. "Find your Larth and squeeze everything he knows out of him while I head off His Nuisanceship as long as I can."

I needed no telling twice.

Karus was one of Domitian's new favourites. A self-serving, nose-poking, loyalty-lacking, tale-telling murderous official. He had been dumped on the vigiles cohorts to carry out an undercover special mission, one so secret nobody was supposed to know its purpose even if he was working alongside them during it. He came and went; the only sure thing was that, whatever he was doing, he held dangerous powers.

I happened to know his background. When the Emperor had entertained doubts about a certain provincial governor, Julius Karus organised an execution; I believed he acted on his own initiative. Snuffing out a serving governor was highly unusual—who knew what reports this secret envoy sent to Rome?—but the upshot was that an important man died, then all his bodyguard cavalry was shifted to a new province, personally escorted there by Julius Karus. Now Karus was here in the city, laden with ornamental thank-you spears. He was the kind of man who would invent a post for himself—and be given it. A lovely chum for Domitian. Bad news for Rome.

Scorpus was forced to work with him; my rule was to avoid the man. So, conducting myself like a member of the public who had sacrificial wheaten cakes to lay upon an altar, I did a bunk towards the upper temples. Leaving the Tullianum jail behind, I nipped up the Gemonian Stairs, then sheered off towards the Arx.

When I could, I looked back. Scorpus and Karus were staring down at the corpse. In deep, sombre conversation, neither glanced up to where I was. The rest of the vigiles had sharpened their stance. I won't say they were drawn up in a straight line, but as they conglomerated in freeform, they fixed humble gazes on their superiors, as if they believed all officers were gods from whom they could learn wonderful things.

That is not what any of them thinks, believe me.

I had urgent work to do. At the place where I had talked to my two witnesses on my first day, I found a sad scene. The other half of the observation tent lay on the ground, thrown down in a rough pile with buckled folds. Its loose guy ropes were tangled. Their pegs had been ripped out, leaving a mess of divots. I failed to find Lemni's mallet. As I peered below the leather, humps under the tent proved to be upturned stools. I saw no sign of Larth.

I stood still, looking around. The ground had been trampled. There might have been a fight. Lemni was active and seemed as if he could handle himself—I had told him so; an assailant could not have found him easy to subdue. I walked the scene slowly, finding only one clue: a tiny bent piece of metal. It was not much longer than a fingernail, originally curved into a tubular shape but now wrenched open, with some sort of brown fibre trapped in its edge. I wrapped it in the napkin I keep in my work satchel.

The Auguraculum is an unwalled sanctuary, large enough for several tents to be put up at a distance from one another when several public events required omens at the same time. (Or, as I now knew, when the portent-spotters were earning backhanders from private clients.) On such an occasion, the tents must look like a mystic horse fair. Today the outdoor space lay deserted. Nobody was observing whether it was a good month to start a war or found a city, or even whether Domitian could expect the sun to shine on his Triumph.

Instinct took me to the huge adjacent temple of Juno Moneta. There, nothing was happening at the outside altar; the stone was cold to the touch. I climbed the long flight of steps. Ignoring protocol, I entered the cella. The light was dim; clean-burning oil lamps flickered amid an aura of very superior incense. Voices murmured.

I had guessed correctly. A group of augurs was anxiously consulting the goddess, though her calm, broad-browed statue looked unimpressed. Priests who failed to catch the sacred geese yesterday were slightly more use here, calming the distressed augurs; one even helpfully held their crooked staffs while they appealed for divine aid.

They are big women, those goddesses of the Olympian pantheon. You don't get to be such a vital force without looking as if you tone up daily with your trainer. Juno Moneta had forearms and thighs like a laundress's, and hips that might safely produce twins. She was the deity associated with marriage, childbirth and the health of the Roman community, but her femininity was muscular. As Juno Who Warns, she was armoured: shield- and spear-carrying in her protectress outfit, which has fetching boots and a goatskin cloak.

I could never imagine settling down in a swing-seat for mint tea and a good gossip with the Queen of Heaven. It was surprising such a chunk of womanhood ever put up with a husband who went out all the time for serial adultery. Surely she was up to the situation with the over-virile Jupiter? After all, this hefty one owned her own golden chariot, pulled by her trademark peacocks (which are difficult birds), not to mention her handmaiden Iris and, I believe, fourteen nymphs; in a domestic brawl, she could definitely summon back-up.

If she had been a client of mine I would have suggested Juno stop being dependent; she should kick out Jupiter tomorrow, even if it meant losing the dowry. Who needs the aggravation?

Most of the augurs beseeching her advice had upraised arms and the constipated expression people think goes well with praying. I found one who was giving his arms a rest and whispered that I desperately needed to find Larth.

He came out into the porch with me. His name was Alichsantre. So he said, rather muzzily. Etruscan is a lispy language. He looked pure Roman to me, a scrawny-necked tenth-generation patrician, with consuls going halfway back to Romulus, himself boring the Senate now for many, many decades.

He said Larth had discovered the tent wreck this morning, with Lemni missing. After alerting his colleagues, Larth had gone down into the city to look for his assistant.

"Where?"

"I cannot tell you."

"Do not know, or will not say?" I demanded. In true Senate style, when faced with an ordinary question, the wimp failed to answer. I decided not to ask him anything difficult in case his angina flared. One day, 600 woolly old grunts like this would be asked to approve the assassination of our emperor. At least half would instantly wet themselves.

Senators are not used to being chivvied by informers. Alichsantre looked anxious. I told him what had happened to Lemni, stressing that it was death by unnatural causes. I told him I was investigating. He turned even more wittery. I suggested that if the augurs felt nervous, they should send over to the Capitol for Nestor, who would give the Auguraculum Praetorian protection.

Alichsantre bridled. To my surprise, he snapped that, from what he knew of Nestor, the man could not protect a bedbug. Concurring, I decided I liked this augur after all.

"So, tell me what you know about Larth and his movements today. If you say he came up here and discovered the tent smashed this morning, he must have been absent for some reason. Where was he before?"

"He went home. It is not necessary to repeat observations every night. We do not live on the Arx."

"Larth lives somewhere in Rome?"

Alichsantre looked surprised at the question. "He has a house in the city. He has homes in many places."

"Of course."

A senator would be worth at least a million sesterces, a trillion or more in many cases; most have estates in their home province, plus villas at the coast, the lakes and the mountains, not to mention investment properties that can be sited anywhere so long as their olive and wine income is good. Larth looked shabby, but I was not misled. To have snaffled an important post as an augur, he knew where all the political strings were, and the right way to pull them. If he wore battered sandals when he came on the Arx, it only showed he had learned that the open ground by the Temple of Juno Moneta was riddled with goose-droppings.

"If you will, Alichsantre, tell me about him and Lemni. From my observation, they were on good terms."

"Lemni was well known to all. He and Larth had a particularly close working relationship."

"They enjoyed long conversations about races at the Circus?" I remembered that from when I first met them. "Did they like a gamble?" That was a tricky question, since gambling is illegal.

"They studied form." Alichsantre toned it down. "They both followed the Green faction." That made sense, even if the Blues were better. No one supported the Golds, of course, apart from my mad husband.

"So where did Larth go to look for Lemni?"

Alichsantre blinked and looked vague. "I believe Lemni has family. Larth must know who they are and where they live, though I do not. He went to enquire of them."

"You spoke to him this morning? Think carefully, please. Until just now, you and your colleagues thought Lemni was simply missing. Now I've told you, was it your impression Larth knew already that Lemni was dead?"

Alichsantre understood my question. If Larth had known the truth all along, it implied his involvement. He would come under suspicion, even as a senator. It also meant that by rushing off "to look for Lemni" he would reach any family members first, taking them the bad news before I could see their reaction. Alichsantre took fright; he was not saying.

I knew better than to accuse a member of the Senate, one who conducted revered religious rites, of covering for his co-worker. I let Alichsantre go back into the cella to assist his other lofty colleagues in cajoling Juno.

Alone in the porch, I looked out towards the Temple of Jupiter on the Capitol opposite. Standing at the top of the temple podium I was suddenly aware of how high up these peaks were. I understood why the Arx felt so near to Heaven that it had become a place for prophecy. There seemed more chance here of catching the attention of any gods who might exist.

They had not prevented the deaths of Gabinus and Lemni. That's the indifference of deities, of course. Don't waste your wheat cakes or sacrificial animals. The job description of gods says they must never care.

Before the elevation made me dizzy, I walked carefully down the temple steps.

XXIX

Whether or not he had found Lemni's relations, Larth was now returning to the Arx. I spotted his tall, black-clad figure ascending the stairs on the riverbank side. His thin shoulders were hunched as he strode up the long flight, obviously breathless. I let him see me waiting.

"Lemni?" he gasped. If he was pretending not to know the assistant's fate, he made a convincing job of it. His voice was less resonant than usual, though he still sounded as if he was asking a sphinx to prophesy a king's fate.

"Found." I spoke evenly, watching his reaction.

"Where?" Larth was getting his breath back. His autocratic manner came with it. "I discovered the tent, vandalised. I feel anxious—"

"I am afraid you should," I said. "Be prepared. Lemni is dead." I have some tact. I could have demanded why Larth's auguries had never prophesied this would happen. Given how often informers are themselves caught out by tricks of Fate, I chose fellow-feeling. It could be my turn next. "I cannot make this easy, sir. Lemni was murdered. His body has been found today below the Tarpeian Rock, enclosed in part of your observation tent. There is no doubt. Someone battered him, then threw him over."

Larth reeled. "Oh, no . . . I want to see him."

"Not yet. The vigiles and a special agent have the body. Because of the similarities with Gabinus' death, I was asked to speak to you if we met first. We have urgent questions."

The augur looked askance. It is true I was pushing my role in any investigation. A good informer does.

"Talk to me. It will be better," I urged gently.

He capitulated.

I wanted to separate him from his colleagues. I had to keep him away from Scorpus and Julius Karus too. Once the officials dug their claws into him, he would be useless to me. Saying it was for privacy, I led him to the Temple of Vejovis. We went inside.

The youthful god, clean-shaven and long-haired, like Apollo, was supposed to be a guardian of slaves and of gladiators who refused to admit defeat. His small temple between the two peaks was a haven for wrongly persecuted people, also dedicated to the protection of newcomers to Rome. A wholesome place. Jupiter gazed down on us with Greek good looks and an air of compassion while we talked. Luckily today there were no guides about, no tourists who might listen in. Luckily I had left my dog at home, so she was not sniffing the cult statue.

"Larth," I began, "your assistant, who seemed particularly close to you, has been killed. The method was different in minor ways, but it may be no coincidence that it follows Gabinus' death. Tell me about Lemni."

"I am not obliged to do that."

This was going to be hard. "No, but it will look bad for you if you refuse. Am I right that he worked with you more often than with the other augurs?"

"Only because we combined well together. I found him pleasant and efficient. He understood the rituals and rarely made mistakes." Larth made that sound as if he had all the choice, though I suspect Lemni let him think it. That relaxed, self-motivated character would make up his own mind whose watch he sat in on.

"You shared an interest in horse-racing," I probed.

"Irrelevant."

Because of the legal ban on open gambling, I guessed Lemni placed Larth's bets for him. Many people flout the law. Having a flutter is a Roman occupation. No senator would be deterred although, just as he had to use an agent for trade, Larth would have to send a runner to act on his behalf if he was betting. It must be someone he trusted, in case he won. He would not want his runner to abscond with a huge windfall.

If an augur won, was it insider dealing? Could bird flocks tell Larth which horses to back? Would other punters feel annoyed? Would bookmakers say he skewed the odds? Must they lay off large risks, whenever Larth participated?

"Had you a gambling connection with Gabinus?" I shot in.

The sonorous one spluttered. He kicked his feet in their ragged sandals. "Most certainly not! I never knew the man. I told you that."

"Did Lemni run bets for him too?"

"He hated him. I order you to cease this line of questioning."

"Why? What inconvenient fact might I unearth?" I kept pushing. "Unless you knew Lemni intimately, how can you be certain? He seems to have been his own man. I take it he never lived in your household."

"Of course not. He was officially employed."

"Larth, he did not strike me as a public slave."

"No. His antecedents were poor people. He was a free man, though."

"So where did he live?"

"One of the tenements beside the Arx." Like Valeria Dillia.

"Is that where you went to look for him today?"

"No." Immediately I saw Larth regret that. "Yes, of course," he corrected himself, without apology. "Lemni was not there."

"Really? I believe you were gone most of the morning. Those tenements are very close to here. So, when you could not find him at home, where else did you go?"

The augur was attempting a cover-up now, and was not very good at it. Having committed himself, he could not bring himself to tell me a straight lie. "I believed he might have relatives so I went to explore, but I never found them."

"Where was that? What neighbourhood do they live in?"

"Oh . . . An old Suburra district. I was unsure where to look. Nobody could help me find the place. It felt dangerous. I came back empty-handed."

"It's not a district for an innocent to wander around, that's true. What relations do you think he had? Did he chatter about his family? Was he married? Parents? Children?"

"He spoke of a sister, and I believe had a brother somewhere."

"You need to be precise." I was annoyed now. "Someone must find these people to tell them Lemni has died. It would be a kindness to give me directions, so I may pass on the news quickly."

"I have no other information."

"They will want to give him a funeral."

"I shall pay for a funeral," Larth intoned magisterially. "Out of my long-standing affection for Lemni."

"And how will you inform his people about the ceremony?"

I watched him mentally snatch an idea. "A notice in the Forum Romanum should suffice."

Now he really was clutching at straws. I gave up on him.

For now.

XXX

I sent Larth down the hill, saying he should make himself known to Scorpus if he wanted to see Lemni's corpse before it was removed.

As soon as the gaunt figure flapped off in his ghastly sandals down towards the Tullianum, I hopped back to the Temple of Juno. The other augurs were emerging, so at the bottom of the steps I battened onto Alichsantre. He looked nervous again. The others scarpered, leaving him in the lurch.

I noticed the diviners acquired assistants as they left—a group I had walked past when I went into the temple. Some were boys, others older, as Lemni had been. They carried the hook-ended divination staffs. One shouldered the material and poles for a tent. The last spotty youth attached himself to Alichsantre, but kept slightly away from us. That might have been politeness, though he was shambling like any bored lad.

I tried to win over Alichsantre by playing innocent. "Just checking a small point that I forgot to ask Larth. I told him Lemni is dead. He was too upset to talk much, but he mentioned that Lemni used to place bets for all of you at the Auguraculum."

Alichsantre blinked.

"Rely on my discretion!" I insisted. "Everyone has a flutter. I can't see that harmlessly playing the odds has any bearing on Lemni's death, but I must check his lifestyle and ascertain his movements."

"He would sometimes take a message," Alichsantre quavered. I hoped he found more self-assurance when reading off an augury.

"Well, I understand. You would be stuck in your tents. You could not nip out to put a silver coin on Belter or the Alexandrian. Mind you, I reckon old Belter has had his day. He runs as if he has a bad case of clunch nowadays. Do you know if Lemni only helped the augurs, or did he run errands for outsiders too?"

Alichsantre apparently lost himself in wondering whether "clunch" was a genuine equine disease. He seemed to be noting my comments, as if I was giving him tips on an unexpected goer in a race that was known to be fixed; he even glanced over at his assistant as if he wanted him to take a note, but the lad was away in a world of his own. Alichsantre eventually admitted Lemni was a runner of bets for most people on the Capitol. Priests, temple-sweepers, trophy-deckers, gate-lockers, even *priestesses*. I let my imagination romp. "If the Vestal Virgins ever came up to conduct a rite of national importance, while they were here they probably took the chance to have a punt, via Lemni . . . And would Lemni's clients have included the dead transport manager, Gabinus?"

"I expect so."

"Gabinus knew him?"

"Everyone knew him."

"And you think Lemni would have run bets for him?"

"Almost certainly," said Alichsantre—though when I had asked Larth, *he* had flatly denied it. Besides, Lemni himself had made out he barely knew Gabinus.

"Help me. Alichsantre—did everyone like Lemni?"

"Why not? Lemni was helpful, discreet, always busy, always on the go . . . We shall all miss him."

I beamed. "That is such a touching memorial . . . which reminds me, his relations need to be found and told. There must be a funeral."

"Oh, Larth will tell them," Alichsantre assured me. "He will be the best person to break it gently."

"Larth knows them?"

"Lemni and Larth used to go for a family supper there sometimes." I was furious to find Larth had lied to me, pretending he barely knew anything about Lemni's family. What was he trying to cover up? Alichsantre only added to it: "Larth has no airs and Lemni was so sociable he would invite him on race days."

"Do you know where?"

"I am afraid not. But Larth will tell you."

Larth would not.

Not willingly.

I was sick of this. I would have to make him.

I thanked Alichsantre and we parted. The young boy, his assistant, looked as if he might want to say something to me, but the augur moved off at speed once he was released from questioning. The boy left with him.

I found myself watching the lad. He shambled rather like Dromo, never thinking what his feet were up to. His poor walk was a legacy of wearing other people's cast-off footwear all his life. Dressed in a tunic made entirely of patches, he had big ears, a skinny frame, more pustules than I cared to count. There were thousands of young men like him in Rome. As with most of them, he had low expectations yet seemed surprisingly tolerant of his position.

He did have a position. Someone fed him, clothed him, told him what to do. He probably knew other slaves like himself, with whom he could share pointless chat, obscene jokes and idiotic feuds.

What else was there? You could become more senior, obtain a salary, have a family, even if most people never met them—but one day end up at the foot of a cliff, trussed in a stiff old sheet of leather.

XXXI

When I left Alichsantre, I saw Scorpus. That saved me having to find him, but now the inquiry chief was in conference with Nestor. They were standing at the top of the Gemonian Stairs so we could not avoid acknowledging each other.

I walked up and found they were not discussing the murder case at all; they were comparing military careers. Typical. I had to wait while they ploughed through details. Nestor had served in Lower Germany, Pannonia, Rhaetia and Africa, where he ended up a centurion; even he said this showed what a crap province Africa had been. Scorpus had had a posting in Upper Germany and was also in Pannonia, though at a different time from Nestor.

I stood there patiently while Nestor quizzed Scorpus on whether he had ever thought of moving up from the vigiles to at least the Urban Cohorts; no, said Scorpus, he had found his niche. Besides, his gammy leg would count against him. Nestor agreed that would rule out the Guard, which was such an élite corps (what—full of deadbeats like him?). However, he reckoned the lower-caste Urbans accommodated plenty of lads with stiff bits, one eye gone, or even missing body parts. Finally becoming tetchy, Scorpus growled, well, that was it. He didn't want to join such duds.

He gave no opinion of the supposedly élite guards; I hoped that meant he despised them. I could not tell from the conversation. But that is how ex-soldiers talk when face to face, especially with a woman listening. Those veterans had to stick together.

I knew men who would have growled, "Listen, Nestor—the guards are garbage!" Meanwhile everyone in Rome sneers at the Urbans, and even I regard the vigiles as tarnished heroes. The fact I had an uncle in the Fourth Cohort only means I know it at first hand.

For two men in military boots, Scorpus and Nestor were a contrast. Scorpus wore a red vigilis tunic that was probably clean but bore marks of much previous action. He had a nightstick pushed through his battered belt and a seen-it-all air, although with a grim undertone, as if he believed life could yet throw up more filthy surprises. Nestor had changed his cloak today, fastening this green one on a shoulder with a brooch; presumably his superior pay scale allowed him to own extra garments. A sword showed under the new one. In a white tunic, long on him and gathered under his fancy belt in heavy folds, he remained everything a Praetorian liked to be: big, threatening, cash-rich and privileged. Scorpus gave an impression of acute intelligence; Nestor looked dumb. Scorpus would help an old lady through traffic, if he could be bothered; Nestor would never even notice her. Scorpus had risen on merit; Nestor survived despite having none.

"What happened to Karus?" I broke in to ask the vigilis lightly.

"I sent him to pick up more flatbreads for the lads." Scorpus must have been joking though he did not explain. I left it. He knew I had wanted to ascertain that the agent was not hovering nearby, observing us.

We had Nestor instead. Impervious to hints that Scorpus and I wanted to compare professional notes, he refused to leave, but stood there, set as a custard tart. Even so, he was less of a threat than Julius Karus. We could ignore the guard or use subtle code if need be. Karus would have been too dangerous to ignore and was probably so fluent in codes that he wrote his shopping lists in numerical encryption. He was that kind of agent. Manic in tradecraft.

"Did you meet with that augur, Larth?"

"Seems a nice man," stated Scorpus.

There are two options when the vigiles describe someone: either they come out and share your scepticism, especially when the subject is of stratospheric rank, or they stubbornly pretend to be impressed by him when they know you are not. This comment was a pretence. I would have to batter my way through a mound of verbal offal if I wanted a real opinion. Never mind that. I would manage without.

I told Scorpus what I knew. I did not care if Nestor overheard. "Decent fellows, those sky-watchers. Very lofty. Plus they can always identify any puzzling bird you have spotted in a bush in your garden, which is so useful . . . Actually, the man is a lying bastard. He claims he has no knowledge of Lemni's family, yet my contacts say he often had supper with them."

"I expect he forgot," said Scorpus, though he flashed me a quick look. We were now having a conversation that was meant to go over the head of the guard.

"No, I get it. A most noble patrician with a national role on the Capitol must feel shy of admitting he's eaten garlic prawns in a tenement."

"Depending on the tenement, so might you be. Flavia."

"Not me. I lived in one for years. Besides, give me garlic prawns and I'm your friend for life . . . Did Larth pinch the body from you?"

"Surprisingly, he did. We had to provide bearers to lug it away, but he saved us the trouble of deciding what to do with it."

"Not his business anyway," I muttered. "Not if he would come clean about Lemni's family. What's he doing, wading in? Lemni's own people may want a say in what happens to his remains, assuming they can afford it."

"They can't," put in Nestor, unexpectedly.

We stared at him.

"So I heard," he added, unabashed.

This had to be addressed. I took him on, while Scorpus listened. "You knew Lemni?" I demanded.

"I met him." Nestor remained brazen.

"Here on the Capitol?"

"Where else?"

"What about his family?"

"Nothing to do with them."

"No idea where they live, then? Did you know he was a betting runner? Did he place bets for you?" That would have explained how they had come into contact.

"I knew he did it." Nestor disappointed me. "Everyone knew. But me and the lads have a man of our own who takes money at the track. We don't use unreliable civilians for wagers," declared the guard. He had such a high-handed manner I could have kicked him somewhere sensitive. But I had to give up street-fighting now I was an aedile's wife.

Tell the truth, Albia: I had been encouraged to calm down for much longer than that—ever since Falco and Helena adopted me. Everyone had warned them it would turn out appallingly; they wanted me to be a refined young lady, to prove the others wrong.

"What makes you call Lemni unreliable, Praetorian?"

Nestor shrugged. No reason, it seemed.

"So what's your team?" asked Scorpus, a natural male question. Now they were into masculine gossip, I would never get any sense out of the guard.

"Greens, who else?" answered Nestor.

Scorpus nodded. It was unclear whether the Greens were his team too, but coming from a Blues family I preferred not to pursue the point.

I made a show of reminding Nestor that gambling was against the law. Scorpus choked at any idea that mere illegality would stop people engaging in our national pastime, or that he should waste his time cautioning Nestor for it.

Then I jumped the guard with a new line: "I heard you saw my husband the magistrate earlier."

"He seems a fine man." Nestor was copying the Scorpus routine, though the dumbcluck had picked up the phrase without its proper tone of irony. Scorpus winked at me. Subtlety is alien to the guards and Nestor could not play our game.

"Yes, people feel privileged to speak to him. Snaring Faustus was not easy! Once I had speared him to a table with a fish skewer, though, he gradually came around . . . Did he happen to ask whether, in your patrols of the Hill, you encountered suspicious types with business links to the late not-lamented Gabinus?"

"You are changing the subject, Flavia!" Nestor complained.

"That's me. Unnerving a witness by picking at something different . . . So did you?"

"Investigate anyone coming to see Gabinus?"

"Exactly."

Nestor managed not to scratch his head as he wondered whether this was meant to entrap him. "I stopped a few. Horse traders mainly."

"You take their details?"

"No reason to bother them." I could see why, despite Lower Germany, Pannonia, Rhaetia and Africa, Nestor had been left stewing at home in the latest campaign, not risked on a tinder-dry frontier. He must be known to be hopeless.

"Horse traders? They lie, they substitute, they steal, they cheat," I listed. "I suppose you could just about say for a transport manager, with a triumph to equip, horse traders' visits were legitimate."

"More or less," interjected Scorpus, chortling. He had been watching with an amused air.

"Well, I personally would not let horse traders wander unescorted near fancy temples that hold valuable, historic contents. But our Praetorians are trusting men, easy-going administrators, unafraid of risk!"

"We are not afraid of anything!" Nestor provided the guards' stock retort. What a cliché-monger.

He had a vague idea we were baiting him. Smart tiger. Since most people are terrified of upsetting the guards, he had never had to learn how to handle ridicule. Nor could he quite believe I was so pally with the vigiles that we might gang up on him. He wanted to despise me as a low-life in what would be a disreputable job even for a man, though he had to respect me as the wife of a highly placed, highly cultured magistrate. He could not believe Scorpus would ever collaborate.

"I hope you took down all their names," Scorpus told Nestor, though he generously did not press it. A Praetorian guard could write, but would he bother? "Lay off him, Albia. Is there something significant in Gabinus and his dodgy contacts?"

I accepted his peace-making. I suppose this is why Scorpus of the First Cohort was a good officer. "There has been talk of a fishy-smelling lot who may come from Tarentum, Scorpus. It would be a real help if Nestor met them and has their details. Nestor, a group of them came up here one night and found themselves locked in after dark. Gabinus had to rouse the keeper of the Porta Pandana to let them all out. Mean anything?"

"Oh, those idiots!" Nestor was so pleased with himself, he burst out with it, then wished he had been cagey in case he had missed some reason to thwart me. He compounded it by boasting he knew more: "They were not southerners. That's bollocks."

"Where from, then?" Scorpus put in for me.

"Down on the coast."

"Near Ostia?"

"Out that way."

"What did sandy coastal prawn-fishers have to do with Gabinus?" Still Scorpus.

"No idea. I stopped them, though they stank so much I never searched them. When they said they were coming to see Gabinus, I lost interest."

"Did you take names?" This was the important question. I made sure it was me who asked it.

"Routine procedure. They were just a family who stank like rats. They said some names. I never wrote them down—what was the point? No call for arrests or follow-up."

Even Scorpus rolled his eyes. I just about managed not to tell the guard he was useless. What I thought might have shown in my face.

XXXII

Scorpus left us. He used the excuse that he had to return to the station-house "to see what was going on." I knew what that meant. He saw no future in further enquiries. He would stomp back up the Via Triumphalis, lounge in his office, dictate a few notes about the Lemni case to his meek clerk, telling the clerk to file the scroll under "pending" for a week then lose it. Job done. Scorpus would call it time to go off shift.

"And what are you planning on next, Flavia?" Nestor made it sound like polite interest. With him, being polite meant patronising. He tried to loom over me, but I sidestepped.

I had no intention of telling him. I pretended I had used up all lines of enquiry, so I would trot off home for a rest and an almond turnover. Since that was his idea of what a woman investigator did, the guard gave a satisfied smirk. I reckoned he would not follow me to check.

I headed off down the Gemonian Stairs. If Nestor returned to patrolling the Capitol, I should get away from him. To be certain and to feel safe, I would have liked to leave with Scorpus, but the investigator had made plain he had had enough of being seen in an informer's company. I respected that. Sharing casework with the vigiles is delicate. I know never to be too clingy.

Anyway, I did not want even Scorpus with me while I went looking for new evidence. That was my real intention.

But for dodging Nestor, it would have been easier to take the steps on the river side of the Hill. This way, I had to trek around between the Arx and the Forum of Julius, through the Porta Fontinalis, where the old Servian Walls ended at the Hill. The Via Salaria, the ancient Salt Road, and the Via Flaminia left the city by this republican gate. Despite the modern overlay of trinket stalls and snack-sellers, the enclave still had a very ancient feel.

Just outside the gate stood a large heroic tomb with four Tuscan pilasters supporting a traditional frieze of garlands and bull's skulls. For the first time, I noticed it contained the remains of a plebeian aedile.

CAIUS POLICIUS BIBULUS,
IN RECOGNITION OF HIS WORTH AND VALOUR
BY DECREE OF THE SENATE AND PEOPLE,
THE SITE FOR A TOMB FOR HIM AND
HIS DESCENDANTS HAS BEEN GIVEN
AT PUBLIC EXPENSE

Hail and farewell, Caius Policius. I wondered how this man had obtained the rare honour of burial within the sacred area of Rome, and whether it meant he had died in office.

It gave me an odd feeling. If Tiberius Manlius had been killed by that lightning strike on our wedding day, as a serving aedile would he now have a tomb inside the city on publicly awarded land?

Don't think about it. Tiberius survived. I still felt weak if I let myself remember that terrible moment of panic when he was struck down, but he was here. He would complete his public service, then probably not attempt to go further since his rank was not included in the Course of Honour. Unlike senators, who go on to bother society for the rest of their purple-bordered lives, we would establish our household and business as private citizens. The likelihood was that one day Tiberius and I would be a couple of eccentric codgers, quietly carried off in old age. Those close to us might honour us, but we would be unknown to many. Our eventual departure would be natural. We would have had full lives, comfortable ones, and by that time be living out a gentle retirement . . .

Two men had died on the Capitol, one loathed, one liked. They, too, must have reckoned on long lives with normal endings. Someone had destroyed that hope. I had always taken Gabinus' fall from the Rock seriously, but when I first started looking into his "suicide" I felt neutral about it; I had simply aimed to establish the facts, whatever they turned out to be. Now, though, I began to theorise that both men were taken out deliberately, and perhaps by the same killer. I saw no reason to think the two deaths were random. There was probably a link. Having two corpses, I began to focus much more intensely on what had happened to them. If there was evil abroad on the Capitol, I was now determined to expose it.

I made my way to the building where Valeria Dillia lived. She was out, though I found a porter. He was the usual misshapen slave, like a pie that had slumped in the oven. I came upon him eyeing up the ground-floor urine tank. He dropped any plan to empty it, though he was not completely idle: he was ready to talk to me as much as I wanted.

Lemni did not live in Dillia's block. Even so, the porter knew who he was. He had seen Lemni come and go; he knew Lemni acted as a race-track runner. He never asked him to carry a bet because he had no money.

Lemni rented a room in the tenement next door, had done for years. The first porter took me along to act as my introduction to his janitorial colleague. I could have managed by myself, but it smoothed the way. I thanked him with a copper. He thanked me for it as though it was a fortune. Nobody normally noticed him, let alone gave him anything.

The second porter, aware now that helping out might pay, eagerly led me up to Lemni's lodging. He opened the door with a latch-lifter that he knew was kept above on the lintel. The door stuck, but he also knew the knack of bursting in with a sudden shoulder push.

I found the familiar small, sparse room with the same battered furniture and the same sour smell as all the rest in this case: another bed-and-bucket bunk-up. By his wonky table, Lemni had two stools, not one. In those tenements it was luxury. It would have allowed him to entertain a visitor, so long as their leg muscles were strong enough to stop the stools wobbling. Larth had sat there presumably. Lemni's sister, or his brother perhaps.

The porter said he had seen Larth come home with Lemni more than once. "There was nothing funny in it!" he hastened to tell me. I was an informer, so he assumed I was looking for scandal. Of course I had not supposed anything of the sort. I had seen the two men together. Rome was rife with mismatched sexual partners, but I was sure that had never applied to them. "They was just mates. They would have a bite they brought in with them, they had a chat, then the tall man always went off, going home presumably."

"I think that's right," I said, to reassure the porter. "They got on well and enjoyed each other's conversation. It can be done."

Lemni's possessions held no surprises, just a few items of clothing, odd tools, a minimal set of household utensils. Two oil lamps, one dry.

The bed was unmade. Nothing sensational, just a squashed pillow and the thin coverlet left open as if someone had recently climbed out. I pulled it straight, no reason not to. It was never a crime scene. No struggle had taken place there. This was simply the room of a man who lived alone and had done so for a long time. He had gone out one evening to his place of work—an unusual place, high on the Arx at night, but routine for him. Behind him he had left the casual untidiness of someone who most definitely expected to come home.

XXXIII

Despondent, I prepared to leave. My heart was heavy for the chirpy soul I had met so briefly. Why was Lemni dead? What pointless quarrel led to this?

On the way out, I asked the porter, "Did you ever see Lemni with other visitors, apart from the tall man, Larth?"

He shook his head.

"Did he ever bring women back?" He looked nervous. "It is allowed, you know," I reassured him.

"Not like that."

"He had a sister, didn't he? What about her?"

It was worth pushing, because now the porter changed his tune: "I seen her a couple of times, yes."

"What's she like?"

"Normal."

"What's her name?"

"He never said."

"Did she come on her own?"

"Most times. Or she had her little nippers. Lemni seemed very fond of them. You could see why he doted. Beautiful children. Well, they took after their mother."

I was not sure how to reconcile this woman being both beautiful and normal, but I let it go. "What about their father?"

I was half expecting the answer, a common enough tale: "Never seen him. I used to hear Lemni having a go at his sister about the man, but she always said she had no reason to leave him, so Lemni ought to stop nagging."

"Do you think he knocked her about? Is that why Lemni was having a go?"

"Not that I saw. She wasn't cowed. She seemed like a woman who would stand up for herself. She wasn't even letting Lemni tell her what to do."

"How many children?"

"Two last time. And a babe in arms."

"Three, then. So what had the brother-in-law done?" I asked, though I could guess. "What made Lemni nag about him?"

"Lemni called him a dead weight."

"He was just no good?"

"No support to her." With three children already, the wife had her hands full and I bet there was a chance of more if she stuck it out with that husband. She must be a tired and anxious woman, kept short of money, often on her own. A good brother would worry about her, maybe even fear he would be called in to provide for her and the infants himself. Of his own accord, the porter confirmed it: "From what I heard when they were arguing, the husband was never around much, so the sister relied on Lemni more and more."

"The pair were close, then?"

"Seemed like it."

"Was he older?"

"Looked to be."

"Might the husband and Lemni have got together and had a quarrel?"

"I don't know."

Hmm. "So there was a sister with troubles—and then I think someone told me Lemni might also have had a brother?"

"Yes, he used to share the room with Lemni, but he moved out." The porter looked as if he was about to add something, but he must have changed his mind. He scratched his groin instead. They all do it. He was unaware of his action; I ignored it.

"Did a man called Gabinus ever come around here?"

"Not that I know."

"In Transport. Not very likeable. Everyone hated him, in fact."

"No," said the porter, in the vague way that made him seem to be hiding something. "No, I wouldn't know anything about anyone like that."

"Gabinus is dead. He's not going to bite you."

Still nothing.

"Do you see all visitors to these apartments?"

"Only if I'm out of my cubicle. Someone might arrive when I'm doing a job in one of the rooms, or if I'm having a lie-down. I wouldn't see them then, not if they came in quietly."

"Of course."

"Doing a job in one of the rooms" might not mean mending a shutter or filling the oil lamps. I had seen the casual way the man could force his way in when an occupant was absent. And from the reek of his breath, drink might frequently lead to him "having a lie-down."

In this he was no different from thousands of building caretakers. They might just about form a deterrent to thieves and others who might not want to be seen, yet on the whole they are just hidden charges on tenants, a distinct liability. Any woman who has lived alone, and even some cohabiting with male partners, will have tales to tell.

I had been in this one's company for long enough. He had made no moves. But experience drew me to the exit.

He stopped me. "I tell a lie."

"I hope not!" I quipped. Light-heartedness was lost on him.

"There was a girl Lemni brought."

"A girl?" I snapped. "I thought that wasn't his style."

"No, he must have made an exception, because this one was a real looker. Young, though. Old enough, if you see what I mean, but she can't have had much time to practise . . . Only the other day it was—how could I have forgotten?"

"Let's hear about it, shall we?" I pressed sternly.

So the door porter stood there, with his turned-up nose, wearing his grimy tunic and his faint leer. He was hoping I would pay him for this. I might tip him at the end; if so, it would be even less than I had given the first porter, who seemed more reliable.

But this loon supplied me with a story. "She was so young, I was very surprised at Lemni. Nothing happened, though, so that was all right." I did not ask how the man was so certain that Lemni had had no sexual activity in his room, either in general or with this young girl. Door porters spy on tenants. Some of them think voyeurism is their right, their perk to top up meagre wages. Some go on to use crude blackmail against the parties involved. This one now came right out and asked me: "Do you pay people for telling you this stuff?"

I applied an expression of regret. I spoke as if what I was saying was routine. "No, I am so sorry. My inquiry is official, I'm afraid, so every aspect has to be seen as purest white in case there are questions about probity. You have a choice: talk to me without hassle, or my clients will send along specially trained men who will put you up against a wall and take it in turns to pound your liver into a smooth terrine. Then you tell them. That's assuming you can still speak, which I believe does not always happen."

He thought about that, looking far from queasy. I guessed people often abused him, so he was less scared than he might have been.

"The young girl?" I prompted. "So this happened very recently, but what was it about her that made her stay in your mind?"

In vigiles parlance, I must have seemed a nice woman. That is, compared to Rome's liver-terrine bullyboys. He decided to tell me. "Lemni came in one night with this little bird, but she didn't stay long. She looked as if she'd been crying—he can't have done that to her, he wasn't the sort. He never said anything, just looked very grim. He brought her indoors in a hurry, then I heard him ask where her family were staying. Not long afterwards they came out again and they left. He had her wrapped up in a cloak of his, so her face wasn't showing. They bustled past me as if I wasn't there, and rushed off."

"Know where they went?" A really curious porter might even have gone after them to find out, but this one was too lazy.

"No. I couldn't follow them. I'm not supposed to leave the building. Anyway, Lemni looked back over his shoulder and glared at me. I was never scared of him—except that night."

I was troubled by all this. "So the girl was extremely young and lovely, and not Lemni's type—if he had a type. It sounds as if he never knew her well, but he did know that she had relations somewhere and he took her back to them. Anything else you can tell me?"

The porter shook his head. It seemed final. Once again, I was on the verge of leaving.

Then he found his voice again. "Whatever she looked like, I'd never have touched her, not me. She smelt like a basket of whelks."

XXXIV

When I came out of the building, Scorpus had arrived to make his own enquiries about Lemni.

"I thought you went off duty?"

"Well, I'm more thorough than you think!"

He was about to go in. I hung around while he, too, inspected Lemni's room. He made no objection to me waiting. Given time, he might even come to enjoy having a wise colleague to talk to about his cases.

His peek at the room was even more cursory than mine. He then made a big event of instructing the porter to lock up and not let anybody else see the place. He found out who the landlord was, saying he would pay him a visit. The man might have knowledge of Lemni's relatives, though we both thought it unlikely.

Leaving the porter untipped, Scorpus and I strolled to a snack bar where we ordered late-morning refreshments to help us forget how gloomy murder made us feel.

Scorpus complained he had not managed to shed Karus from the case. The agent had stayed up on the Hill, making his secret importance widely felt. He would be asking anyone who worked in the temples whether they saw anything last night when Lemni and his assailant must have had their fatal confrontation.

"That should ensure no one there will be willing to share their evidence!" growled Scorpus, glumly. "No point me going back up the Hill. Co-operation ruined. I give up!"

I sat quiet. I was picking apart a fruit tartlet. The pastry was stale; I would eat only the contents, even though it was difficult to tell what berries these were.

"Borage tea? I don't know how you can drink that muck, girl. You could have a go, after," offered Scorpus. His shy magnanimity was sweet. "On the questioning, I mean. Dip a toe in. If bloody Karus hasn't entirely put their backs up, Flavia, they might still talk to you. Sorry, I should've said Albia."

"Thank you," I answered meekly. "I can certainly try."

"If you run into that bastard, bloody Karus, don't say I said to."

"No, Scorpus."

It went without saying that if I learned anything I was supposed to report on it to Scorpus, without telling Karus. Maybe I would. That depended on what crumbs of information I picked up.

"How are you getting on, Scorpus, having him on your neck?"

Scorpus spat out an olive stone. This passes for repartee in Rome. His style was slick: he achieved controlled acceleration. The stone bounced off the counter marble, then zinged accurately into an empty saucer. I clapped my hands silently.

"Getting on with Karus? Badly. Bloody badly, Albia. When I'm ready to swing a hatchet at his throat, I go off by myself and catch bath-house thieves. My prefect is amazed at the sudden upsurge in our clothes-snatchers clear-up rate."

"Proves it can be done!" I remarked. Losing your tunic at the baths is a perpetual problem. The worst bath-house keepers sell off stealing rights as a franchise. For the public, left standing nude in the street, the only recourse for their missing clothes is yelling about the keepers' dishonesty and the vigiles' complete disinterest in this awful crime. If you train a dog to sit on your stuff in the clothes manger, thieves often steal your dog too. Ditto your little slave if you leave one. "Want to tell me which places you have made safe, Scorpus? Or is it obvious from the advertisement: *Only bath-house in Rome where the mangers are guaranteed thief-proof, due to vigiles' interference?*"

Scorpus gave me a nasty look. We paid up and separated.

———

I stayed on. I ordered another beaker of borage tea at the counter. He was right. It is filthy stuff. I had only asked for it in the first place to stop Scorpus developing ideas that if I had wine he could get frisky. In fairness, he had never done that. I had simply worked in Rome so long I expected the worst.

Julius Karus struck me as a stubborn brute. He would stay up on the Capitol until somebody told him something, even if a consortium of altarboys finally put their heads together to invent a big lie just to get rid of him. Then, if they had any sense, they would ritually purify any ground he had stood on.

When I thought even Karus might have cleared off back to his own dungheap, I went quietly back up the Hundred Stairs. I spent a couple of hours interviewing priests, temple sweepers and occasional tourist guides. Workmen making arrangements had thinned out but I spoke to a couple of spare soldiers. With all of them, I showed an interest in their work, assumed they wanted to be helpful, used good grammar, always said thank you. Most seemed grateful to be talking to someone who made no threats, not even silent ones. I kept going until I ran out of human witnesses and was talking to statues. None of them knew anything, either about Lemni or even Gabinus.

I then made enquiries at the Tabularium, the huge building above the Forum where Rome's archives are stored. The reception staff told me there had been excited talk after Gabinus died, but nobody had seen him fall from the Rock. As for Lemni's murder, the building closed when darkness fell so no one would have witnessed events that we believed had occurred at night. They promised to let me know if they heard anything. This gave them a genuine excuse to gossip with clerks and visitors, so they were happy.

As I left, I discovered Karus had not yet given up. I spotted him having a face-off with Nestor. The guard looked his usual truculent self. The secret agent's sinister manner failed to quell Nestor's bombast. Nestor was giving Karus his usual routine: investigating deaths on the Capitol ought to be his job.

I guessed another report on him would soon whizz along to his superiors at the Praetorian camp. The word was that Karus hunkered down in another barracks, the Castra Peregrina, which was set up for spies, but his authority would weigh. The Praetorian Guard's two prefects might curse Karus as imperial embuggerance, but they and the Peregrina snoops were brothers, bonded in crushing the public. If Karus fingered Nestor, Nestor would be flattened like a beetle in an olive press.

Since the pair were together, one wide loop allowed me to dodge both. I hooked around towards Juno Moneta, where I went looking for Feliculus. I braved a train of hissing geese, to whom I returned the traditional threat of "Onion sauce!" Pretending to have no idea what I meant, they veered away snootily.

Feliculus was by the poultry pen. In one cage, a goose lay curled up limply. He was stroking its head, receiving little response. Another goose had been sitting on the roof; it flopped down and came towards me, but was half-hearted. I shooed it off.

The bird Feliculus was tending looked extremely sick. I had a feeling it might be the one I fell upon, though he did not accuse me.

"This is Florentina. Under the weather, aren't you, darling? She seems to be developing a cold today."

"Is that common?"

"We suffer terribly with our sinuses, don't we?" Feliculus asked both geese rhetorically. They disdained to comment. "Any diseases are a worry in young birds, but Florentina is old enough. She ought to get over it, but I'm trying to avoid her being stressed."

The goose guardian was anxious; Florentina had depression too. They made a moody pair.

I asked politely what her symptoms were. Problems had come on suddenly: thirst, watery droppings, ruffled appearance, no appetite, stomach-ache—how did Feliculus know that, I wondered, since the goose could hardly have spelled it out for him? "She kept leaning forwards to ease the pain, but that was last night. Now she doesn't want to move at all."

I remembered my father complaining that geese were as tender to look after as a flock of two-year-old children. Any disease spread rapidly among them and could be transmitted to the humans who looked after them. I advised Feliculus to wash the cage out frequently, then wash his own hands well. He nodded but was visibly dispirited.

I managed to persuade him to answer a few questions. Had he heard or seen anything last night when Lemni died? No, he had gone down the hill for a drink with a friend. When he came back he realised he had forgotten to put the geese to bed before he left, but they were patiently waiting up for him, without mishap. But poor Florentina was so out of sorts he had stayed up with her all the rest of the night.

"I am glad to hear you are getting out to enjoy yourself sometimes," I interrupted. "I am sure Falco would say it will help you overcome your troubles. Isolation is no good for somebody as sensitive as you." With little real interest I asked, "So who was your company last night, Feliculus?"

"Him I told you about. The gatekeeper who used to be on the Pandana. He came over to tell me he's been given his old job back, now Gabinus isn't there to keep complaining. We had a jar or two to celebrate."

I experienced a slight qualm: a man who suffered from black pits of despair should not go out downing quantities of wine. Since he was so miserable, wiping the eyes and beak of his snuffly goose, I held back from issuing this warning. It is never popular. He was an adult. You cannot save everyone.

I left Feliculus with his patient, while I took myself to the Porta Pandana. The newly returned gatekeeper was a wheezing old slave; he must have been pensioned off here, where he held what passed for a useful position but was rarely called upon to do much.

He remembered the fishy visitors. Unlocking the gate for them was his only excitement for the past three years; since it had lost him his job temporarily, it would stay in his mind. After breathlessly cursing Gabinus for a vindictive, ungrateful, power-hungry swine, he then usefully confirmed a fact. As Nestor had said, the visitors had come up to Rome from the coast. They lived and worked south of the port at Ostia. The gatekeeper knew they had come to see Gabinus about something connected with their trade.

"What trade is that?"

"They do dyeing. From the seashells."

My family owns a much-loved maritime villa on that part of the seashore. It nestles among pirates' retirement palaces and senatorial off-duty spreads; my grandfather bought it so he could go fishing. "Fishing" was his euphemism for landing valuable statues on his beach, instead of at a port, so he could dodge the import tax. Falco discontinued this illegal practice once he took over the auction house. Of course he did.

After Father inherited the place, we often spent holidays there, taking excursions to places of interest nearby. One educational visit had given me a clue to the smelly people's whereabouts. We went to a remote spot, deliberately stuck away from habitation, where they were allowed to work. However, we left quickly with no lecture and no free samples. That industry stank so much my young sisters held their delicate noses, squealing. My little brother actually threw up—although, being Postumus, vomiting at will was a talent he had taught himself. My siblings were ordered to stop making an exhibition of themselves, and the Didius family fled to the villa of a rich friend who served iced fruit sorbets.

What we had missed was a demonstration of people manufacturing imperial purple dye.

XXXV

It says much for my husband that a day out, even to a stinking dye-works, struck him as romantic.

The first time Tiberius and I surrendered to our pent-up feelings and slept together happened when we were travelling in pursuit of information. We were newly in love, so had been full of nervous inhibitions. Being outside Rome freed us. The mansio at Fidenae, known privately ever since as the Cow with No Tail, made a drab setting for a tryst; it was a bad travellers' rest with flea-ridden beds, while the journey we were taking at the time ended poorly for several people, some of them friends of his. But for us, our trip through Fidenae was imbued for ever with intimate nostalgia.

"We are married now," I scoffed. "Sex is no longer thrilling. Don't get ideas."

"Too late!" quipped Tiberius, cheerfully.

After a moment he asked, with a more uncertain air, "You are teasing. Tell me it is still exciting."

"Of course it's lovely, darling," I replied. Roman wives know how to keep them guessing. "I don't expect I shall even think of taking a lover for, ooh . . . months yet."

"Good to know!"

Tiberius went off to organise transport. Roman husbands on the hop like to bury themselves in manly tasks.

For my head of household, arranging transport meant he snaffled the two-mule carriage that belonged to his uncle, without telling Tullius. The alternative was for me to borrow my father's auction delivery cart; that was all right if you were a cupboard. In either case, the vehicle came with a po-faced driver, who plainly disapproved of us. Father's cart sometimes contained three chickens and a cement-coated plank. The uncle left behind the cushions he had lolled on, which held a curious whiff of patchouli and dubious practices.

Uncle Tullius, being a top-of-the-pile businessman, owned a comfortable conveyance so we preferred that. He only travelled within Rome so the mules were up for stretching their legs with us. Even their driver perked up.

Rome to the coast can be done in a day. Lawyers even hare down to their airy villas after the courts close. Since we started out early, we hit the Didius homestead in the hours of daylight, giving us time to roust out slaves and announce we were overnighting. After they had bounced with outrage at me turning up without warning, along with a stranger I claimed I was married to and a dog they had never seen before, they grumpily began to prepare a bedroom and a meal for later. In theory staff left in charge of country homes are supposed to have houses in readiness all the time. This is in case a consul who knows their master arrives unexpectedly with letters of introduction and a hundred hangers-on. Being prepared never happens. Home slaves are so busy enjoying themselves and lording it over the harder-working farm-labourers, they are easily caught out.

We left the mules to rest. Their driver walked about, sneering at my family's seaside hideaway. It had a shabby air; he could not tell that it was discreetly stuffed with choice antiques. He just thought it was a dump.

Instead of the carriage, we saddled two elderly donkeys, who were as affronted as the slaves when their lazy routine was interrupted. Tiberius had partly grown up in the country so he believed himself expert at animal management. He had not met ours before: Castor and Pollux had established a myth that they responded only to my grandfather; since he had been dead for twelve years, they wanted total idleness. In my experience rural parts are stuffed with such intransigent beasts. I cling to being a city girl; I try to have nothing to do with them.

Tiberius and the two donkeys had an altercation in a field. It was their field, which they had no intention of leaving. He was acting magisterial, which only works in situations where you can impose huge fines. I suggested that to exercise authority he should have brought his curule stool; he answered with something I did not quite catch.

Slaves came out to watch. One skivvy sat placidly shelling peas; this oddly enraged Tiberius. They had all known me since I was a girl, but were behaving as if they had never met me: me, their master's eldest daughter, the sensible one in that generally crazed family.

I reminded them that I was a British import, saying I had friends among those hairy, head-hunting horse-lovers far away. Unless they made Castor and Pollux move, spirits from my homeland would put a spell on them. The slaves just stared, then drifted back into the house. The deadbeat donks refused to budge.

Barley had had enough of this. My dog crept up behind Castor in her silent way, then nipped his ankle. He took an involuntary step; Tiberius threw himself into the saddle. Barley let out a short bark at Pollux, who turned, wild-eyed, but at least also became mobile. I put up Barley into a big pannier, one of a pair I had set on Pollux for that purpose, then somehow managed to wriggle aboard.

"Walk on!" instructed Tiberius. One donkey brayed derisively.

"Get going, you dopey pair of long-eared idiots!" I yelled. That was the kind of language they were used to, from my young brother Postumus. After a few pointless circles, we finally set off. Tiberius muttered that Barley had probably given Castor windpuffs above the fetlock. I said, "Serve him right."

We took sandy paths along the coast. By now it was mid-afternoon so the November sun was waning, its light less intense; we had little time to spare. We dug in our heels to persuade Castor and Pollux to travel as fast as possible. Donkeys are in fact extremely intelligent, so they must have grasped that the sooner they took us where we wanted to go, the sooner they would be returned to their field.

On our approach to the murex works, we soon knew we were in the right location. First we passed rows of transport amphora and smelly mounds of spiny whelk-like shells. The smashed remains ponged of old seawater, though that was nothing like the vats we soon came to, where woollen cloth was being double-dipped in liquor. It was the same odour I remembered from the palace, when Hylus had shown me Domitian's triumphal robes, but here the horror was stupendously intensified.

Tiberius was wincing. "Jupiter! Let's make this quick," he appealed to me. I would have replied that interviews have to be as long as it takes, but at that moment I was suffering from the smell too much to speak.

Compared to production at Tarentum in the heel of Italy, what happened south of Ostia could only have been a cottage industry. All Italian dye production paled into insignificance beside the ancient trade of Tyre, Sidon, Crete, Troy, Cyprus or North Africa. I had heard that the most abundant murex crop was hauled out of the eastern end of the Mediterranean. Those fishing grounds were fought over. Taxation on sales was so lucrative that territorial treaties over harvesting molluscs were made internationally.

Here on our own western coast, a struggling industry was established. Banished to an empty stretch of shore, the dyers made their ghastly product and, because the colour was too unstable to transport it in liquid form, they soaked cloth in situ. The state of the track that led to the works told us they must receive regular deliveries of molluscs, bales of wool, and presumably provisions for themselves. Finished cloth would be collected. But passing trade must be rare.

I knew Tyrian purple material was sometimes available in Rome, from freedmen's stalls in the Vicus Jugarius and Vicus Tuscus close to the Forum, or from the fancier indoor markets. It was ferociously expensive, hardly ever bought—leave aside moments when emperors like Nero banned the public from wearing it (having first bought up the stock for imperial use). Even so, holidaymakers at the coast must rarely drop in here, whether from curiosity or specifically bargain-hunting: the smell was too bad. I saw no stalls set up for outlet sales as would happen at a pottery or a cameo studio. Apparently, visitors from the outside world were so infrequent that when Pollux brayed a greeting the entire complement of workers came out of their low-roofed huts to stare.

XXXVI

At first, we played it like casual tourists. A man who must have been in charge came forwards, so as Tiberius dismounted he called a greeting: "Hello, there. Mind if we look around? I am Manlius Faustus. The wife and I are staying locally." That left it vague until we were sure what we were dealing with.

The dyers' spokesman was called Ostorius. He was a thickset coastal character with an accent that demanded concentration. If he was aware that everybody stank, he made no reference to it. They were probably so accustomed to it, they gave it little thought. Ostorius offered his hand to Tiberius, who was not a man to refuse a test. After I slipped down from Pollux, I joined them and bravely shook hands as well. Now I had to remember not to touch anything I valued.

Everyone there had blue or purple palms and fingers. Every palm and every finger stank. When we shook hands, the high odour clung to us. Once I fully realised how bad it was, I didn't bother wiping my hand on my skirt. There was no escape.

I left Barley in her pannier on the donkey's back, where she sat, intermittently barking at the air. Young children went close to stare at her, not speaking. As far as I knew the dog would not be aggressive; the children seemed fascinated but harmless too. I could tell they were youngsters who worked with their elders. The rest of the group, who were of all ages, comprised women with their sleeves rolled up and men carrying dye-vat dollies. The atmosphere was friendly, though with an undertow of suspicion.

Tiberius waded straight in to ask about the process. He was soon being shown how the shells were opened to extract their purple. These molluscs, varying in size but not a large species, were seriously spiny, with pointed tails. Ostorius said they were predatory creatures, devourers of other sea life. I could not tell at what point in the extraction process they died. Clearly they did.

When the workers lost interest in us and went back to their tasks, we watched them opening shells with special small stone hammers, then nipping out glands. Even the children wandered back to join in. At the point of extraction, the glands emitted a secretion that was colourless and odourless, but we were told exposure to sunlight would quickly transform the secretion so its ability to colour rapidly perished. For this reason, the people worked inside dark hutments. Retrieving the glands seemed an easy task, which even the youngest children managed at speed, turning out hundreds every hour. But the glands were tiny. To obtain a useable quantity of colour required hundreds of thousands.

Salt and potash were added; the mixture was heated for three days, though must never reach boiling point. The dye remained very unstable in the vat, easily affected by light or air, which would make results blue rather than the coveted deep purple. Therefore a good source of wool had to be available close by; other fabrics such as linen, cotton or silk shrugged off the colour, but wool absorbed it best. It was steeped in dye baths for seven to ten days, with repeated immersion to give the best colour. A woman, Ostorius' wife Cincia, was testing small samples in a vat that had been in use for some days; she showed me how the square of cloth now looked blue, which meant the dye was exhausted and should no longer be used.

The deepest regal purple required prolonged soaking in the strongest liquor. Since it took thousands of shells to make an ounce of dye, we understood the extraordinary cost and how purple robes became a symbol of divinity. Even a basic bluish or reddish hue cost a fortune but the blackish shade likened to clotted blood, as magnificently worn by emperors, was worth ten times that.

When the vats' contents reduced by evaporation, their smell significantly increased.

We were walked along a row of dye tanks to experience this feature.

Holy hypobranchials!

I needed to come up with a precise set of questions for my case. Nothing would drag me back to this gastropodic putrefaction to ask supplementaries.

I held off the interrogation as long as I could, while Ostorius regaled us with interesting seashell stories. Gesturing to Barley, still queening it in her pannier, he told us how Hercules supposedly discovered the secret of murex. His dog had been gambolling on the shore eating seashells, then had come back to him with a purple muzzle; Hercules had fallen in love with a nymph called Tyre, for whom he made a wondrous dress that was dyed with his discovery.

Other dyes, said Ostorius, were made from other materials: blue from a different kind of murex shell, pale blue from grape hyacinths, crimson from crushed insects, a cheap fake purple from various plants. Expensive colours were often faked: indigo with pigeon dung, reds with madder, red ochre substituted for true vermilion. The noble fan-shaped pinna shell produced long strands of anchoring fibre that could be woven into a precious, delicate amber-coloured fabric; this sea-silk was only available in such small quantities that nothing larger than a hat or scarf was ever made from it.

Used shells could be incorporated in building lime, although Tiberius said that his men hated it unless the shells had been long exposed to air to reduce their oceanic smell.

As our tour ended, we were taken to a warehouse to be shown bolts of finished cloth in different qualities and hues. Clearly we were expected to buy some. No pressure, said Ostorius. He gave his tour of the works for no charge, only grateful when people showed an interest . . .

We knew what to do. Tiberius agreed to purchase a length of deep blue fabric to make an outfit for me. "We don't see ourselves as wearers of imperial purple, I'm afraid! Anyway, blue is my wife's favourite colour."

"That's very observant," I said, in surprise, as he fetched out his purse and paid up. He had no clues: I was in rust that day, a safe dark tone to disguise travel stains. "I do love blue, my darling, though I am not aware I ever told you."

When Ostorius congratulated me on my thoughtful husband, I explained he was still very new.

Tiberius enjoyed his coup. "Can you find someone to sew you a gown, Albia? Or are you intent on making our clothes yourself at home, like a good Roman matron?"

We exchanged banter about the traditional wifely role of working a loom in the atrium; I wormed my way smartly out of that suggestion.

Finally, I took advantage of the good mood in our gathering and tackled what we had come for. "Ostorius, we have loved hearing about what happens here and I shall wear my new gown with much pleasure." Well, I would do—once I had hung it out of doors to air . . . "We won't keep you much longer. But I must admit we had a purpose in coming to meet you."

Almost as if they had been expecting trouble, a group of workers, including Cincia, clustered around us. There were a couple of girls I would categorise as children; none were as stunning as the description of Lemni's find that night in Rome.

The mood was quiet enough, though I felt wary. Tiberius stood with his thumbs in his belt, a relaxed posture. He had dressed to look unofficial; indeed, he had wasted much anxiety on choosing his outfit for leisure at the coast. No toga, of course. Instead of a crisp white tunic, some shapeless garment Dromo had produced from the bottom of a chest, in a shade even Tiberius described as camel-piss. He had a multi-purpose tool hung on his belt. There had been a hat of unutterable ghastliness, but it was in Barley's pannier, making a bed for her.

Tiberius and I looked unthreatening. After our tour of the works, we were all smiles. When I began asking questions, I kept it light. But my easy-going enquiries were less fruitful than I wanted.

I owned up that I was being employed to investigate two deaths on the Capitol, one of them that of Gabinus. I said I knew Gabinus had had visitors who worked in their industry; I was certain it was them.

Ostorius reluctantly agreed. He and his family had gone to Rome in the hope of obtaining a contract to supply imperial purple. The suggestion had come originally from a chance meeting with Gabinus at Ostia; Gabinus made out that he had influence at court. He claimed he knew someone who controlled the orders for purple cloth and might be looking to take on a new supplier. But Gabinus was shamming. Any contact he did have must have told him to get lost. Once the dyers showed up in

Rome, expecting much from Gabinus, of course he could not deliver; they realised it was a swindle.

That was the end of their visit, declared Ostorius. He agreed they had found themselves stuck on the Hill for a time, until the gatekeeper released them. Despondent, they had returned to their lodgings overnight, after which they came home.

"You must have been very angry with Gabinus," Tiberius suggested.

"We felt like fools."

"Did you quarrel?" I kept my tone neutral.

"Not much point." Ostorius was honest about being duped, yet played it down phlegmatically. "We could see we had been stupid ever to believe him."

"He told Gabinus what we thought of him, all right!" chipped in his wife, who was more outspoken. Cincia was a short, wide-faced, assertive countrywoman with the stained arms they all had. She had been paying a lot of attention to how Ostorius handled my questioning. "It cost us, going all that way—and for nothing."

"Did Gabinus apologise?"

"No way!"

"Did he explain why he had led you astray?"

"He pretended that since we first met at the port, he had found out the purple supply was in the hands of powerful agents. He claimed he had tried to break into their cartel but couldn't budge them. The material for the Triumph was already ordered and the cloth being embroidered, in any case. So we were too late for that and there seemed to be no opening for us. We should have known!" complained Ostorius, bitterly.

"The contract is with Tarentum?" I sympathised, letting him know I already possessed information. He nodded, not bothering to curse their rivals.

"Are they good?"

"Pretty fair."

"So are we! We'll get that contract one day," Cincia announced firmly. There was a strong sense of her stiffening Ostorius when his hopes flagged. She gave the impression she regularly yearned for a take-over from Tarentum. Perhaps visiting Gabinus had been her idea.

Cincia must be nearing the menopause, I reckoned. She might be seeking more to show for her life than a line of pug-nosed offspring—even wanting more for them than extracting glands from murex shells just as she and her forebears had always done. She believed these dye-producers deserved better, and she was right. They led a disgusting life; from the state of their hutments, rewards were few. Yet they must be well aware how much profit their dyes earned for somebody else, further down the line.

Tiberius looked around the group. "Did you take the whole family to Rome?" he asked, sounding as if it was an innocent question.

"None of us had ever been there," Cincia told him. "We decided we would like to see the place."

He smiled. "A good experience. Especially for your children. Widen their horizons. Are these all yours?" On a quick count there were nine.

It was Cincia's turn to nod, though first she flashed a look at Ostorius. Cincia had seen our point. Ostorius then added almost sheepishly, "Couple of cousins came as well. So as not to feel left out."

"Are they here today?"

"No." Ostorius left it at that.

With no alternative, I declared our interest: "I assume one of those cousins was the lovely young girl who has been mentioned by my witnesses?"

Silence.

"Come on. I know she exists. I know she had some kind of adventure, and that it was very upsetting for her. Somebody rescued her. Someone saw them. Who is she, please?"

Ostorius accepted that the game was up. "Oh, you must mean Susuza," he answered casually. "Silly thing got herself lost, that's all it was. She wandered off, couldn't find the rest of us, had a bit of a panic. Someone did give her directions to where we were staying, so she found her way back. Nothing to get excited about. Nothing at all."

Now it was the turn of Tiberius and me to exchange a glance. Neither of us believed this story. And neither of us cared if the murex family saw that we were sceptical.

XXXVII

We could no longer stay. The dye-producers were intransigent: Susuza was not theirs. The girl led her own life. They claimed they had no idea where she might be that evening. Anyway, she had nothing to say about anything, they assured us. It only heightened my interest.

The mood had changed. Ostorius brought our cloth; he threw the package, harder than necessary, into a donkey pannier—a good-riddance gesture. He wanted us to leave.

With nothing to lose, I tackled him: "When you were telling Gabinus what you thought of him, exactly how far did it go?" As I let him hear my implication, he assumed his cautious look. "Was there a fight? You must have been furious he had lured you to Rome for nothing—rightly so. Did you have proper fisticuffs?"

Ostorius shrugged. I could see Cincia preparing to back him up, but he replied strongly enough of his own accord: "I don't like violence. Things never came to that."

"We had the little ones with us," Cincia reinforced him, almost as if without the children she would have weighed in herself to assault Gabinus. "What does it matter, anyway?"

"If there was pushing and shoving, I want to know."

"Who cares?"

"I do. The city of Rome does. If his Triumph has been polluted, the Emperor has a deep interest."

Cincia looked startled. "What's so important?" She was bright. She had guessed.

"Because Gabinus hasn't simply died. Somebody pushed him off the Tarpeian Rock."

Cincia clapped her Tyrian purple hands. "Oh, well done, whoever that was! But it was not us."

"I may believe you," I said quietly. "So tell me this: how will Susuza, your cousin or niece or whatever she is, react when you tell her Gabinus is dead?"

"She won't say anything," Ostorius declared. "Why should she? He was a stranger—she only met him once."

"Anyone says otherwise," his wife added, "I'll push them off a rock too. That will be after I dunk them head down in a dye vat and leave them stewing for a week."

It was too big a threat. She must be protecting the girl. They were lying about whatever had happened.

Tiberius and I took leave of them, remaining as polite as we could. There was nothing else we could do. We had been taken on a full tour of the works, so we had seen everybody present, yet never encountered anyone who could have been Susuza. We rode off slowly. Once out of sight, we stopped to confer.

While the donkeys munched grass where they could find it, Barley sniffed maritime plants, making feints as she tried to find one that was acceptable for a city dog to pee on. The gross smell of dead murex had accompanied us, suffusing our clothes, our hair, our skin. We felt we would never be rid of it. How much worse it must be for those who worked with it—the children whose little fingers prised out the glands from hundred after hundred of seashells, the women we had seen on their knees, hand-wringing newly dyed wool.

We stared back at the outlawed huddle of buildings, so isolated from the world where their produce was so valued. There, in the airless dark, the luxury fabrics stewed to their deep, sought-after sheen. From this stinking environment came the fabulous hues that would mark out great men and the women associated with them. In Rome, our self-regarding Emperor stalked marble corridors in a haze of marine odour. The vestments of priests or tributes paid to world leaders began life amid thousands of dying molluscs and the horrendous stench of dye baths, worked by exiled souls who were universally shunned.

"Their trade stinks, but why should that prevent ambition?" Tiberius reflected. "They went to Rome in a gang, dreaming they might pull a flanker on Tarentum. Of course, if they really know their market, any hope of that must have been slim. Why did they fall for it? Surely they understood there are ways things are done? Palace freedmen control purchasing as a fine art. Imperial patronage would never be handed out by a transport manager, even one who had snaffled a prime location for his site hut."

"Perhaps they felt desperate," I mused. "Tarentum has an entrenched hold on their trade. Gabinus offered them a way in, through a magical back door. They wanted to believe it. They wanted to trust him, even if that meant behaving like idiots. Did they think they could bribe him, or somehow pay off his supposed contact?"

"He may have let them think so. But would they have that kind of cash?"

"Probably not," I said. To myself, I was wondering what else they might have had to offer him. I supposed I knew: the lovely young Susuza. The thought was extremely unpleasant.

Arms folded, Tiberius turned his face to the ocean. Bathed in twilight sun, the Tyrrhenian Sea lapped imperceptibly on its sandy shore in the long, straight stretch that runs south towards Antium. Low dunes carried patches of scrub between the sea and the line of the often wave-battered coastal highway. Behind us the heights of Latium were visible as long purple shadows, with their ancient hilltop towns and Alba Longa, where the Emperor infamously had his citadel. We were at the northern end of this stretch of coast; sluggish rivers drained old salt lakes but brought sand to pleasant enough beaches, which supported a fringe of substantial villas and imperial property. Much further on, the Pontine Marshes lay behind this shore, full of flies and fatal disease.

"This is a pleasant spot," said Tiberius. "You and I could take advantage, darling. Better than fighting bedbugs at the Cow with No Tail . . ." He held out his hand and I came to nestle against him, though I merely pecked his cheek, too dispirited for love. He seemed keener. A man with an only recently married wife has preoccupations. So does she, of course.

He would settle down. Maybe even I would stop wanting him so badly . . .

For practical reasons, I was gently resisting. "We need to get back before dark, love."

"Have to make it quick, then!"

A bloodsucking insect landed on my arm. I slapped it away. "Ugh! Call me a spoilsport, but my family's villa has gorgeous antique beds with soft, wool-stuffed mattresses. By now the domestic manager will have been rousted out of the bar he favours. He will have brought in fish to grill on the beach, aired musty rooms, fired up hot water and found us a palatable flagon from my grandfather's investment cellar."

Tiberius capitulated. "What are we waiting for? Get a move on, girl. Let's go!"

However, it was end-of-the-day for everyone. Before we persuaded Castor and Pollux to stop grazing, four or five boys with shrimping equipment came swinging along on their way home. With wet hair and damp tunics, amid much happy joshing, they had clearly been out enjoying themselves rather than seriously collecting dinner. As they passed us, we saw that their bucket of seawater contained such a small catch it would serve only a hundred-year-old granny with a pitiful appetite.

A short distance behind them trailed a girl they were ignoring. Tiberius and I might have ignored her too. She was not what we thought we were looking for. The ungainly teenager stomped along and had pudding features. But as she drew level, we both caught our breath. In the words of the tenement porter, she smelt like a basket of whelks.

XXXVIII

"Y ou must be Susuza!" I held out my hand to stop her. "Stay for a word, will you?"

She was theoretically a child. She had yet to grow to her full height; she was all puppy fat and perturbation, but she had the fully developed bust of a twenty-five-year-old grown woman. It happens.

I groaned. She was no beauty. It was the big bust that attracted male interest.

She wore a rumpled, purple-streaked tunic, too short and much too low on top. Her hands and arms were stained with dye. Her dark hair had been crudely speared up with pins in a fanciful topknot that she had spent hours creating; odd pieces of plait trailed. I might have expected eruptions of spots, though her skin looked surprisingly clear, as if a diet of seafood and local greens protected her from hormonal rampages.

She wanted to be with those boys but they did not want her. They knew her; she had grown up in their circle. But with that weighty bosom she could never again be one of the lads. Those mature breasts scared them; still pre-pubertal, they were not ready to venture. Besides, they must sense that in subtle ways she was miles ahead of them.

Even so, the five boys now lingered, watching what happened.

Susuza broke my heart. She was heading to a life of loss before she understood how much she wanted the alternative. The first man who showed an interest would seduce her. Her first time would make her pregnant; her first child spelled her doom.

"What do you want?" Curiosity, so dangerous in other situations, had made her agree to stop.

"I need to talk to you."

"Oh, that's a shock. Who bothers with me?" She spoke up, not so nervous as she had looked when she first came sauntering along, dragging her heels so as not to catch up on the boys too closely, in case they shouted at her.

"We have been to the murex works to see Ostorius and Cincia. They showed us around. But, really, I wanted to meet you."

Tiberius moved away from us, pretending to walk the dog. Barley looked up at him with refined surprise.

"What for?" Susuza had no balance between self-confidence and aggression. As she stood her ground with me, she verged on too much truculence, given that she didn't yet know what I wanted.

I made her sit down on a sand dune with me. "The people we met at the dye vats seemed unsure where you were today. What are you doing out here?"

"I hate the work I have to do." Susuza waved her dye-stained arms. "I bunk off when I can. Still, you have to eat." She had an odd manner, as if she made a habit of listening in on adults.

I made no comment, then told her: "I want to hear what happened when you went to Rome."

"Why?" she demanded, in her gauche, blunt way. She was staring at me with open calculation. "What's so special?"

"I shall tell you in a moment." I decided to hold off saying that she had met two men who had now died. "First, explain that trip to me, please." "Please" might have been a new word to Susuza. Still, she took my good manners as her right. She was an oddly composed creature. "You went to the city with your relatives, who had hoped to secure a contract from a man who let them down."

"He was no use. He was horrid."

"Yes," I said pleasantly. "I have met quite a few people who thought that. The more I find out about him, the more I sympathise." She was eyeing me up, making a judgement. My rusty brown travel outfit failed to impress. This trapped girl dreamed of city life. In a woman from Rome, she yearned for glamour: stunning colour, wide embroidered hems, rich draping stoles, masses of jewellery—big jewellery, huge gems chained to crushing metalwork . . . When she looked over to Tiberius, he made the same poor impression: too old, too casual, too unexciting. I hid a smile.

"So," I broached, more sombrely, "you met Gabinus."

Now Susuza had the intelligence to wait, finding out how much I knew before she gave up her story. I gazed at her, as if considering how much to reveal. "Did he make an unwelcome move on you?"

Susuza nodded cautiously.

"Surely that was all right," I suggested. "You had people with you."

"Oh, they were no help!" she scoffed.

"No good?"

"They pretended they hadn't seen anything. He was all charm and they went along with it."

I tutted gently, letting her know I understood. I was on her side. Still, I decided against the full sisterly heads-together routine. We had only just met; for that, you need much more in common than we shared. "I am thinking about Cincia, how she was when I saw her this afternoon, Susuza. She seemed like a broody hen with her children. Naturally protective. But you are not hers. Does that make a difference?" Susuza had enough loyalty not to answer. "Are your parents alive, Susuza?"

"Both dead. I live with whoever will have me. I get passed around quite a bit."

It would not help that she was so awkward, so loud, so hard-edged when she spoke.

I had been a street child, at the mercy of anyone; I was around her age when rescued from that life. I, too, had been self-reliant and stroppy, though it hid my terrors of the world. Of course she struck a chord with me.

I did not believe this young girl was being seriously mistreated, although I recognised her loneliness. She had come to think life held nothing good for her. She might sound brash, but she had no real self-confidence.

"All right," I said. "Let me tell you what I suspect. Gabinus had let everybody down, but they were desperate. He looked at you, he made some innocent-sounding suggestion. 'You seem like a bright girl. Would you like to see some interesting temples, Susuza?' Your people thought maybe there was a chance for them after all. They struck an unspoken bargain with him about you, which you perhaps did not understand, or not immediately. Perhaps they are good people at heart, so they blinded themselves to what they were doing. When they left the Capitol, you stayed behind. I guess that was because you did not know how to escape the situation—"

"Anyway," Susuza broke in, "I did want to look at the temples. I thought he meant it. He knew how to behave with the old folk, so he sounded safe. He had already told us he was going for a drink later, so we thought he wouldn't spend long with me."

Internally, I sighed. "What happened?"

"He started off nice, after the others went out of the gate. Then, quick as a wink, he jumped on me. I'm not daft, whatever you think. When I saw what his game really was, I kicked out. He wasn't expecting that. I hauled myself out of his filthy grasp and ran away, fast as I could. He was too surprised to stop me. It was dark on that hilltop. I didn't know where I was going."

"Somebody found you?"

"I found them. I ran into a tent. I nearly sent it flying. There were two men inside and I was scared I had just dived into the same problem with them. But once they stopped cursing me for spoiling their sky-watching— which was what they were doing, though they had a pie and picnic cups— they let me explain about Gabinus. They were very angry over what he had tried to do to me."

When she ran out of story, I took it up for her: "The man called Lemni led you down off the Hill to safety. He brought you to where he lived, calmed you down, wrapped you up so no one could see who you were, then took you to where Ostorius and Cincia were staying."

"How do you know all that? They were so glad to see me," Susuza said. "They must have had a change of heart. I think they had been arguing about it. Cincia started being really nice to me. She is still doing it, when she remembers. Mostly she just treats me the same as usual, like everybody does. I'm Susuza. I look like trouble. What are they going to do with me? . . . Lemni said some very stern words to Ostorius before he left our inn. Ostorius looked shocked at the way he spoke. After that, no more was said about anything and we all came home first thing next morning."

"You never saw Gabinus again?"

"No. Thank goodness."

"Or heard anything about him?"

"No, why would I?"

"Has anybody told you he is dead, Susuza?"

The girl stared at me. Her eyes, in that soft-featured milky face, were dark brown, flickering as she thought about what I had just said. It would be wrong to dismiss her as a bumpkin. She was bright enough: she saw at once that something about Gabinus' death was significant. She was busy interpreting my tone. But she waited for me to explain.

I told her he was murdered the next morning, which she accepted without excitement. Then I said Lemni had been killed, too, more recently. She went rather pale over that, looking unhappy. I made it plain these deaths were being investigated, so anyone who had had contact with both men might come under suspicion.

"I never killed that Gabinus," Susuza argued, in a low voice, immediately aware of the threat to herself. "He was a filthy lech but I never did anything to him. Why would I? I had run away. I got myself in the clear. And that old Lemni, he was kind to me. I wouldn't want anything bad to happen to him. I'm sorry if it did." She paused. "Was that my fault?"

I reassured her. So far, I had no idea whose fault it was. Although I felt Susuza's adventure might be tied up with both murders, I could see no direct connection between them and no obvious link to her.

"Do you remember anything about that night with Gabinus? Anything Lemni and the other man in the tent said to you, or to one another, after you burst in?"

Susuza shook her head. Her reaction was quick enough to be convincing. "No. When I was sounding off about Gabinus, they just kept shooting looks between them. They knew who he was. It was like they were never surprised by anything Gabinus did. It was like they had already talked about what a rotter he was. Then the tall one took over. He told Lemni to take me down the Hill and find my people for me."

"His name is Larth. He acts as an augur. He understands omens. Is that all, Susuza?"

She hesitated. "No. Lemni didn't want to go, not at first. Larth said leave it all to him. I could tell he was the one in charge. Lemni had to follow his orders while Larth was going to deal with things. He would go to find Gabinus and speak to him. So does that mean . . ." The girl was even sharper than I had thought. "Does that mean Larth went over to where his hut was, and *he* did Gabinus in?"

I told her it seemed unlikely. Larth was an important man with a special position in Rome. Anyway, Gabinus was not killed at his hut.

Tiberius had taken as long as he feasibly could, pottering with dog and donkeys. He joined us, then pointed out that he and I needed to return to Father's villa before nightfall. Since he saw Susuza and I were still talking together, he suggested Susuza come along, in case she had anything else useful to tell me.

She rounded on him in a flash: "I have a job, you know. I don't want to leave them in the lurch. You will have to make it worth our while!" Tiberius looked rueful, but nodded patiently. Susuza then said, rather eagerly, "You might have a bit of work I can do, nicer than the murex shells?"

"That's quick, even for you!" Tiberius said to me, with mock admiration.

Scrambling to my feet, I told the girl openly, "He thinks, whatever case I am on, I pick up helpers. I was a stray soul myself once. A couple took me in to look after their children. But don't get ideas, we have no children. You come along if you want, Susuza, so we can talk some more about Lemni and Gabinus. If you do, your people must be told where you are going, so they are not anxious."

At once, Susuza jumped up too. She marched over to where the group of boys were still hanging about, then loudly ordered them to tell Ostorius and Cincia she was needed to give evidence in an important inquiry.

While she was out of earshot, I murmured to Tiberius, "According to the porter's description, I was expecting her to have a lovely face."

He grinned. "You are so innocent."

"Rarely said!" I snipped back.

"Ah, no," he replied fondly, tickling under my chin. "The others make superficial judgements. I'm the man who knows you, Albiola. As soon as you first bumped into me, then bounced off down the street pretending you had not noticed nearly cracking my ribs, I saw through the carapace."

Carapace? Not a word you expect to hear while trying to round up a donkey on a deserted beach.

Susuza was back.

"Right. That's settled. I'm going to come with you in case I can be helpful."

"Thank you," I said.

"He wanted me," she asserted suddenly. "That Gabinus. But just because they think they're getting something doesn't mean you have to give it them, does it?"

I told her that was a very fine attitude to hold. Then the girl jumped up behind me on Pollux and we set off for home.

XXXIX

For Tiberius and me it had been a long day. After a modest supper, we retired to bed.

Susuza was different. She darted about, exploring the house as much as the slaves would let her. From time to time we heard her voice, questioning them about who lived here and the family's way of life. Eventually she must have gone to sleep somewhere. I felt sure no one had given her a guest room. Grumblings about our mollusc-fragrant guest would reverberate for a long time.

Mother would understand. Father would have the time of his life thinking up wisecracks. My twelve-year-old brother would ask her straight out why she stank so badly and how many seashells it took to produce the ingrained pong . . .

Postumus would have his chance to sniff the girl, then keep little spidery notes about her, because Susuza intended staying. In her way, she was as unworldly and single-minded as my brother but normal life was her dedicated aim. Overnight she planned not only her next move as my witness, but her full career thereafter. She told me openly: "I shall have to come with you to Rome. You need to ask that Larth about what he did that night after Lemni had gone to look after me and find my people for me. Larth said he was off to sort Gabinus out. You need me to say I heard him."

"That's true," I agreed, with caution, as I ate a breakfast roll. "My husband and I are returning to Rome today. It is certainly my intention to interview Larth again."

Susuza had already piled so much honey onto her roll it was dripping in slow rivulets down all sides. She was licking them up greedily with a long tongue while she talked. "Well, you want to have me there with you. That way old Larth can't deny he went to see Gabinus, because I can pipe up and say it's what he definitely did. So then you can ask did the old fellow do Gabinus in, or what?"

Susuza bit into her bread. With her mouth crammed full, she immediately continued: "He's bound to say no. You'll have to nag at him, so he owns up."

"Assuming he did it. Which I doubt. Chew nicely, Susuza," I found myself saying. "Chew first, then talk." I had turned into my mother, without noticing it happen.

Tiberius, who had been watching us quizzically, cut fine slices of cheese neatly. He handed them around, using a knife blade to serve. He beamed at me, saying nothing in a way that said it all.

Susuza took my intervention well. She had a fully formed agenda for her own advancement. As soon as she had swallowed her mouthful, or most of it, she pressed on unabashed. "I'm glad I met you yesterday. This is a useful turn-up for me. I ought to come to Rome and have a job in your house." She looked me up and down. I was wearing the same brown dress as yesterday, with my hair loose. It was certainly not imperial-court fashion. "I can see you haven't got a maid. You can have me to do things for you."

I managed to ask whether she had any experience.

"No, but you can organise it for me. Send me to people who can show me. What I would like," Susuza informed me, "is training in how to do hair. I am very interested in styles and fixing. I could be quite good at it. So this would entirely be for your benefit," she said frankly. "I can choose your jewellery as well. You must own some. If not, he can buy it for you. Then I can tell you every day what you need to have on so as to match your outfit. You need some poshing up."

"Flavia Albia does wear smart things," Tiberius put in quickly, as if defending my appearance. "At home in the city, where smartness is appropriate."

Susuza looked disbelieving. Still, for once she said nothing.

Most women who have decided to add a maid to their staff visit a slave market where they pick out some young, meek, virtually silent foreign girl who will do their bidding. It seemed for me things were different.

"*If* I give you a trial," I imparted to my own new treasure, as sternly as I could with Tiberius grinning at me, "you need to understand this: I tolerate no one who bosses me about."

"That's the best idea," answered Susuza. As my maid she intended to engage in honest heart-to-hearts. "I do the same, Flavia Albia."

XL

Rome, on our return, was heaving. We had taken the usual route from the *villa maritima* to the city, travelling on the Via Laurentina. Our approach from the south should have been well clear of all the nonsense taking place in the northern areas in preparation for Domitian's big event. But there was always heavy traffic coming up from the port. Uncle Tullius stabled his mules near the Ostia Gate because a wheeled carriage could not enter Rome in daytime. So we knew we would hit the inevitable slowdown where we joined the Via Ostiensis, though we had not anticipated quite such a jam.

By the time we could see the big dump of olive oil amphorae near the gate, and that odd old tomb called the Pyramid of Cestius, we were worn out. Throughout most of the journey, Susuza had been travel sick, which had not helped. Apparently, she had been almost as bad when she visited with Ostorius and Cincia, but had not thought to mention it so I could make her chew root ginger.

"Well, that's it, Flavia Albia. I can't go through that anymore. I am never going back again."

"You can go home any time you want," I assured her, though I knew I was losing the battle. "We can find a way!"

"No, don't worry. Now I've managed to get myself here, you are stuck with me!"

Lovely.

———

We left the mules at their stable and went on foot. It took us a while to pass through the gate. It was gridlocked with bodies: the inbound stream of people was held up by seriously morose soldiers pretending to check them. Nobody seemed to grasp that these guardians of the state had stationed themselves there in the hope of backhanders. Half could not find their money because thieves by the gate were also preying on the stationary visitors.

Tiberius refused to hand over a bribe. He demanded to speak to an officer. Of course that was pointless because the officer in charge was planning on a big cut from the "donations for military heroes" that travellers had to offer. Tiberius said what he thought about us being locked out of our own city—a city with an all-welcome public policy. The troops grew chippy with him. I thought he would be arrested, but after half an hour of arguing, his grave persistence wore them down so they waved us through with sneers.

We then had a choice of what should have been a quick step up to the Lavernal Gate or the Raudusculana, either of which gave us a short sharp climb up the main Aventine peak, along the Vicus Armilustrium, and home. Of course, all the sailors, visitors, hopeful traders and petty thieves who were pouring into Rome had endured the same slog along the final stretch of highway so when they broke free of the soldiers they stopped in their tracks, right inside the Ostia Gate. Once arrived, none of them had any idea where to go. As they milled around searching for lodgings, or simply a snack bar at which to recover, we had to force our way through an unyielding mob.

If anybody asked us, Tiberius suggested they might be able to camp in the Grove of Stimula. It had fine river views, he told them. A few fed off leftwards in search of this haven, unaware it had once been the scene of Bacchanalian orgies and was even now sacred to Semele, the mortal mother of Bacchus. "For Heaven's sake, you're an aedile!" I raved at him. I was hot and tired, and had lumbered myself with an untrained maid I didn't want. "Try not to encourage wild social drinking all over our neighbourhood!"

"It's all goads and scourges nowadays. Serious stuff, not an orgy."

Tiberius tried to convince me. Suspecting he thought this claim was a joke, I would have kicked him, but was preoccupied. After we left the carriage, I had somehow ended up in the classic wifely role: carrying most of our baggage.

Travellers continued to block our way; they foolishly thought we people who really lived here were sneakily trying to jump the queue for bed and board. Crowds seemed to have surged up through the drains, as if Rome had some ghastly blockage in the sewers, which forced scum out of the manholes and into the streets, with no possibility that the human tide would seep away again by nightfall. Aimless, mapless, dehydrated and desperate, they moved at a snail's pace with their porters, donkeys, children, chickens, immeasurable quantities of luggage and oddly muffled-up associates. They had come in unsuitable clothes. They barely spoke Latin. If they had brought an address where someone at home had told them they might be given shelter, it was in some other part of town that nobody had heard of.

As our scrawny Aventine dogs barked at these frustrated people, mine picked up the idea and joined in. Even Susuza yelped. Thinking she had been groped, I swung around with the baggage packs I was lugging. I did not care who I aimed at. Never tangle with a woman who has been stuck with two garment bags, a picnic tote with a broken toggle, a satchel full of hard-cornered waxed tablets and a dog lead. Never feel up her maid. Not even if the girl has a phenomenal bosom and you thought she looked as if she'd let you. You thought wrong, buster.

Eventually Tiberius, playing manly, grabbed the impedimenta off me. I fought him for it, as you do. "I can manage!"

"Give it here, you idiot!"

Such a loving couple. Marriage is about sharing. Sharing the insults, normally.

I turned around for an angry exchange of views with the person I had bashed, only to notice Susuza had gone missing. Scylla and Charybdis, we had lost my best witness. Almost the only witness I had, in fact.

Tiberius and I pushed this way and that through the press, growing hoarse as we called to her. Suddenly we saw her by a shop where she had been staring at horrible trinkets. "Oh, there you are, you two! I thought you'd given me the slip!" While the shopkeeper leered, Tiberius grabbed her arm and pulled her away with us.

We reached our house. Nobody heard us knock. We went through the ritual of kneeling in the porch while we unpacked onto the ground two garment packs, a picnic hamper, a satchel, various purses and belt-bags, because nobody could remember where they had put their door key. As soon as all our belongings were spread over the doorstep, the double doors were opened from inside.

Gratus, our urbane house-steward, glanced briefly at the stacks of stuff we had piled about, giving us a reassuring leave-it-to-me look. He went into his well-honed smile of welcome. It transformed to a horror-stricken rictus as he caught the ripe fishy odour of Susuza.

"Witness," I said.

"New maid," she told him confidently.

Utterly unmoved, Gratus told her, if that was the case, she should carry in my things for me.

XLI

Travel is such a luxury.
So why does it take three days to recover from a two-day trip?

Next morning Tiberius and I hid upstairs for as long as we could, feeling sluggish. Eventually I set open our door and window shutters, but still lurked in private while early light brightened our room. It was painted chalk white, with fine lines of fantasy candelabra and garlands. Delicate colours picked out the ceiling and coves. Tiberius had chosen the scheme as a surprise for me; his taste was elegant and relaxing. One day we would manage to finish our whole house like this. It ought to be an incentive to work, though not always.

I lay quietly in bed, listening while our disturbed household began daily life. Tiberius awoke, briefly cocked an ear at the sounds downstairs, winked at me, then hauled himself out for a few stretches and lunges on the bed-side mat. Soon he flopped back with me.

We could hear domestic adjustments taking place. Whenever Dromo passed anywhere near Susuza, he signalled this by letting off an explosive cry of "*Phwoar!*" If she wanted to stay, she would have to learn for herself how to deal with him. I refused to be bullied into acting as a peacemaker: you can never win.

Dromo was a slave; Susuza was not. The moment when she realised what this meant would be interesting.

We heard Gratus establishing rules. Fornix must serve menus entirely without fish for a week. Susuza was to go to Prisca's baths twice a day.

Dromo had to take her, with no cakes if he moaned. Gratus would allocate her a cubbyhole to sleep in, once the shellfish stink faded. He spoke matter-of-factly, so she sounded unoffended.

Susuza's clothes would be destroyed as soon as Gratus found new ones that fitted her. This both solved the smell problem and would provide more modest covering. In any normal household, a maid inherits her mistress's cast-offs but my clothes would never work on Susuza. I liked the way Gratus avoided the real problem, stating only that I was "too tall" . . .

He renamed her. Thank goodness. The whispering sibilants imposed by her daft parents had already started driving me nuts. According to Gratus, a new name was routine. This was Rome; like it or go home. The girl might offer suggestions if she was quick about it, but since she hadn't expected the question, my steward made his on-the-spot decision. Gratus called her Suza.

Tiberius and I were forced to descend for breakfast when Larcius, the building foreman, arrived from next door. His whole team had come with him. Apparently, they needed Tiberius to make a tricky decision about soffits for the refit they were working on in Salamis Street. Larcius said everyone might as well take part in the discussion, to know the plan before they made a start . . .

It was nonsense. The men had all come for a look at my new girl's big bust.

At that point, I bounced downstairs to give them shirty looks. I told them she was only twelve, so I expected them to be fatherly. When they ambled off, I could hear them agreeing that Suza was quite something. It was said in a friendly fashion. The toothless, bow-legged group liked being part of our easy-going household; they were thrilled by our new acquisition, a wonder over whom they could gloat to outsiders.

I myself took Suza to Prisca's bath-house the first time. After two days of travel I felt ready for pampering; besides, I wanted to give the proprietress an explanation. I had known Prisca and her staff for a long time. "That does not give me the right to send along someone who reeks like an oyster barrel!"

"Too right!" Prisca answered baldly.

"I appreciate your help, Prisca."

"This will cost you!"

"Get away, your baths are always full of fishwives." There were some, though most of her customers were housewives, or at least engaged in social trades like cushion-stuffing.

Prisca was slight, approaching fifty, hardworking, a good business woman. Today she was in her usual sleeveless tunic and sandals, with a scarf tying up her hair. Suza took a good look at her chain necklace and big hoop earrings. "What makes you think you can trust her?" demanded Prisca. She spoke her mind, which supposedly was why I liked her, though brutal honesty could be inconvenient. She never cared. She owned her own business; she could be as rude as she liked.

I had outlined where Suza came from and the cause of her smell. Professional discussion ensued. "I could wear scent!" Suza piped up.

"Then you'll stink of fish and ghastly scent," Prisca countermanded. While one of the washing attendants was giving her a thorough oil and scrape, Prisca subjected the girl to her own kind of scouring. "You keep your prying little fingers out of Flavia Albia's jewel caskets, my girl. Lock 'em up, Albia, you've got some nice things you don't want to go missing. She's a stranger, you know nothing about her, or whether she has morals. I hope you're listening, missee!"

I explained that as Suza was so keen to be a maid, she would be trying hard for approval. Prisca retorted that I was an innocent. All this was happening in Suza's hearing, though we never invited her to defend herself.

I had in fact already turned the tiny key in my jewellery box. I hoped I could remember where I had hidden it, so would not need to enlist Suza in a search.

"What have you picked up this wonder for anyway, Albia? Is it some juicy case you've been keeping from me?"

I explained. It was always worth consulting Prisca about my investigations. She liked to gossip. For all I knew she even kept whatever I told her private; there had never been unwelcome fallout afterwards. Occasionally she was a help, but even if she had nothing to contribute it kept her sweet so she would open up out of hours, or find me a massage even when I had forgotten to book.

I told her that Suza had been assaulted by a man who was subsequently killed. I said who it was.

"Ha!" scoffed Prisca. "I heard about that. I don't suppose you've thought to consider, have you, Albia, whether it's this girl who shoved that beggar off the rock?"

Fortunately I had. Suza was taken back to the inn where her relatives were staying, then next morning, when Gabinus died, they were all on their way home. I could time his death, because the old woman, Valeria Dillia, had seen him fall. Also, I knew that Suza was on the coast at the murex complex when Lemni died later. As a young girl, she hadn't the strength to fight with Gabinus on the top of the cliff. Nor could I see her bundling up Lemni in half a tent, even if she had bopped him on the head with his mallet to subdue him.

"You never know!" replied Prisca, thrilled by the possibility.

Subdued at being discussed as a suspect, Suza was watching us. Her skin looked red all over where she had been forcibly scrubbed and strigilled; Prisca's staff had enjoyed their task too much. Nude, the young girl was, of course, fully displaying her attributes.

Prisca sniffed. "You wouldn't catch me having anyone built like that in my house!" After a moment, she relented. "Just cover her up from the neck down. The men will soon stop showing any interest." Suza was gazing longingly at a snack-seller; he was looking startled as he noticed her for the first time. "Put her on a proper diet," Prisca advised me, as she shooed off the interested man with the tray.

Relenting, she sent one of the manicure girls to ask her statuesque mother-in-law if she had a gown she no longer wanted, or one she would lend temporarily.

"Adolescence! Who needs it? You and I can thank the gods we got through that safely, Albia. Life holds enough struggles. I'm having fun with the menopause—and what about you, with that randy new husband? Are you pregnant yet?" Before I had time to shake my head, she dropped her voice. "Bloody hell, I hope you're using something . . . I could have found you a proper maid, if I had known you were looking, Albia. One who could tidy up that hair of yours . . . I just don't see why you're making so much fuss of this girl from the coast."

I repeated that the awkward orphan was a useful witness. That being so, I was determined not to lose her and didn't want her out in the city by herself. I asked Prisca to send someone to escort Suza home safely while I went to try to find more evidence.

XLII

I walked over to the Capitol. Rome was seething; the Triumph was now definitely close. After I had shed Suza, I walked down from the Aventine on the river side, through the meat and vegetable markets, then up onto the Arx to the Auguraculum.

I wanted to speak to Larth. I had not taken Suza because I was keeping her in reserve. I would tell Larth that I knew all about the night Gabinus made a grab for her. I had found her, and I had brought her to Rome to give a formal statement. Knowing the part Larth and Lemni had played in her adventure, I wanted the full story.

Larth was not on the Capitol. However, I finally found someone who told me his proper name: Gellius Donatus. I even discovered where he lived.

His house was small but secluded, a neat property off the good side of the Clivus Orbius. It was not far from the Capitol. The road ran along the back of the new Baths of Titus; it once edged the Suburra, a famously grim district. Buildings that escaped demolition for Nero's Golden House now benefited from proximity to the Flavian Amphitheatre. If the owners could endure constant work being carried out to create new imperial fora, they might bask in their position, about as close to civic grandeur as it was possible for a private home to be.

Last night, they nearly burned it down.

Amazingly, I learned this from Scorpus, whose cohort attended the blaze. Their siphon engine was still standing outside, along with a few bored vigiles. I recognised Taurus and Zenon and, of course, Scorpus himself.

"Arson?" I asked hopefully.

"You've worked with low society too long, girl. Nobody hates these people—their house is so discreetly hidden, no arsonist could find it. No, it was a funeral."

The Gellius home was indeed on a modest scale, though fancy enough to possess an interior garden. It would serve to grill a kebab supper, at least until neighbours complained. This desirable block, clinging on at the edge of imperial monuments, must be full of educated people who were well up on property law.

As the Gellii had now proved, their interior was too small for a cremation. Flames had set ablaze a fig tree. This prized possession, a mature provider of both shade and fruit, filled most of the peristyle, or at least it had done. The First Cohort had hacked it down with fire axes. Huge burned branches lay out in the street, where the firemen had dragged them. They had saved the house, though that did not stop the ungrateful owners wanting compensation for their tree. Scorpus was lingering outside, ready to field any further complaints.

"The pyre is still in situ. They are waiting for the bones to cool—unexpectedly mingled with cindered figs. The unripe ones fell off and were hard as hell underfoot. There was a lot of incense slopping around too. Not to mention torches. All being manhandled by amateurs. No idea. Bloody nightmare. I'm stuck here until we can sign off everything as made safe."

He sounded grumpy. He must have been in attendance most of the night. He spoke bitterly of a boundary dispute: he reckoned the Clivus Orbius belonged in the Fourth Region, assigned to the Third Cohort. They were, said Scorpus, bone-idle scum, who sat on their rat-arses doing nothing. I thought it best to agree meekly that this was what I, too, had heard.

Scorpus bleakly continued his moan. Unlike the renegade bastard Third, *he* was conscious of the horrible proximity of the Urban Prefecture. This tripartite edifice contained not the Urban Cohorts in person (since they were barracked out of town with the Praetorian Guard) but their ancient archives, the grandiose office of the Urban Prefect, and the tribunal where he issued his noble decisions.

What worried Scorpus? A simple fact. In our city's stately hierarchy, the Urban Prefect was the immediate superior of the Prefect of Vigiles. The Urban overlord would be very concerned about a house fire on his own doorstep, especially if it involved a fellow senator. The Prefect of Vigiles had probably already been called in for a "friendly" meeting, which might not be friendly.

The fact that Gellius Donatus had caused his own fire would not affect the Urban Prefect's assessment. We could imagine his watchful eye on the fire brigade, his junior colleague's down-at-heel force. He would take a view on the fate of the much-loved fig tree. This view, inevitably, would be as unreasonable as he could make it.

"So the Clivus Orbius should never have been your shout," I sympathised with the despondent Scorpus. "Yet here you are. What happened? Were your men just strolling past on their way to evening duties in the Forum, and they happened to smell smoke? Or when the fire started, did the householder send a message for help to the wrong station-house? Good grief, why did a fire start at all? Whyever was anybody holding a cremation here?"

Scorpus sighed. "It's not illegal, Albia."

"It's ridiculous."

"It's crap. But you know what nobs are like. Someone they feel affection for has died, so they offer their nice garden. Most have more spacious grounds than this, but still there's no law that says you have to own a park. So long as no corpse is actually buried inside the city walls, people can do what they like. Burn your brother. Flame your freedman. Immolate your sodding eunuch . . . It was out of doors. They thought that was enough."

I was scathing. "That's criminal. We could have had the city on fire again."

"If they had asked first," Scorpus agreed, now calming down as he unloaded his pain, "I would have advised against. Too confined, plus a big risk of hot air and sparks being funnelled past the upstairs bedrooms—which is exactly what happened. But who gets a check from the experts? They expect us to handle the crisis they have caused, then blame us afterwards."

"If this street is under the Third's jurisdiction, you could have sent a runner for them then left them to it. They would have the lost-tree complaint instead of you. So how did you and the First get stuck with it?"

"I couldn't bloody well not call in my lads," growled Scorpus. "We had flames shooting up like a chimney, the whole house was at immediate risk, and neighbours were screaming it would be their places next."

"I see that. But why you?" I insisted.

Scorpus might have looked sheepish, though he wasn't a man for regret. "I came to the house on official business. They told me about the funeral, so when they invited me, I accepted."

"You mean you were right there in the garden, politely eating the roasted sacrifice, when the fire went up?"

"Can't deny it. I ought to have called a halt when they were frizzling up the sow for Ceres on a portable altar, but it smelt pretty good and I was hoping for a nice piece of crackling."

"Did you get it?" Even he looked slightly abashed. "I hope it wasn't you who put the downturned torch to the oil-soaked brushwood." I made free with my grin. "Scorpus, you have shocked me! So, was it on *your* orders that unruly lads with fire axes destroyed the much-loved fig tree?"

"Only thing we could do," replied Scorpus, tetchily.

XLIII

Nothing so rough as a caupona was allowed in this stretch of street. I dragged Scorpus across the road to where a barber had defiantly set up stools, blocking the pavement. He had a customer, but we shooed him off. From here we could see that the Gellius home had a well-disguised narrow doorway. Cypress trees were currently set up on either side, to indicate bereavement. The front door was standing open, not an invitation to enter but to assist with smoke escape.

A couple of small windows over the street had heavy old bars. Otherwise nothing drew attention to this being where a senator lived. There were no stone benches where clients could await admittance, no shiny knocker, not even a grille for a porter to squint through. No porter was in evidence, nor any other inhabitants.

"My house is smarter than this!"

"Well, you did all right for yourself, Flavia. You married a building contractor. Of course he's added a nice porch to yours—he probably pinched a pediment from a client."

"Only the doorcase. Salvage."

"Has he told the customer?"

"You know Faustus. Pious and right-thinking."

"I know that he's a builder. Pious my arse."

We discussed whether to send the barber to buy drinks for us, but with a claim for compensation hanging over him, Scorpus was too downhearted. He stretched out his legs on one low, shifting stool. I sat neatly on another. Hugging your knees can help control a wobbly perch.

"Come clean." I was firm. It was probably pointless. "I know this is

Larth's house. Why had you gone there last night? What has been going on?"

A typical vigiles officer, Scorpus was unrepentant. "Mind your own business."

"Don't make me pull rank."

"What rank?" he scoffed.

"Husband. The aedilate."

"Jumped-up losers! Losers who do up their houses with doorframes they have pinched." He seemed obsessed with his scenario about how Tiberius Manlius worked.

I was reduced to wheedling. Informers do a lot of that. "Come on, Scorpus. What's the big secret?"

"Can't tell you."

"Not the old myth 'operational reasons'?"

"Don't get all riled up," Scorpus admonished me, as if I was the one being unreasonable. "You can hardly blame me, if you went gadding off on a spree with your lover while things started happening."

"One, he is my husband. Two, it was a mission to find a witness. Three, I got her, she is at my house, you can see her if you want to. And what things happened? You can tell me—in fact, you *should* tell me, if it affects my inquiry, which, four, I remind you is official."

"Five, a piece of evidence was found," said Scorpus, which at least proved he knew Latin counting.

I noticed he did not say he found the evidence himself, nor assign its discovery to one of his lads. "A clue? At last! Who found it?"

"Who do you think?"

"Not Karus?"

"Bloody Karus."

We both sat for a moment, reflecting on life's unfairness.

After a suitable pause for mutual depression, I said at least that explained the "operational reasons" farce. Scorpus, who had not in fact used the phrase, felt no loyalty towards the special agent. He came clean.

After they inspected Lemni's body at the foot of the Tarpeian Rock, Julius Karus had taken it upon himself to stiffen up the inquiry with his version of leadership. While Scorpus merely suggested discreet temple-to-temple enquiries, Karus plunged in, ordering a disruptive search, covering the entire Capitol and Arx. He brought in mysterious resources, evil-eyed troops Scorpus had never seen before. The men poked in everywhere, making as much racket as they could: temples, Auguraculum, Record Office, goose pens, huts. They even slit open the special grain sacks for feeding the Sacred Geese, incurring the wrath of Feliculus. In reply, the troops duffed him up.

"Juno, he'll be having a nervous breakdown!"

"Don't worry. I told his geese to look after him."

"Oh, nice touch, Scorpus."

In the Jupiter caretaker's special hut, now the transport manager's site office, Karus found his evidence. I would get no credit, but it was what I had told the vigiles to look for: a tent mallet, still with human material clinging to it. Remains of Lemni. That was what must have been used to bash in his skull and kill him.

"I hope you didn't bring the mallet last night to show Larth?"

"Flavia, the face of it was blood-soaked. Lemni's oily black hair was sticking out of the clots. That," said Scorpus, "would have been insensitive." He paused. "I just toddled along to inform the augur that we'd found the murder weapon that had killed his friend. I wanted to see his reaction."

I nodded. "Standard stuff."

"Karus might have come to do it, but he's fresh from the military so he never thought of it."

"You came to show him up."

"I came because it was right to check. Do you want to hear me, Flavia? I was specially glad I didn't have the bloody peg hammer stuffed under my tunic when I got to the house and found it was the night they were holding a funeral—to be precise, Lemni's."

"No, it wouldn't have felt right. So that was why they invited you, and you stayed." I cursed myself for missing the event. Although I had said nothing out loud, Scorpus grinned. "So, who came to the funeral?" I enquired, trying to sound unconcerned.

"Not many. If ever you get allowed into the house, you'll see there was no room. Their garden is only a tiddly sitting-out space, and it's filled up with a bloody great tree."

"A dead one now!" I was not really cruel. "Don't worry, fig trees are rampant. It will soon sprout back."

"It had better! All I saw was lanky Larth, born Gellius Donatus, and his wife, a high-class woman, name of Percennia. They live here with just a couple of skinny old retainers and some young slaves, who were tending the pyre." Doddery attendants, I supposed, might have been part of the trouble with it blazing up too strongly. "There was a good-looking woman with young children who came. She must have been Lemni's sister, from the way she was crying her eyes out, then being comforted."

"Name and address?"

Scorpus tutted. "Not the time or place to ask. Anyway, why bother?"

I whistled through my teeth. "For a wonderful moment there, I had forgotten I was talking to one of the vigiles! Don't you care why Lemni copped it? Don't you think his relatives might fill in the picture for us?"

"Cool it, Flavia." Scorpus shook his head. He seemed relaxed, in his embittered way. "Doesn't matter what I think. Karus has already arrested a suspect. Done deal. His killer is at our station-house, and even though he seems a bit slow about cooperating, we're all waiting for him to confess."

"He will?"

"He will."

If Julius Karus had solved my case for me, I would curse. But Karus was an impetuous type. He knew it all. His word was law. For that kind of agent, a rapid solution is better than the truth.

I said it sounded as if Karus had been brilliant. Scorpus said Karus was a god of investigation—though not as brilliant as he thought. Being only part divine, Karus had decided that since he found the mallet concealed in the custodian's hut, it must have been put there by the man who currently lived there, the man who slept in the bed under which the murderous tool was hidden. Karus had arrested Egnatius.

To Karus this was obvious. To us, lunacy.

According to Scorpus, Julius Karus could not see that if Egnatius did have a motive for heaving someone off the Tarpeian Rock, it would have been envy directed against Gabinus, his predecessor, whose post

Egnatius coveted. We knew of no connection with Lemni. We saw no reason for Egnatius to take a mallet to his head.

Besides, Scorpus and I agreed what Egnatius himself was now shouting from his cell: anyone who knew the hut was there, or who just happened to run past that way, could have broken in with the blood-covered mallet and pushed it under the bed before escaping. For his part, Egnatius claimed he had been out when the mallet must have been dumped; he was looking at stables in the Campus Martius.

"Have you checked for witnesses who saw him?"

"That would suggest I doubt the miraculous Karus."

"Yes, Scorpus, but have you?"

"Of course I bloody have. And found plenty. Egnatius was at some stables. He was haggling with the owner, so it took a long time."

Being fair, if he had killed Lemni, Egnatius would be ridiculous to draw attention to himself by hiding the weapon under his own bed. He had personality defects, but stupidity was not one of them.

"So what will Karus do now? Subject Egnatius to unbearable torture until he admits something? Even though he didn't do it?"

"That's a good traditional method," Scorpus replied drily. "Karus will know how to leave no marks . . . He is averse to risk-taking, however, at least when it might rebound on him. Egnatius is an imperial freedman, needed for Domitian's Triumph. Even Karus sees the implications. How would it look if the big procession went wrong because of some horse problem, then Julius Karus was revealed to have the transport man in custody? With my bright boys mentioning all along that he could be innocent? Dangerous scenario," said Scorpus. "The special agent's orders to us are to keep asking Egnatius nicely, just in case he decides to own up."

"Which he will never do."

"Probably not. On the night before the Triumph we are to release him, without requiring bail."

"No charge?"

"Charges deferred."

"Indefinitely?" I was laughing.

"No need," came the solemn reply from Scorpus. "We won't have to prosecute Egnatius because by the time the Triumph starts *you* will have given us the real killer, won't you?"

I swallowed. "How long have I got? Has it been announced yet? What day is the Triumph?"

"Tomorrow, I believe, Flavia Albia!"

"*Tomorrow?*"

"So I shall leave you to get on with it," he answered, not even bothering to smirk.

XLIV

The barber wanted his seats back because he was losing business. Scorpus pulled me up by the arm and surrendered mine. His, he handed to his man Taurus, whom he whistled up. Taurus was told to sit there, as if he was waiting for a shave. If anyone came out from the Gellius house carrying what looked like an urn full of funeral ashes, Taurus had to jump up and follow where they went.

"See? I have my methods, Flavia."

I saw. "You think Lemni's remains will be sent to his family? What if they are planted straight into a niche in a columbarium?"

"Every columbarium has a custodian. He keeps a list of who has visitation rights."

"You made that up!"

Scorpus shot me his world-weary look, the one that said informers gave him heartburn. If so, that would be because we are right.

We parted company.

I took myself into the house. With no porter to annoy me, the first part was easy. I did knock, of course. Quietly.

I reached and inspected the peristyle. It was certainly snug. A neat pyre, now cool, stood in the centre of the garden area. The surrounding colonnades and house walls were blackened and heavily soot-streaked. Windows and a balcony had been lost. Repairs would be feasible, Tiberius would say, but for now this home was unliveable.

Apart from large trampled leaves carpeting the ground, all that was left of the fig tree was cut ends of branches where its multiple arms had come up from the ground. Any remaining soft wood was shredded. The vigiles were hackers and hasty smashers.

I still thought growth might resprout. The roots were undamaged. Figs are monsters, very hard to kill. But this one would take several seasons to become useful again.

Larth emerged to check the pyre.

"I can suggest a reliable firm of renovation builders," I offered, after greeting him.

"I cannot bear to start thinking about that." He had never commissioned much work to his house in the past, or he would have leaped on that word "reliable."

"It is only property," said a new voice. An elderly woman who must be his wife, Percennia, appeared. She too was tall and, like her husband, so thin that they must simply nibble small bites of food after their slaves had reminded them enough times that they ought to eat. "No one was hurt and we still have the building."

Larth, or Gellius Donatus as he was at home, introduced me to his lady. He then slumped into unhappiness. The loss of Lemni, followed by a night of fright and damage to his home, had crushed him. Even the first time I met him, he had been in his own world, letting Lemni do most of the talking. Now it would have been even harder to squeeze anything out of him, but Percennia took over. She led us indoors to a salon that had partly survived the blaze. We sat gingerly on damp couches, trying to ignore the smoke haze.

It was the kind of house where nothing had been bought new for fifty years. All the furniture must have been inherited. Some of the vases and dusty statuettes on side tables were rare antiques, but they had always been there so the owners barely noticed them. The battered couch bolsters were wrong; that, too, was a discomfort they were used to. Renovation was overdue, but they would hate it.

"Gellius, tell the girl what she wants to know," Percennia instructed Larth. "Then we can get on. We are going to stay with friends as soon as my husband completes the funeral formalities," she explained to me.

Percennia had a round, open, clear-skinned face on which she wore absolutely no cosmetics. Her dress was quiet, her jewellery discreet. Her way of speaking was polite, sensible, yet firm. She never stressed her noble position, but acted as if people of all ranks were civilised. If she ever met someone who was not, she would continue with her own high style, thinking it rude to treat them differently. She reminded me of Mother. Women like that never lower their standards.

"What do you want to know?" Larth asked me obediently.

I outlined events when Gabinus assaulted Suza. "You sent Lemni to take her to safety and find her folk, the murex workers. You instructed him not to tackle Gabinus, because you would do so. Please tell me why, and if you found him, what transpired."

The augur spoke in his sombre timbre: "Lemni could be hot-headed, which caused me concern. I overruled his desire to confront Gabinus, gave him a useful task with the girl, and to satisfy him I promised to deal with Gabinus myself."

"Deal with him how, sir?"

"In a rational fashion."

"Not pushing him off the Tarpeian Rock, you mean? The man subsequently died. Why you and Lemni were so angry with him is critical. The girl was in distress, yet she was a stranger to both of you. You treated her kindly, yet your response to Gabinus over her seems exaggerated. Out of character, too, if I may say so."

"The Arx was being defiled by Gabinus and his lewd behaviour," offered Larth. As an explanation I thought it feeble.

"Did you find Gabinus?"

"No."

"Suppose you had," I asked, trying again, "what would you have done, Augur?"

"Taken him to task."

"In what capacity?"

"A concerned citizen. A member of the Curia, a man of authority. A representative of the College of Augurs, whose sanctity Gabinus had affronted."

"No other concern?"

"Nothing else," he responded.

He was lying. His wife knew. She remained tight-lipped.

I recognised their kind of marriage. They must have been together for thirty years; there was no indication they had ever had children but I sensed the strength of their partnership. They lived side by side, accepting, content, even though Larth had probably seen more of Lemni than he did of Percennia. I guessed when they were both at home, when Larth was not officiating on the Arx, each moved around the house independently. Actual conversation might be limited; they communicated in unspoken ways simply by knowing each other so well. I could see they rarely argued. When he dug in his heels, as he was doing over Lemni, she stood by in silence.

"I failed to find the man," declared Larth. "I came home to my wife. She will confirm that. I was in some anxiety about the episode with the girl. Percennia and I discussed it."

I glanced at Percennia but did not bother with her confirmation. "You could have reported Gabinus to the authorities. You, or at least Lemni, appear to have had a personal motive. I ask you again. What was it?"

Larth lifted his chin and looked lofty.

I persisted. "Will you clarify our previous discussion, please? You and Lemni both assured me you had no prior link to Gabinus. That was untrue. Lemni built up an elaborate lie that he had only ever heard about him from the custodian of Jupiter Custos. You have since assured me Lemni never ran bets for Gabinus, yet other people say differently. They reckon he almost certainly acted as his messenger, just as he did for everyone. Why did Lemni pretend they were strangers?"

Larth simply shrugged.

"This is hard to believe, Larth. My witness, the girl, says neither of you showed surprise when Gabinus behaved badly to her. She thought you both loathed him already and Lemni was wound up further by this new offence. What had Gabinus done before? What had he done to Lemni?"

Still no answer. I glanced at the wife, Percennia. She seemed embarrassed by this situation, but had an austere old-fashioned loyalty of wife to husband. I had been taught to respect that; I did not try to persuade her.

"So after Lemni took the girl to safety, you say you failed to find Gabinus that night?"

"Neither Lemni nor I saw him alive again," stated Larth. "Next morning we were preoccupied with setting up our tent anew, since the girl's abrupt invasion had polluted the ritual. We were seated inside while I prepared myself for a new observation. We heard Gabinus cry out when he fell from the Rock. I summoned people to go down to recover the body, though we did not descend the Gemonian Stairs ourselves. The body was taken away. I had no other involvement."

"And Lemni had never confronted Gabinus?"

"No, I told you. He took the murex girl to safety. What are you suggesting?" For the first time, Larth appeared perturbed. He almost glanced at his wife, but managed not to do so.

I told it as I saw it: "From my impression of Lemni, once he left Suza at the inn, he would have found it impossible to rest. Lemni was thoroughly worked up. He harangued the leader of the murex workers furiously, then must have left the inn while still very upset. Don't pretend: even though you had tried to stop him, I believe Lemni went back to the Capitol later, looking for Gabinus."

"He never found him," Larth insisted. "You are right, he did try. He failed to find him, just as I had done. Next day he admitted this to me. Someone told Lemni that Gabinus had gone off drinking. Apparently he went down the hill to meet an acquaintance at a bar."

"Who said that?"

"Lemni never told me."

"And who was Gabinus meeting?"

"I do not know. Lemni knew the bar, and he even went there, but there was no sign of Gabinus."

"What bar?"

"Lemni did not say."

"People tell me nobody liked drinking with Gabinus. So it matters who he went to meet. This drinking partner might be the person he quarreled with on the Rock next day. If he exists, I need his identity."

"I agree, but I cannot help," said Larth. Presumably he wanted the unknown boozer found in order to exonerate Lemni, so I felt he would have told me if he could. "Everything seemed quiet again on the Arx. There were clear skies. Lemni and I resumed our duties. We were both inside our tent next morning when Gabinus died."

I had no option but to accept that. I had run out of ways to nag at him. Larth must be covering up for his friend, as if he really knew Lemni was guilty.

Now Lemni was dead too. Larth appeared genuinely shocked by the second murder. So what about him? His alibi for the first murder was Lemni; he had none for the second. However, I could not believe the augur would ever have harmed Lemni.

"One last thing," I concluded wearily. "It is clear to me, despite all denial, Gabinus and Lemni had a personal feud. Lemni had some motive to hate Gabinus. Any investigator would think their deaths must be linked. But with Gabinus dead, who do you think had a motive to attack Lemni?"

Nothing. I was wasting my time here.

I thanked them for letting me ask questions. Lemni's ashes must be ready for collecting from his pyre. If they had no objection, I said, I would remain here for that, since I had met the dead man and liked him. Afterwards I would leave them in peace.

XLV

I waited while Lemni's remains were formally collected by Larth. It gave me time to think.

The ritual seemed to stiffen the augur. Covering his head, he slipped easily into the calm persona he must use for his duties. Its gravity seemed to comfort him.

Their ancient slaves were helping Larth. I stood quietly with Percennia. As her husband carefully placed the ashes and bone fragments in a round glass jar held by one of his younger retainers, I murmured that he would clearly miss Lemni very much.

At first I thought Percennia would not reply. Eventually she said, "Theirs was a good, rare friendship." I wondered if she had been jealous, though she seemed too generous. Suddenly lowering her voice, she went on, "I hope you will drop any foolish suggestion of my husband killing that man, Gabinus."

I inclined my head, though in silence.

"Even if Gellius had found him and remonstrated with him, it would never have ended in violence. He is not the type!" his wife insisted. I let her think I accepted it. I knew that, when pressured by circumstances, anybody is the type.

She left the subject. Instead she told me sadly, "We were intending to hold a funeral feast here in the garden. Now I don't know . . ." She tailed off.

By this stage, Percennia and Gellius were showing elderly fragility. They both seemed bowed by trouble; they must have been dealt a serious blow by last night's events. Trying to remain composed, Percennia gave the old female slave instructions for bringing their luggage as they prepared to stay with friends. A practical woman, she told me an address in case of further queries.

The couple's unexpected departure to someone else's house would probably affect them further. Once they were sitting in some senatorial guestroom with time for reflection, shock would catch up with them. I found myself hoping they came to no harm.

A large plain glass cinerary urn had been placed in the basket of a pull-along trolley that the old male slave must use to collect shopping. He was spry enough, though past his best. A boy was to accompany him; their destination was not mentioned. Without more ado, I said goodbye to the householders and politely left. They must have thought I had finished here.

Scorpus had left Taurus with the barber. I had seen him give the barber money to cover use of his stool, though he said the vigilis must not have a real shave, because he might have to leap up to follow someone. I was intending to give Taurus the nod. When I came out into the street I saw that, despite his orders, he was under a napkin, head back, oblivious.

I parked myself discreetly in a doorway and wrapped my stole around my hair as a gentle gesture to disguise. It often works.

On emerging from the house, accompanied by the young boy, the first thing the old slave did was look around to see if his exit was being observed. He even glanced over at Taurus as if, regardless of the shave in progress, he knew why he was there. The rest of the vigiles had now left, taking their siphon engine. Scorpus was long gone. Pulling his trolley behind him, the old man set off, not noticing me. He was walking fast, deliberately evading Taurus. The young boy scampered with him.

We crossed the Argiletum, a teeming, sordid street. It had always been a main thoroughfare but led into the bad area called the Suburra. Julius Caesar was supposed to have lived in the Suburra but from him, always a maverick, it was raising a finger at the establishment. Nobody who could do better would expose themselves to this place of many trades and pervading crime.

Caesar defied Fate. Few enemies would have dared attack him; if they had, he would not have cared. Less arrogant, I tried to take precautions. It was tricky. The Argiletum was clogged with both normal traffic and visitors. Shops spilled out across the pavement, regardless of the regulations. In between untidy piles of metalware, basketware and amphorae sticky with food or wine, people offered trays, selling congealed snacks or small religious statuettes. Every tourist coming for the Triumph had to go home with a mismatched set: two versions of Jupiter, one rude eastern Venus, a faux-bronze bull with one horn missing, an amulet against the evil eye, a model womb in case of gynaecological disease . . . Once their mouths were crammed with Lucanian sausage and gherkins, people were incapable of saying, "No, thanks."

When we turned off into back-streets, the congestion grew worse. The old man with the trolley was given a pathway; the skinny boy managed to slip through. A lone woman faced greater problems. As I tried to balance following my targets with keeping safe, I was often buffeted. It might have been unintentional. Probably not. I was wearing sturdy walking shoes so whenever I spotted who did it I could graze their shins; if they looked too brutal, I just took the punishment. I had no time to stop for an argument.

I had done worse in my time. I stayed cool, ignored my bruises and pushed on after the slaves.

They ended up at a basic lodging-house, a featureless doss packed with cheap rooms. They took the trolley indoors with them. Thieves would show no respect for Lemni; they wouldn't want his remains. The glassware that held the last fragments of him was another matter, an alluring target. Emptied out, it would be saleable.

While the boy guarded the trolley, I saw the old man come out, go up a staircase and return with a crone, who must have been the concierge. She had something in her hand, like a latch-lifter. After a time they all came back out into the street, where the old slave added a new bundle to his trolley. Whatever he brought was wrapped in a piece of woollen blanket; he had clutched it in both arms, staggering under quite some weight, then positioned it very carefully. While the crone waved amiably after them, he and the boy set off again. The trolley must have been harder to drag; they slowed down.

This was a mistake. Struggling with their unwieldy load signalled them as vulnerable. Dubious do-gooders offered to help. The boy knew his job, but his polite rebuffs were being ignored. Surprisingly, the old fellow drove off the first would-be street-thieves by standing his ground and letting out a loud yell.

The pair set off again, now hauling the trolley together so they could move faster. Members of the public were crowding them and trying to peer in at whatever they were carrying. Hands pulled at the cover around the second bundle. The old man let go and shooed people away, waving his bony arms above the trolley to protect its contents.

They turned the trolley around so they could push it. With some gusto, they shot off again. They sped along, heading west. Emerging into the civic area, they went around the Forum of Augustus and the Forum of Caesar, until they passed the Atrium of Liberty where the censors' records used to be stored. They turned right on the Vicus Argentarius. The prison was behind them. They were further along than the metal-workers' head-quarters. They were closing on the Porta Fontinalis, where I had been the other day, the day I saw the aedile's tomb.

At this point, they thought they had shaken off trouble. I could see they were wrong, though I was helpless to warn them. A couple of deter-mined luggage-lifters had dogged them all the way. When they hit the pinch-point at the ancient gate, these predators jumped them.

One clipped the lad, another shouldered the old man. I put on a spurt but was too late. It was over in an instant. The old slave fought back; they put him on the ground. The boy found himself in a headlock. Before any-one could do anything—assuming the public had wanted to (joke!)—the first held onto the boy while the second had the trolley away. Then the boy was flung aside as both muggers disappeared.

I did not stop to check on the slaves. I hared after the trolley-thieves.

XLVI

The slaves had been heading past the gate as if intending to turn around the Arx. The thieves did a rapid double-back. After they had zipped around, burying themselves in the crowds, they slowed down, laughing as they congratulated themselves. They sauntered right past me. I took a close look, unsure whether to tackle them. Nobody had protested when the slaves were attacked; no one would help me.

They were not exactly white-tunic clericals: a lean, mean-faced goon in dusty work garb, whom I wouldn't hire to shovel horse-shit, and a harder, fight-scarred no-brain wearing a more upscale tunic that he must have pinched. Having seen them in action I knew they would fight dirty. Being female would give no protection. With two of them determined to hang onto what they had stolen, even a man would think twice.

They looked back over their shoulders but saw no sign of the Gellius slaves and did not recognise me. I tucked in behind them while I wondered what to do.

The stately Clivus Argentarius, bounded by the Capitol and the imperial fora opposite, lacks dark alleys down which gutter rats can dive. These two were brazen, however. When they thought they were safe, they stopped right in the middle of the street to investigate their loot. As they bent over to inspect the trolley contents, for me it was now or never.

I thought I heard a whistle, like the vigiles calling for back-up when they have sniffed out an overturned oil lamp. I didn't stop. I ran right at the thieves crashing into them hard. At the same time I loudly screamed, "Rape!"

Don't knock it. Even street pickpockets use this distraction. As a trick it works. People are guaranteed to cluster around in a circle, wanting to watch.

I had failed to knock the two men over, but they both staggered. This was helped by them being off balance as they straightened up with armfuls of something weighty. Each had one bundle from the trolley; when I collided with them, both were dropped.

I had an advantage of surprise. It didn't last. Of course they both turned on me at once.

I had really done it now. This was deeply dangerous. From the expressions on their faces their response could be fatal. Street muggers in Rome like to avoid attention, but when cornered they become feral. They may back off from a sting they haven't started, if something about it looks too public, but once they are hanging onto stolen goods, they refuse to let go and turn vicious. Only an idiot would take them on. Now I was that idiot.

I had never been afraid of death, only any pain that precedes it. I cannot say what I would have done if I really had been alone. Fortunately the Fates were not ready to snip my thread of life. Help arrived.

Taurus and Zenon, vigiles of the First Cohort, powered up the Clivus just as I was preparing to be torn asunder in foul ways. With sturdy legs in solid boots, their sprint was an athlete's dream. Used to patrolling the top end of the Forum, a genteel beat unless someone fell off the Tarpeian Rock, the pair were keyed up for a fight. Rescuing me would brighten their morning. Using their usual arrest tactics—unnecessary and protracted punching—they reduced the two thieves to jelly, then according to custom kept hitting them until they (Taurus and Zenon, that is) had had enough. They exchanged signals that they were prepared to stop. After a couple more punches to prove they were winners, they did.

I thanked them, expressing mild regret that it had not been necessary for me to get my hands dirty.

They were both short and muscular, Taurus with sharp features, Zenon chubbier. Taurus said they had been following all along. Scorpus, he reminded me, "had his methods." Still grateful that I was alive, I conceded that they worked. The methods must be more sophisticated than I'd originally thought—or those two got lucky. I made a pale attempt to pretend

I had realised the troops were there, though we all knew I had not thought to check.

To get over my poor street-craft, I turned to examine the thieves. One was kneeling in the road, coughing blood as he clutched his battered guts; the other just stood bent over from the waist, hideously groaning.

"What shall we do with them?" asked Taurus. Zenon leered, full of unpleasant ideas. His excitement was greater since the vigiles so rarely catch anyone.

The thieves had happened on the trolley slaves by chance, so in a way they were irrelevant to me. As muggers they ought to be punished, though, and I could bear witness that they were very violent.

"Throw them into the condemned cell in the Tullianum," I suggested. "If they are still down there alive when the Triumph ends, the jailer can strangle them. It ought to be Dacian captives, but Domitian won't be bringing any."

"We haven't done anything!" one thief moaned, trying it on in the classic style of Rome's more pathetic criminals. Given the chance, he would probably say his mother had neglected him as a baby and his stepfather was cruel.

"You defiled the dead," Taurus retorted. "What you've stolen is ashes that were bound for a necropolis. Don't you have any conscience?"

"Rhetorical question!" I snorted.

"We weren't to know!"

"No excuse. You're going in the jail, like the lady said."

To emphasise the wickedness of the crime, Taurus and Zenon gestured to the stolen goods. In one case, the result of me rushing the criminals was a disaster. The dropped glass urn that had contained Lemni's ashes lay smashed in the road. Among glittering shards, Lemni was now spread around on the Clivus Argentarius.

I had had dealings with corpses in my work. This was the first time a victim had ended up like wet-weather anti-slip gritting. Since the day was sunny and the roadway dry, poor Lemni was in fact acting the other way; his knuckle bones and teeth caused pedestrians to skid. Pieces of his shattered urn were waiting to amputate toes.

The vigiles responded with care for the community. Leaving me to guard the prisoners, Taurus commandeered stools from a snack stall to form a rough and ready safety barrier, while Zenon found a road-sweeper and borrowed his broom. Soon they had Lemni pushed together again in a neat pile, even though the pile also contained stones, glass and pigeon droppings.

I looked for the other bundle from the trolley. I was just in time to snatch it back from a sly youth who was seizing his moment to lift it from the gutter. He cursed me. I asked if his mother knew he talked like that. He strutted off, reduced to nothing.

This object, still cushioned within its piece of blanket, had survived intact. Zenon and Taurus gathered around while I squatted down beside the parcel, which was quite large; I untied some string that secured the wrapping. Inside, was a big, bulbous, reddish-coloured ceramic pot. It had a small base and a raised lip into which its lid fitted snugly.

On one side was an incised picture of a round face: straight nose running up to arched eyebrows, slits for eyes and mouth, even lined-out ears. Calm and blissful, these were the stylised features of somebody asleep in death. When I gingerly pulled up the lid, inside were more grey ashes.

I gazed up at the vigiles, each holding a slumped prisoner. "Well, boys, here's a puzzle. If that's Lemni you swept up in the road—who in Hades is this?"

XLVII

The anonymous remains were in a fine Etruscan-style container that had cost some grieving person a goodly sum. When similar items came up at the auction house, Father always declared they were of immense antiquity; they could easily be more recent, and often were, because such pots were still being made to their centuries-old design; with ceramics, nobody can prove it either way. This one was very clean; it looked new to me. But well made.

Whoever was in the face-pot now acquired a lodger. Taurus and Zenon decided it would be indecent to leave Lemni at the side of the road where dogs would pee on him. They made the road-sweeper pick up the remains on his shovel, then delicately filtered Lemni and associated road dust into the pot too. They had just finished this solemn act of piety when the two Gellius slaves, whose master had loved Lemni so much, came limping down the Clivus. Zenon whipped the lid onto the overflowing container.

We stopped them. Taurus quizzed them. They seemed reluctant to tell us either where they had been for their first stop or where they had intended to go next with their trolley. Larth had told them not to talk to us.

In Rome it is unacceptable to blame slaves for obeying their master's orders. Mind you, the vigiles are always allowed to swear at them nastily.

It was decided that, as I had suggested, Taurus and Zenon would free themselves from hassle by depositing their prisoners in the Tullianum jail. It was locked up still, but they broke in, just as they had the other morning when they needed to fetch those long hooks to recover Lemni's body. After a few yells, the two thieves were pitched down into the cell, which is notoriously deep and escape-proof. The vigiles shouted the traditional farewell that they had better behave themselves, adding sternly that prison was too good for them. They reapplied the locks on the outside door, or made it look as if they had.

Taurus had to report to Scorpus. He took the face-pot for safe keeping at the station-house. Zenon would escort the old slave and his empty trolley back to his master and mistress, since his ordeal had nearly finished him. I reminded them that Larth and his wife were now staying with friends, whose address I passed on. The old man must know, but he seemed confused, no longer fit for anything. The boy was reluctant to part from him, but was told he had to come with me. I wanted him to show me where they had meant to take the trolley next.

Under compulsion, he trotted along with me up the Clivus. He had been nervous of the vigiles, but reacted better to me. Along the way I played it friendly, luring him into conversation. I told him I had a brother of about his age, which I put at around thirteen. That is supposed to set lads at their ease, though most don't care.

This one said he was the old fellow's grandson, name of Marcellus. He was thin, well-mannered, biddable. He had been born into service with the family. Gellius Donatus was a kindly, if slightly distant, master; Percennia was a good mistress. Marcellus, with his young sister and both grandparents, helped around the home. It was light, undemanding work. He liked his job. He thought himself fortunate. He hoped one day to gain his freedom so he could run some kind of business. Import/export, he suggested, though perhaps with little idea of what that cliché meant.

I managed to persuade him to reveal where they had gone first: the tenement was where Lemni's sister lived. She was out; she had to work. But that had been known in advance; they had been told to fetch the old biddy who acted as a caretaker. She let them in to pick up the face-pot, which the sister had left for them. Their instructions were to take both sets of ashes to another member of the family.

"And who is that? If we are going there now, you may as well tell me." I did not want to arrive cold. The boy mumbled something, scuffing his feet with his head down.

He was trying to keep things to himself, admitting he was sworn to secrecy. My brother, a more independent character, would have invented an alternative story, offering it with a convincing straight look, even if he had peopled his fantasy with lion-headed demons.

Before I could press, we reached our destination. I was flabbergasted. I recognised this building. It was the tenement next door to where Valeria Dillia lived—Lemni's lodging house. The porter I had spoken to before was even coming out to greet us in his nosy, mildly inebriated fashion. The boy hung back.

"Marcellus, buck up!" I snapped. "Are you telling me you were supposed to bring the remains of Lemni to his own room?"

"No," said the boy, unhappily.

"What, then?"

I was so cross, he gave in. The slaves were supposed to bring both urns to another man who lived here.

"What man, Marcellus?"

With the porter on hand, ready to pipe up with the answer, Marcellus could no longer refuse. "Lemni's brother."

Luckily this was not a complete surprise, because I did remember that someone had mentioned another sibling. I challenged the porter who said yes, it was true.

"What's his name?"

"Gemellus."

"Oh! Is he a twin?"

Nobody knew.

"Porter, when I was here the other day, you never mentioned him."

"You never asked," the porter whined. "I don't know every tenant in the place. Only the ones the landlord can't make pay their rent. I hear him cursing them."

"Don't talk rot. You know Lemni's brother is Gemellus. You should have seen I was interested. Stop prevaricating. Tell me where to find him."

This brother lived two floors above Lemni nowadays. They used to share, said the porter. He had in fact mentioned that before, though on the first occasion he omitted to tell me the brother still lived there with a widow. I managed not to grind my teeth. It only wears them down.

While they bunked together, Lemni had had the bed by day after he came home from augury, while Gemellus took over by night. That was do-able while they were young men, but it had become bothersome later. They wanted to avoid paying extra rent. A solution was found when the brother took up with a widow who let him in with her. She was old enough to be his mother, but the porter assured me it wasn't incest.

I said I was glad to hear that Gemellus was only a miser and a gigolo. My husband wouldn't want me going into an apartment where unnatural relations took place. The joke was lost on my audience.

I had no qualms about men who preyed on women or indeed women who took advantage of men; in my work I had met plenty—ambitious play-boys improving their lives and foolish widows who wanted to ignore be-ing past their prime.

The porter had reeked of alcohol last time, but he seemed a little more sober today. I left the boy downstairs with him, while I went up on my own to visit the lovers.

XLVIII

The widow was called Callipina. She was a busy, tidy, tiny woman who must have been over sixty. She kept her minute apartment spotless. Even my grandma would have passed her on hygienic housekeeping. Despite that, Callipina kept apologising for the state of the place. She was not only sharing it with her lover, but she had her grown-up son staying with her at the moment due to problems at his place of work. There was a lot of masculine clutter, though I had seen worse.

Both the son and the lover were out, working, yet the two-roomed place seemed cramped after I entered. At her urging, Callipina and I climbed out of a window onto a narrow ledge that passed for a balcony—"It's all right, once you get used to it"—where we perched for our conversation on seats that had to be kept outside because there was nowhere else for them.

A passing pigeon thought about joining us, but he could see there was no room. As he flew off sulkily, I pondered the fact that this was the second time today I had put my life in danger.

"Just try not to look down."

"Thanks, Callipina." I hoped no one used the cosy platform when they had had too much to drink.

Our daredevil niche faced towards the Vicus Pallacinae. We could see the Campus Martius, from the Circus Flaminius at this end, then all the way up to the Saepta. If my father had been taking his oil flask to the Baths of Agrippa behind the Pantheon, I could have waved to him in the distance. Once the Triumph began, the glamorous procession would come straight towards this building before it swung around into the Circus Flaminius.

Callipina would have a glorious view down the Via Triumphalis though not much scope to hire out her so-called balcony to sightseers. She groaned that since only two people could fit on the balcony, she was facing daily arguments about whether her son or her lover would be allowed to join her to watch.

"My son thinks it's his right, because he was brought up here. In any case, he keeps hoping Gemellus will leave."

"They don't get on?" I could see why the son kicked off. Especially if he thought her fancy man had homed in on free lodgings and a sighting of any savings she had collected. If I ever got to meet this son, I might offer to check out the lover for him. But even if I proved she was being preyed on, his mother would probably not listen.

"I do understand what he worries about," she admitted, as if she realised I was sceptical. "Gemellus is a little bit younger than me. I suppose anxiety is natural. Still, having white hair doesn't make you lose interest. I am entitled to find company for myself, aren't I?" I nodded. Into her stride, she continued with surprising honesty: "Besides, I have known Gemellus and his brother for years, so it's not as if I brought a stranger into my home. It is just bad timing at the moment. Normally my son never needs to get in our way, because he is supposed to have his own accommodation, for his work."

"What does he do?" I demanded.

Callipina was still too absorbed in self-justification to answer. "I was lonely, I admit that. Anyone likes a bit of male comfort. Not that we . . . you know . . . very often. Though it has been known to happen, and I don't think I have to be bashful about that. I say it's nobody's business but mine."

"Quite," I managed to interpolate. Though her personal grooming was as immaculate as her housekeeping, nothing could change her thin white hair or that she looked as if close manoeuvres from a lover would crush her ageing bones.

"It's not as if he is going to end up with any little brothers or sisters to put his nose out of joint."

"No. That would be one for the marvels page of the *Daily Gazette*!"

"Not at my time of life, thank you, Juno Matronalia!" I felt it polite to join in with her cackle. "It's just very awkward that my son needed to come to stay, after I thought I had seen the back of him. Not that I mind having him, never. He will always have a home with me if he needs it. It's just temporary, so we are all trying to rub along together until he gets his own place back."

"What happened about that?"

"Oh, someone wanted to borrow it. It's not for ever—it goes with my lad's job, everybody knows that. But he doesn't carry the clout to say no. Not to the nasty piece who pinched his hut."

"His *hut*, Callipina?" I had been hearing a lot about huts.

"Oh, didn't I say, dearie? My son has a very important role up on the Capitol. It's a position his father and his grandfather both held. He is a caretaker. The Emperor built a beautiful little temple where the old hut used to be, called the Temple of Jupiter Custos because Jupiter had saved his life. So my son lives in his own official hut attached to Jupiter Custos."

"I see," I breathed, when the proud mother finally fell silent. This was a turn-up. "Let's be clear: we are talking about the hut that was grabbed by the transport manager? I must have met your son; we had a talk about Gabinus." I was quickly consulting my waxed tablets. "Is his name Callipus?"

"That's right," said his mother. "He said he met you. He still tells me everything even though he left home years ago, or I thought he had. My son is the caretaker of Jupiter Best and Greatest."

Unexpected aspects of this enquiry suddenly began to come together.

Recovering, I asked did his mother know where her son had been on the morning that Gabinus fell off the Tarpeian Rock. She immediately gave him an alibi. Callipus had told me she would: he said he was here with her, having an argument about her lover, whom he could not stand. To me, his mother called it "having a late breakfast." Still, that would do to place him.

Since this lover had unexpectedly turned out to be the brother of Lemni, who also perished on the Rock, I asked where Callipus was that night too. Here at home, his mother assured me. He had slept here every night since his hut was commandeered, unfortunately for her love life.

XLIX

No alibi given by a mother really counts. But much had been made of Callipus having to stay with his mother after he was turfed out from his hut, so it made sense. He was here. He was having his argument when Gabinus died, and since Gemellus had his old room (when he was not cuddling the widow), Callipus was sleeping on the floor the night Lemni was killed.

I nodded at the fond mother's statements. My old Aventine granny would reappear from the grave to give me a right earful if I dared to doubt a woman who kept such a spotless home. Dear old Junilla Tacita would even have championed the right of a widow to take a younger lover.

"Can I check something else? Your son told me Gemellus was here too, on the morning when Gabinus died?" I congratulated myself mentally on how smoothly I turned my questions to the lover. "So when you and Callipus argued about Gemellus, Gemellus listened in?"

Perhaps Callipina looked embarrassed. "My son is a bit short on tact. Yes, Gemellus had had a late night. He had been going out with his brother but Lemni kept him waiting, so he came in very late from the bar and didn't go to work in the morning. My son calls him lazy. Well, he tries to call him a lot of things, but I refuse to hear it."

"I see. I'm sorry Gemellus isn't here. I would have liked to meet him," I said, intending it to sound less like politeness and more like a threat. "By the way, I have a lad downstairs who had the sad task of bringing Gemellus the ashes of his brother."

"That's right," confirmed Callipina, who knew all about it. "Gemellus is going to the necropolis, but it's outside the Porta Triumphalis. We'll have to look after the ashes here until the Triumph is over. I keep telling him he'll never get through at the moment. He and his sister will have a plaque made later, once they can afford it."

"Money is tight?"

"Money is always tight. But there has been some argy-bargy about the inscription on the plaque. Gemellus and his sister having a set-to," Callipina clarified.

"Care to elaborate?"

"No, it's not for me to say. They both know their minds. Gemellus and Lemni always called their sister soft, but she is so upset that Gemellus has caved in and will do whatever she wants. The poor girl is all on her own now, with three small children and another on the way. She has work at the moment so she's busy. Gemellus thinks she will go to see the grave later, once they have a plaque to install."

"What is the sister's name, by the way?"

"Naevia." Why did that sound familiar? Someone must have said it. I queried the news that Naevia was now "all on her own": "So her husband has died, as well as her brother?"

"That's right." Callipina spoke without much sympathy. "Two lots of ashes."

"That's sad for her. Was it recent?"

"Yes, she is still coming to terms."

"What happened? Do you know?"

"Bit of a tragedy. He got himself drunk—which happened all the time with him—then he must have picked a quarrel with somebody. One time too many."

"A bar fight? It must be her husband's ashes that were picked up from her house today. They are in an expensive face-pot."

"That will be him. Too good for the swine," declared Callipina.

"Lemni and Gemellus, her brothers, thought he was a wastrel?"

"It was much worse than that, dear," Callipina whispered, even though out on our balcony nobody else could hear her. "He was *not* a nice man. Let's leave it at that, since he's gone now. Whatever he did, she never left him—which must count for something, mustn't it? And she still did the decent thing when he died. We all had to go to his funeral; she wanted a good crowd there. A few from his work turned up, though they didn't stay. She says she doesn't want her children to think poorly of their father. That's why they must have a good memorial for him."

"So it won't say, 'This plaque was put up by his heartbroken wife, well deserving of her'?" I guessed. All the time I was thinking that many of these details were oddly familiar.

Callipina winced with me. "Sounds right. Gemellus is going to let her have both deaths on the same plaque, just as she wants, never mind what Lemni would have thought."

At last I asked the question: "I hope it isn't out of place to ask. Do you mind telling me, was Naevia's husband called Gabinus?"

"I thought you knew that, dear," said Callipina. "Naevia was married to the man who borrowed my son's hut. He fell off the Tarpeian Rock. Bit of a coincidence, really—since her own brother died horribly later, in just the same place."

L

I took a moment for thought, as my investigation jolted onto a new path. Callipina merely carried on talking. "Gemellus will carry the other ashes to the necropolis for Naevia as well, when he trots along with Lemni."

Recovering, I mentioned that the burden would be lighter, since both dead men were accidentally sharing the same face-pot. Callipina winced again. She said she would let me tell Gemellus. I did not look forward to explaining it was impossible to separate the remains of his admired brother from those of the loathed brother-in-law. Still, I asked innocently when I was likely to see Gemellus.

"Any moment now," replied the man-in-question's lover. She had spotted him below in the street, coming home, as he did every day, to have his lunch. He enjoyed his meals, and liked to have them served up promptly.

We climbed back indoors, so she could have a bite ready for him, on the table. All dainty. His own bowl, knife and napkin. It could have been Valeria Dillia spoiling Nestor, or my own grandmother looking after anybody who called.

Half an hour later we and the lunch were still sitting there. Gemellus had not arrived.

I went down to the street to look for him. I was told that when Callipina's lover learned from Marcellus and the porter that I was upstairs, he'd done a runner.

I sighed.

I returned to ask Callipina where her sweetheart was likely to hide up if he was in trouble. She claimed she had no idea. Nothing like this had ever happened before. He was a good man, who never mixed with bad company. He only ever went out for a drink with his brother, and now he wouldn't even be able to do that . . . She started to grizzle, thinking the ungallant Gemellus might have left her. No chance. The man was set up in a much too cosy roost.

Since he refused to come home, I ate his lunch.

Apart from saucers of olives and walnuts, the food comprised bread rolls and cheese; the cheese tasted as though it had been sliced with a knife that had recently cut onions. It reminded me of Lemni.

I remembered how Lemni had let me share his snack in the observation tent. He was so friendly and easy-going, and from my enquiries so well loved by everyone; it was painful to think he might have killed Gabinus. But it was where all my clues were leading me. Lemni hated what Gabinus had done to his sister. Gemellus knew what Lemni must have done, so now he was avoiding me.

"Callipina, tell me more about these brothers and their sister. Is it right that Lemni was constantly nagging her to have no more to do with Gabinus? That Gabinus failed to support her, especially financially? I was told a tale of a woman, who must have been Naevia, going up to his workplace on the Palatine and appealing to him. She had taken her baby. But he cruelly pretended to colleagues she was not even his wife. He rejected all her pleading. I was even told he threatened to push her about."

"He never did hit her. She hardly ever saw him, anyway." Callipina was rapidly cooling on me. Gemellus' failure to appear disturbed her. Now she blamed and distrusted me.

"She saw him enough to be pregnant again!" I pointed out. "Did that annoy her brothers? It sounds to me as if Lemni was incensed when Naevia let it happen."

"I don't know about that."

"Don't you discuss such things?"

"I tried to keep out of it. Gemellus never says much."

"Lemni took the lead in family arguments?"

"He was the older one."

"Older by how long? Gemellus is a name for twins—were these brothers twins then? With Lemni just born first?"

"I never heard they were—Gemellus is quite a youngster." Callipina boasted of her catch. "Flavia Albia, I need to get on. If you have asked all your questions . . ."

I had plenty more, but sometimes there is no point in trying to ask them.

Callipina had been too unhappy to eat, so I took her lunch down for the slave-boy Marcellus. Now he really was a good boy.

Mind you, he might change entirely once he hit puberty.

The boy had been taken into the porter's cubicle, where they were chatting. I had to call out quite loudly to attract their attention. Anyone could easily have crept past the gossipy porter unnoticed . . . If somebody did, I could guess who he would be—and where he would be going.

I gave the new friends the food to share. I told Marcellus he should go to find his master after he finished eating. I instructed the porter to take Callipina's platter back, well washed; he would enjoy nattering to her about my visit.

I slipped quietly back to Lemni's room. On my previous visit the porter had revealed how to find the latch-lifter above the lintel; I remembered how he had shouldered the door to force it open. I could do that. As I expected, when I suddenly burst in, a man was lying on the narrow bed, wondering what to do with himself. He looked despondent; he looked rebellious. However, he did not look particularly like Lemni. There must have been quite a few years between them; Gemellus definitely must be twins with Naevia.

"Hello!" I cried. "I had a feeling I might find you lurking here as if you own the place. Of course you and Lemni shared it once."

He swung himself upright but stayed sitting on the bed. The game was up. He had failed to elude me. Now Gemellus, brother of the late Lemni, grumpily accepted that he would have to talk to me.

There were similarities, when I inspected him closely. Gemellus and Lemni used to go to the same barber; this brother had chosen a different hairstyle but used the same thick oil, also plastering it on like axle grease. His shifty air as he faced up to me reminded me that even Lemni had come across on first meeting as potentially shady. Once he found his voice, Gemellus piped up with the same cheeky confidence: "If you're going to nag me, get on with it."

I seated myself on a stool, smoothing my skirts impassively. "You tell me."

"Tell you what?"

"Oh . . . many things, Gemellus. Start with why you ran away just now, why you were hiding to avoid me."

"I'm in bereavement." He was playing up the drama. He sounded very sad for himself. "I don't feel up to seeing people."

"Poor you. I am sorry for your loss! Well, I'm sorry about your brother—I met him and liked him. I don't feel the same about your brother-in-law. No one does. From all I hear, he was deplorable. Do you think Lemni killed him?"

Gemellus started. "Lemni would never do that!"

"Too easy-going?" I pretended to agree, but I laid out the facts: "Yes, except just before Gabinus died, Lemni found out he had assaulted a young girl. By all accounts Lemni was zinging with fury—and if Gabinus was married to your sister, it makes sense." Gemellus upgraded his shifty look to utterly untrustworthy. "The girl who was assaulted says Lemni was sympathetic to her, but I think he was really livid about the injury to Naevia. Gabinus had tried to violate a teenager, even one who stank of decaying shellfish so horribly no man with any self-respect would go near her. But the bastard was married and fathering children he refused to support. It must have been the last straw for Lemni."

Gemellus agreed eventually. Now he was speaking in a serious voice, sounding more reasonable, less defiant. "We talked about it. We had to discuss whether to tell our sister."

"Was she told?"

"She knows now. When she was mithering about his funeral, I let it slip." Trust a man, especially when it no longer served any purpose to tell her. Discovering this would add to the poor woman's grief. Gemellus, of course, made out he'd had no choice. "She needed to know. She keeps carrying on about how Gabinus was her husband, so she must give him proper rites. She was up to her neck in debt already because he never gave her any money, even though he kept hanging around her. Now she has been to loan sharks, just so she can pay for his funeral. Me, I'd let him rot like a traitor on the Gemonian Stairs. We should have just left him there."

I said quietly, "I will assume it was not your sister who pushed him off the Tarpeian Rock?"

Gemellus looked startled. "Hang on! Don't start calling her a suspect. Naevia has enough to cope with."

"She had cause," I warned him. "But if she didn't know until Gabinus was dead what he did with the murex girl, I can rule her out. But I can't ignore her having a devoted brother who was incensed on her behalf."

"She had two," Gemellus pointed out.

I nodded. "Don't worry, I won't forget you! But Callipina assures me *you* were upstairs with her and her son that morning."

Gemellus muttered, yes, Callipina was right. So Gemellus had his alibi. The same could not be said for Lemni.

"If Lemni killed Gabinus, either on purpose or accidentally during an argument, how do you feel about that, Gemellus?"

"If he did, it has caused us a lot more trouble. But that filthy turd deserved it," Gemellus swore. "Someone should have done for him a long time ago. Lemni was ready to, I know that much."

"Pointing the finger at your brother—that's nice! So who do you think murdered Lemni?"

Gemellus, back in surly mode, said it was a complete mystery.

I tried to explore why it happened. Did his brother have enemies? Not as far as Gemellus knew. I asked whether any of his brother's business of carrying bets might have gone wrong. Gemellus was sure that was impossible. Lemni had been known for his straight dealings and everyone liked him for it.

"His was a violent death, Gemellus. Has anybody told you? Someone cracked Lemni very hard on the head, then wrapped up and disposed of his body, chucked him over the cliff-edge like a piece of meat. This was not accidental, like a street mugging or a bar fight. It was not a stranger-killing. It was all very deliberate."

I had wanted to see if the younger brother was upset by the details. Something else was on his mind, though. "Did it mean something," Gemellus asked me intently, "that he was thrown off the cliff—just like Gabinus?"

I had to say I thought it did mean something. Gemellus seemed upset by that. Lemni's manner of death was a message. It had to be a message *to* someone, so it looked as if that could be him.

We sat in silence for a short time.

Gemellus then began to talk about Lemni and their sister, in the cathartic rambling of the bereaved. According to him, there had never been any antagonism between the brothers. They had been close. From childhood they were always wonderful friends. Even before their parents died, they shared responsibility for their sister too. She was close to them, until she made the wrong choice of husband; in view of that, they continued their moral support.

Why did Naevia fall for him? I asked, since from all I had heard, Gabinus was a stinker. I imagined he always had been. Yes, said Gemellus, but when the bastard wanted something, he could sweet-talk convincingly. (I remembered Suza spoke of him charming Ostorius and Cincia.) Naevia was easily fooled. Then once she had their first child she seemed to feel permanently bound to him. He immediately lost interest—which, needless to say, came as a surprise to Naevia. Classic.

Afterwards, Gabinus would never entirely leave her alone, but each time the brothers hoped he had finally left for good, he kept reappearing. Naevia always gave in to him—which by then was no surprise to anyone. Gabinus openly gloated. Now she had two further children, plus a new one on the way.

"Does she work, Gemellus?"

"She does a bit of sewing. It never brings in much, and what she gets soon goes. She tries to manage without paying for minders. The people she works with often help with the elder ones, but she has to look after the baby." Gemellus seemed to be a fond uncle, for he hung his head and mumbled that they were lovely children. I had heard this from other people.

"Lemni thought the same?"

"Yes, he adored them."

It was a common situation. The only person who was never endeared to his beautiful offspring was their absentee father. His idea of family life was simply having sex, foisting new ones on their feeble mother. I had cousins who grew up in the same circumstances. They struggled with life; two died too young; the rest had learned nothing from their parents but would perpetuate the same miserable cycle.

I talked more about the brothers. Gemellus confirmed that even now he lived with Callipina it had been regular for him to visit a bar with Lemni. They went for a drink and a chat, often about Naevia and her troubles. They always patronised the same place, the Centaur; it was a dump but had the advantage that it stayed open all hours. If Lemni was watching for planets with Larth or one of the other augurs, his brother would wait up; on his return, they would pop out for a quick one even in the dark. Callipina had never raised any objection. Now I had met him, I wondered if in truth she was glad to get Gemellus out from under her feet.

In conclusion, Gemellus formally declared that in Lemni he had had the best brother in the world. It seemed to make no difference to him that there were two awkward anomalies. One: although everybody liked him, Lemni was an increasingly prime suspect for having had a furious row with Gabinus on the Tarpeian Rock during which he sent Gabinus spinning off. Two: for unfathomable reasons, Lemni had upset someone enough to be himself deliberately murdered.

I left Gemellus in the room they had once shared, still sitting on his brother's bed. He had his head in his hands and seemed as troubled as I was.

LI

As I was leaving that tenement, I saw Valeria Dillia about to go into hers. Against my better judgement, when she waved I paused to ask how she was. She remained an important witness to Gabinus' death. I had to keep her sweet.

When she tottered over to me, she seemed to have the same bits of fluff clinging to her dark gown, the same faint whiff, the same strands of hair flying loose. Luckily she was so nosy about what I had been doing next door, I was spared a diatribe on aching bones. I mentioned that her friend the Tullianum jailer might discover someone had left him a present. Dillia, who had just come from cleaning there, said he already knew. The two thieves in his cell were caterwauling; the jailer had threatened to shut them up by strangling them then and there.

"As soon as he likes to do it," I encouraged, feeling heartless.

"He has to have an instruction!" the old dame corrected me, shocked that I could countenance such a breach in procedure. So, in Rome it was quite acceptable to rape virgins and massacre captives—but only with the necessary paperwork. I said if my crony Scorpus knew the right form of words, I would remind him to send a cover note.

"Two!" chirped Dillia, since the jailer would need one for each thief he eliminated. Two fees for him, two cuts from him for her. She would, after all, be required to mop up twice as much mess after the terrified prisoners shitted or threw up.

I changed the subject hastily. I asked how she was, and did she still see Nestor? Yes, that lovely, generous Praetorian was still looking after her.

Dillia worried about him; he was feeling low. Thinking of the goose-boy, Feliculus, with his permanent depression, I reckoned working up on the Capitol might affect people badly. Too much dazzle off the golden temple roofs? Or at least a sense of isolation.

That could be, Dillia gloomily decided. On the other hand, Nestor, poor thing, was suffering because of a recent death in his family.

I had been facetious. I pulled myself together. Even Praetorian guards, I said gravely, would feel a bereavement. Tough men were sometimes ultra-sensitive. They were trained to hide their feelings, but grief had to come out so it must be very special for Nestor that he had a sympathetic friend to share it with . . .

I was almost ashamed of my hypocrisy. "He lost nobody close, I hope?"

"Yes . . ."

I sensed that Valeria Dillia was about to launch into a long family trag-edy. Curses on her guard! I could not face a sob-story of fatal childbirth, chicken pox or food poisoning, so I cut her short. At this time of year, every time you stopped for a gossip with someone at the baths or on a street corner, they would bore you with another malaria victim who had col-lapsed on holiday.

Shifting the subject, I said admiringly that widows around here seemed fortunate in finding younger men for company. Apropos of Callipina's fling, I wondered if Dillia knew Gemellus or Lemni.

As I suspected, she knew both; in fact, she had lived there so long her memories went back right into their childhood, including their sister. Their parents, now dead, had been nice people who had lived close by. Dillia remembered how the children used to go out to play, the three of them heading down the road with some toy, Lemni always in the lead, the other two closely following.

"Did you know the girl had married?"

Dillia had heard so, but Naevia moved away, to the Suburra, where folk from here would never venture. It was only a few streets away, yet its bad reputation meant she spoke with horror. She presumed there had been no money in the marriage; even so, for Naevia, who was brought up in a decent home, the Suburra was a terrible comedown. Dillia had not seen or spoken to her since, though she believed the girl sometimes brought her children to see their uncles.

"I have something sad to tell you." I tried to break it gently. "Her husband held a good job at the palace, but he treated her very casually. She was virtually abandoned with the children to look after, and now is expecting another. She has had a hard life, but he was a brute who never cared. I just discovered who he was. That man you saw falling off Tarpeia's Rock, Gabinus, I am afraid he was Naevia's husband."

The old woman's jaw dropped. For once she had nothing to say.

"If you knew Lemni," I offered thoughtfully, "would you say he was very close to his sister? Would he have been angered on her behalf when she was mistreated?"

"Oh, both boys adored Naevia, and Gemellus had the special bond you always get with twins." Before I could follow that up, Dillia rushed on: "Naevia always looked very sweet and was lovely-natured. Hardworking too. If that husband wasn't helping her, she was bound to have mucked in however she could, to do her best for her little ones. Well, it's how we were all brought up, decades ago, weren't we?"

It was rough for me, when I was an orphaned infant, but that was in the distant past and private. I concentrated on the siblings here: "Lemni would have hated Naevia having to work so hard, with no help from her man?"

Dillia nodded. "He would have been disgusted."

"I have heard Lemni could be hot-headed, Dillia. How far do you think he would have gone?" I asked. "If some new outrage made him flare up enough, might he have attacked Gabinus?"

"Oh, yes!" she assured me at once. "If Gabinus was being a brute to his sister, Lemni would have ripped his head off."

"In that case," I put to her quietly, "remember, you are the witness and I have to ask this: regarding the second man you saw up on the Arx with Gabinus when he fell—could that man have been Lemni?"

She did not want me to ask. Everywhere I went, people tried to protect this family. Yes, it could have been him, though she hated saying it. Valeria Dillia had not recognised him at the time. And now she would not give me a firm identification.

"I only had a glimpse. Who I saw up there, well, it could have been anyone."

I remembered that this was the woman who once mithered that she didn't want anyone to be in trouble because of her evidence. She had never made a convincing witness. That had not changed.

LII

I managed to extract myself from Dillia. I could see her fretting over something I had said. She was saddened by Lemni's death, Naevia's marital disaster and now my accusation. Any or all of those were causing her worry. I had nonplussed her, so at least she became less clingy. With the Triumph now so close, I needed to move on. Soon it would be physically impossible to visit people to ask questions. Besides, I wanted to close the case.

As I had been intending before I saw the old dame, I next made my way to the Suburra. While following the slaves with the trolley I had tried to memorise their route, so fairly soon I found where Naevia lived. Someone told me which door was hers. She was still not at home. I managed to work out where the concierge lived. No answer there, either.

I was about to leave despondently, when I heard children's voices. I discovered that the building was set around a large courtyard. It was probably cobbled, but the setts sat in mud, which turned to dust in hot weather. This neglected communal space, like those in many commercial tenements, only really provided extra light to inward-facing rooms. The landlord ignored it. Tenants found it too far to come down and unappealing if they did. No one had planted anything, no one brought out seating. People up above had hung bedclothes to air on their windowsills, but that was the only sign of life—apart from three little people.

In this bare playground, a baby was lying in the shade in a basket, while his very young brother and sister sat on the ground. They had no toys; they were amusing themselves in the dust. They seemed happy enough, chuntering to one another as they pushed dirt around in patterns that must have made sense to them.

When I entered through a big gateway that had lost its doors, they looked up. Their faces fell when they saw only a stranger. All over Rome children were left on their own out of doors until called in. They were safe enough if they stayed here. At least they would not be run over by a heavy builder's cart, and probably not kidnapped. The baby's presence might indicate that someone who looked after them was close at hand, though I guessed the elder two were supposed to be in charge of him. The boy looked about five, his little sister more like three.

The baby was awake; he was big enough to be struggling to stand up in his basket. It was clear to me he would soon be climbing out. His brother and sister had not noticed. Just as he succeeded in squashing down a basket side and was making his break for freedom, I reached him.

"Whoops! Come here, little traveller." I scooped him up. Though he wriggled in exasperation, he accepted me thwarting him. I carried him over to the others. While he cooed and dribbled at me, I squatted down to talk.

The baby was naked, apart from a bracelet of very tiny beads. Now I had captured him he busied himself trying to eat it. I had seen his loin-cloth back in the basket, where I left it for the same reason that this vigorous infant had squirmed out of it; he had needed changing.

His elder brother and sister were dressed in matching tunics that had probably been cut from one worn adult garment. It was neatly done. No fraying. Hems a good length, not so long as to trip them up, even though infants in poor families need to grow into their clothes. An existing length of braid had been incorporated into the boy's. Both wore amulets to protect them against the evil eye. They were barefoot. They had dark eyes, with dark curls, so even by the handsome standards of Roman children, they were exceptionally sweet. That would help them in life; from what I knew of recent history, I was glad of it.

One of the things my father had warned me off when he was training me to be an informer was interviewing children. You are heading for strife from their guardians. You can never believe anything they tell you. The twisted ethics that will govern their adulthood are in evidence from when they are six months old. A few nasty monsters may even accuse *you* of filthy practices.

"I know," said Falco at the time. "You will think, *None of this applies to me. I know what I am doing.* Listen to your wise old pa: don't try it."

That was more than ten years ago. I had learned in the meantime that, whatever the subject, if he gave advice I should listen. He was certainly right that I would think no sensible rules were relevant in my case.

I should be fine here. I knew two of these.

"Hello again!"

They had forgotten. They looked shy and anxious. Still, everyone had told me they were lovely children. I left them space to run away if they were scared.

"Not playing Dacians today! You are in your own clothes, not those beautiful outfits I saw you showing off to Quartilla the other day. You know what I mean—the costumes for when you are being prisoners' children on the float in the parade . . ."

They neither remembered me nor wanted to be reassured. My knowing about the Triumph was not enough. Things were already sticky with the elder two, though I was convinced I would soon win them over. If any passing pervert can woo an infant to go off with him, holding his horrible hand trustingly, surely a nice lady they had met before was no problem?

It was the baby who ruined it. The villain decided to take against me. He began bouncing in my arms, flinging himself around with bruising results. Then he started screaming.

The other two picked up the idea. Soon they were also crying as if utterly heartbroken. Anyone would have thought I had done something dreadful to them.

The old biddy who must have been minding them turned up at a run. She snatched the baby. He clung to her as if he had been rescued from unspeakable doom. His brother and sister flew to her, clinging to her tunic, subtly increasing the level of their tears and terror. Since she now had her hands full, she kicked out at me with her battered sandals.

I tried to explain, but she wasn't having it. I was seen off. I found myself out in the street alone.

Well, that would teach me. Father was right. Don't try it.

LIII

Hey-ho. Start a new game of soldiers. At least I had learned something useful. Since I recognised the children, I knew where their hardworking mother was currently employed.

I headed to the Diribitorium. That meant I must turn back across the bottom of the Vicus Longus and through the decayed tangle of republican buildings that has since been swept away, then once again up the Vicus Argentarius. I seemed to be criss-crossing through the same streets interminably today. I was tired of this. In fact I felt tired altogether. I hired a chair. It took longer than walking but I could rest, which meant I could think.

The journey was dire. In fairness to my bearers, the streets were stuffed with official traffic for the Triumph. It paid no heed to the normal laws about wheeled vehicles; this upheaval was for the Emperor, so get out of the way. All the paraphernalia that I remembered Tiberius once cursing was now being finally assembled, both human and inanimate: "Musicians, dancers, masses of incense and strewing flowers. Each full of potential for chaos. Two white oxen to be sacrificed. *Spare* white oxen for when the originals get tired. Medics to stretcher off people who collapse. Law-and-order located at suitable points for unavoidable arrests . . ."

With half a day to go, this stuff was already causing chaos. We had to negotiate the carts trundling incense and flowers. It seemed too early to bring the strewing flowers, which would be brown when they were finally chucked at the procession, though those carts were dripping as if buckets of water had been thrown over them. These were lopsided, axle-dropping transports with horrible drivers. The best must have been mustered somewhere ready for the procession.

Open wagons carried musicians and dancers: half-naked, painted, ribald creatures, who seemed already drunk or drugged. Reeking of low morals and weird sickly perfumes, while they travelled towards their early assembly points they rattled sistrums at pedestrians, then twanged stringed instruments mockingly if the pedestrians shouted back. I never saw white oxen. I did hear lowing above the clamour, plus neighing, braying, barking, swearing and occasionally screaming. Anything that called itself a law-and-order detail was standing at a bar counter, watching but keeping out of it. Exhausted pickpockets, taking their break, went over to have a drink with them.

I was lurched into the Vicus Pallacinae, then gave up. Beside a long line of decrepit shops, many with their shutters closed, I stopped the bearers, paid them off, then walked. At the crossroad with the Via Flaminia I could hardly move for men erecting scaffolds upon which sightseers would perch to view the coming procession. Some eager idlers were hanging about already, to make sure the seating matched their requirements. As they demanded extra space for their aunties, I cut off into a large open area where once Rome's armies would gather; an altar to Mars was sited there. Poor old Mars, Rome kept him busy. We must give him more war than even he wanted.

The space was crammed: vehicles, groups of bored soldiers, roped-off enclosures with stored materials of many kinds, people in normal clothes still trying to go about their daily life, fanciful people who had dressed up in peculiar costumes, foreigners whose odd, brightly coloured attire probably felt normal to them. I stopped to brace myself before forcing my way through.

A wall of heavyweight monuments faced me. Coming up from the river beside Tiber Island were the Theatre of Marcellus and the Porticus of Octavia, with the Circus Flaminius behind them, then the Theatre and Crypt of Balbus and another grand porticus that contained a small temple, behind which lay the Theatre of Pompey. Further on were the Diribitorium and Saepta. All of these mighty works had been destroyed by the terrifying fire nine years before when Titus was emperor. All had been magnificently rebuilt by Domitian.

Taken with his dramatic reconstruction of the temples on the Capitol above, no critic could deny that he had grandified his city with generosity, not to mention skill and taste. Even if the aim was enhancing his own reputation, our tyrannical ruler's achievements were fine. Some were at his own cost. Perhaps he deserved thanks, even acclaim. I only wished I had not heard rumours that he was coming home even crueller than before.

A double triumph? Once he settled back among us, some people had no idea what we were in for.

Inside the Diribitorium, the uproar was louder. Everyone was even more frantic than last time. Everything I remembered seeing had altered immensely. Floats were finalised. Half were standing ready on the flatbed carts that would carry them. Nobody was clearing away their equipment yet, but as I passed among the weary workers I sensed there was nothing more they could do. Variation orders for finishing touches, dropped on them by finicking administrators who had no idea, would not happen. Time had run out.

Only the costume-makers were still madly stitching.

With some of the fake captives having last-minute fittings, my visit was ill-timed. As she demanded that they stood still while she adjusted pins, Quartilla looked flustered; she made no pretence of welcome. When she discovered I wanted to meet Naevia, I was viewed as an utter menace.

"Can't you leave her alone?" She pushed a Chattian warrior on his way. He was sucking a thin salami stick and eyeing up a Dacian maiden.

"I need to talk to her. I am sorry to do this. I know she has a lot to endure. I understand you were protecting her before, but it is best if things are brought into the open."

Storing a needle by pushing it through the shoulder of her tunic, Quartilla disagreed. "Albia, her husband died, her brother died, she has no money and she's pregnant! I need her. She needs the work I've given her."

"The Triumph provides, but once it's over, people are stranded?" I acknowledged the difficult truth.

"Too damned right. God knows how Naevia will manage then. Don't upset her any more, or I'll kill you."

I said sourly there had been enough killing.

I could not see this ending well. Sometimes my work is hateful. If I started suggesting to Naevia that her brother had murdered her husband, the woman would despair. I would not blame her.

Visibly reluctant, Quartilla pointed her out. I went over and introduced myself. I ought to have spotted her myself: even though she was so short of money she had a long black veil up and over her hair for mourning, like a priest making a sacrifice.

Naevia was sitting on an upturned barrel, speeding her way around a hem that needed shortening. Her stitches were neat, stabbed through the cloth with skill, though her fingertips were red raw from plying a needle too much. She was a sweet-faced, worried-looking, tired young woman. Although her eyes were puffy from constantly crying, she must be striking to look at normally. I could see why Gabinus had hung around, even after he had little use for her.

On edge even before she knew who I was, her wide eyes blinked too much in the shadow of that veil. Her strain confirmed everything I had heard of her misadventures. If there were no physical bruises, I could still see she was a defeated soul, running out of strength. From what I knew of her life, its future outlook was grim.

I said I was sorry for her losses. I only wanted to help by finding out who had caused her grief. She showed no reaction, so I simply started. When I gently pried about the morning when Gabinus died, she said she was working here with the others; Lemni came to tell her. When I tried asking about the night before, when Gabinus encountered Suza, she blanked the subject. Instead she kept talking obsessively about losing her husband. It had been terrible trying to organise his unexpected funeral. He had left her no money. Not that there was anything different in that.

What about the night her brother was killed? She was at home with her children. Next day it was Larth who told her what had happened to Lemni; Larth was, Naevia said, extremely kind to her from then on. He and his wife had promised some financial help with funeral costs, so she could be freed from the moneylenders. Otherwise she had no idea how she was going to manage, even if her other brother helped her out. He had his own life to lead, and now there was a lady friend . . .

She had nothing to tell me that I did not already know. Two people close to her had died. In any situation like this, I had to look at relatives. But it was clear this woman had neither wanted nor conspired in either of the deaths. Why would she? Naevia was now in even more trouble than before. She had been left in greater poverty, facing much more loneliness.

"Are you named Naevia Gemella? Is Gemellus your twin?"

Almost fearfully, she nodded. "He hasn't done anything!"

"I never said he had. And what about Lemni—that cannot have been his birth name?"

"No, but everybody called him that because of the work he did. He was Naevius. I must have Naevius on his memorial stone, but it will seem very strange." She was obsessing about memorials to keep herself sane. Once the plaque was in place, she was likely to fall apart.

"You are a good sister, and Gemellus will be a good brother to you now. People want to help you, don't worry."

It was trite, but what else could I say to her?

Her co-workers were watching. They sent her little supportive looks, implying that if I was pressing her too strongly, they would make me leave. Naevia was liked; she was loved; many in her circle tried to protect her. Perhaps that would give her the strength she needed, if she could only see it.

I did not suggest to Naevia that Lemni might have killed Gabinus. I saw no point.

The theory is, check everything, question everybody, push them if they seem reluctant. Sometimes, though, it is the wrong thing to do. Sometimes even an informer has to have a heart.

I was ready to leave. Seamstresses swooped around Naevia, gathering her into a safe huddle. Quartilla marched me to the edge of the vast hall. It must have looked as if she was seeing me off the premises. In fact, once she recognised that I had not been hard on Naevia, she softened towards me. Before parting, I did tell her my suspicions that Lemni had killed his brother-in-law. Quartilla nodded, though she said nothing.

Then I remembered something. I fetched out the strange piece of metal I had picked up on the Arx, just after we found Lemni's body. "As an expert in dress, would you have any ideas about what this is? I found it near a crime scene."

The well-padded woman with that air of competence took my find in her hand. She turned it over and over with gentle fingers. Inquisitively, she pulled at the single thread of fabric that remained caught in it, peering closer. "Brown. That's a big help! You'll get in a pickle, trying to match that." She gave me back the metal object. "This is an aglet."

"What's that?"

"A sheath on the end of a lace to stop it fraying."

I saw that she was right.

"When it was new, it would have been crimped together with pliers . . ." Quartilla cocked her head, looking wise. "A shoelace would probably be leather, not fabric. This is probably off someone's garment that they close down the front, not with brooches. My guess would be, it has eyelets. Metal eyelets would make their ties easier to push through, especially with aglets on them." She touched the single fibre again. "Look after that, if you might want to match it. It's been in the wars," she pointed out. "This poor little aglet. Somebody tugged so hard they ripped it off and opened up the metal."

"The lace itself wasn't there. Not where I found this. I would have seen it."

Quartilla laughed ruefully. "All a bit foreign, if you ask me. Most people use a fibula for cloak-fastening. Or if they have ties they just dip the ends in wax. Much cheaper. This is like something I could have put on my Dacians and Chatti. Bit fiddly, though. Foreign," she reiterated, "or else it comes from some poser who loves metal. Buckles and toggles. Lugs and loops. Any kind of grommet. Stupid male embellishments." She gave the aglet a look of derision. "The military!"

Then she said it for me: "That isn't going to help you much, is it, Flavia Albia? Not with the whole of Rome awash with soldiers!"

LIV

I came out of the Diribitorium into streets that were choked and impass-able. With no interview follow-ups beckoning, I wanted to go home. It was still only mid-afternoon, yet I felt I had been out for hours. Then, as I set off glumly walking, I heard cries of "Make way, please! Make way, you bastards!" I recognised the voices, with their easy-going attitude that if people did not move of their own accord, they would be barged aside and no compensation paid for broken ankles.

As I turned, I found a familiar conveyance running me down. It was a heavy litter in neutral colours, of such great age it had been used by my grandfather, that unrepentant rogue Didius Favonius, also known as Geminus. I think it was old when he was given it, as some shady payment in kind. Heaven knows what he had done to receive some-thing like that. He used to loll inside on the beaten-up mattress, behind the sagging curtains, pretending to impress customers with his stand-ing in society. As an auctioneer his standing was so low, nobody was fooled.

The webbing had failed and his bearers were little better. Geminus had let them take the strain when he was tired or tipsy of an evening. They brought him home, either to his house by the Aventine or his big spread on the Janiculan. They rolled him indoors over the threshold; if anything remained in any flagon he left behind in the litter, they were allowed to drink it. That only added to their liverish pallor.

I hailed them. They were glad to pause. My father owned this monster now. It was being humped to his house, Grandpa's old one, though Falco was not with it since he had been called urgently to the Capitol. Some disaster involving geese, I learned. The sickly bird had died. The goose-boy was distraught. Pa had run off to help him get through it.

Even without him, the litter was lurching heavily. Father had filled it with valuable stock that he wanted removed from the Saepta during the Triumph tomorrow. This booty was being taken to his house on the Embankment for safety. I asked the bearers how much I would be paid for not telling the Aventine Guild of Cat Burglars. They grinned, replying that I might as well pop up for a ride because the weight was already killing them. More would make no difference. I could grab any vases that tried to slide off.

I had to climb in over strongboxes, then fight a bunch of faux Greek statues for a place on the pillows. As they and I snuggled intimately, I pondered my case. Leaning my notebook on a naked nymph's backside, I went through my evidence. One treasure was a bust of Homer but he turned a blind eye.

Gabinus was murdered. At least I could say I believed my witness: his fall from the Rock was not suicide. I thought it most likely Lemni had pushed him, in which case I could understand why. So long as Larth, an important figure, continued to give his friend an alibi, I would never be able to prove it.

Then Lemni was murdered too. I suspected it was linked, but I had no idea who had done that or why. The vigiles had arrested someone. Pointless: it would never come to court.

At least if I learned nothing else, I could report all that to the aediles with an air of finality. End of inquiry. Call it a family tragedy. Rome should move on. Thank you, Albia, here's a reward for solving very little!

They would hardly be surprised by sketchy details. Most people thought informers were always useless.

The litter swung on, making me queasy. I tried to take my mind off it.

I knew what Quartilla had meant about men who collected metal fittings. Rivets, studs, hooks, hinges, bosses, loops, ferrules, tangs . . . Rattling made them feel masculine, because their ornamentation was heavy to wear. Among retired or off-duty soldiers, a bangle or a fine nielloed silver belt let them show off their high army pay so they felt superior to civilians. For other men, who lacked a military background, flummery let them pretend.

As for lacing, it was not entirely "foreign," as Quartilla thought: I knew it was the standard way of fastening the front of a soldier's cuirass. The plates of *lorica segmentata* were front-tied with a double-ended, criss-crossing cord from gullet to waist.

I had seen nothing like that recently. There were soldiers who came and went every day, all over the Capitol. Like the legionaries who were making a nuisance of themselves along the Via Flaminia, they carried no visible weapons because within the city soldiers must be unarmed. They were in plain red tunics. Their armour must be rusting in a heap some-where, a dragon's hoard of girth hoops, collar plates and shoulder guards. Legionaries' front ties probably never had aglets because they passed through fairly large fixings. Anyway, if the ends frayed, any soldier I ever knew would stick the wobbly fronds together with a blob of spit.

I did know this. I was married to a soldier once. Wounds had forced him out of the army, but Lentullus thought of himself as a legionary until the day he died.

The soldiers on the Capitol were transitory lads. Given a task in the morning, they were moved elsewhere by noon. I had seen them around a lot, but never recognised the same ones twice. It was unlikely any of them had even encountered Lemni, let alone wanted to kill him.

Whoever did kill him had wanted to do it very much. Every aspect was deliberate. Chucking Lemni off the Tarpeian Rock was planned. Ge-mellus was right. The Rock was the point.

Thinking again about soldiers, only one stuck himself up on the tops regularly: the Praetorian guard, Nestor. I had seen him in a couple of cloaks, though never laced into one. I thought I had seen him in brown, though I mainly remembered a green garment, brooched on one shoulder, which was the guards' standard fashion in Rome. As far as I knew, Nestor had barely met Lemni. I saw no reason why he would have attacked him.

Besides, all Praetorians ignored the rules. They did carry weapons. They did not care who knew; they actually liked letting people know. With everybody else unarmed, they revelled in it. Nestor was constantly flash-ing his gladius, like the bully he was. So why would Nestor have hit Lemni with a mallet, when he could have used his own sword?

The litter lurched again.

What else could I ask? Where else could this task go?

Unhappily I began to accept that I had covered all the possibilities.

We reached my parents' house. Stiff and sickly, I was helped out of the litter, a courtesy only so the bearers could unravel me from armfuls of precious things, without incurring damage to the treasures. Never mind my welfare. I was expected to make my own way up the Aventine steps to home.

"There's no way we are staggering up that cliff! You'll see your pa later, by the way. He told us he would snaffle that dead goose. Unless it was carried off by some horrible plague, he's going to bring it over later. It can be roasted on a spit at your house; he says you have a courtyard that is absolutely made for the job. And you have a celebrity chef to cook it. So everyone is coming for a feast at yours after the Triumph. That will be tomorrow tonight, won't it?"

"How nice!" I remarked sarcastically. Fortunately our courtyard had no fig tree to be set on fire. "Right, I'm glad I've got you here. Tomorrow morning my husband, the aedile, needs to be collected from the Temple of Isis after he greets the Emperor. He has been quite unwell—"

"We heard about the lightning bolt!"

"Then you understand. I know Falco will agree to this. Please pick up Tiberius Manlius and bring him safely to our house. If you wait in the Meleager Porticus he'll find you. He's very sensible."

Guffawing that carrying someone sensible would make a nice change, they readily agreed, since it clinched their invitation to our feast. "You are not to worry about the rest of the food and drink," they reassured me. "People will bring everything. Falco said he knows you are a poor new bride with a tight-purse husband."

Somewhat coolly, I thanked them for the ride then said I must be off, since my miserly husband was more important than my father seemed to think. Tiberius Manlius would need me to help arrange his toga tonight since he had to go out before dawn to greet the triumphal Emperor. When I saw him, I had better warn him we were offering open house.

"That's all that matters, isn't it?" the bearers told me happily. "Family!"

LV

Ilet myself in, to be met with silence. I might as well still have been living alone. My entire household was missing—even the dog kennel was empty.

I walked through the atrium. Out in the courtyard, Tiberius and henchmen of his had been making trestle tables. That was a bonus of living next to a building yard: wood always to hand. One table had already been finished. It was positioned centrally, standing there as a template. Though rough, it had been covered to see how it would look, while other folded cloths were piled on it, magicked here by somebody. My mother, I guessed.

I continued exploring my tomb-like home. My father's a fast worker. In the kitchen, a dead goose already lay on its back on a platter, neck off, feet off, plucked. A bucket contained its down, which would make superb cushion-stuffing. Another bucket, under an upturned platter, probably contained bits Fornix had removed. Intestines? I preferred not to look. If this deceased honker was the one called Florentina, at least she looked anonymous. I never like eating creatures I recognise.

Emerging from the service corridor, I crossed to the yard door. When I opened it Drax, the watchdog, walked to the end of his chain, gave me one wag, then lay down to sleep again. He must have had a busy day getting excited, because a firepit and huge metal cooking spits had been created in the middle of the yard. At least that meant my house would not burn down, or not until the yard had long preceded it.

I walked back then shouted loudly, "Barley, come off that bed!"

For a moment the silence continued. Then soft, skittering paws announced my pet, scrabbling down the stairs from the next floor, half guilty but more pleased to see me.

"Where are the people, Barley dog? Why aren't they all here squabbling?"

She wriggled. I fussed her. Answer came there none. I let her follow me back upstairs, then we went to sleep on the bed together. There was a nice warm patch where she had been before. Hardly was I comfortable and dropping off, when the household began to pile back noisily.

Dromo brought water buckets that he had filled at a nearby fountain, a precaution for the firepit. He was taking a dangerous interest in that, telling me all the ways the fire must be looked after, as if he thought he would be in charge. Suza, still whoffing, sauntered home from the baths, swinging the oil-flask I had given her. Apparently, despite my instructions to be escorted, she now went by herself. Apparently she was entitled to have a manicure at Prisca's on my tab.

Fornix and Gratus walked in together, followed by slave-boys from local provision suppliers, carrying enormous baskets, wheeling handcarts with amphorae, and grinning. I pointed out that they were a bit premature because the feast was not until tomorrow; they looked surprised that I quibbled.

"Yes, Gratus, but I have been told people are bringing stuff, all we shall need."

"Never wise to rely on promises." The steward must have been caught out before. "Do you know how many your father has invited?"

"I have no idea. I haven't even seen him."

"Fortunately," replied Gratus, somewhat heavily, "I did see Falco when he dropped off the goose, so I interrogated him."

"A throng?" I said in that case, I was confident I could leave preparations in his capable hands. Gratus agreed: he liked to be given his freedom. We understood each other. I had known that when I hired him.

I agreed we owed the world a party. "My parents gave Tiberius Manlius and me a magnificent wedding feast. We should have followed up with entertainments ourselves, but when a bridegroom is struck by lightning, you tend to imagine you have been let off."

"Deferred!" said Gratus, smiling wisely. "By the way, I have not yet questioned Fornix about his previous experience. Will he know how to cook this goose?"

At that moment Fornix emerged from his kitchen corridor, carrying something on a titbit saucer. He overheard Gratus. There was a tense stand-off between the round, bulky cook and the tall, slim steward.

I quickly explained to Gratus that, although it seemed unlikely for people like us, Tiberius and I had secured the services of a master. "Fornix was previously the top chef at Fabulo's, a celebrity restaurant over on the Quirinal, where his culinary feats were legendary. Gratus, I should have mentioned this earlier. You have come to a favoured, almost fashionable home."

"I can roast a goose!" For once, Fornix was dour. He knew his worth.

"I am slavering with anticipation, dear Fornix!" Gratus assured him, tactfully vanishing with eel-like sinuosity.

"Save him a wing," I murmured to my chef. "He was not to know."

Fornix ignored that. They had issues to negotiate. Running a household was such fun.

Getting over his coolness, Fornix told me he was planning a pre-triumph supper for Tiberius and me: curly lettuce in a mask of goose fat, sprinkled with chopped goose gizzard, which, when prepared by him, was a heavenly delicacy.

"Yum! I am really glad we have you, Fornix."

"You can cut the flattery! While I was cleaning the bird, madam, I found something. Since your father said I was to look out for any signs the goose had died of disease, I thought you would want to know."

With a small flourish, Fornix proffered his saucer. I recoiled.

"This was in the crop. She must have eaten it, couldn't digest it, and it slowly killed her. Poor thing," added the chef, kindly. "Still, it means we can safely roast her."

I thanked him. Then I asked him to clean the item since I had better keep it. He was surprised—even more so when I explained that he had just found me a clue.

The poorly goose Florentina had died because she had eaten a long, narrow piece of fabric. In form it was tubular. Even after being inside a goose for several days, it still looked like a lace with a frayed end. Its colour was a rustic brown. And when laid near the aglet I found on the Auguraculum, it still matched the single thread that was caught in the bent metal.

LVI

Tiberius came home hot and bothered from his last meeting about the Triumph. I sent him out to the baths. He came home again, cool, clean and cursing.

We sat in the courtyard. Fornix produced the goose gizzard salad, plus other perfect snippets. Gratus poured wine. He had chosen a good one. Tiberius settled.

"What a stinking day. The Greens have been bellyaching to the City Prefect that their faction was unfairly locked out of tendering for the chariot horses. They were shunted on to the aediles because nobody else knew what to do. We ruled that nothing improper had occurred. The Whites' team will be used tomorrow with the Reds' in reserve, according to advice received from experts. The Greens stormed off, muttering that this was a lousy fix by supporters of the Golds."

"Word has got out then, darling?"

"What word?" he growled.

"Was your name on the response to the complainants?"

"Yes, I happened to sign it."

"It was your day to have the pen? Or do the other three aediles simply know when to dodge?"

"I don't follow your logic."

"The Greens are loons, but I expect they have scouts to research a complaint. Everyone does it. If you had a murky past, love, they would probably try to blackmail you." Unsaid went the fact that his past was of a less pious shade than his present. Tiberius had topped it off by marrying an informer, but that had been announced in the *Daily Gazette*, so was no use as sleaze.

"The bloody Greens can leave my past alone. I need another drink!" Gratus whipped in to pour. I warned Tiberius to stay sober, since it was only a few hours until we had to dress him up formally. He groaned. Sipping slowly, he grumbled more quietly, "It was all that damned freedman, Aepolus. Remember the ghastly man who came here? *He* lobbed the complaint our way. I put it down to spite because you treated him so snippily."

"I can't see it. But, just in case, I apologise."

"You are so reasonable! So . . ." he asked, lightly enough, ". . . what's new, precious? Have you solved your case?"

I reminded Tiberius it was his case first, then pretended to have reached conclusions for him. All of my household drew in closer to hear of my progress, like children waiting for a bedtime story. Even Barley curled up against my foot.

I summarised everything I knew. Although it had felt like endless struggle, I was surprised how far I had advanced while out on my own today. The certainties I had reached while in Pa's litter sounded good. Impressed, they all listened without interrupting. Once I had finished, I picked clean the last nut saucer, which I had balanced on my knee. Dromo licked out a salad bowl. He managed it without slurping. The boy was learning.

As twilight fell upon our tired but peaceful gathering, a blackbird sang full-throatedly from a ridge tile, claiming territory. Our enclosed space was quiet, a private haven, although on the Aventine noises were always audible. This was the Hill of Freedom, centred on the Temple of Liberty; raucous celebration happened even though it was rarely from liberated slaves. All Rome was now collecting itself for tomorrow's festivity; the Aventine stood apart, yet that never stopped the party here. Raw life, some of it even happy, resounded everywhere.

Tiberius had watched me listen. As if I had spoken aloud, he began to talk about this too. "Here we are in our cut-off courtyard, but we can hear music and laughter, smell other people's food grilling, catch the air of expectancy." For a quiet man, he had moments when he enjoyed talk, playing the paterfamilias. I was simply happy he was pain-free and could do it. "I'm thinking about those other peaks, the Arx and the Capitol. Sweetheart, how different a picture you give for them. No streets, no tenements, no shops, no stalls, no baths, not even brothels. Nobody lives there, apart from a few caretakers. So what do those people do, Albiola, when they want to be sociable?"

I laughed. "They go down the Hill for a drink. Some of them meet up with exactly the same cronies, every night. They aim for the same ghastly bar, like a ritual, even if they have to wait hours for their pal. Everyone seems to do this."

Tiberius looked quizzical. "Do they all congregate at the same place?"

"That I don't know. The one place I heard named is the Centaur, which people admit is a dump, but it stays open all night."

Tiberius chewed his thumb.

Until now, Suza had heard us in silence. I had noticed her taking it all in. She fixed on not only what was said but how we said it. Her capacity for absorbing manners and behaviour was immense—the complete opposite of Dromo, who would never own any sensitivity, so never any tact. Suza had already learned how to hold her fingers when she ate, even drying them on her napkin—if she remembered she had one.

She leaned forwards. I might have imagined it, but a faint waft of murex shell escaped. I hoped it was diminishing, or would do soon. She was less bouncy than when she had come here, less forward, less loud. If Suza had been invited to a house where an obscenity was used every other word, she would be aping that. But no: "I believe I have heard something about the Centaur," said Suza, as if in an elocution lesson.

"What's that, Suza?" asked Tiberius, in surprise.

As she became excited, she lost her new intonation. "That night I was on the Capitol. When Gabinus had got rid of my people, he was very short with me. As soon as Ostorius and Cincia left, he mumbled, 'We have to make this quick, girl. I am due at the Centaur for a drink.' Then he said, 'With my brother.' At first I thought he meant showing me the temples had to be quick, but I soon learned he was after the other thing."

I breathed slowly. Tiberius swirled wine in his beaker.

"Gabinus had a *brother*!" I murmured. Picking up on sudden tension, Suza looked stunned that she had caused it.

Tiberius raised his eyebrows. He drawled, with deliberate thoughtful-ness, "So, Flavia Albia, information queen, what do we know about *him*?"

"Nothing. Absolutely nothing. No conniving swine I have talked to ever managed to tell me some brother exists."

Tiberius put down his cup on a portable table. He stood up slowly, stretching. "Right. Since I have to be ready to applaud Domitian's con-quering, I need a nap first. Here's what I suggest. I ought to start off early in case the crowds are very thick—but if my loving wife wants to come too, I should like that. Just to see me on my way to the walk of misery," he pleaded winningly. "If we can get near the start nice and early, then be-fore I pack you off home again, there should be time, darling Albia, to stop at a bar for a drink."

I smiled. "So much for me putting you into your toga, then jumping back between the sheets for a luxurious lie-in! Well, fighting Barley for the bed. Do you have a bar in mind? Some favourite, perhaps?"

Old grey eyes gave me the grin I liked, all innocent—yet wicked with it. There was an advantage in marrying a man with a hidden past. "I thought we could just set out on spec," he said, "then find somewhere we like the look of. I have heard of a place that stays open, somewhere below the Capitol."

LVII

Of all the bars in all the world that pride themselves on being duds, the Centaur was a frontrunner. Even with so many to choose from, it throbbed with lack of promise. It made the Stargazer, which my family owns, look chic.

This popular local meeting point was more of a hole in the hillside than a winery. You could not go inside. It had grown like a weed in a dead-end alley that was stopped off by the ancient Servian Wall. Its seats were placed out in a dark passage. Any entertainment happened street-side, as did the lavatory functions of neighbourhood dogs. A beggar limped by, but he kept going.

While Tiberius had been resting at home, we had sent out Paris to find this place. I must have been past it many times, not on this case but in general life, because it lurked at the back of the Vegetable Market, near the Porta Carmentalis. This had been an ancient swampy area; at the Centaur we could still smell hints of damp. While less horrid than murex shells, it made me think of flooding, fevers and other misery.

We were arriving while it was still dark. Because of the Triumph there were plenty of people about in the streets, though being charitable, this may not have been the best time for the Centaur. With Tiberius in full fig, we could hardly appear casual, but we engaged in light-hearted banter. It was a ploy Tiberius and I sometimes used, mainly because we liked bantering. We had brought Paris with us; he just listened with a baffled grin.

"This is the kind of bar where your friend mutters, 'Keep your hand on your purse!'"

"Uncle Tullius would say, 'Keep your hand on your privates'—but he just likes being obscene."

"He was quite well-behaved at our wedding."

"You only think that because you walked out halfway through." I decamped from our ceremony to interview a murderess. Well, she was leaving for the coast. Sometimes you just have to do it.

"If this is your idea of a marital treat, I should have run away for good . . . What happened to their signboard? It looks as if ten years ago a customer was sick on it and the cleaner can't reach."

"Half man, half horse—and difficult to say which end of him needs to be taken to a vet. I blame the painter."

"He calls himself Sludge. This is his vomitorium period. Apparently the idea is to look unpleasant—it challenges hidebound preconceptions. Quite sought-after among knowing connoisseurs."

"Not the art for me. I know what I don't like . . ."

We need not have bothered with our glittering wit, because nobody took any notice. Hopeless customers slumped. The very few snack dishes were empty. Oil lamps were lit but dying. The owner did not waste money on waiters, since he could use his two grandsons for free. He believed in giving talent its head, which meant he never bothered with training them. When he came here the bar was his pride and joy, so for thirty years he had supposed that was all it needed from him. He intended to pass on this gem to his children, but was surprised to find none of them wanted it.

He was here tonight. It was beneath him to serve anyone, though he was trying to unbodge the wax in an amphora, banging away as if he had never done it before. While we waited for a sad serving-boy to wander close, Tiberius engaged the owner with his other brand of patter: offering to remodel what passed for a bar counter. "I don't often see anything as bad as this! Your grouting is completely shot and this crack is a disaster waiting to happen . . . Someone did you a lousy job here. Ideally all your mock-marble needs to be taken out with care, then reseated properly. Don't worry, we do this all the time. I run a specialist company. I can easily send my estimator to take a look for you . . ."

The bar-owner did not seem to find it odd that the conversation was with a well-shaved man who was formally togate, including a purple stripe and magisterial bearing. Well, we were coming up to a triumph. He probably thought it was fancy dress.

Tiberius did not really want to work here. In our house, "I'll send a man to look at it" was a phrase we now used if somebody had a bright idea that someone else was intending to ignore.

A waiter passed within reach. Tiberius grabbed him; I ordered. The weary child claimed there was a list of wines on a wall inside, but when I craned over the counter I could not even see the board, let alone read it. Interior walls appeared to be rendered with primeval dirt. Cobwebs held up the beaker shelf. I nearly chose water for myself, but I opted for their house wine, so something stronger might kill whatever was swimming in the water. If not, whatever floated in the wine would have to die quietly inside me.

Paris helped collect seats and even a small table. He found the table with a leg off, but he and Tiberius pushed it back together. While we waited for our order, we all looked around. There were a few customers. Some had never managed to obtain a drink; they might yet go home without one. Patrons of the Centaur whom I had met would say they came for the company. They must all have very optimistic natures.

Perhaps lively ones came at lunchtime. After dark, subdued customers sat in small, desperate groups. Some hardly spoke. Others talked, but with the banalities of people who had been meeting each other for so long they had run out of anything to say. Newcomers did nod on arrival to those sitting there. It was friendly enough, but just dead.

I recognised several, from questioning them up on the Arx and the Capitol. One priest on his own raised a beaker to us; he called over that it was very quiet tonight. He reckoned everyone who worked on the tops would be going up there in the morning, to look down at the procession. They were saving themselves now.

"You can have too much jollity, can't you?"

Not at this bar, sunshine.

The landlord must have sorted the amphora bung; he sat down with us to see why we had landed at his bar. His tunic needed pensioning off, so he hid it under a grimy apron. That was on its last legs too. A towel was stuffed into it to make him look professional; it must have been the wrong kind of towel. One corner of his mouth quirked up as if he was constantly sneering.

"I know who you are!" he declared to me, as if claiming a prize.

"Flavia Albia." I played it demure. Tiberius and Paris exchanged glances.

"That's right, Flavia. You are the crazy who has been trotting all over the Capitol, asking questions. Did anybody tell you anything? No, I thought not. Never mind, you finally got down here to the Centaur with me, Honest Romulus. I'll give you any answers you want."

I murmured, "Thank you, Romulus."

Tiberius joked that he hoped the landlord was not descended from the legendary founder of Rome, since his own watchword as a country man was, "Never trust a shepherd." That broke the ice, for this Romulus was utterly a man of the city. His alley accent said it all. Luckily I had lived in Rome long enough, so I could more or less translate.

Some Romans are brusque. We had a chatty one. At least we could occupy ourselves while he talked at us, because our drinks came. Paris tried asking for a bowl of nuts; he was more of a comedian than we had realised.

The wine was the kind of vinegar Fornix used to clean his griddle. My father and Uncle Lucius would have called it "promising," meaning its subtle undernotes made promises of after-midnight acid reflux.

"You want to know all about what happened when Gabinus topped himself!" Honest Romulus informed me. I did not mention that we no longer viewed it as suicide. I kept my cool, letting him run. It seemed he did have useful things to say. "Well, it was all going down at the Centaur *that* evening, I can tell you! You're on about the Naevii, aren't you? They were in. They came in late, though that was usual for them. Old Lemni was ranting. That was him, though. He rocked it out, then afterwards he let go of it, whatever was bugging him. Absolutely might never have happened. Nicest fellow. He never let anything eat him up—that was one reason everybody liked him. Always a pleasure to speak to, old Lemni."

"What about Gemellus?" I managed to chip in.

"*Not* the same." Honest Romulus had a decisive way of speaking that made me want to show him up, but I played nice. "Ab-so-lutely not the same. The opposite. Gemellus sits and broods to himself. He has been doing it a lot lately, all on his own, since Lemni passed. Well, he would, of course. He misses old Lemni, the way we all do. That was horrible, I have to tell you. Lemni never deserved to die like that. Ask anyone who comes here, we were all shocked."

"So the night before Gabinus died—"

"The night before that bastard popped off, those two brothers come in for a drink, don't they? Lemni is furious, spitting fire."

"And Gemellus?"

"Gemellus just looked dark."

"Could you tell what they were upset about?"

"That's your job, isn't it?" Honest Romulus really knew how to get on my bad side. I could see Tiberius grinning. "Well, everybody knew, of course. For one thing we could hear what the two of them were saying and, anyway, nothing that happens on the tops is a secret. Gabinus had had visitors—we all knew what he was playing at with those murex people. And then he tried it on with the girl but she gave him the brush-off—well, we knew about that afterwards, though come to think of it, we may have heard the tale from Lemni while he was here, ranting. Took her down to his house first, so he could tell Gemellus he would be late due to looking after her. Then the brothers came in here some time afterwards. Both steaming about what Gabinus had done."

I tried to speed up his story. "Did the Naevius brothers stay long?"

"No. No, not long. Well, not Lemni. He had to be up with Larth next morning for bird-spotting, so he went home to bed. He had calmed down by then. He told Gemellus they would sort it, the nasty business with their sister. That was nothing new either. Those brothers always wanted to do something for her, but she never let them. So it seemed the same thing all over again—I mean that they hated how her husband was, but they were stuck. 'All in good time,' said Lemni, after he calmed down. He was always reasonable. Old Lemni. Such a loss. I really liked him."

"And what did Gemellus do?"

"He stayed on here for a bit. Staring at his cup as if he thought we'd put poison in it. They had asked me for the reckoning, so both put down their share of it. Normally they left together . . . Well, they lived close, in case you don't know that. But on the night, Gemellus sat longer, all on his own, moving the money around on the table. My boy didn't like to disturb him, so he didn't take up the cash as normal. You can't leave it sitting there, it's asking for someone to swipe it . . . Then suddenly Gemellus jumped up and left quietly, without a word to anyone. If I didn't know better," opined Honest Romulus, "I'd say he was off to do Gabinus in that very night. Only of course Gabinus jumped off the Rock next day."

"In the morning. He didn't jump, he was pushed. But," I said, "Gemellus has an alibi."

Honest Romulus looked surprised, though he was unabashed by my tone. "Well, Flavia, you need to think again. Alibi? If that's the caretaker's mother, she was never going to land her lover in trouble with you and lose him, was she?"

"Two people," I specified, still terse.

"Oh, and the other must be Callipus! Well, you can forget him, Flavia. He is notorious for always doing what his mother tells him."

While I pursed my lips, pondering, Tiberius broke in with a change of subject. "May I ask you, Romulus, what you felt about Gabinus dying?"

The landlord did not bother with customer loyalty. "Tell the truth, Legate, I absolutely thought he stank. Horrible man. I was sorry when he got himself that hut, and started coming down here every night. Nobody could stand him, and my two boys never wanted to serve him. If he could moan, he would—the place didn't suit him, the liquor was off, and he was always on at my boys for the way they looked after him."

Honest Romulus leaned forward, jabbing a finger in my face. He had strong feelings to communicate. "You know what? I am known for my love of my customers, you ask anyone. Famous for it. But I hated that man. I absolutely hated him. He drove my clients away. People just want a quiet night out, with a decent drink to help them forget their day. He came here, always upsetting everyone. He did it on purpose—he enjoyed making them unhappy. In the end I had to say to him, that very night I had said it, I'd rather he took himself to the Venus in the Clamshell sometimes."

"This was actually the bar Gabinus came to?" I demanded quickly. "The night before he died?"

"Just said to you, Flavia. Luckily he was in and out before Lemni and Gemellus or we'd have had a right barney. I don't know what might have gone down if they'd turned up and seen him, not after what they heard about him and the busty murex girl. But Gabinus had already stormed off, swearing that was the end of his custom here. Knowing him, he meant it. He had no call for that. I had to have a quiet word. You've seen how I am with people—me, Honest Romulus, all charm. I hate having to bar any-one—I had been quite pleasant with him. So if the bastard was pushed off the Rock by somebody, then I congratulate whoever did it. But you listen, Flavia," Honest Romulus instructed me, being very, very earnest now, "don't you go looking this way for your murderer. It was not me."

It was so long since anyone had made this declaration, I almost didn't see it coming.

LVIII

"Now I suppose," Romulus careered on, "you'll be asking me about Gabinus and *his* brother?"

"Yes, do tell!" Tiberius thought he had the weight to impose himself on the garbled torrent. "We know Gabinus had one, and the pair drank here together some nights."

Romulus was not about to relinquish command of the tribunal. "Let me stop you there, Legate! I'm your man for that. We had them in here every night. Until I had a gentle word with him, anyway. He liked a quaff, did Gabinus."

"His brother too?"

"Well, they do, don't they, in his line? That was part of the trouble. They both liked it far too much. Put them together, other people fled. The way I heard it," Romulus imparted, leaning in and lowering his voice in imitation of discretion, "that was why them two started coming here in the first place. Gabinus told me his brother had fixed himself up with a job on the Capitol deliberately, in order to be near. Then they could go out together, instead of him getting bladdered with his mates. The mates had given him the push. A lot were away all summer, of course, so he was feeling left out of manoeuvres. But then even the duds who had been left behind, who he *thought* were his mates, complained they were tired of him. After they took a vote, he was chucked out of where he drank before— some place up by the camp, where the guards all go together, some dive called Nino's."

———

"Gabinus had a brother who is a Praetorian?" I tried not to croak in surprise. "His brother is *Nestor?*"

"I would have thought you would know that, Flavia," confirmed the landlord, smugly.

"Yes, darling, I am very surprised you never found that out!" Tiberius joined in. He at least had sweet laughter in his eyes; I was meant to know he was teasing.

Our runabout, Paris, had something to contribute now. "Nino's isn't bad. Their liquor is very drinkable. I suppose you would expect that with soldiers. I had to go there," he informed Romulus. "Business enquiry."

"During which we learned something," I reminded them. "The landlord at Nino's claims that the night before Gabinus died, Nestor was up there with his pals—the whole time."

Romulus shook his head. "Not on. Couldn't have been. Nino got that wrong."

"He is very bribable!" I confirmed.

"Gabinus and Nestor were here," Honest Romulus insisted. "Then they moved to the Three Mallards. I know for a fact—old Duckie at the Mallards told me: after I had chucked them out for bad behaviour, they hunkered down there annoying him all the rest of the night. By the time Gabinus rolled back up the hill to that hut he stole, it must have been light. Somebody found him still snoring, dragged him out for a set-to. The bastard was too drunk to avoid being skimmed off Tarpeia's Rock like a pebble. But that's the other end of the Hill from here, so none of us ever saw it."

"You would have gone to cheer?" suggested Paris, sharp-featured and curious.

"Not half!"

His trip for me to Nino's seemed to have given Paris proprietary rights in the guard. He banged down his beaker. "Why did Nestor stick around here afterwards? Once his brother was dead, I don't see the point."

"Well, I am very surprised you don't know that!" retorted Romulus, baring his teeth in a lop-sided sneer. He exonerated Paris; he aimed this at me, the flawed female investigator. "Old Nestor is obsessed, that's why. He is determined to know who murdered his brother. He wants to avenge him. His superiors have ordered him back to the camp, but he sticks around, because he is intent on solving it himself. He was very put out when you were appointed, Flavia." He didn't want me to discover the answer first, I thought. "When he finds out who the killer was, he's going to kill them."

"Did he say so?" snapped in Tiberius.

"Too canny. He looks stupid, sir, but he can be deep."

"Why, though?" mused Paris, still harping on Nino's bar. "Why did Nestor need to fake an alibi for himself?"

I checked with Romulus. "Were Gabinus and Nestor always on good terms? Or were they brothers who had fights?"

"Bonded."

"So nobody would ever have suggested it was Nestor who pushed Gabinus off the Rock?"

"Opposite. It left him devastated. All Nestor did after his brother was lost was rant that he would have revenge."

Nestor was utterly heartbroken, according to Honest Romulus. On the other hand, Nestor was also an idiot. Nestor would always get anything wrong if he could. The alibi was my fault. I had asked where he was that night, which he took as a personal threat, so he had invented a lie purely to double-cross me.

Paris had not finished. "He was wearing a cloak." We were learning about our runabout: he could be obsessive too. "When I saw him at Nino's, he had muffled himself up furtively. He had a cloak with a hood, fastened up to his chin. It was brown. It had ties on the front."

"No, that's not right, son," disagreed Romulus, flatly. "The guards always fix their cloaks one-shouldered, with a heavy brooch. You'll never see any of them do anything else."

Paris, who obviously had seen it, shot me an appealing look. I nodded, reassuring him he had my trust, never mind a barmy barkeeper. I knew Paris was observant. It had been his first solo commission. He was watchful at the time and now he remembered everything about it.

Ignoring Romulus and his set ideas, I said to Tiberius and Paris, "Increasingly it looks as if Nestor attacked Lemni. They grappled in the Auguraculum, and Lemni managed to wrench off the tie with the aglet. I found the metal piece, but Florentina had waddled along on her morning walk. She swallowed the lace before I got there. Nestor, being bigger and angrier, had bashed Lemni with his own mallet to subdue him, then disposed of the corpse. That's assuming Lemni died of the head wound. It's possible the fall from the Rock actually killed him."

Paris shuddered. He was observant, but not tough. Well, not yet. Working for me would stiffen him up. At present he looked as if he was thinking, *What if Nestor had spotted me spying at Nino's?*

I turned back to Honest Romulus. "I don't suppose you know where Nestor is tonight?"

"No, he is still barred," the landlord told me. "He won't show his face. He tried to come back after his brother died but he was so cut up and gloomy, he was deadly as a customer." How could anyone tell? They were all dreary.

"I hope you will be careful if he does show up," Tiberius suggested, in a low voice.

Romulus did not get it. "Why should I? I know old Nestor—he's always a pain, but I can handle him. I've been doing this job for thirty years. Nobody scares me."

As if he sensed our views on that claim, Romulus suddenly felt the call to attend to other customers.

"I must get going myself." Time had gone by: Tiberius needed to leave in a hurry to join the other dignitaries. If one of the aediles was missing at his ceremonial breakfast, the Emperor was bound to notice. He would be counting members of the Senate on his tight mental abacus, then checking the magistrates too. "Domitian may not know me personally—but if he sees an aedile is absent, he's soon going to identify who it is. I dare not risk offending Our Master, or as a family we are finished."

I liked that "as a family."

He had been thinking about the situation. "This is not easy. Arresting a Praetorian may be impossible."

I agreed. "Nestor's crime will have to be put to the Praetorian prefects. The fact Lemni was so close to the augurs ought to provide leverage, though. Once Larth knows Nestor killed Lemni, he will jump on it. The Praetorians always try to protect one of their own, but this goes beyond covering up."

"It sounds as if he was insubordinate in appointing himself to the Capitol. Things must have been slack, with the main Praetorian units away on the Danube. But Nestor has already been recalled to camp. Refusing to obey that order won't have helped him." Tiberius reached fast conclusions: "Here is what we can try. Once I've done my duty at the Temple of Isis, I shall be close to the First Cohort's station-house. While the procession sets off, I can go to find Scorpus and report on this."

"Julius Karus would be even better," I admitted, for once prepared to use his special influence. "He must carry weight at the Praetorian camp."

"It won't be safe to go looking for Nestor," Tiberius warned. He gazed at me gravely while I nodded like a good wife. "Let the authorities catch him. Promise me, Albia."

"You want me to go home."

"We have our arrangements," he emphasised. "Your father's litter is at the Saepta and will bring me."

"No change to our plan," I assured him. "I am going home now to wait for you, Tiberius."

"Will you?"

"Or what? Go tramping around in the dark, trying to apprehend a volatile, angry, armed soldier with élite training, who has already murdered someone?"

"You're daft enough!" Tiberius scoffed briefly. Then he gripped my hand. "Don't just say what I want. I dread how many times I shall hear you are running alone into danger. 'Nipping off to see a killer. Home for supper . . .' I won't even mention our wedding." The lightning strike during our marriage procession had blotted out many memories, but he never seemed to forget that one. "Flavia Albia, daughter of Marcus Didius, wife to me, I love you. Think of that, will you? Please tell me I do not have to worry."

I kissed him; I made it lingering. "Manlius Faustus, you do not have to worry. I mean that."

I did too.

Being honest, I can say I meant it at the time.

LIX

You guessed. Possibly he guessed too. I meant it when I said it—then a crisis intervened.

I waved him off, thinking how fine he looked when togate and conducting formal business. He always said if you sought a high position, you could not shirk its responsibilities. Office involved more than seeing your name in the *Daily Gazette*. It was about more than enjoying your power, imposing eye-watering fines on feeble people. If a man was elected as an aedile, he must accept it came with crud.

Once he left us, I sat and thought some more. Paris had another drink, while trying to persuade one of the young waiters to run out to another bar to borrow nuts or olives. The boy said he would, yet looked vague. He would not go. I stopped watching.

I had talked to a large number of people in this inquiry, many more than usual. Mostly it was casual questions about whether those on the Capitol saw anything, rather than deep interrogation of any part they personally played. Just as the triumphal procession would be a series of tableaux, I had encountered a series of participants in the victims' lives.

Almost without me noticing, the focus had narrowed down. My area of interest shrank until what had happened on Tarpeia's Rock concerned only two families linked by an unhappy marriage. Two pairs of brothers, one sister. Two dead, three left behind to grieve.

Several very young children were affected, but I guessed the elder ones were at this moment excitedly putting on their jewelled Dacian tunics, unaware that their mother and two uncles had been touched by tragedy for ever. Their father was dead, but they had never seen much of him anyway.

Their loving uncle was lost, but they were young enough to forget. To the toddler and the unborn baby, Gabinus and Lemni would only ever be names on the memorial plaque.

Naevia seemed the kind of woman who would take them to the necropolis. Visiting the place where the face-pot was deposited would be a regular family trek. Naevia would make everyone leave flowers, feast with the dead, appease their souls, remember them.

I reckoned Gemellus would often accompany them. He was Naevia's twin. They had that special bond. That bond . . .

Now I thought more about Gemellus. The landlord here had painted a picture of him after Lemni rescued Suza. Even though they had lived in the same building, Lemni went home first, with his rage cooling and with words of resignation. Gemellus stayed, brooding darkly. *On the night, Gemellus sat longer, all on his own, moving the money around on the table . . . Then suddenly Gemellus jumped up and left quietly, without a word to anyone.*

I had been wrong. It was not Lemni who had pushed Gabinus. Larth and Lemni had spoken the truth when they said they were in their observation tent when that hated man died. What they were keeping from me was a different secret: Larth and Lemni had both been sure that Gemellus killed him.

I pictured it. They heard the cry. They ran outside. Perhaps they even saw Gemellus on the top of the cliffs, immediately after the event. Whether shoving Gabinus had been pre-planned or an accident, Gemellus was now in deep trouble. Valeria Dillia had told me she looked up after the body fell: *There was a commotion. Some temple officials popped up on the top and had a look down, gabbling and pointing.*

That was Larth, Lemni and Gemellus. Their agitation was not simply because Gabinus was dead: Gemellus was still standing there in shock, guilty. The augur and his brother must have yelled at him to make himself scarce. He rushed home to hide. Back at the tenement, at some point, on somebody's suggestion, Gemellus persuaded his lover and her son to provide him with an alibi for that morning.

This meant one terrible thing: If it was really Nestor who killed Lemni, the guard had murdered the wrong brother. *Nestor was utterly heartbroken . . . Nestor was also an idiot . . . Nestor would always get anything wrong, if that was possible.*

For me, this coloured the augur's odd behaviour over Lemni. Larth had seen the horrid truth: his good friend's murder was mistaken identity. Determined to protect and help the family, Larth could not tell me that. He could never find justice for Lemni. Larth must continue to conceal what he knew about Gemellus.

With hindsight, I decided that Larth—Gellius Donatus, the old-fashioned elderly senator—had probably told his wife, Percennia. She backed him. Hades, if I could, I would do the same. They would know Gemellus had acted against Gabinus for his twin sister; he was no danger to anybody else.

Paris was still maundering on about the lack of nuts. "I told him what he ought to do. He's taken no notice! Come here, boy!"

"Leave it, Paris. We have snacks at home. Around here they will only be rancid."

Abruptly, I dropped a hand on his arm. Tiberius would have known what I meant. Paris kept going, then gradually took my point and hushed. Two new customers had turned up.

The young waiter said in passing, "Valeria Dillia. And her boyfriend."

I waved. They came over. Dillia took the seat that Tiberius had vacated. As a gesture to her evening out, she had rearranged the fluff on her dress and added a decrepit necklace, which she wore lopsided. Her companion took the seat Romulus had been using.

The man whom people at the Centaur called Dillia's boyfriend was definitely not Nestor. Calling him that was a joke—I think.

He was in his sixties, so dapper he would have been out of place anywhere. He had a thin moustache that my mother would call the adulterer's version, small feet in very polished shoes, his hair lashed down with wax, then ploughed with heavy comb tracks, and he was sucking a fragrant-breath pastille. This fellow was like a highly committed finance officer, who needed to get out more. However, that was not his role in life. Valeria Dillia introduced him as her long-term chum, the Tullianum jailer. The prospect of being strangled by him must feel like facing a tricky business audit.

"Well, this is a night of surprises!" I tried to sound cheery. "I thought you never came round to the Forum Holitorum, Valeria Dillia?"

"I never trust their overpriced veg—but I have a little drink at the Centaur. A nightcap with Genialis."

Yes, Genialis was the jailer's name. The Empire's strangulation king was no plug-ugly bruiser who smelt of body odour and menace; once you accepted that, his name seemed less satirical. His manners matched. He could make himself welcome anywhere, though some hosts might be wary.

We conversed politely. In a bar this is expected. It turned out that, like everyone else with a job on the Capitol, Genialis had inherited his position. He was the latest in a line of friendly family jailers, proud of his calling, nonchalant about his special skill. His father had trained him by taking him to a funeral director who let him practise on corpses. Since they were already dead, he joked, it did not matter if he bungled the job a few times while learning. To him, as to Dillia, what he did was not at all sinister.

He thanked me for putting him in possession of two trolley thieves he could use tomorrow as faux foreign chieftains. His gratitude was heartfelt. Knowing Rome, it came as no surprise that, with no Dacian or Chattian prisoners to hand, substitutes from among the criminal fraternity would be quite acceptable. It was the ritual that counted.

Genialis was glad he had them in advance because he had been able to give instructions on death-cell deportment. "I want a good clean expiry. I'll make it quick for them, but we have to have a lot of screaming. The crowds like that, and it attracts divine attention. After all, this is a sacrifice to the gods who have protected Rome."

I saw Paris blenching.

"So," I managed to venture as their wine came, "what has happened to your other young man, Dillia? Where's Nestor?"

"Off on his own tonight." The old woman spoke frankly, even in front of Genialis. The jailer did not appear to view the Praetorian as a rival.

Dillia seemed less eager than usual to give extra information, but she grumbled, "I don't know what he's playing at."

"I do!" scoffed Genialis. His cynical view reassured me. As they had known each other such a long time, I hoped he would protect Dillia.

"You said," I reminded her, "Nestor has been upset about a relative's death. It was his brother." She nodded, once more reluctant. "Has he told you who his brother was?"

"That Gabinus," Dillia admitted. Then she revived. "So what? It doesn't change anything. Nestor stays near me because I was the person who saw his brother fall. Knowing me is his link to his brother's last moments."

"He cosied up to you for a reason," I warned. "He wants to know if you recognised who argued with his brother. Who pushed him."

"Well, I can't help. My old eyes are not that good."

"Keep saying that!" Genialis urged her heavily. "Don't be involved. That man is trouble."

"He has been very nice to me!" Dillia wailed plaintively. Her friend humphed. Clearly his affection was genuine. He was pressuring her over Nestor, with some chance of prevailing.

Genialis turned to me. Even though he looked like a second-rate ledger clerk, this man was sharp. He glanced at Paris, checking whether to trust him. I nodded. So Genialis the strangler, with an air of relief to be sharing this, told me the bad news. "Nestor has been hanging around the tenements looking for Lemni's brother, Gemellus. I think we know what that is about. He sees himself as a holy instrument of justice. The Praetorian is out of control. He's armed and dangerous."

I shared my own concern. "Gemellus has not been at the Centaur tonight. So where is he? Does anyone know?"

Facing up to the guard's real motives freed Dillia's tongue. "His lady love persuaded Gemellus to start being more friendly with her son. When the Triumph ends tomorrow, Jupiter Custos will be back to normal again. Callipus went up to clean his hut, after those horrible transport men. His mother convinced Gemellus to help him out. She said they can settle their differences over a dirty task together."

"Nestor has another target, too," warned Genialis. "Take care, Flavia Albia—he blames you for hampering him while he was looking for his brother's killer."

I groaned. "I can look after myself. But I shall have to do something about this. So Gemellus is up on the Capitol—and Nestor is tracking him? When did Gemellus go?"

"Just now. We passed him on our way here."

My heart became heavy. If nothing was done, I foresaw another trag-edy. Like me, Nestor had figured out his mistake over Lemni. No one needed an augur to see what Nestor had in mind.

With the whole of Rome intent on Domitian's Triumph, there was lit-tle hope of finding someone in authority to take an interest. So that was why I went myself. Nestor wanted to punish Gemellus fatally. I must try to stop him.

I did my best. I told Paris to run after Tiberius, who should have reached where the magistrates were gathering. It was hopeless, but if Paris did make contact, Tiberius might be able to send reinforcements. I had nobody else to call on. There was no time for elaborate explanations to troops who would not want to know. There was no one I really trusted.

I did not even have my dog. When we left home, Barley had put her nose out of the door, but she found the smell of the night too dangerous and ran back to her kennel.

Good dog! That was the right idea. On the eve of the Triumph, the very air was tingling with hazard. Nobody with any sense would now climb the Capitoline in darkness, all alone, following a vengeful killer.

LX

Rome was ready for Domitian now. Crowds must have been throng-
ing the entire triumphal route. All the way down the Via Flaminia,
around the huge monuments by the river, down along the mighty race-
track of Circus Maximus, then up the Forum on the Sacred Way. Even
here by the Capitol, which the procession would not reach for a whole day,
they had clustered. Camaraderie flowered everywhere. Well, except when
young men without futures decided to stab one another. Or wives found
their husbands having holiday recreation with the wrong people.

Those who wanted to watch the procession had decided the only way
to ensure a good view was to sleep on the streets. Many lay on pavements,
wrapped up in blankets with flagons and picnic baskets, remembering old
wars, then telling anyone mad enough to listen how much they adored the
imperial family. Some had brought pictures of Vespasian and Titus, not
caring how much Domitian—the younger son, the less than charismatic
brother—would hate that. They started sing-songs. Occupants of apartments above threw down cabbage ends and worse. Glued to their spot on
the edge of the pavement, the advance spectators would be outraged later
when other people simply turned up and parked large families in front of
them in the roadway.

The nearest gate to me lay below the Temple of Faith, where soldiers'
honorary discharges were stored. It was the Pandana, the gate in the Capitol's fortifying walls that had been locked against the murex dyers. *The
Porta Pandana is always closed at night . . .*

I hoped the night before a triumph might be an exception. I was wrong.
The reinstated gatekeeper was either not there or deaf to my banging.

Surely staff would have preparations to make at Jupiter Best and Greatest. Would the gatekeeper not be on duty for once, for them? No. The old man, perhaps with his old compadre the goose-boy, had locked up and bunked off. With Feliculus grieving his gullet-blocked goose, this would be a kindness. They had toddled down the Hill for a pre-triumphal, don't-feel-suicidal-old-mucker drink.

I had to find another way. Hurrying as best I could, I pushed down the Vicus Jugarius. Fighting the throng around three sides of the Temple of Saturn, which is massive, I made it to the Clivus Capitolinus. Barriers were keeping the road clear, ready for Domitian's chariot. I ducked under a barrier.

As I went up, I left behind the moaning hum of a city that would never sleep tonight. With gradual elevation came stillness and silence. Given the slope, I never tried to run, which would rapidly have exhausted me. I walked. I had come out in serviceable shoes. Their tread was soft upon the worn old road's slabbed pavement.

It was very dark. Because this was the processional route, torches lined it, but they were all unlit, waiting for the Emperor's late finale. Every masculine informer I have ever met would swear that on a jaunt like this he always brought his kit of useful implements: his folding knife, a length of string, his military pocket multi-tool, and certainly his flint for striking sparks. I had nothing. I would not manage to fire up a bitumen torch by rubbing together a cheap string of beads. Tonight's were definitely not amber.

Don't blame yourself, Albia. Hell, you only came out for a simple drink with your husband. Theoretically you were not working . . .

I could only just find my way. What happens to moonlight when you need it? Starlight, even? If you believe them, my male colleagues would all have pinched a torch by now—thereby rendering themselves, with their moving dot of light, a target. Better without: I thought I heard footsteps following. I was afraid: it sounded like a soldier's boots. The last thing you want when you are chasing someone is to find that they are really chasing you.

I stopped. The sounds had gone. I kept moving.

I was still afraid. I am human.

I passed the Tabularium. Its three-tier bulk, blacker than the surrounding night, helped me know where I was going. At the top of the Clivus stood a monumental arch, set up for himself by Scipio Africanus, greatest of all triumphal generals; he built it at his own expense, after defeating Hannibal at Zama. That was before he retired bitterly from public life due to charges of corruption and treason. He said the charges were false. He would. Perhaps they were. Indeed, that was likely. Such is politics: envy and back-stabbing. Disgusted, Scipio refused to have his body buried in Rome but he left this stonking monument to remind us of what Rome owes him.

By the arch there were flaming lights on stanchions, in case anyone wanted to see and be impressed. Scipio's memorial to his deeds was set into the wall around the temenos, the ancient fortification that secured the sanctuary. Fortunately, the arch's passageways had no metal gates blocking entry tonight.

Once inside the sacred area, I picked my way on rough, narrow paths through the confusion of altars, statues and trophies. The Temple of Jupiter loomed above, from which I found my bearings; from memory I came to the little shrine of Jupiter Custos. At Domitian's folly, crackling flames were providing an eerie light. I recognised voices, which eased my nervousness.

Callipus and Gemellus were burning possessions left by Gabinus and Egnatius. Egnatius might have something to say about that, but they thought they were safe because he had been arrested by Julius Karus. I knew his stay in vigiles' custody must now be over. Already Egnatius would be in the Campus Martius, no longer lording it nastily, but behaving as a busy transport manager should at a double triumph: filling in for his dead predecessor, frantically sending men in all directions, gesticulating to the grooms in charge of horses and oxen, checking his stable lists, running around like a half-swatted fly, all in pursuit of his reward bonus.

As their fire crackled up, I greeted the caretaker and his mother's lover, now acting like old friends. Boys will always bond over a bonfire. They were in fact around the same age, well into their forties if not older, but they made a drippy pair. They were supposed to be cleaning the hut, but both had flagons.

"Your mother should have supervised you, Callipus."

"She's gone for extra equipment at the kitchen supplier."

"Not tonight, surely? Will she find one open?"

"She's his regular. We call him another of her boyfriends. She has a 'special arrangement.'" I thought Callipus was joking, though perhaps not.

They wanted to stand staring at the flames, but I had no time to waste. I quickly warned Gemellus about Nestor looking for him. "You know why, Gemellus!" I made it clear that I knew, too, though I was not suggesting any action against him. Even I was surprised by that.

For a moment more, I found myself musing: "This was a case about brothers. Now here we are on the very hill where Romulus cheated on Remus. Twins must have been different then. Now it's lovey-dovey loyalty to your siblings. You and Lemni and Naevia—Gabinus and bloody Nestor."

"Rome is a city of brothers," Gemellus joined in. "Don't you have one?"

I thought of my brother, smiling. "Yes, though mine is only twelve and quite a character."

"But he looks after you? Wouldn't he kill your husband for you, if he knew the brute deserved it?" Spoken low, while he stared fixedly into the fire, this was Gemellus making his confession.

It would never apply. My husband was decent; Postumus took against many people for his own weird reasons, though not Tiberius Manlius. However, my brother did once stand up to someone I knew whom he disliked. It turned out the man was pathologically evil, a serial liar, a threat to me, deadly to others. Looking back, yes, it gave me a warm feeling that my brother had taken him on and spoken out for me.

Murder was different. I would never want that. Forget the sanctity of life: murder brings too many consequences. If I left Gemellus with his secret now, his sister would have somebody to support her. But he and Naevia would never really escape what he had done. The sombre knowledge would eat them up. They were trapped. And he would have to carry what his deed with Gabinus had done to Lemni.

His fate was very nearly snatched from me. We heard a furious cry. Roaring for vengeance, Nestor burst out of the darkness.

He ran at us, with his sword out. He was careering full tilt. Only because the fire blazed up suddenly between them did Gemellus dodge what was coming. Callipus dragged him sideways, as Nestor made maniacal feints. The guard was bigger, angrier, well used to fighting.

The three men pranced, feet apart, like exotic dancers. Callipus had pulled out a burning stave from the fire. He waved it but was not a natural brand-wielder. Nestor dashed it to the ground with a swipe of his gladius. His quarries were tipsy. As Callipus got in the way of Gemellus, Nestor capitalised on their stumbles. He was homing in on Gemellus, but his move was stopped by a newcomer: distrusting men to tackle home-hygiene properly, Callipina appeared, bearing a brand-new broom for them.

"Now I shall kill you, Gemellus!" shouted Nestor, clearly about to do it.

Wrong words, Praetorian. Never utter threats like that before a Roman mother, a Roman widow with her lover.

"You had better not try it!" Callipina did not falter. The fastidious housewife knew her tools. She gripped the besom by its long stiff bristles, using two hands. Holding the broomstick straight out in front of her, she galloped at him. She struck Nestor full on. It was a direct hit in the midriff, with her weight behind the sturdy rod. The rest of us gasped for him. Even the soft sponge that passed for Nestor's brain registered horrific pain.

LXI

He was bleeding. Not much. Not enough, maybe.

The pole must have gone into him. With better luck his wide belt would have deflected it, but military equipment was for fending off barbarians. It had never been designed against a raging mother with a broom.

While Nestor bent double, I grabbed Callipus. He still clung to his flagon, but I knocked it aside. In an urgent undertone I ordered, "Take Gemellus into the hut and hide him." He looked dumb. "Move, Callipus! That's what your precious hut is for. Here is a hunted fugitive—get him in. Shove him under your bed, bolt the door—save him!"

The guard was still distracted. Callipina had not finished. Nestor clutched his midriff with one hand, while trying to fend her off with his free arm. Doggedly, she kept thwacking him.

Straightening up, he caught the end of the broomstick, refusing to let go. Striving for possession at besom's length, they circled slowly.

It would not last. Callipina would be badly hurt. I had to help.

A monumental trophy stood nearby. I fell on it, trying to drag out weaponry. No use. The ancient swords and spears were welded together by rust and time. I could not free anything. Exasperated, I flung myself at the weather-worn construction, using one shoulder. The tall collection of captured armour wobbled drunkenly, then the entire thing fell over with a deafening crash. I tugged at a shield; it was too heavy for me. I managed to haul out a helmet. I hurled that at Nestor's head. It made contact. He yelled. With a supreme effort, I wrenched out a long spear from the trophy tangle.

The guard lost his hold on the broom. Callipina fell over, still clutching her treasure. She landed on her back, thrashing her feet, like a downed beetle.

"Try somebody your own size!" I challenged Nestor. He was half as high again as me, and muscular with it. No one was doing arithmetic. I laughed mockingly. That generally works.

He had lost his sword when the widow first poked him. He bent, with a pained grunt, and tore the broom from Callipina. "*Run!*" I said to her, then saw the widow roll over on the ground, crawling off into the darkness as fast as she could, fleeing from him, like a demented land crab.

I spoke quietly as I taunted him. I needed to draw him away from where Gemellus was now hiding. "Nestor, the game is over. Forget Gemellus. If you really want justice, why kill him? You inflicted more anguish, greater punishment, by what you did to his brother. Gemellus has to live with the endless thought that Lemni, who was innocent, died because of him."

Still holding his stomach, the protesting guard groaned. I could see him starting to turn his anger on me instead.

"Call yourself a guard? No wonder you were grounded when the decent ones went off to the frontier. You are useless—I hear even your mates at Nino's have decided that!" I jabbed towards him with my spear, though I started inching backwards. I needed to leave the area with the caretaker's hut. More pressingly, I had to put myself well beyond Nestor's grasp. "Everyone knows what a fool you are. I worked out who killed your brother ages before you did."

He swung with the broom.

"Ridiculous!" I scoffed, even though it was the only thing available. The injustice would enrage him more. "It's over," I told him. "I shall report that you murdered Lemni."

"Prove it!"

"Nice cloak!" I retorted. He was wearing a brown garment. A large brooch pinned it at the neck: round, large central garnet, smaller cabochons around it, slightly uneven in their spacing. "That brooch used to be on your green one, so what's it doing here? Eyelets up the front, Nestor, but why no lacing? Oh, look! One of your ties has gone missing!" I saw horror as he worked out what I was saying. "That's right, man. I have it. Plus another witness who saw you in that cloak. You are finished. At the very least you will lose your job, cashiered without a pension. For you, life in the Praetorian Guard is over. All gone. All lost. Complete disgrace."

Finally he came at me. I smashed my spear down on the broom handle. The broom only broke but the spear shattered. As the hundreds-of-years'-old war trophy disintegrated into rust, I scrambled further out of reach. "Give up! You won't catch me, Praetorian!"

I turned and ran.

He could not help himself. Like a dog seeing a rabbit race away, Nestor came pounding after me.

I had really done it now. I had been in some stupid situations, but this beat everything: high on the Capitol, symbol of Rome's indestructability, all on my own, being chased by a maddened Praetorian guard who had no option but to kill me.

LXII

Once he committed to chasing me, I knew he would not stop. Having accepted the challenge, he had to catch up and deal with me.

I had no plan. Always have a plan. I had had no time to formulate anything so fancy. My sole aim now was not dying.

It was dark. I can run, but I ran carefully. I could not risk a fall. Sprawling helpless on the ground was asking for the worst.

If there were people up here, I never saw them. There must have been. Lovers, temple thieves, altar-boys who had forgotten to go home, soldiers sleeping here ahead of tomorrow. I would welcome even a seedy priest or his sleazy, spotty acolytes. I thought I heard a male voice shouting, over by the Porta Pandana; it sounded urgent but was too far away and could be no one who might help me.

I ran at the Temple of Jupiter Best and Greatest. At dawn, all the temples would be thrown open, so the gods could join Domitian's party. Maybe, since this was the prime temple in the world, some attendant would be on duty. With Nestor behind me, I hurtled up the mighty steps. Each cella was closed. Not a single god at home to visitors. Thank you, Jupiter, Juno and Minerva! Thanks a lot, Olympian Triad! No wonder people honour different gods on the Aventine. No wonder I pray to none at all.

A few lamps dimly lit the porticus, so the guard and I dodged around the huge columns playing hide and seek. Eighteen columns on the front, in three rows. Such fun, nipping in and out of them, wondering if my next turn would bring me face to face with a man intent on killing me. Further columns lined the temple sides, but I would not venture there in case he trapped me against an end wall.

I managed to evade him enough that I could skitter down the steps again. At ground level I set off, running faster, back towards the Arch of Scipio. Nestor worked out where I had gone. I could hear him much too close now, as I turned onto the Clivus Capitolinus.

Taking the curve on the top of the Saddle, it was time to thank Romulus bitterly. None of his groves remained in the Place of Refuge to conceal me. No asylum here for me! Never trust a shepherd . . .

Halfway down the long slope towards the Forum came the Tabularium. I knew it well. There is one door at the roadway end, which should be locked at night. I placed one hand on the boss. At my lightest touch, the heavy door swung silently so I could slip inside the building.

I was in the great corridor. Raised fifty yards above the Forum Romanum on its massive substructure, it runs the whole width of the Forum. By day, the huge vaulted corridor would be lit through small windows. Everyone has seen them from outside, where the three levels have those arches with columns in the architectural orders, which form a decorative treatment and provide scale.

Indoors at night there could be no natural light. Slaves had left occasional oil lamps. It is well known: some clerks never sleep. *I* knew that clerks who work in a building that commands a good view of a procession always turn up with a bag of provisions, plus family and neighbours, to take advantage of their special access. That was probably why the door had been left open. I was hoping to find occupants, but no luck.

I walked along. It was chilly. The Tabularium forms a structural link between the Capitol and the Arx. Alone in the dark, I could feel how these concrete arcades had been built snug against the cold Hill; I sensed the huge weight of the gallery above me on the second floor, plus a temple high above, which Domitian had remodelled. Linked underground to the Temple of Saturn where the Treasury banked the state's reserves, this was where religious and civic buildings met. The lower storeys housed public records. The name says it: tablets. Military diplomas ended up here in hundreds of thousands. Room after sealed room slumbered, while one frightened woman with no right to be there invaded their quiet.

I continued walking the long vaulted corridor. To my horror I heard footsteps back in the murk where I first entered. I was sure I knew that heavy-booted tread.

When I first set out on this chase, I hoped to go back to the Forum, hide myself among the crowds, be amid warmth, noise and safety. I had headed downwards. Now I was stuck going up again. The far end of the corridor has no exit. I had to climb to the next storey. It helped that I had been here before and was familiar with the layout. As I found the stairs then hastened up, I heard the relentless steps of my pursuer. I reached the next level where the vast hall is.

Arched windows gave access outside above the Forum. I stepped through one, but nobody below would see or hear me if I waved for help. I turned back.

Suddenly, a shock. My first human contact. A clerk blundered out of the darkness, terrifying both of us. I pointed behind me. "I am being pursued. Say I went down the Forum steps!"

"That way is closed!" I knew. A long flight of entrance steps used to give access from the Forum to these upper levels. It still exists but has been blocked up at the bottom since they built the squashed-in Temple of Vespasian and Titus.

"He won't know. Say it, please."

The clerk took the point. He would help me. While Nestor was discovering it was a dead end, I would gain time. I hurried away. There is an exit from the Tabularium, which was unlocked, and I took it, though this brought me where I had not wanted to be again: out on the Asylum, close to the Temple of Vejovis, now on the Arx.

I was starting to think I could never escape from this hill tonight. Tired out and frustrated, I began to lose hope.

LXIII

Out on the dark peak, a cool wind lifted my hair. I detected a faint change in the sky: the approach of greying daylight.

I was facing the river side, though to reach any of the steps down I would have to cross over, either down in the Asylum or in front of Juno Moneta. Neither was attractive but I stayed up on the heights. It felt exposed. Unhappily, I made my way across to outside the Temple of Juno, where I crouched by the big outdoor altar, hoping I was out of sight as I listened for sounds of pursuit.

Now in the intimate darkness I knew the Triumph was starting.

I could sense it as I heard new movement far below. Large crowds had assembled, down on the Via Flaminia, especially around the Triumphal Arch. Before the Triumph began they had nothing to do but stand around. It would be chaos in the processional streets. Several hundred senators, all mature, some ancient, had to be brought out from the city centre to the Temple of Isis where Domitian had spent the night in sleep and prayer. He would be offered a substantial breakfast, though in his mean-spirited way he was a modest eater. Hylus would dress him in those glorious robes.

The characters I had interviewed at the Diribitorium would be witnessing the success of their labours. Quartilla and her staff, the painters Successus and Spurius. Lalus would be creeping close to the chariot, anxiously in attendance with a touch-up pot of liquid gold. The Whites would bring their four beautiful horses.

Below on the Campus Martius, they would soon have their triumph with all its seediness, fakery and making-do. The spectators would mock but accept it, even the furniture they knew had been foraged from imperial houses and the reused old props. The wild day was beginning. Braggart soldiers, sordid crowds, knockabout actors and musicians, tiring noise, smells, then the self-satisfied man in his chariot. Tiberius saw this as a massive fraud. Its honorand and his audience would not be complaining.

I stood up now, beside the altar, planning to make a move. For the senators' walk to greet Domitian's return, flustered soldiers would be opening a tunnel through the human mass that clogged the road, forcing a highly élite rat-run, down which the purple-bordered togas could make their stately waddle. Down there, where Tiberius should be, I thought I could make out pinpoints of light: torches so they should not stumble, imperceptibly progressing. It was like when you stare at stars and cannot decode whether or not they are moving. The first ranks were neat, the rest straggled. These were self-satisfied men who held opinions; they had no truck with formation marching. Thinking of Tiberius among them, I suppressed a sob.

My brief respite was over. I would never escape Nestor. I heard him. Once I knew where he was, I even thought I could see him. Somehow, despite the decoy I arranged, he had managed to come out of the Tabularium, then passed me, lower down the Saddle. Bulky, determined and murderous, he would block my way to the Hundred Steps. What was the point of being so near to Heaven, if the gods were lying on their couches, sated by a night of screwing their sisters, turning nymphs into trees, blowing up storms to destroy innocent sailors? Wake up, you degenerate crew: a desperate woman needs divine intervention!

No luck. Nobody to help. I must still use my own resources.

I turned back on myself, now planning to descend on the Gemonian Stairs. If Genialis had returned to his jail, I could seek refuge.

Perhaps I kicked a stone inadvertently. Perhaps instinct was working for him. I heard Nestor shout insults, his voice seeming much nearer than I had hoped. He must be directly following me again. There was only one thing left for me. The gods had taken no notice. Nobody else knew I was up here. Forget the gods, I was at my limit. Soon I would no longer have strength to run. I could no longer save myself. I needed to attract attention—and I thought of the only way that was certain to do it.

Gasping for breath so much it hurt, I struggled to where I could just make out a line of cages. For security, their fastenings were intricate, but I knew how to work them. Keys were never used because this was a sacred area. When I began rattling metalwork, I heard soft cooing. The Capitol's guardians did not want to leave their beds, but one by one I pulled them out. They knew me of old, so I had to be rough with them.

"Get going!" I pleaded, whispering in case Nestor heard me. "All that pampering isn't so you can walk about, shitting on grass and pecking people. Do your job, geese!" Puzzled, they huddled together. I threw my last dice, the loaded one. Imitating the cutest possible small child, I squealed at them the words they hated: *"Nice birdies!"*

And so I set them off. Running around the sanctum in search of infants to threaten, the big white creatures Rome had honoured for centuries now remembered what they were famous for. Those wonderful birds did it for me. Flapping their wings with heavy beats and honking their hearts out in hideous cacophony, the Sacred Geese of Juno raised the alarm.

It was too late. There was no time for help to come. While I had been freeing the birds from Falco's cages, the Praetorian had crept up on me. He rushed me, then, with a grunt of exultation, pinned me in a suffocating grasp. Immediately he began trying to drag me across the Auguraculum. It was now too light to see the stars, though too dark for flights of birds. The ground was rough, but Nestor in his military boots never stumbled.

I fought him. I fought him like the street child I had once been in Londinium. I had a good life now: I was not ready to relinquish that. But he was bigger and much stronger so I knew what he was going to do. He forced me all the way across, heading for the edge of the clifftop . . .

Then an excited gander came out of nowhere; flying low, it crashed into him. Nestor flung up an arm to protect his face. I bit the other arm hard, twisted, kneed him viciously in his unprotected privates. He lost his hold.

We had broken apart, though it could not last. I had no energy. He knew it. I was finished. "Just one thing." I played for time pathetically. "Why didn't you use your sword to kill Lemni?"

He scoffed, deluded into believing I could not appreciate his forethought and finesse. "Only the guards carry weapons in Rome. That would have pointed straight at me!"

He carried no sword now, yet he would manage. He started his last move towards me. Brother of Gabinus, killer of Lemni, his only chance to avoid his own fate was to destroy me.

A shadow moved behind him. Someone came fast towards us across the Auguraculum. I remembered the voice I heard shouting by the Porta Pandana. I guessed this was that man. At the last moment, Nestor knew what was happening though he had no chance to react. He may have been taught how, when the geese signalled where the danger was, Manlius Capitolinus had burst on the scene and hurled the first Gaul off the battlements. Every Roman has heard that story.

No word was said. Only a man came out of the darkness, running hard. Full of wrath against the threat to me, my own Manlius threw the Praetorian off the Tarpeian Rock.

LXIV

Stand near the edge. Distract or overpower your victim, then a sudden big shove. Step away quickly . . .

Until then I never knew he had the courage, never thought he had such strength. Once it was over, I felt no surprise. I knew him and loved him. I knew how much he loved me.

We stood in the Auguraculum together, recovering, locked in each other's arms. *"Caius Policius Bibulus, in recognition of his worth and valour by decree of the Senate and People, the site for a tomb for him and his descendants has been given at public expense . . ."*

"Who the heck is Bibulus?"

"An aedile who earned the right to be buried inside Rome. He must have been like you. Nobility comes with the job."

"Daft woman," Tiberius said comfortingly, as I wiped my tears. If he ever died before me, I would pay for an enormous tomb and a huge plaque citing valour and worth. If I could not afford it, maybe the Gold faction would acknowledge his support by chipping in.

We heard people approaching.

Someone would have to round up a flock of agitated geese. The body could be left to rot, moved among the others on the Gemonian Stairs, just one more fake captive given up to the gods in the Triumph.

As for us, we had solved the puzzle. A report would be written, if anybody cared any longer. Over on the Aventine, the plebeian hill, we had our house: new staff, new dog, new décor, happy new lives together. Family would join us there tonight. It was our private retreat, where we could quietly be apart from any commotion that engulfed the rest of Rome.

Dawn broke. The procession had slowly started moving. It was not for us because Tiberius and I had better plans. We were going home.